ELVEN QUEEN

ALSO BY BERNHARD HENNEN

The Saga of the Elven

The Elven

Elven Winter

ELVEN QUEEN

THE SAGA OF THE ELVEN

BERNHARD HENNEN

translated by Edwin Miles

Text copyright © 2014 by Bernhard Hennen
Translation copyright © 2019 by Edwin Miles
All rights reserved.

Previously published as *Elfenwinter: Elfen 2* by Heyne Verlag in Germany in 2014. Translated from German by Edwin Miles. First published in English by AmazonCrossing in 2019.

Published by AmazonCrossing, Seattle

www.apub.com

Amazon, the Amazon logo, and AmazonCrossing are trademarks of Amazon.com, Inc., or its affiliates.

ISBN-13: 9781542094054
ISBN-10: 1542094054

Cover design by Mike Heath | Magnus Creative

Printed in the United States of America

CONTENTS

OF FALCONS AND WOLVES

Duke Alfadas looked back down the long, winding path they had been following for hours. The army had been making its way uphill for a day and a half. At first, their route had taken them through forests and along the gently rising slopes of the foothills, but it soon grew harder. The path twisted among rocky crags before rising along the face of a precipitous cliff. On the left, the cliff dropped away into an abyss so deep that the men felt already as if they were high in the sky. On the right loomed the sheer rock wall, and the sky directly overhead was a radiant blue.

Some of the men had lost their nerve and were blindfolded—the sight of the chasm had been too much for them. Three, unable to go on, lay tied to the dogsleds. Was it the beauty of the land stretched far below their feet that robbed them of their senses? This world felt so different, to say nothing of the amulets that took the bite out of the wintry world. This place was not made for humankind. Only death would allow a man to stay here forever.

Alfadas wiped the sweat from his brow. From far above him came the distinctive chopping of ice picks. Sparkling cascades of ice periodically blocked the path, and the elves had sent an advance party to clear these obstacles. Count Fenryl was a capable leader, and he had shown himself to be surprisingly receptive to the humans. So far, the different races had managed to get along very well. *One less thing to worry about, at least,* Alfadas thought. He was also convinced that their approaching rendezvous with the refugees was no coincidence—it had been planned from the start because, like this, the humans could think of themselves as protectors. But against whom did the fleeing elves have to defend themselves out there on the ice? The troll fleet was still hundreds of miles away, Count Fenryl had quietly told Alfadas. The refugees needed no escort, and that must have been clear to all the elves. The duke hoped that his men would not see through the subterfuge. If they did, they would probably feel as if they were being treated like children.

Chunks of ice tumbled with a roar over the side of the path. Alfadas watched them ricochet off the gray cliffside below and disappear in a shroud of glittering silver shards. Ahead, a signal horn sounded: the way was once again clear. Slowly, the long train of elves, humans, and dogsleds began to move again.

He found it oppressive to march through a winter landscape and not feel even a trace of cold. The wind slapped him in the face and tore at his heavy red cloak, but its fangs did not sink into his skin as they should have. Winter had had its teeth torn out. It was certainly more comfortable—no doubt about it. Alfadas saw the hoarfrost in the dogs' fur, and he could imagine how murderously cold it had to be. If he were not wearing an amulet, he knew, his breath would probably freeze in his beard. The cold would wear his little army down and probably even kill the weakest among the men, so it was good that the elves looked after them. And yet the feeling remained that it was not right to walk through a world of ice and snow and not feel the cold at all.

Alfadas clambered over a boulder on the path. Life was too easy if he had time to fret about a hardship they'd been spared. The path hacked from the rock was growing narrower and narrower. *How long must it have taken to build this path up the cliff?* he wondered. He saw no signs of pickaxes anywhere. If anything, the path seemed to be a natural formation, but no cliff he'd ever seen came with a convenient walkway! The winding route had probably been formed by magic.

He looked below to the forested hills they had left behind. So that was Silwyna's homeland. He had never visited the Slanga Mountains before. They were considered a wild and inhospitable place, and nowhere else were there as many souled trees. Many were the tales told about the forest. It was said the magic in it was so strong that spontaneous supernatural phenomena were not unusual. Just as one never knew where lightning would strike in a thunderstorm, in that enchanted forest one could never be certain of not falling victim to ungoverned magic. Silwyna had told him many stories of strangers strangled in the night by wild, thorny tendrils, and he'd heard of wanderers infected by a mania that made them walk in circles forever after. Now and then, the forest drained the very life from those who entered it, turning them old in a single night. The land was as dangerous and unpredictable as those who lived in it. No one in their right mind went there voluntarily.

Silwyna had been keeping her distance from him for the past two days. It seemed she had understood correctly his parting words to Asla in the human world. He was in Albenmark because he was forced to be there, and he wanted to return to his home. The bond that had once connected him with the elf woman had been cut—and he was not the one who had cut it. She should not have any false hopes!

Alfadas slipped and had to brace against the rock wall to stop himself from falling. The path was icy. The advance party had strewn sand and ash from the last campfire—a stopgap better than nothing, but not by much.

Never in his life had he been so high in the mountains. Neither trees nor bushes grew. Again he thought how out of place humans were here. It was too beautiful. The Maurawan forced her way into his mind against his will. He would do better to watch where he put his feet than brood over her. She was not supposed to have any place in his head now. Why was he not able to separate himself from her? He had a wife who loved him and two wonderful children. What could Silwyna offer him compared to that? Disappointment, no more.

His gaze swept the wild mountainous country they were leaving behind. There was something uncanny about the abyss. It beckoned him, and Alfadas had to make an effort not to stray too close. Was it the same for the other men? Climbing so high, so close to the heavens, made him feel like a bird. It was almost as if he could fly.

The ascent was taking more out of him than he had reckoned. His breath came in pants, although he kept the tempo slow. Something was robbing him of air. The other men around him were the same, puffing and wheezing along as if an army of old men were struggling up the mountain.

He looked ahead. Another fifty steps to a switchback. Several men were moving very close to the edge of the abyss. The new world and the magic that protected them from the cold had made them high-spirited. Others marched half-naked and had painted their bodies with grotesque faces to look like berserkers. He would have to talk to the men before they broke camp next day. High spirits could cause trouble.

A cry startled him, and a man rushed past barely two arm's lengths away, his eyes wide and shining. His arms outstretched like the pinions of a gull, he plunged into the depths.

Now Alfadas stepped close to the path edge. A long way below, he saw the unfortunate man strike the rock wall. There was a spray of blood, and the man kept falling until he disappeared into the haze farther down. While Alfadas was still staring into the depths, a second cry rang out. Shriller, wilder. Its wings tucked close to its body, a snow-white falcon plummeted from the sky. It, too, vanished into the mist at the foot of the cliff.

Shaken, the duke stepped back from the edge. "Onward!" The entire column had stopped in its tracks. With a few harsh words, he drove the men on and marched with them, not wanting to think about the dead man. Alfadas had forgotten his name, but he could still remember how he had come to him in Honnigsvald. At first, the man had been quite reserved, but after a while he had spoken with more and more fervor. He was the blacksmith who had conceived the poleaxe.

What bothered Alfadas most was the expression on the man's face. The smith had not fallen. He had jumped. And he had looked happy.

The duke peered forward. Another hour, perhaps a little more, and they would have the cliff behind them. Whatever delirium had seized the smith, he hoped it would not infect any more of his men.

Alfadas had underestimated. It took them more than two hours to reach the broad, snow-covered plain at the top of the cliff. While he was organizing the men into groups as they left the cliff path, Ollowain and Count Fenryl came to him. In their white garments, the two elves almost blended into the snowy background of the plain.

Fenryl had warm pale-brown eyes. His full lips and wild curly hair made him look less indifferent or aloof than the rest of the elves did. He wore a plain but elegant white tunic and a silk cloak that billowed with the slightest breath of wind. Only on second glance did Alfadas notice the falconer's glove on Fenryl's left hand.

"It will be night soon, Duke," the count began, dispensing with pleasantries. "I would suggest that we keep the army marching until dark to put some distance between us and the cliff. I'm worried."

"Why?" Alfadas looked sharply at the count. Had the elf been keeping something from him?

"It's the air. It's different at altitude. For most elves, it makes no difference. We just breathe faster when we exert ourselves. But your men . . . I don't know what effect it will have on them. Kobolds are known to become intoxicated to the point where they are no longer masters of their own senses. They suffer hallucinations and imagine the strangest things."

"That they can fly, for example?" Alfadas asked sharply.

Ollowain, abashed, avoided his eye. But the count nodded. "Yes. That has happened."

"You should have told me that in advance."

"We thought it would not affect you humans because you are so much bigger and stronger."

"Is there anything else you think won't affect my men, Count? I would be grateful to you if, in future, you could tell me in good time when you know of any minor details you *think* might possibly be a threat to their lives!" Alfadas had grown louder as he spoke, and a number of his soldiers were already turning to look at them. They had been speaking in the language of the elves so that the Fjordlanders would not be able to understand. Veleif Silberhand looked across curiously, and they had caught Lambi's attention, too.

"Please lower your voice, Alfadas." Ollowain had raised his hands placatingly.

"Might we face other problems that are bound to particular hopes on your part?" Alfadas persisted. He was finding it difficult not to become loud again.

"The light on the ice," Ollowain said. "It can blind you."

"It's only temporary," Fenryl added quickly. "We do indeed have your men's well-being on our minds. The light on the ice does not represent a danger, only a hindrance. We know it from the centaurs and fauns. It does not affect kobolds at all. Besides, it is easily avoided. Your men only need to wear eye masks of leather with narrow slits cut in them to see. They protect the eyes."

Alfadas looked up at the sky. Clouds had gathered in the last few hours. The sun was low on the horizon, night not far away. For today at least, snow blindness was no longer a risk. He had heard of the condition before. Hunters who risked the perils of the far north in winter spoke of it. Such blindness could last for days.

"I'll make sure my men protect themselves. Anything else I should know?"

The count smiled. "Forgive me. I should have taken the thin air into consideration, but I have no experience with you humans." He paused. "There is something else. If we find ourselves in a snowstorm, make sure your men know that they should stop where they are when the storm hits. The amulets will protect them from the cold, but marching on is almost a guarantee of losing one's bearings. The column would fall apart and end up scattered in all directions. In a storm, it is crucial to simply stay put and sit it out, in which case I will temporarily assume command. My lieutenants will tell your men what to do."

"What does that mean? That I lose command when it starts to snow?"

"Only in case of a storm," Ollowain said, trying to clarify. "You cannot imagine how devastating a force of nature an ice storm here on the plain can be. If you don't find shelter, you can be simply blown away."

Alfadas did not understand why he should now concede to Fenryl's demands. "We will decide that for ourselves if we get caught in a storm." He nodded in the direction of the clouds. "Is one coming?"

"No, only driving snow." Fenryl abruptly raised his left arm. A white falcon landed on his gloved hand, a blood-smeared amulet in its beak.

Alfadas looked at the bird in astonishment. "That's from the blacksmith, the man who fell off the cliff! You've trained the bird to recover amulets—you knew what would happen!"

"No, no, no!" Count Fenryl shook his head adamantly. "I have merely trained Snowwing to recover lost amulets. They are extremely precious, Alfadas, and it takes a long time to create such a talisman. We have to get them back for our children. They cannot simply be replaced. I thought it likely that some among us might die with no easy way to recover the body, so I brought my falcon along. I can't see into the future, Duke. I knew no more than you that someone would die during our ascent. But even without magic, it was clear to me that there would be losses. There must be. That is simply what happens in war."

Alfadas turned and walked away without a word. The count was right, and what he had done was only sensible. Yet Alfadas found it hard to accept that the elf had deliberately prepared for deaths among the humans, the first of which had caught the duke off guard.

He was suddenly aware of how long he had been away from Albenmark. And at the same time, he wondered, with shock, if the people of Firnstayn perhaps looked at him in the same way as he himself now saw the count, whose foresight was certainly practical. But making preparations to recover amulets from hard-to-reach corpses seemed to Alfadas deeply inhuman. His mistake. What else did he expect from the elves? How were they supposed to be "human" at all?

"What's the matter with you?" Ollowain had followed him.

"Nothing!" Alfadas waved Ollowain's question away tiredly. He wanted to be alone, as much as that was possible for a duke among an army of marching men.

"Count Fenryl would like to know if he has offended you somehow. If so, he would like to apologize."

"I have some things to think about. Tell the count that everything is all right." That was a lie, but Alfadas did not have the strength to carry on a debate with the elf about something that no one could make him understand. The matter with the falcon . . . it made perfect sense, yet it horrified him.

Alfadas marched with the men. Like all of them, he carried a bag with emergency rations, and he turned down the offer to ride one of the few horses. It bothered him that he could not remember the blacksmith's name. He talked with the simple farmers who had never seen a landscape that consisted only of ice and rock, a land in which nothing would ever grow and for which, still, war was waged. He talked with the young soldiers from the king's bodyguard who had joined forces with them at the end. They were burning for their first battle, hiding their fear behind swagger.

But Alfadas preferred to be with Lambi and his men. The war jarl wore an impenetrable armor of grim humor. He gave his men the impression that nothing could knock him down, and it gave them courage. Somehow, one felt things could not get too bad if Lambi was close by.

Alfadas wished that he was more like Lambi. The men of his army held him, their duke, to be invincible. That was a fragile claim to fame. He would much rather have been the man who, even in defeat, could come up with a bawdy joke about his enemy and make his men confident that the next fight would turn out differently. But their first defeat would erase the men's trust in Alfadas. And how were you supposed to win against trolls?

He kept his thoughts to himself, moved on, and helped the men set up camp. They stretched tarpaulins as protection against the wind. It was impossible to start a campfire on the bare ice, but the elves set up large copper bowls on legs and lit fires in those. And although no one was cold, the humans gathered around the braziers. Their light was the promise that the darkness would pass.

Alfadas gave the order for several sheep to be slaughtered. The death of the blacksmith had shaken Alfadas's men, but the smell of roasting meat was enough to raise their spirits again. They sliced the meat into broad strips and threw them onto the coals in the braziers until a dark crust formed.

The duke saw how Ronardin, the watchman from the bridge in Phylangan, observed the humans with a mixture of fascination and repulsion. In all the centuries Ronardin had been alive, he had no doubt never eaten a piece of meat burned black on the outside and still raw and bloody inside.

The elves passed around light apple wine that did not go to one's head but was still delicious and herbed bread, dried meat, and a little honey.

Alfadas heard Veleif's voice at one of the fires. The skald was singing about a hunter who went out stalking one lonely winter's night to save his family from starvation. All Veleif needed was two verses and everyone around him fell silent. Even the coarse laughter from Lambi's men faded.

Alfadas walked a short distance away from the camp, fleeing from thoughts of Asla and their children. If they were to be victorious, then he had to be like Count Fenryl. He had to think ahead. Lambi and Veleif would keep the men's morale high. His job was to be coolheaded, to calculate how they could win against unequal enemies. It was good that, at first, they would only have to defend a fortress whose walls protected them from fighting the trolls hand-to-hand.

Suddenly, the snow in front of him began to move. A figure rose from the white powder, well camouflaged inside a heavy white woolen cloak. Silwyna.

"Why aren't you in camp?" Alfadas asked in surprise.

"Staring into a fire spoils your night vision."

"Do we need someone to watch over us tonight? Fenryl says the trolls are still far off."

Silwyna sniffed disdainfully. "He's just a Normirga. I'm a Maurawan. I know that a hunter who underestimates his prey is no better than prey himself. In Vahan Calyd, everyone thought they were safe, too. Now I know that the trolls have returned to Albenmark, and I know that they want to return to their old homeland. Those are two good reasons not to just lie by a fire and sleep in the Snaiwamark."

Alfadas thought about how close the two of them had once been. "You're always on guard, aren't you? What did I do back then to make you leave me?"

"This is neither the time nor the place to discuss that," she said sharply, and turned away into the darkness.

"Will there ever be a time and place to discuss it?" he shouted after her. But his anger was not just directed at her. He was just as angry at himself that only a few words with her were enough to make him lose his self-control.

Silwyna stopped. Slowly, she turned back. "You speak truly, Alfadas. It will never be easy to talk about what was, and in a few weeks, we might both be dead. You have a right to know. Why do you think I came to you in the Other World?"

Another question that Alfadas had asked himself often in recent weeks. He had found no answer.

"Perhaps because Ollowain asked you to?"

She was standing very close to him now. "No," she said, smiling. "He would never do that. He was actually worried about taking me with him because he was afraid the sight of me would make you angry." Her wolf-like eyes held his. She was as beautiful as ever. At least to him. "I went to the Other World to see what kind of father you are. I knew you had a wife and thought that you would probably also have children. I wanted to see them, wanted to know how you were raising them. How you are with them. How they look at you."

Alfadas felt a lump forming in his throat. He thought of Ulric, how he listened with a serious expression whenever Alfadas talked to him about how a man fought with honor. And he thought of how Kadlin's exuberant laughter could dissolve his anger at all the small catastrophes she dragged Alfadas into.

"You have another son," Silwyna said softly. "His name is Melvyn."

That was impossible! Her words took his breath away like a fist to his gut. His mouth felt dry. "Humans and elves are not able to have children." He could barely speak.

"That's what they say, isn't it? It's . . . unnatural? But he was conceived in love. Is that unnatural?"

Again, a flash of anger overcame Alfadas. "Why did you run away? Why didn't you say anything? You stole him from me. Why are you telling me about a child I will never see?"

As suddenly as his anger came, it dissipated again. He thought of all the lonely hours of his own childhood in which he had wished for a father. Ollowain had truly done his best, but a father was something else.

"I had to. Because of Emerelle." Silwyna's lips trembled. "Noroelle's son. He was another child who should never have been conceived. A bastard, a half elf. She ordered his death, and she exiled Noroelle until the end of days. You know . . ."

"Yes." Alfadas's voice was little more than a despairing croak. He knew what had happened. He was among those who had finally found Noroelle's son, after all. And he'd been able to understand very well why Farodin and Nuramon had refused to carry out their queen's order.

"I was afraid that Emerelle would also condemn our child to death." Silwyna was speaking quickly now, her voice breaking, and Alfadas realized how long she must have wanted to say these words. "My love for you never died, but I could not say a word to you. You would not have let me go, and if you had come with me, our secret would have been discovered. You were too closely bound to the queen's court to simply go off to the Slanga Mountains with me. Emerelle would have found out what happened. But because no one knew about it and I disappeared one morning without a word of good-bye, everyone thought the moody Maurawan had simply gone off after the call of the wild, that she didn't care a damn that she had broken the human's heart. I know what the other elves think about my race. It's safe to say that nobody at court was surprised at my disappearance."

"No," Alfadas admitted. He remembered that even cold, aloof Emerelle herself had tried to console him. *The Maurawan are like the wind,* she had told him back then. *They are simply not made to spend much time in one place.* It had not helped. The only thing that had brought him back to life again was meeting his father. Going with Mandred on the search for Noroelle's son was a welcome opportunity to get away from the queen's court, where everything reminded him of Silwyna. In the end, he had turned his back on Albenmark and never returned.

"What's he like, my son?" he asked, and tried to imagine a child whose face blended Silwyna's features with his own.

"He has my eyes," she said with a smile. She stroked his hair. "And your ears. He doesn't like that. He thinks it's a flaw that his ears look different from mine or the wolves'. I've never been able to convince him otherwise."

"Why does he compare himself to wolves?" Alfadas asked, perplexed.

"Wolves look after their cubs well. The entire pack watches out for their young. If anything happens to the mother, the other females in the pack raise the cub."

It took Alfadas a moment to understand what she was trying to tell him. "You . . . you gave my son to a wolf pack? That's—tell me that isn't true!"

"It wasn't like that. I went to the pack and became part of it myself. I hunted and lived with them. I did not hand Melvyn over to them, and I was almost always there."

"You raised him among wolves!" Alfadas could not believe what he was hearing. "Among beasts!"

"Those beasts have never treated him like a half blood, despite how different he is. Of the litter he grew up with, only one old she-wolf is still alive. They accepted him as their brother, and he had his place in the pack. He would not have had that anywhere else! I never dared show him to my race, not once, because I did not know how they would react. They might have sided with Emerelle. There has never before been a boy that is half elf, half human. It was possible that even the Maurawan would have decided to kill him. So I withdrew to the forests at the foot of the Albentop. No one goes there. People think it is cursed. None of my people questioned it; it is not unusual for one of us to go off and live a solitary existence. They could accept that, but could they have accepted the boy, too? I don't know. Telling anyone about Melvyn would have meant risking his life."

Alfadas tried to imagine an infant lying among wolf cubs. "They could have torn him to pieces. A child safe in a pack of ferocious wolves . . . how could you think of raising a child among animals? Are you so coldhearted? Does his life mean nothing to you?"

"You don't know what you're talking about." Silwyna looked at him despondently. "You don't really want to hear what I'm saying, do you? It doesn't interest you."

"How can you say that? He's my son. He—does he have more of me than just the ears?"

Silwyna smiled mildly. "Yes. Much more. He asks about you all the time. That's why I went to Vahan Calyd. I wanted to meet Ollowain and ask him to help me get to the human world." She shook her head. "But he had a request

11

for me instead. He entrusted me with watching over the woman I feared more than any other inhabitant of Albenmark: Emerelle, from whom I fled into the wilderness in the first place."

Alfadas looked around to make sure they were still alone. Only then did he ask, "Was it you? Did you shoot at the queen?"

Silwyna looked at him for a long time without answering. With every passing heartbeat, Alfadas grew more uncertain. This was not like the Maurawan. In the past, she had invariably been open with him, her answers coming without second thoughts or second guesses. And she had always spoken the truth, though it might harm herself or others in the process. Was she struggling now with a lie?

"I did not shoot at Emerelle," she finally said. "She is the queen. It is not my place to kill her. Still, Ollowain could not have found a more unsuitable guard for her. I did, in fact, see the assassin on the quarterdeck of her ship, and I did nothing to stop him. Emerelle is a danger to our child, Alfadas. I cannot protect her."

"But you helped them escape the town. You . . ." Alfadas faltered.

"I helped Ollowain because I trusted him to find a way out of the inferno, and he did. I didn't care what happened to the queen. I wanted to survive, and . . . I wanted to get to you."

"But by helping Ollowain, you saved Emerelle," Alfadas persisted. He did not want to believe that Silwyna had pitted herself against the queen.

"That may be," Silwyna said calmly. "But it counts for nothing because it was not my intention to help *her*. And she would do well never to rely on any help from me."

"Does Ollowain know this?"

"He doesn't have to. He doesn't trust me, and he's right not to."

Alfadas could not really grasp Silwyna's thinking. She hated Emerelle and feared for their child. She did nothing to protect the queen, but she did not try to do anything to hurt her directly. "Where is my son now? Did you leave him with the wolves? And how old is he? He isn't still at that mountain with such a terrible reputation that even the Maurawan won't go near it, is he?"

"*Our* son is experiencing his twelfth winter. And he is safe among the wolves. They would tear themselves apart to protect him. I . . ." Her voice failed, and she turned her face away. "I can't trust anyone."

12

Alfadas stepped closer to her and stroked her cheek gently. "You can trust me." As he touched her, all his anger melted away, and the thing he had feared the most came to pass: all the images of the half a year they had shared came back to him, vivid and unvarnished. It was the first time in his life that he had been truly happy.

Asla had been the one to heal the deep wound that Silwyna had inflicted with her sudden disappearance. He had cursed the Maurawan, looking for her week after week. But even in the beginning of his search, he knew he would never be able to find her unless she wanted him to. When he finally gave up, he at least tried to understand her motivation, but even that was denied him. No one understood the Maurawan, it was said, and he had finally shared that opinion. And then his father had come. Riding with Mandred, leaving behind everything that reminded him of Silwyna, had been a welcome change. And it had brought him Asla. She loved him from the very first day. And he?

Asla had been good for him. He found peace with her. But every time he looked up to the stone crown on top of the Hartungscliff, he was conscious of what he had done to her. She had had to fill the gap left by Silwyna. He loved his wife, but it was a different kind of love than what he felt for the elf woman.

Silwyna kissed him. It was a fleeting touch, and yet filled with passion.

"I will not stand in your way," she said, her voice raw. With quick steps, she disappeared into the night.

SKIRMISH IN THE STORM

He had hardly slept in the night, and they were on the move again well before dawn. Heavy, driving snow hid the plain from sight and shrunk the world to just a few paces across.

Alfadas thought of Asla. He had been happy with her all these years, though he could not shake his memories of Albenmark. Had he been fooling himself? He wished he had not made Silwyna talk to him the night before. Now he marched in the middle of his column of men, a lost black figure in a long row of black figures. He stared at the cloak of the man in front of him. The wind tore at the threadbare fabric. Snow gathered in the deep folds at the shoulders. The only good thing about this miserable weather was that they had been spared from having to wear the snow masks. With strips of leather over their eyes and only narrow slits to see through, it made little difference if one were really blind or not.

He waited every moment for an emissary from Count Fenryl to arrive and request him to hand over command. How much heavier would the driving snow have to be before the elven prince saw it as a danger? It would be wiser to call a halt where they were.

Alfadas stared at the back of the man in front. He told himself that when he could not see the folds of the man's cloak clearly anymore, he would give the order to halt, whether the count was still vacillating or not.

He pressed his fingers to his chest and felt the elven amulet beneath his chain mail shirt and padded leather vest. Without those enchanted small gold pieces, half of his men would probably have frozen to death in the night.

However bad things looked for the elves at that moment, a race that could create such miracles would never be defeated by a mob of unwashed trolls. They had to win, just as they always had in the past!

Mag came up and joined him. The war jarl's cloak was crusted with snow, and he ducked slightly as he braced against the wind.

Alfadas blinked at him. The snow stabbed his face like a thousand tiny daggers. "Everything all right?" He almost had to shout to make himself heard over the howling wind.

"Yes," the erstwhile ferryman said. Then he suddenly shook his head. "No. My men asked me something, and I don't know how to answer them, so I wanted to put the question to you. Will we—the farmers, fishermen, and craftsmen—also enter Norgrimm's halls if we fight heroically? In the old stories, it's always jarls and kings or at least famous fighters that Norgrimm calls to join him." He took a deep breath. "And now that we're here, so far from the Fjordlands, will we even be able to find a way to his Golden Hall?"

"We'll teach him that courage has nothing to do with a man's standing in the world," said Alfadas. He could see that his answer did not satisfy Mag. "Have you ever met someone who returned from the Golden Hall to report on it?"

The young war jarl looked up in annoyance. "Of course not. The heroes will return to the Fjordlands with Norgrimm only when the last of all battles is fought. There's no coming back before that."

"So how do we know about the eternal feast of the warriors and the magnificent hall of the war god? Only from his priests and from the skalds who tell us stories about the heroes. We have our own skalds, and Veleif Silberhand is considered the best in his guild. He will write a magnificent epic about us. And I can promise you that in his heroic saga, everyone who has fought bravely will find their way to Norgrimm."

Mag's brow furrowed. "But is it the truth?"

"Who save Luth, the weaver of fate, knows the truth? I don't know if the Golden Hall of the gods exists, Mag. But I know one thing with certainty: when Veleif returns to the Fjordlands, then the grandchildren of our grandchildren will tell stories about the men who went to fight at the side of the elves. King Osaberg himself and all the other heroes have not earned more renown. Their stories have lived on beyond their deaths. Maybe that is what makes the Golden Hall—it is the place of the ones not forgotten."

Mag knocked the icy snow from his shoulders. "They say you don't believe in the gods. Maybe I should have asked someone else for advice."

"You're not asking for your men, are you? You came because of your brother Torad."

Mag looked at Alfadas in surprise. After some moments, he nodded. "Is my heart always so easy to read?"

"Is it dishonorable not to be able to hide the truth?"

The young war jarl sighed. "It's easier to catch the wind in your hands than to get a straight answer from you, Duke."

"Only if you ask me something to which you already carry the answer in your heart." Alfadas had to smile. He could understand the young war jarl's despair. He himself had suffered through dozens of conversations like this with his swordmaster and foster father, Ollowain. Back then, Alfadas had been the one despairing at the answers. Only with the passing of the years had he learned that Ollowain's words were more than mere excuses to avoid uncomfortable questions. He had since learned to follow the voice of his own heart—most of the time, at least.

Lysilla, the white-haired elf woman, appeared like a ghost from the driving snow. Leaning low over the mane of her white horse, she charged past the men.

"They're spooky," said Mag. He spoke so softly that the storm almost swallowed his words. "Ever since we were on the golden path, my brother has been terribly afraid of dying. He fears it's like the darkness we passed through, an endless horror."

Alfadas hesitated briefly, then decided on a lie. "All of us saw the path, the golden light, when we passed through the darkness. The same path is in all our lives. Generosity, courage, and our sense of justice are the signposts along it. If we never leave the path, it will lead us beyond life to the halls of the gods, just as the golden path led us through the darkness into the world of the Albenfolk."

Mag nodded earnestly. He seemed relieved.

Alfadas felt miserable talking fervently about something when he was not really convinced. Mag, however, seemed to have forgotten completely that he had just charged Alfadas with not believing in the gods at all. But who could claim to know an honest answer? What came after death was a question of belief, no more.

"Duke!" Ollowain came galloping along the line.

"Here!" Alfadas stepped clear of the row of marchers.

The swordmaster reined his horse to a halt and sprang from the saddle. "They're here. Less than half a mile ahead. The trolls! It has begun."

Several men had stopped and were looking at them, but Alfadas was certain that they could not hear what was said over the howling wind. "How many?"

"I don't know. Lysilla discovered them. They're attacking the elves from Rosecarn. We have to help."

Alfadas's mind raced.

"Stop the column," he bellowed to the lines of men. "Call the war jarls together!"

His plan had been to have the trolls attack a wall of pikemen through a hail of arrows, but everything had been turned on its head. Now they themselves would have to attack, and fast! Archers would be all but useless in the stinging, gusting snow, and the large formation of pikemen would fare little better because they were too cumbersome to attack an unseen enemy.

As his officers gathered, he ordered the archers and pikemen to build a defensive line behind the rest of the troops. Alfadas formed those armed with poleaxes and swords into loose lines. They would lead the attack, and the elves were to distribute themselves along the battle line and give what support they could to their brothers-in-arms.

Apparently calm, Count Fenryl stood with the war jarls and observed as Alfadas's orders were carried out. An eternity seemed to pass before the battle lines had formed. One had to look very closely to see the count's hand clench and relax on the grip of his sword. Somewhere out there were his wife and child, and he had no choice but to wait until the humans were ready.

Alfadas strode along the entire row of men before he gave the order to attack. Their first engagement could not fail. The men's morale would never recover. Lambi's and Ragni's fighters formed the first row. Behind them came the young men from Horsa's bodyguard and only then the men with the poleaxes.

The duke drew his sword. The storm limited his sight to ten paces. He had forbidden his men to use any horn signals. Their attack had to take the trolls by surprise. Alfadas swung his sword once in a shining arc over his head, then he pointed forward and took the lead. Lambi came up beside him. "I hope you don't think we're going to treat 'em like we did those steers."

Alfadas looked at Lambi with incomprehension. "What do you mean?"

His comrade grinned. "Throw me in chains if you want, but I'm not about to eat a dead troll."

Some of the men around them heard the jarl's words and smiled. Even Alfadas felt a little of his tension drain away.

"I think I'll do with them what my father did with some of his enemies: he'd cut out their liver and feed it to the dogs."

Lambi shook his head disapprovingly. "These dogs aren't the curs we have in the Fjordlands," he said. "I can already picture 'em heaving up their guts and lying sick on the sleds, and then we'd end up in the harness, pulling 'em along. Better for all of us if some of your good father's habits don't become a tradition, even if he was the damned hero who slew the manboar."

Alfadas stepped over a small figure lying in the snow: a kobold with a knife clutched tightly in its fist, its dead eyes staring toward the sky. What courage did it take to face an enemy seven times taller with such a pitiful weapon?

From somewhere ahead came the sounds of battle, but the enemy was still hidden from view. The snow kept the battlefield out of sight, revealing only individual scenes of the horror. Alfadas made his way around an upturned sled with a gray mare still harnessed to it. A blow to the horse's back had broken its spine. Its hind legs lay grotesquely twisted on the ice. Whinnying quietly, the beast tried to push itself up with its front legs and had already rubbed itself raw on the shafts in its desperate attempts to stand. The duke stroked the mare's mane and spoke to her soothingly. With a knife, he gently opened the swollen artery at her neck. She would not suffer much longer.

Behind the sled lay an elf, trapped when it overturned. His chest had been smashed in, and snow had already gathered over his eyes and in his nostrils. Not much longer and winter's shroud would cover him completely.

"Can you do me a favor?" Lambi asked, his voice hoarse.

The duke looked up. "What?"

"If I'm wounded, don't worry about me." The warrior smiled wryly. "I don't want to perish like that nag."

Alfadas nodded. "Are you scared?"

From in front of them came a long, primitive cry, like the roar of a bear greeting spring after its winter sleep. The sound of weapons rang out.

Lambi rubbed his mutilated nose. "Of course I'm scared. I'm all but shitting in my breeches. I wish we'd finally get to fight. The trolls can't be as bad as I picture 'em. Having one of the bastards in front of me will be a relief."

"You're sure I shouldn't feed any troll's liver to the dogs?"

Lambi grimaced. "Could you keep your bloodthirsty stories about your father to yourself until we're done with this? It might surprise you, Duke, but before a battle, my stomach is always very sensitive."

Alfadas looked at him in dismay. "Really?"

Lambi nodded earnestly. "Yep. About as sensitive as the belly of a blood-hound when it's gnawing on a deer's guts." The war jarl let out a ringing laugh. "Do I look like a man who pukes in the snow because of a bit of blood on his sword?"

In front of them lay a smashed chest. The wind tore at a delicate dress that had caught on the splintered wood. Crates, barrels, and even items of furniture strewn across the ice bore witness to elves trying desperately to lighten their sleds to escape the trolls.

Lambi lifted the delicate cloth to his ravaged nose and sniffed at it. "Mmm, delicious!" he called to Alfadas.

An elf woman in a lime-green dress staggered toward them. Her red hair was tousled, her eyes wide with panic. A fine thread of blood ran down her neck from one of her long, pointed ears.

"By the gods! Luth has listened to my most secret wish!" Lambi cried, hurrying toward the elf woman. Suddenly, a bellowing roar drowned out the howl of the wind. An enormous figure materialized from the white flurries of snow. It was more than half again as tall as a man. Its skin was rock gray, and like a rock, the deadly cold seemed not to bother the monster in the slightest. It wore no more than a loincloth of filthy matted fur. For a moment, the troll seemed surprised. Then it raised its club, let out a marrow-shaking cry, and charged straight at Lambi.

The diminutive fighter saved himself from the first powerful swing by dropping flat on the ice. Alfadas stood as if petrified and stared at the troll. Nothing he had ever heard about these fearsome monsters came even close to the reality. The others around him were as frozen as he was, as if looking death itself in the eye.

Lambi rolled desperately to one side. Just a few fingerwidths from his head, the great club hammered the ice. The war jarl had lost his sword. He rolled helplessly from side to side, doing his best to dodge the troll's attacks.

Alfadas finally overcame his initial shock. His friend was about to die.

"Over here, you filthy freak!" he cried.

BERNHARD HENNEN

The troll whipped its head around. Its narrow, lipless mouth twisted into a smile. The duke lunged forward and ducked beneath the giant's club. His blade sank deep into the troll's thigh, but his adversary only grunted. Then the back of its hand hit Alfadas in the face. It was no more than a slap, yet it was the slap of a giant. Alfadas was jerked off his feet and flung a short distance through the air. His sword still protruded from the troll's thigh.

The monster now charged the other fighters. A swing of its club smashed the skull of one of the poleaxemen. Groaning, Alfadas rose to his feet.

"Attack it together!" he screamed. "Or it'll kill you one by one!"

"Take this!" Lambi was back on his feet, too. He pulled an axe out of his belt and threw it to Alfadas, who caught it adroitly in the air and hurled himself back into the battle. From the corner of his eye, he saw Lambi follow, armed now with just a knife.

The men's poleaxes stabbed forward, jerked back. The tips of the weapons were equipped with long, four-sided iron spikes. They dug into the troll's arms and chest but were not able to injure it seriously. The giant was swinging its club in an arc, smashing the shafts of the men's weapons if they did not jump back fast enough. It bellowed something in a deep, throaty language. *Was it afraid?* Alfadas wondered.

Lambi crept up on the troll from behind and stabbed his dagger into the back of its knee. With a shrill scream, the monster collapsed to one side. Poleaxes rained down on it. The broad blades opened gaping wounds in its shoulders and back. Even in its death throes, the monster was still able to grab one of the weapons. It yanked the blond fighter wielding it forward and smashed his chest with a butt of its head.

A poleaxe blade came down on the back of the troll's neck. Alfadas heard the splintering of bone. Its arms spread wide, the giant sank forward, burying the dying warrior beneath its body.

Alfadas stepped forward and pulled his sword out of the troll's thigh. The duke looked around. Two of his men were dead and two more so seriously injured that they would not be able to fight again for a long time.

"Victory!" Lambi bawled. "Victory! They're flesh and blood like us, just too damned much of both."

"Silence!" Alfadas cried. The raging storm had abated somewhat. A throaty shout rang out. Right and left of them, they heard the sounds of battle, the screams of someone dying.

"This way!" He stormed off in the direction of the screams. They found two more trolls battling the men of the Fjordlands. The snow was red with blood.

Ronardin, the keeper of the Mahdan Falah, was trying to distract the two trolls from an injured man crawling over the ice.

Without hesitating, Alfadas moved in. His sword slashed in a glinting half circle and left a bloody line across the back of one of the trolls. In the same moment, he heard the crash of metal. Ronardin fell to his knees, struck by a war hammer. His breastplate caved inward deeply. Blood brimmed at the elf's lips, even as he swung his sword powerlessly at his adversary's knee. A second hammer blow knocked the sword from his hand.

"Hey, rockhead," Lambi shouted. "Your sister spreads her legs for everyone!"

"It can't understand you," Alfadas cried, just managing to dodge a low swipe by the troll he'd injured. "Enough nonsense!"

The troll with the war hammer ignored Ronardin now and turned around. Its chest and legs were covered with bloody handprints. A broad strip of flesh hung from a meat hook on its belt.

"If you get the tone right, they don't need to understand the words," Lambi shouted back. He flailed his sword manically. "Here, you overgrown toad. Let me tell you what it's like to screw your sister."

Alfadas ducked beneath an abandoned sled to dodge the other troll's stone axe. The monster wore breeches made from pale leather, and at its belt hung a bow cover and a quiver. Its stone axe shattered the sled's bench seat.

The duke rolled through between the runners. For a moment, the light vehicle was in front of him. Then the troll, with an angry cry, hoisted the sled into the air and held it high over its head.

Alfadas began to run. When he heard a second cry, he threw himself to the left, colliding hard with a wooden chest reinforced with bronze. The sled just missed him. Bits of the wreckage flew through the air, and a twisted runner clanged against the wooden chest. Alfadas's leap had saved his life.

A shadow reared above the duke. No, his leap had only extended his life by a few moments. The troll stood over him, its legs apart. Alfadas tried to stab upward, aiming for the troll's crotch, but a savage backhand swing knocked the sword from his hand.

The giant grinned and raised its stone axe. Without warning, an arrow shaft suddenly jutted from its right eye. The troll trembled. Dark blood ran down its cheek and gathered at the corner of its mouth. Its grin remained.

Slender hands reached for Alfadas and dragged him aside. The duke could not take his eyes off the troll. The hand holding the stone axe opened, and the heavy weapon fell to the ice.

"It's over," said a familiar voice. Ollowain.

"Thank you," Alfadas managed to croak. The troll began to sway. Its uninjured eye stared rigidly at him. Suddenly, the giant collapsed forward. For a moment, it lay without moving. Then its right hand reached for the axe. Its fingertips touched the shaft before the huge body emitted a deep sigh and did not move again.

"Don't thank me," said Ollowain gently. "She saved you." He pointed to a white-robed slim figure holding a long hunting bow. Silwyna. The elf woman was standing beside Lambi, who was breathing heavily and supporting himself against the wreckage of the sled. The second troll had vanished.

Ollowain kneeled beside Ronardin and grasped his hand. The face of the guard of the Mahdan Falah was as white as the snow all around, but his lips were red with blood.

"They did not make it across the bridge, did they?" His brown eyes peered intently at the swordmaster.

"The bridge has not fallen," said Ollowain in a steady voice. "You did your job well."

Foamy blood pearled on the elf's lips.

"Please . . . the queen sent the lady to rescue Phylangan. Ask her for forgiveness. I did not mean to offend her with my gaze." Ronardin tried to sit up, but Ollowain pressed him back gently.

"She was never angry with you, my friend. Rest now. We will take you back to the stone garden so that you can continue to guard the bridge."

"She can't . . ." Ronardin's eyes widened. "You must . . ."

Ollowain held him a moment longer, then folded the dead man's hands over his chest.

"What did he mean?" Alfadas asked.

"He seemed to think he'd been fighting on the Mahdan Falah. He was the keeper there for many years."

The storm had now receded completely. Only a little snow still fell, and the wind had died. Before them, graceful figures began to appear from the whiteness. Carriages and sleds moved toward them: the Rosecarn refugees.

The human fighters burst into jubilant cheers. They had won! Lambi came and clapped Alfadas on the shoulder. "We gave their asses a damn good kicking, didn't we?"

Alfadas nodded tiredly. "The alliance has passed its first test. That's a good sign. We were able to save the elves, at least these."

Lambi laughed. "What do you mean, *at least these*? This is just the start! We'll follow the trolls into the hills and finish 'em all off. I've got a score to settle with that one with all the handprints on him. No one gets away with pushing me around."

The duke felt the ice tremble beneath his feet. Had the enemy returned with reinforcements? The battle was not yet won!

THE BATTLE ON THE ICE

"They came on us by surprise, Pack Leader," said Brud remorsefully. "We were caught off guard."

The chief scout was on his knees in front of Orgrim and obviously expected to be punished. But Orgrim said, "On your feet. No one could have known. It was smarter to bring our warriors back here than to sacrifice them in a senseless battle, as honorable as it might have been." The pack leader looked out over the plain. Far off, an extended black line was forming on the ice. It looked as if they were readying for an attack. "You're sure it was humans?"

The scout nodded. "Yes. And it seemed as if they were prepared for the fight."

"Centaur shit!" Gran swore. "They surprised us, and they were lucky." The giant warrior snatched a strip of bloody meat from the hook on his belt and bit off a large chunk. "We ought to go down there and smash in their skulls," he said, both cheeks full. "You have more than two hundred battle-hardened warriors, Pack Leader. We'll bash them to a pulp if we attack. They're just humans. They can't stand up to us!"

"What makes you think they were prepared to fight us, Brud?" Orgrim looked searchingly at the leader of the scouts. Was he trying to make excuses for his defeat?

"They didn't seem surprised when they saw us. And some of them carried strange weapons, axes on long poles. They could use them to attack us without getting near our clubs."

"What do you think, Mandrag?"

The aging troll looked out over the plain for a long time before he answered. "I think the elves must be desperate if they have to use humans as allies."

Orgrim nodded his acknowledgment. He hadn't looked at the situation from that standpoint.

"We should catch one of the humans," Birga said. "I'm sure he'll tell me everything."

"The question is, who would understand him?"

The shaman eyed Orgrim calmly. "Forget not who I am, whelp. I can speak ten thousand tongues if I want. I understand the sighing of the trees and listen to the whisperings of the crows on the battlefield. Get me one of those humans, and I'll tell you where they come from and why they're here."

"I did not mean to offend you," Orgrim said, eager to reassure her. He wished he could look the ugly hag in the face and read her expression, but as always, her face was hidden behind a leather mask.

"Look! Something's happening out on the ice."

Boltan's words gave Orgrim a welcome opportunity to turn away from Birga. Orgrim shaded his eyes with his hand. The clouds had dispersed. The tips of spears glinted in the sunlight.

"Riders," Orgrim said.

"No, centaurs," Brud corrected him. "About three hundred, I'd say."

Gran laughed. "More to slaughter. Let's get off this hill and cut them to pieces."

"No," Orgrim said decisively.

"Lost your courage just because our scouts were surprised by a few men?" Gran goaded him. "Send the warriors down there, and you'll see. This time, we'll win."

"Didn't you run from the fight, too?" Orgrim asked, smiling.

"I didn't run. I followed the order to retreat. A good warrior knows to obey."

"And a good leader owes his warriors victories," Orgrim replied. "The arrival of the centaurs has shifted the balance. If we go down and attack, we might win, but at what cost? Our casualties would be high. They may wipe us out entirely. But if we stay up here, we can only win."

"That sounds like the yammer of a coward!" Gran turned to face Orgrim's retinue. "I can only win if I sit on my ass and do nothing," he said, aping the pack leader's voice. "You know what we lose if we follow this order? Our honor. And our pride as warriors."

"Did the humans kill off your common sense in that last little skirmish?" Orgrim said. He cursed the day he'd decided to take Gran on board the *Wraithwind*. "If we stay here on the hill, we force our enemy to make a decision they don't want to make. If they attack, their losses will be far worse than if they defend an attack by us. And if they stay down there on the plain and wait to see what we do, then we are tying up an entire army that I can tell you with certainty has something better to do than sit there and watch us. If they retreat, it will look like they're running from us, and it will demoralize their fighters. An enemy that runs once will run again. On top of that, Brud will follow them and make sure they don't sleep a single easy night. Did that go through your thick skull?"

"I don't like deciding battles like this," Gran grumbled. "There's no dignity in it for a warrior."

"Dignity is something that each of my warriors decides for himself, through his actions. The dignity of the pack leader lies in one thing: victory."

"Well spoken," Birga said, unexpectedly backing him. "You should keep your mouth shut now, Gran."

On the plain, there was movement in the enemy ranks. The centaurs swung out to the right flank while a mass of foot soldiers mustered in the center. Spear tips gleamed above their heads. The enemy's left flank seemed to be their weakness, guarded by two small groups of fighters.

"Are your men ready?" Orgrim asked his artillery chief, Boltan.

The pack leader looked with pride over the formation of his troops. The battle had certainly gone differently than expected, but it made no difference— the elves and their allies would fall into his trap. The long caravan of refugees had re-formed and was moving clear of the battlefield. But if he were victorious in the hours ahead, he would catch up with them again.

His warriors stood in a long double row along the crest of the hill. Behind them, out of sight from the plain below, waited eight of the new catapults they had looted from the battles at Reilimee. The first salvo would take the enemy completely by surprise.

Orgrim looked at the looted weapons with satisfaction. Boltan had jacked the catapults onto heavy wooden feet, making them easier for the trolls to oper- ate. The cocking levers on the winch had also been reinforced. The catapults were built for stones the size of an elf's head. When a locking lever was released, the stone was pulled along wooden rails. The catapult arms were made of silver steel. They were inserted into two drums that held what looked like lengths of rope twisted into each other. The bronze drums protected the ropes from moisture. Orgrim had been there when the artillery chief had opened one of the drums. He had wanted to find out what was behind the extraordinary tensile force of the catapults. When Boltan released the twisted ropes, however, he managed to destroy the drums, and one of his assistants had been decapitated in the process by the whiplike cords. The artillery chief could neither reconstruct the drum with its ropes nor understand the mechanism. In the end, Boltan decided he could live without the knowledge, or he would end up with no useful catapults left.

He had turned his attention to ammunition instead. The elves fired beautiful polished spherical stones, each one laboriously crafted. For a field campaign, however, they were unsuitable because they were too difficult to replace and too heavy to carry in large numbers.

Boltan had carved wooden molds in which he could make balls of ice. In the cold of the Snaiwamark, they would not melt, and the ammunition could be replaced in a matter of hours. The balls of ice would certainly do little against a fortress or even a ship, but against softer targets—the bodies of elves, for example—they were as deadly as any stone ball.

When they had landed in Whale Bay, they had loaded the catapults onto cargo sleds. It had taken time and energy to get the heavy sleds over the coastal ranges, but Orgrim was convinced that the effort would be worth it.

The pack leader watched as the enemy's formations advanced. He could now clearly see the spears of the large mass of the humans in the center of the battle lines. They were unusually long. Orgrim had never seen spears like them before. Apparently, the humans had thought about how to make up for their lack of strength in a battle against the trolls. He could not allow them to get too close!

"Aim at the centaurs first!" Orgrim ordered his artillery chief.

Boltan nodded. The catapults, standing in a row on the top of the hill, swung a little to the side and realigned.

A cloud of arrows came down on his men. Archers had concealed themselves behind the spearmen and were now firing at the battle lines of the trolls.

Orgrim raised the heavy wooden shield that lay in front of him in the snow and pushed his left arm into its broad leather loops. Then he gave the trumpeter a signal. Two long blasts sounded. The lines of trolls moved forward ten paces and halted.

Pride filled Orgrim. His warriors were the best in Branbeard's army. No other detachment of trolls could have been brought to a halt once they were in motion toward the enemy.

A second hail of arrows hissed down. Most of them buried themselves uselessly in the warriors' large shields.

The catapults returned fire. Balls of ice exploded in silvery showers. The first salvo was low, just in front of the centaurs. Shards of ice slashed between the manhorses' legs. Many went sprawling. Their orderly formation fell apart. The second salvo was already on its way, but this time Boltan had instructed his soldiers to fire a little higher.

The balls of ice carved bloody gaps in the centaurs' rows but also fanned their thirst for battle. They surged forward in a wild gallop, leaving the ranks of the humans behind them. A single blast of the trumpeter's horn was the command for the trolls to advance.

Orgrim took his place among his warriors. A third salvo hissed overhead. This time, the mass of spearmen was the target. The archers had stopped firing, as the centaurs now blocked their view.

The opposing forces plowed into one another with a deafening roar. Many trolls went down. The centaurs' hooves stomped them where they fell. The air was filled with screams and the clash of weapons.

At close quarters, Orgrim could not swing his war hammer well. He rammed the hammer's head forward into the chest of the centaur in front of him. The bearded manhorse dropped to his knees. A strike with the shaft of the hammer hit him above his ears, and he went down completely. Orgrim set the edge of his shield on the manhorse's neck and leaned on it. His weight was enough to all but separate the centaur's head from his shoulders.

Another centaur saw that Orgrim had opened his cover and took his opportunity. A spear thrust caught the pack leader in his upper arm, and the thin blade of the weapon sliced a bloody furrow in his flesh. Orgrim jerked his shield upward, shattering the shaft of the spear. Then he dropped his war hammer and snatched at his enemy's weapon, wresting it effortlessly from him. He turned the shaft in his fingers and stabbed the shattered end into the centaur's chest.

The ranks of the centaurs began to falter. Their hooves found little grip on the ice. The trolls forced them back, and panic suddenly spread among them. Orgrim saw a black-bearded fellow with a longsword cursing and trying to hold the battle line together. But finally he, too, had to accept the inevitable. The attack had been repulsed.

The trolls all around him hurled insults after the fleeing centaurs and set upon the wounded. The humans had also retreated to escape the lethal catapults. The dead lay all around on the ice.

COURAGE

Alfadas had ordered his men to retreat on the double from the small group of hills. A charge against the catapults' position would have been tantamount to suicide. He had been unable to hold back the centaurs, and they had paid heavily for their eagerness. Breaking off the attack had been the right thing to do. All his plans had been turned upside down. The trolls were supposed to charge their pike formation beneath a deadly rain of arrows, but instead the enemy commander had forced *them* to attack. *Who is he?* Alfadas wondered, and he'd had to admit that everything he had previously thought about the trolls had been profoundly wrong. Until today, he had considered them to be something like predatory beasts, creatures driven by nothing but instinct. But whoever was in charge on the other side knew what it meant to think, and though the attack should have taken the trolls by surprise, their commander had managed to turn everything to his advantage.

The retreat had shaken the men's morale. Yes, they had saved the fleeing caravan of elves from the trolls, but then they had run from the enemy themselves—the same enemy they had trained so hard to fight. Alfadas knew that he had to speak to the men. The way things looked to them now, all the long, hard days of training had been for naught, and they were facing an enemy able to butcher them without even getting close enough for hand-to-hand combat. He could not allow the night to pass without buttressing the men's courage!

They stretched heavy tarpaulins and set up a number of braziers as they had the evening before, giving themselves some shelter. The refugees, too, arranged themselves for the night. Some of the children watched the humans curiously. Some brought small gifts as thanks for being saved. But few of them were able to make themselves understood to the strangers.

Alfadas was about to climb onto one of the sleds to deliver a bracing speech when Lambi held him back.

"Don't do it, Commander. You make good decisions, and you don't owe anyone an explanation. You'll only hurt yourself if you apologize now."

"Something has to be said," Alfadas insisted. "They can't think of themselves as failures."

Lambi rubbed his mutilated nose. "The way I see it, the orders you gave saved us from defeat. Let me talk to the boys. I'll straighten their heads out. Trust me!"

Alfadas hesitated. When a villain like Lambi said "Trust me," the words had exactly the opposite effect. Lambi seemed to be well aware of that.

Smiling, Alfadas eyed Lambi as if the war jarl could see into his mind. "Speak," he finally said. They would only survive this battle if they did what Lambi asked: they had to trust each other.

Thirty-seven fighters had fallen to the catapults. The losses had left a deep gash in the men's confidence. Maybe Lambi was the healer they needed? The fighters under Lambi's command, at least, had taken the retreat in stride. They were already laughing around their fires.

The war jarl climbed onto the sled. He cleared his throat, but only a few of the men took any notice. It was worse than Alfadas had expected. Most of the fighters did no more than stare into the flames. They didn't want to hear anything.

"I was actually planning to tell you about a woman who's waiting to get laid," Lambi called out, and he let out a laugh. "But I can already see I'm going to have her all to myself."

"Are you planning to ride the king's whore?"

The war jarl laughed again. "Not tonight! I'm talking about a woman so temperamental that I'm damn sure our old king wouldn't be able to ride her anymore. I'm talking about Svanlaug, Norgrimm's daughter, mistress of victory. She's laughed in all our faces today. But when I see you moping 'round the fires like that, then what am I to think? Am I in an army of the blind? Did none of you see that glorious woman at all?"

"All I saw was a mob of cowards creeping off," called a deep voice from the cover of the crowd.

"Damn right, man! Let's talk about cowards and not about women. I'll be straight with you. I only used Svanlaug to get your attention. D'you really think old Lambi would tell you how to get to that strapping young wench? That road's just for me, because when I meet Svanlaug, the last thing I need is a few hundred horny goats breathing down my neck. Especially if they've still got their noses, and compared to me, they're as pretty as a virgin's tits! So let's talk about cowards. Today I came across the biggest coward I've ever faced as a soldier. And I really do mean the *biggest*, because next to those gray-skinned brutes, we look like babes in arms. I'm telling you here and now, I shit my breeches full when I saw the first of 'em in the snowstorm."

"Then you should have took 'em off afterward, y'old stinker," shouted the red-bearded warrior from Lambi's squad. Several men around him laughed. The tension began to ease.

"Hey, I thought I'd be seeing Norgrimm himself today, and I'd rather meet a god in shitty breeches than none at all. The god of war knows well enough that men let themselves go in their last battle. I'm sure of that. But if I was to stand in front of him with no trousers on, he might think I've given up the ghost midhump."

"You'd have to find a blind whore for that!" Ragni shouted.

Lambi gripped his chest theatrically. "Just 'cause I'm the deadliest soldier in this motley mob, you think I don't have a heart, Jarl? Jests like that cut me to the quick. But I forgive you, because I hear in your words that when it comes to the trials of love, you're still as green as a leaf in spring, or you'd know you can have a lot of fun without having to look your woman in the face."

"Shut up about women, Lambi, and see things for what they are!" Ragni puffed angrily. "For me, the cowards are the one who slunk off the battlefield with their pricks between their legs."

Lambi grabbed himself by the crotch. "Everything's still in one piece here, greenleaf. Nothing pinched, nothing jammed. And I'm wondering, were we even in the same place today? I was there when a man—a man who was a baker's assistant just a few days ago, mind you—damn near hacked a troll's head off. I saw hundreds of men march with courage, though they knew a terrible enemy was waiting somewhere in the driving snow." He slapped one hand to his forehead. "Oh, yeah. I almost forgot. I saw a troop of trolls, too. Must have been two hundred or more. They stood on a hill and didn't have the balls to come down off it. They're bigger than cave bears but didn't have the guts to come down to a plain defended by bakers, farmers, and ferrymen. We stood down here and waited for 'em. And what did they do? They shot chunks of ice at us from a distance. That was as far as their courage went."

"And then the brave men ran away," Ragni shouted back.

Lambi raised his hands to the sky. "Oh, Luth, what did I do to you? Why do you send me so many idiots and so few beautiful women? What does courage have to do with making yourself a target for trolls, Ragni? Thank the gods our commander is blessed with more brains than some of his war jarls! I don't see myself as a coward because I didn't wait around for a few trolls to shoot my head off. If we'd stayed put, we'd have gifted the trolls an easy victory." Lambi pointed out into the darkness. "But where are they, the supposed victors? They don't even have the guts to follow us, those *brave* stoneskins. Look around. I see dozens of elven women, children, elders. The trolls' booty. We stole them from under the trolls' noses! Can you call a man a loser if he leaves the battlefield with the loot?"

"No!" cried someone in the crowd. "No!" several other voices chorused. "No!"

Lambi spread his arms wide to settle the rising voices. "Maybe they'll send a few scouts after us, skulking through the night to try to frighten us. That's the way of cowards afraid of the daylight. The trolls will only earn my respect again when they face us in battle. Before they get close enough for me to see the whites of their beady eyes, I spit on 'em for the gutless brutes they are!" The war jarl sniffed noisily and spat in the snow. Then he looked around with a grin. "The brighter ones among you might've noticed that I'm rather a disrespectful fellow, and I'm damned glad that I'm a war jarl, because I don't like dancing to anyone else's tune. There's only one man that this don't apply to: the man who managed to turn a useless mob of layabouts and laborers into an army even the trolls fear. Until today, I was damned sure that my last day would come when we met the troll host that wiped out an elven city." Lambi pointed at Ragni. "I know you hate my guts, Jarl, but I'm willing to bet, on this one point, that you and I didn't think any differently this morning. Nor you, Veleif Silberhand—you thought the same, didn't you? And you, Rolf Svertarm. And you, Yngwar."

But for the low crackling of the fire, it was deathly quiet. Many of the men nodded, lost in their own thoughts. Lambi stayed silent for a few heartbeats, letting his words sink in.

"Next time I face the trolls, they should learn that their fears have a name. They should know who the man is that cut their battle balls off. His name will be my battle cry, and I want them to tremble when they hear it. Alfadas Trollkiller! Come on, let the trolls creeping around our camp right now hear it!" Lambi drew his sword and jabbed it toward the night sky. "Alfadas Trollkiller!"

The war jarl's call was picked up by hundreds of voices. The men rose to their feet, crowding close to Alfadas. Their new battle cry rang out over and over, and they finally lifted Alfadas onto their shoulders. Lambi, too, was hoisted high by the crowd. He whipped up the men again and again with his battle cry, and it seemed to Alfadas that an eternity passed before the men finally settled down again.

Dozens invited the duke to drink with them, and he went from fire to fire almost until dawn, speaking with the men. All were burning for another chance to fight the trolls. Finally, Alfadas sought out Lambi and found him some distance away, lying in the lee of a sled. The war jarl was asleep, a half-empty wineskin pinned beneath one arm.

The duke looked down at him in silence and wondered how Lambi would surprise him next. Suddenly, he opened his eyes and blinked sleepily.

"No rest tonight for you, I guess," he said.

Alfadas shook his head. "I wonder: Was all that just pretty words, or do you really believe what you told the men?"

Lambi grinned mischievously. "What am I supposed to believe? That Svanlaug is laughing in our faces? The mistress of war is a whore. You never know whose bed she'll lie in next."

"You know I'm not talking about that."

Lambi sat up. His breath reeked of sweet wine, but his voice was clear. "A good commander is one that knows best who to put where and when. And a *very* good commander knows not to hold that man back once he's decided for himself that his time has come."

"You don't have to flatter me, Jarl."

Lambi let out a short, ringing laugh. "Do I look like a flatterer or a boot-licker, Commander? Learn to see the truth for what it is. And don't let me down. You're the man to make sure we kick the trolls' asses so hard that they taste the soles of our boots on their tongues. I believe in you, Alfadas."

THE LAST LINE

Landoran, prince of Snaiwamark and Carandamon, watched the envoy stride down from the Mahdan Falah. Sandowas was the last emissary to return to Phylangan. The elven prince waited for him in the small pavilion close to the bridge.

Gravel crunched beneath the emissary's feet. As soon as he entered, he dropped to one knee and threw back his long cloak. Sandowas had gold-blond hair held in place by a silver circlet. He wore boots of suede leather that reached above his knees and a dark-green doublet studded with pearls. His red cloak was hemmed with a broad band of gold.

A little too grand, thought Landoran casually as he looked the young elf over. The sword and dagger, the cross guard of which had been designed to resemble a shell, were also rather showy. But like so many things, taste was a question of age. The prince wondered for a moment whether Sandowas had been the right man for the mission to the heartland. On the other hand, it had been a simple enough task, and the youngsters had to start gathering experience somewhere.

"What do you have to report?" Landoran asked, skipping the usual formalities.

"We can expect no support from the heartland. As long as nothing is known about the queen's whereabouts, Master Alvias is in charge. He fears an attack on the castle and cannot spare a man."

"Doesn't he know that the troll fleet is sailing north?" asked the prince in annoyance.

Sandowas spread his hands in a gesture of helplessness. "He knows it very well. Hundreds of refugees entered the heartland through the Albenpaths just before Reilimee fell. The guards on the sea walls defended to the last man. They did everything they could to keep the path to the gateway in the Shell Tower clear. The trolls wreaked havoc in Reilimee, even worse than what they did in Vahan Calyd. Only those who made it to the Shell Tower escaped alive."

"Then is it somehow unclear to Master Alvias that we have to stand against the tide of these monsters with all our might? If each of us fights his own battle, we will all perish. We can only succeed against Branbeard and his butchers and drive them out of Albenmark again if we work together."

Sandowas allowed himself a smile, which Landoran felt was out of place. "The queen's chamberlain requested that I inform you that we are to send all our troops to reinforce his own. He says that because the trolls are now able to move along the Albenpaths even aboard ships, the direction in which they happen to be sailing means nothing. They could appear anywhere at any time. He is convinced that their next goal will be Emerelle's castle."

Exasperatingly, that line of reasoning is not so easily dismissed, Landoran thought. The prince looked to the Mahdan Falah, suddenly concerned. The stoneformers were still hard at work on the huge defensive tower that was intended to secure the end of the bridge. Already almost twenty paces high, the massive construction destroyed the harmony of the Skyhall. Two hundred archers and crossbowmen were supposed to occupy it. If the trolls dared to set foot on the Mahdan Falah through the Albenstar at its end, they would be met by a storm of arrows. The bridge would run red with their blood, which would pour down its snow-white columns.

Landoran sighed. Maybe all their preparations were in vain. He looked down at the hundreds of kobolds busily watering the Skyhall's gardens. Dark clouds had gathered beneath the roof of the cave, and the air was as humid as a mangrove swamp in Vahan Calyd. Not even the power of the Albenstone had caused their fortunes to change.

Sandowas cleared his throat softly.

"Yes?"

"Might I be permitted a question, my prince?"

Landoran smiled with amusement. "Now that you have already asked one question without my permission, you are granted a second."

The emissary blushed. "I . . . what about the other races? Who will send us help?"

"The centaurs have not forgotten the old bond between us, but how much use are manhorses when it comes to defending a fortress? Maybe some of the Maurawan will help, but you can never tell what's going on in their heads, let alone who they think their allies are. The host of humans will soon reach Phylangan. That's it. Those are all the allies we can hope for."

"But all our sister races? They can't—"

"Branbeard has sent out emissaries of his own," the prince said, interrupting the young elf. "The trolls have changed a great deal since we drove them out of Albenmark. Branbeard inflicted his cruelties on Vahan Calyd and Reilimee very deliberately. He intended from the start to sow the seeds of fear, and his harvest has been abundant. His emissaries are promising that only we Normirga and Emerelle need fear the wrath of the trolls. But whoever supports the queen and her clan will perish like our brothers in Reilimee." Landoran's face stretched into a mocking smile. "Some of our elven brothers at least had the decency to hide behind the lie that no decisions could be made until the line of succession had been determined. Others said openly that they had no desire to bleed for the feuds of Emerelle and our people. So we will have to hold Phylangan with the help of the humans and centaurs, and that is all. We are the last line of defense."

"Can we win, my prince?"

Landoran laughed. "This is the strongest fortress in the north. It does not matter how many trolls there are. One of our warriors is worth four of theirs."

Sandowas paled. He was clearly imagining how he would fare in battle against four trolls.

"The strength of our walls will help us, boy. The trolls probably won't even make it as far as the Snow Harbor. Besides, we all know that Carandamon is as good as defenseless if Phylangan falls. Branbeard has sworn to wipe out our people. He should not have done that. Everyone who fights here knows that there is no turning back. The stone garden will not fall!"

"Where is my sword needed?" Sandowas asked, newfound defiance in his voice.

"Report to the Snow Harbor. Defense preparations are being organized there. You may go now, Sandowas."

The young elf bowed once more, briefly, then hurried away.

Landoran looked up at the dark clouds beneath the dome of the Skyhall and thought about how much more relentless the power was against which Lyndwyn fought. In the end, it might be she alone who decided whether Phylangan was destroyed.

THE SNOW HARBOR

They had been marching up the glacier through the wide valley for more than half a day. Slowly, the mountains on both sides closed in, joining to form a towering barricade of stone at the end of the valley. The narrow slits in the snow masks meant that one could only ever see a small section of the mountain panorama. Sunlight sparkled from the snow-covered mountainsides and gray-blue ice of the glacier—the army was wading through light. The sheer dazzle and splendor of it all was overwhelming for human eyes. And though the blinding light did not inconvenience the elves, they seemed to have lost all sense of wonder at the mountainous world around them.

Alfadas was relieved that they would soon reach Phylangan. Lambi's predictions had proven correct. On several occasions, small parties of trolls had tried to attack by night but had been repelled easily each time. Two nights before, however, a pair of sentries had vanished without trace. It did not fit with the style of the other attacks. Silwyna had tried to pick up the trolls' trail, but heavy snowfall had wiped out any traces. Patrolling centaurs had found neither the sentries' bodies nor the trolls that must have been behind their disappearance.

Alfadas stepped away from the marching column and climbed a low hill that rose like a large boil from the glacial ice. Having the world reduced to what he could see through a narrow slit was getting to him more and more, but he resisted the urge to remove his snow mask. A few more hours and they would reach the safety of the fortress.

His gaze drifted to the horizon. He could not understand why the trolls had not tried to attack them again. Since the battle on the ice, he had expected a renewed assault at any moment. What was holding them back? Were they too weak? Had Lambi been right with his fiery speech?

Even though no serious attack had taken place, the commander felt constantly as if he was being watched by something other than his men and the elves. Something was lurking on the ice. It was never far away, and yet it stayed out of sight. He had talked with Ollowain about it, and the elf had confided that he felt the same. It could have just been the trolls' scouts, but an inner voice warned Alfadas that something else lurked out there, something far more treacherous than trolls.

Alfadas looked ahead, toward the end of the valley. Just a few more miles. The wall of rock rose almost vertically. These were natural walls, higher than any human could have built. Several broad outcrops jutted like domed towers from the faces of the cliffs. Snow lay on narrow ledges and in cracks. There was no way up. The Snaiwamark ended with this valley. Beyond the mountains lay the high plateau known as Carandamon. The elves could not afford to lose this fortress. From the east, it was the only way to reach the high plains. If the fortress fell, the plateau beyond was all but defenseless. The forts of Carandamon were smaller and had not been built to withstand a determined attack.

He recalled the evenings in Honnigsvald, when Lysilla had talked about Phylangan—its towering halls, the labyrinth of passages, two large harbors, and all the other marvels that were there.

Alfadas descended the hill again and joined the shepherds accompanying the army. Their herd of sheep had shrunk considerably. Fewer than a hundred beasts remained, and those that did were skinny and exhausted. The duke shared a few jokes with the men and after a while went to speak to Egil.

"Well, Ralf," he said, addressing him by his alias. "The shepherds' work will soon be done. What would you like to do next?"

Horsa's son looked around cautiously. Only when he was sure that no one was within earshot did he reply. "I've spent years training with the sword. Take me as a soldier."

"The other shepherds say good things about you. You've earned their regard, although they suspect you're of noble birth. You can't hide your birthright. The way you talk, the things you know, even the way you move—it all gives you away. But they have kept your secret to themselves. Do you want to leave these men behind?"

Egil sighed. "Should not every man do what he does best?"

"Are you sure you have discovered what it is that you do best? Even today, I am plagued by doubts about whether I have followed the right path in my life."

The king's son laughed. "You can't be serious, Alfadas. You're an incomparable swordsman. There isn't a man in the Fjordlands who can measure up to you, and you are renowned as a commander. How can you doubt the road you've taken?"

Alfadas smiled. "None of that counts here. Among elves, I'm an average swordsman, at best. But perhaps I would have been an incomparable fisherman or hunter? What I'm trying to say to you, Egil, is that you should give yourself time. You already know how good a soldier you are. But can you be a friend? The other shepherds don't know who you really are. Enjoy the freedom you have! One day, when you sit on your father's throne, you will never know who is truly a friend and who is just a flatterer with no interest but their own advantage. You will do well to be distrustful—kings have very few friends."

Egil looked toward the other shepherds. There were only five of them, hard-bitten fellows. Sun and wind had made their faces dark and craggy. "What will they do when we get to the elven fort?"

"I'll ask them, but I do have plans for them. There's a weapon that is easy to master and no less deadly than a sword. When we get to the fortress, I want to train them in its use. Do you want to stay as one of them?"

Horsa's son looked down, abashed, at his snow-encrusted boots. "I don't know."

The duke clapped him on the shoulder. "Don't listen to reason. Listen to your heart. You've pleasantly surprised me in recent days. I'd have been willing to bet that you'd give me nothing but trouble. I trust you; I know you'll make the right choice."

Alfadas dropped back to the very end of the column. On the dogsleds lay the wounded from the battle. Dalla tended to them. The mere sight of a human woman seemed to work wonders for most of the men. Veleif, too, spent much of his time among the wounded. He had them tell him about their lives—the skald had given himself the goal of getting to know every man and his history.

Veleif got around with the aid of a walking stick made of pale wood. He wore a fine linen shirt that looked like it had come from one of the elves. His long gray hair was not tied, and the winter wind toyed with it. On his back, safely wrapped in leather, was his lute. As with the rest of them, a broad strip of leather hid his eyes. He seemed to be in a surly mood.

"Ah, Father of Songs, is today not a good day?" Alfadas joked.

The bard pointed ahead at the steep rock wall. "Why should I be in a good mood today? I talked to that snow-woman, Lysilla. She told me about the splendid elven castles to the south and about Emerelle's palace with its garden of enchanted trees. And where do I end up? In a rocky nest about as fetching as an empty aerie. Nothing here reminds me of the magnificent elven castles of our faery stories."

"Don't be too quick to judge. Just wait! I'm quite sure the elves will manage to surprise you yet."

Veleif edged closer to Alfadas. "There's something here," he whispered. "Most of the men don't have senses fine enough to notice it, but have you?"

Alfadas did not want this particular story spreading. He shrugged. "The elves say that the air up here is so thin that it makes us see things that aren't really there. I'm tempted to believe them. They know their land."

The skald swept a strand of hair out of his face. "Making people see things is my stock in trade. Thin air . . ." He snorted. "I know what I know."

Suddenly, the valley reverberated with the solemn sound of golden lurs, large trumpets with mouths designed as dragon or horse heads. In the cliff in front of them, a gap opened, growing wider and wider, as if some gigantic monster was opening its maw. From inside radiated a silver-blue light almost as bright as the sun, but it did not blind the eyes.

An ice glider pulled up beside them, its runners crunching in the snow. Ollowain waved to Alfadas. "You should enter Phylangan at the head of the column. As commander, it is only right."

"Would you like to come along, poet?"

A smile finally appeared on Veleif's face. "Maybe you were right about elven surprises, Duke."

The two men climbed onto the steel runner of the ice glider, and Ollowain pulled them up beside him. The strange vehicle looked like a sled on which the builder had fixed a slender mast. It was controlled with a lever fitted at the bow that allowed the runners to be adjusted and thus to either slow the glider down or steer it in a wide curve. The glider was no more than five paces long. There were no sides to help passengers hold on, but wide leather loops on the deck provided grip for the feet, and there were ropes to hold on to as well. Sailing on an ice glider was like riding an arrow in flight.

"Hold tight!" Alfadas warned the skald. Then he slipped his feet into a pair of the leather loops and grasped one of the ropes with both hands. The large triangular sail swung into the wind, and with a jolt the glider began to move. As if flying, it shot along beside the marching column. The wind burned in their faces as they sped toward the silver-blue light. In Alfadas, the thrill of speed fluctuated with pure terror. To fly as fast as a bird was sublime, but if he fell overboard in a moment of inattention, he would break every bone he had on the hard ice!

The ice glider sped over a bump and was momentarily airborne. Veleif, grinning with delight, let out a whoop! He went so far as to let go of the safety rope with one hand and wave to the troops as they passed. *You bastard!* Alfadas thought. How would he look, playing second fiddle to their bard?

Alfadas waved with both arms, hoping that the deck loops alone would be strong enough to hold him. It was an exhilarating feeling! Slowly, though, the sense of speed faded. Could he use a glider regularly once he got used to the speed? Ulric and Kadlin, he knew, would love to go sailing over the frozen fjord on such a vessel.

The duke looked ahead. They had almost reached their destination. A tall elf on a white horse was waiting for them at the gate of the fortress. His white hair fell to his shoulders, and he wore a long robe the color of fresh cream, but his face looked emaciated. Alfadas had never encountered a man who looked so tired. A guard of honor accompanied the prince of Phylangan. Soldiers in white tunics and long silver chain mail shirts flanked the gate, lining a wide entrance that led into the enormous cavern that had opened in front of the approaching army.

Ollowain slowed the ice glider and turned the sail off the wind. Alfadas heard hoofbeats, and Orimedes, Lysilla, and Fenryl galloped up.

"I bid you welcome to the stone garden," said the elven prince, greeting them with a slight bow.

Alfadas noted that even men standing far away looked up at the elf's words, although Landoran had not raised his voice. Maybe it was because of the valley or maybe the elf had worked a spell of some kind. Whatever the truth, Alfadas had the impression that everyone who heard Landoran could understand him, although he spoke in the language of his race.

"I am grateful to our allies, the humans and centaurs who turned misery and death away from my brothers and sisters. And I mourn with you for your companions who paid for their bravery with their lives. Now enter our bright halls and lay your weary heads to rest. If the day comes when your courage is once again put to the test, then know that the stone garden has never yet been conquered. However strong our enemies may seem, they must first defeat the mountain before they fight us. And what is a troll compared to a mountain?"

Alfadas silently wished that the prince had managed to put a little more of Lambi's fire into his speech. Yes, his words of welcome were friendly enough, but they did little to stir enthusiasm.

He looked around the hall they had entered. Ollowain had already told him what to expect: when they traveled up the glacier to Phylangan, they would come first to the Snow Harbor. Although Alfadas tried to imagine what Ollowain described, he had found it impossible to picture a harbor inside a mountain. Now, as he looked around, his amazement grew, for even in Albenmark he had never seen a place like this.

The Snow Harbor was a cavern so immense that it was easy to forget that you had stepped inside a mountain. A singular spell the Normirga cast made the roof of the cavern disappear. In its place, an unsteady silvery-blue light flickered like a torch in a storm. The light made men and elves look paler than they actually were, and the breath that stood in bright clouds before their mouths took on an unreal, magical look.

The floor of the broad hall was a plain of grooved crushed ice, and the distant walls appeared to be covered with hoarfrost and ice flowers. At its northern end stood stone piers where huge ice gliders, as big as ships of trade, were moored. Some had three masts. Their sails were reefed, and long icicles hung from the rigging and yards; these ships of eternal winter looked as if they had not sailed for a very long time.

Along the piers waited loading cranes with towering wooden cogwheels, and dark openings in the rock may have led to storerooms.

In the same way that scavenger fish, at times, accompanied sharks, the large ice ships were surrounded by a throng of smaller vessels like the one on which Alfadas had entered the Snow Harbor. Their masts stood as dense as trees in a forest. Alfadas guessed there were almost a hundred of them.

On the other side of the yawning cavern was a fleet of sleds all sizes and shapes, some so big that Alfadas was at a loss to imagine what beasts could possibly pull them.

Landoran's speech was met with solemn silence, but when the refugees from Rosecarn entered the harbor, a din arose that Alfadas only knew from the royal city of Gonthabu, when traders from every land gathered there in late spring. Hundreds of kobolds helped unload the sleds and small ice gliders, and while families were reunited and the elves embraced one another in eloquent silence, more kobolds launched into a musical cacophony of guitars, strange wind instruments, and hand drums. A magician regaled the children with whirling colored lights and was rewarded with squeals of glee.

Alfadas's men marched into the great cave with remarkable discipline. The war jarls had organized their respective troops into rows of five and had made sure that each man had polished his weapon. But all their efforts could not conceal the ragged appearance of the allies from the Fjordlands.

The men looked around in wide-eyed wonder. They found a place close to the ice glider where they were not in anybody's way. Only Lambi's men strolled casually around the Snow Harbor. They kept no formation and acted with all the self-control of a mob of seamen finally allowed to disembark among the brothels of a harbor town.

Alfadas turned to the elven prince, who waited with Ollowain and endured the arrival of Lambi and his men with solemn composure.

"What is the function of those large gliders?"

"We used to use them to ferry supplies from Whale Bay to Rosecarn, across the great ice plains. In recent years, however, most of our trade has arrived via Windland and is transported with the centaurs' yak caravans. The ships have not been used for a long time. Why do you ask, human?"

"Would you put three of them under my command?"

Landoran frowned with annoyance. "I don't know what use you expect to get out of them. You're welcome to have three ships, but I can't put any windsingers at your disposal. Right now, they are indispensable, and without one of those sorcerers, it would be irresponsible to take one of the ships out on the plains. You would be at the mercy of winter's moods."

"Then would you let me have a few men who could instruct mine in how to handle one of the ships?" Alfadas persisted.

Landoran looked him up and down with disdain. "I see no benefit in learning to control an ice glider that will never leave this harbor."

"Send me the men, and at the council of war that Ollowain is going to call for two hours from now, I'll teach you about the tactical approach to a superior enemy preparing for a siege," Alfadas replied calmly. *Miserable bastard,* he thought. *I can see I'm going to have a lot of fun with you.*

Landoran breathed in and out deeply and straightened his shoulders. For a moment, he looked as if he might lose his composure but then seemed to have himself under control again. "What do you mean? What council of war?"

Alfadas responded before Ollowain could get a word out. "If I've been informed correctly, Lyndwyn has command over Phylangan, though she has not done us the honor of welcoming us here in person. She, in turn, has delegated control of all military matters to Ollowain. As I'm sure you would agree, it is advisable for the commanders of our alliance to meet in a council of war as quickly as possible." Alfadas knew about the strained relationship between the swordmaster and his father. He gave Ollowain a pleading glance and hoped that he would let himself be drawn into his stratagem. It was crucial that everyone knew who was in charge in Phylangan from the very start.

"Because you are unable with your own power even to protect yourselves from the cold, by the laws of my people, you are children," Landoran explained condescendingly. "No adult Normirga will be prepared to fall in with your whims."

"We are three races that are supposed to fight side by side, Father," Ollowain said. "You don't think it unwise to insist that *all* the laws of our people apply? How long do you think our alliance will hold if the only words that matter come from *adult* Normirga?"

"The council of war will convene in two hours in the Pearl Room," Landoran said harshly. "This is no place for a dispute. Only children have so little self-control that they air their differences of opinion in public." He patted his horse softly on the neck and rode off toward the refugees. Lysilla followed him but looked back at Ollowain and Alfadas with a smile.

"Arrogant old snake," Orimedes muttered. "Who does he think is going to protect his precious fortress if we *children* decide to leave again?"

"There's one thing he's right about, my friend," Alfadas said. "We should save our quarrels for the war council. It would be bad for the morale of the troops if they saw how united we really are."

"Duke?" Count Fenryl had dismounted and was walking toward Alfadas. "I am deeply in your debt. Thanks to you, my wife and child—and all my clan—are alive. There are windsingers among my people, too. I will put them under your command, along with the two cargo ships that sail under the flag of Rosecarn."

Alfadas dismissed the offer. "You owe me nothing, nor do I want you to be at odds with your prince on my account."

Fenryl was not willing to accept this. "I trust your judgment as a commander. The Normirga have already been driven out once by the trolls. I am certain that it is better for my people this time if someone else has supreme command. You have a plan, don't you? Tell me what you need, and I will make sure you get it."

For a moment, Alfadas thought about whether he should wait for the decision of the council of war. But who knew how many hours they still had before the main army of trolls arrived? Every one of those hours mattered.

"Find me every windsinger you can. And I need the carpenters and the blacksmiths who made the runners for the ice gliders. Most of all, I need men who are not afraid to face an enemy that will outnumber them a hundred to one."

OF WHISKER WAX AND DEATH

S hahondin watched as the long column disappeared into the cave. Was she here? The tremor in the Albenpaths had drawn him as the human army marched through the void. When he discovered Ollowain, he knew he was finally on the right trail. Where the swordmaster was, the queen would not be far away. All he had to do was follow Ollowain. Sooner or later, he would lead to Emerelle.

The beast in Shahondin mewled, wanting food. The prince stretched. He was concealed almost completely inside a snowdrift, with only his big head extended. The elf was once again unpleasantly reminded that he no longer had a body of flesh and blood. He had grown accustomed to everything else, but his spectral form annoyed him. There was little left of the beast inside him. Like a feeble glowing spark in a fire that had burned out hours before, only the faintest glimmer of that strange creature's consciousness remained. For two days, Shahondin had submitted to it to learn from it; then he had all but crushed it out of existence. What did that filthy troll shaman think? That he, Shahondin, prince of Arkadien, would allow a primitive beast to rule over him? He was older than most of the forests of Albenmark. The troll bitch had been able to capture him only because she possessed an Albenstone. If not for that hidden power, she would have ended her days a slobbering idiot. He would have snuffed out her mind the moment she came in contact with his. But that damned stone had acted like an impregnable shield, and he had been forced to submit to her will.

The beast inside him wailed in its hunger. Miserable thing! A disembodied specter did not need to eat. Taking the life-light of some creature of flesh and blood did not sate him. It merely gave him pleasure. Twice, he had given in to the urge. The first had been a troll sent after the humans as a spy. The second had been an elf woman and her three children. In the driving snow, when the trolls had attacked the elven convoy, he had leaped onto their sled and murdered them all. Killing children was a special joy. Their light was purer.

But he stayed away from the humans. Without fail, they carried iron, and though it might be no more than a knife or the tip of a spear, something about the way they worked metal was deeply unnatural and disturbed the flow of magic. Shahondin—cautiously, with an outstretched paw—had once touched one of the weapons left behind on the battlefield. He had paid for it with searing pain, as if a blue flame had taken hold in his heart. It had stolen something of the essence of which his magical body was made. The iron of humans could kill him. He had to be on his guard against them.

Fortunately, he could scent their iron from a long way off. It left a disharmony in the structure of the world. Everything in Albenmark was permeated with magic, and its invisible pattern became distorted wherever a human passed with his iron weapon. Shahondin wondered why the elves did not notice it. It might be that his senses were infinitely finer inside the form that Skanga had forced him to take. He was a creature of magic, bound far more deeply with the magical part of the world than he had been as an elf. This meant that he could protect himself from the humans' weapons as long as he kept the beast inside him in check. He suspected that the creature, in its craving to kill, would throw all caution to the wind.

Shahondin thought about the leader of the trolls. An exceptionally capable savage! The prince reminded himself that Orgrim had witnessed Skanga's transformation of him. The trolls were no threat. They detested iron weapons, or any metal weapons for that matter, yet they were still very good at slaughtering humans.

The elven prince's eyes wandered over the looming rock wall. The trolls would pay dearly if they tried to storm Phylangan. Maybe he could help them? It would be easy for him to spread fear in the hearts of the defenders.

He moved toward the rocks, and his body glided into the stone. Darkness surrounded him. He allowed himself to be led by the network within the magical order and sensed a distortion in it, far above him. The Normirga did not smash their way through stone with force. They reformed it magically, creating tunnels and chambers in the mountain.

Shahondin let himself rise through the rock, exploring the hidden fortress. A long tunnel had been formed through the face of the cliff that flanked the glacier. The broad outcrops that jutted from the cliff were like towers, with several levels arranged on top of each other. Embrasures there were fitted with wooden shutters, and the shutters had been roughly plastered, camouflaging them, making them all but invisible against the bedrock.

On the various levels of the towers in the rocky outcrops, the elves had prepared catapults that targeted the ice. A single tunnel connected these positions with one another. Shahondin discovered pulley systems that allowed sections of the tunnel to be blocked with thick granite plates. In other places, deposits of rubble and stone dust had been left. Adding water to the stone dust and mixing in rubble made an easily workable material that hardened quickly. Sections of the tunnel could be filled overnight, and getting through it would take no less effort than burrowing through the bedrock itself.

The prince, in his spectral animal form, glided out of the rock and studied the cliff on the other side of the valley intently. In the last light of the evening, he made out shadows in the rock, spaced at regular intervals. *So that side also has its defenses.* If the trolls stormed up the valley, they would find themselves in a murderous crossfire before they even reached the gates of the Snow Harbor. Skanga needed to know this! A thoughtless attack would cost hundreds of lives, maybe thousands. Even the connecting tunnel, which ran close to the surface of the rock, had numerous embrasures where archers could be stationed.

Shahondin glided back into the rock. He moved around a branching vein of metal ore and avoided the caves and the tunnel. Only occasionally did he venture to look out of the rock but was careful to remain undiscovered.

The defensive positions were manned mostly by kobolds. It was not unusual to find far more kobolds than elves in an elven settlement, of course. But the longer Shahondin spied out the fortress defenses, the more surprised he became. In Phylangan, the disproportion seemed to be especially pronounced. In the end, he realized that the disparity he saw probably was due to most of the elves being gathered down below in the Snow Harbor to give the humans an impressive reception.

The prince discovered an abandoned storage room in which a few bundles of arrows still lay. He found it more comfortable to be in an open cave, although in reality it made no difference where he was because he had no physical body. Still, he felt uneasy inside the rock walls—it would take quite a long time, it seemed, for him to truly get used to his spectral form.

He had no intention of inhabiting it long enough to do that.

Was Emerelle perhaps somewhere in the fortress? The Normirga were her people, after all. Where else would she have fled? And Ollowain was here!

Phylangan was the strongest fortress in the north. She would be safer here than anywhere else. On the other hand, this was also where one would look for her first.

But the answer to another question was more pressing. Shahondin knew that betraying the Normirga would not cause him any sleepless nights, but was it wise to tell the trolls too soon about what was waiting for them here? If thousands of their warriors perished in the crossfire on the glacier, their army would be too weak afterward to do much more damage in Albenmark. But Shahondin also knew that if, by some senseless stroke of fate, Skanga were killed during the battle, he would be trapped in that spectral body forever.

And how would the shaman react if she realized he had seen the massacre coming and had not warned them? He had no choice: he had to look for Skanga.

The defenses alongside the glacier had a vital point of weakness. All the supply chambers, troop quarters, and defensive positions were linked by a single tunnel. They were lined up like beads on a string, and that could make them a deadly trap. If one managed to block the start of the tunnel, then all the troops would be sealed off. One only had to find another way into the stone garden and ignore the route up the glacier.

Shahondin slipped back into the rock. He followed the course of the tunnel, which rose slowly. Although he kept a little distance between himself and the tunnel, he could clearly feel the disturbance in the rock, the resonance of the magical powers the Normirga had used to create this section of the fortress. Finally, he reached a small chamber from which a door led out to a lookout point. The tunnel ended here, more than a mile from the Snow Harbor gate.

He slipped out of the wall cautiously. The guardroom there was lit by a single oil lamp. In a wide recess was a powerful catapult beside which stood a number of stools. From its dimensions, he could see that the catapult had been designed to be used by elves, but the stools allowed even kobolds to operate the winch and the locking lever and thus load and fire the weapon.

Beside the catapult stood a row of clay jugs, some of which were wrapped in strips of linen. The mouths of the jugs had been carefully closed and sealed with wax. The prince sniffed curiously at one of them. A sharp odor stung his nose. Incendiaries!

A snuffling sound followed by a soft gurgling made Shahondin turn. Along the opposite wall stood five bunk beds with curtains of heavy brown woolen blankets. The musty smell of clothes worn too long lingered in the air, and mixed with it was the faint scent of whisker wax. A large table and chairs and two long chests that served as benches filled the rear of the chamber.

Shahondin pushed his head through one of the bed curtains. A kobold lay inside, curled up and fully dressed, snoring. The elf allowed the beast inside him free rein. He felt like a bystander as the creature devoured the kobold's life-light. The small figure withered, his skin stretched across his skull. He died without waking.

The beast glided up to the bunk above. The kobold there was sitting up with his back to the wall. He had wrapped himself in a blanket and had a wide strip of cloth around his face. For the space of a heartbeat, Shahondin thought his victim was awake—for some unfathomable reason, he had *expected* him to be awake. He observed how the kobold's chest rose and fell evenly. The small fellow did not move: he was sound asleep. The odor of whisker wax was more intensive up there. Now Shahondin understood what he was looking at. The kobold had twirled the ends of his moustache artfully and had tied the cloth around his face to stop the elaborate construction from losing its shape. Maybe he had plans to meet a female when he was off duty and wanted to impress her with his striking whiskers. Maybe it would be amusing to let him live? How would he react if he woke up as the only survivor among all his dead comrades? Would he be paralyzed with fear? Would he run out screaming? And would he spend the rest of his life wondering why he alone had survived? He would surely never come to the conclusion that his swaddled moustache had saved him.

The beast inside Shahondin rebelled. It had no sense for such malevolent pleasures. It wanted to kill! Filled with contempt, the elf stifled the witless beast and set upon the other sleeping kobolds, murdering eight of them. Not one of them awoke. They went straight from sleep into eternal darkness without ever suspecting what had happened to them.

Satisfied, Shahondin withdrew to the darkest corner of the chamber. He was curious to see what would happen when someone discovered the guardroom filled with the dead—all but the kobold with his proud moustache, who could explain to no one what had happened. Killing like that was more gratifying than roaming through the fortress and murdering indiscriminately. The prince began to plan how his next victim would die. He would raise his assassinations to the level of art, and his applause would be the horror that spread through the mountain fortress. As an invisible, nameless bringer of death, he was infinitely more terrifying than the army of trolls that was soon to gather at the fortress gates.

THE BOOK OF THREADS

7th day of the wolfmoon. Alfadas left us today, a day somber and sad. On the other side of the gate of light lay a terrible darkness. I would not have wanted to pass through it. May Luth stand by the duke and his men. King Horsa did not want to linger in the village. He left before dark.

9th day of the wolfmoon. Kalf found the dog breeder Ole deep in the woods. Ole was attacked by his own dogs, it seems. He is terribly injured and talks deliriously. I cleaned his wounds. Asla has taken him into her house to care for him. The big black dog had to be shut outside.

11th day of the wolfmoon. Galti the fisherman has disappeared. His boat was found abandoned on the western shore.

12th day of the wolfmoon. Erek and some of the men in the village have killed the dogs in Ole's cage, but two were missing. Asla threatened the men when they came for her dog. I had difficulty settling the matter.

13th day of the wolfmoon. Two slaves disappeared early in the morning: Fredegund and Usa. The village council met in the evening. Every face was fearful.

14th day of the wolfmoon. The body of an old woman washed up on the shore. She wore Usa's clothes. No one can explain how that could be. Many seek my help, but I cannot interpret these threads of Luth.

15th day of the wolfmoon. A strange scourge has befallen Erek's goats. They were found in the stall with nothing left of them but skin and bone. Ole's fever grows worse. He babbles about a white elk cow.

16th day of the wolfmoon. Solveig has not returned from gathering brushwood in the forest. The council, at Asla's urging, has decided that no one else is to leave the village.

17th day of the wolfmoon. Kalf cornered one of the missing dogs in the woods and killed it.

18th day of the wolfmoon. The men went through the woods, looking for the missing hound. They did not find it.

21st day of the wolfmoon. There have been no mishaps for five days. The fear is starting to fade. Luth be praised!

From *The Book of Threads, a Chronicle of Firnstayn*

By Luth priest Gundar

Volume Seven of the Temple Library of Luth in Firnstayn

THE WOLFHORSE

Halgard pulled on her hide boots grumpily. The little girl hated being dragged out of bed so early. They'd stayed in Asla's house until late the previous evening, along with the rest of the village. Gundar had addressed them and prayed with them. Halgard loved the old man's strong, warm voice. For her, it was like sunlight on her face: simply a pleasure.

Still tired, she rubbed the sleep out of her eyes.

"Come on!" Her mother hurried her along, pressing a chunk of hard bread into her hand. "Stop dawdling. I've been up for an hour, and you don't hear me complaining!" Halgard's mother helped her get the wide leather straps of the woven laundry basket over her shoulders, then tucked the shawl in warmly over her body and the basket. Mother must have hung it in front of the fire. Halgard sighed and rubbed her cheek against the wool. If only she could have stayed in bed a little longer.

The door creaked open. The cold breath of the fjord pushed its way into the little hut. Halgard felt her way along the table and banged her knee against the bench. Mother had moved it from its rightful place. Again!

"White fog is coming up the shore," said her mother in a droning voice.

Halgard pulled the door closed behind her and followed the voice, which went on ceaselessly as it described what her mother saw. As she had hundreds of times, Halgard wished Mother would talk about things that Halgard could understand. But that never occurred to her. Halgard could not really imagine clouds. They must be very large, and somehow they wandered across the sky although they had no legs. One could see them readily enough but could not touch them. And what was white? Another word with no meaning, like so many words Mother used in her never-ending descriptions.

The path they followed was soft and muddy. Halgard liked the slurping, sucking noises her boots made after rain. It sounded as if her feet were giving the earth a wet, high-spirited kiss with every step she took.

"That black cat is lurking behind the rain barrel at the corner of Erek's hut again. It looks to me like she's been waiting for us. Funny that she's standing there almost every morning." Her mother's footsteps stopped. "If I catch you feeding her, you're in for it!" Her voice sounded a little different—she must have turned around. "We don't even have enough to feed ourselves; we don't need to also start fattening up some stray beast."

Halgard bit into her bread and shrugged. It was pointless to try to talk to her mother. She would calm down again faster if Halgard simply said nothing at all.

"Cats can look after themselves perfectly well," her mother went on.

The cat purred quietly and rubbed around Halgard's legs. It was a wonderful sensation. The girl bent down and felt for the soft fur. The cat kept purring and pushed its head against Halgard's hand and licked her fingers.

"I don't have any fish today," the girl whispered. "Maybe tomorrow." She broke off a tiny piece of her bread and held it out for the cat, though she knew that her little friend did not really think much of bread. But it was all she had, and she did not dare give it nothing at all because she was afraid that the cat would stop waiting for her altogether if she failed to feed it even once.

"Where are you?" her mother called.

"See you tomorrow." Halgard patted the cat's head one last time and hurried off after her mother, whose feet were already crunching on the gravel. She heard the basket scraping on stone and the sigh that Mother produced every time she put down her heavy load.

"It's completely dark out," her mother explained. "The sun is still hiding behind the mountains. The wind is starting to stir the fog."

It's always completely dark for me, thought Halgard angrily, and she wished Mother would finally stop talking to herself all the time.

As if her mother had heard her thoughts, she suddenly stopped talking. Laundry rustled softly. Her mother would now sort it all out into small piles and weigh each pile down with stones before she set to work. Halgard's mind drifted back to the wonderful days before she had to get up ahead of the sun every day, when Father was still with them. In spring of the year before, he had gone off with the jarl on a campaign and never came back. Ever since, hunger had been a constant guest in the house.

Halgard thought of her father all the time. His voice was always slightly hoarse, and his big, bony hands had often stroked her hair, and then she had been the one to purr like a little cat.

In the evenings, when she could not sleep, she listened to the sounds of the night. She still hoped to hear his familiar footsteps one day. He had been so tall and strong. Who would ever have been able to kill him? He just got lost somewhere along the way. He was sure to come home again. There just had to be someone who still believed it would happen. Mother did not. She was so infuriatingly pigheaded! Halgard had heard herself how Jarl Alfadas had offered her mother to look after both of them, but she didn't want that. Instead, she took Asla's laundry and washed it by the fjord early in the morning. She took in the laundry of a few other women, too, and in return for her labors, she received bread and cheese and sometimes a little meat. Mother didn't like the other women watching when she did their laundry. She acted as if nothing had changed since Father had failed to return, but everyone in the village knew the work she did.

"Are you dreaming again?" her mother snapped at her, and then came that most hated of sounds: the sodden splat of a wet piece of laundry on the wash stone in front of her. Reluctantly, Halgard felt after it. Its size and weight told her it was a shirt. The cold gnawed at her hands. She did what she could to wring out the wet fabric while her mother dipped the next item into the fjord and rubbed the fabric together over a rough stone.

After a morning like this, it felt as if her hands would never be warm again, not even in front of the fire. Halgard groaned. She took out all her anger on the laundry. She twisted it as hard as she could and felt the icy water dribble over her fingers. The cold ate its way deep into her bones, and the best she could manage then was to travel far away, to ride off in her mind to somewhere so distant that she didn't feel anything anymore.

Asla was nice. Sometimes, the jarl's wife slipped her a honeycake when Mother brought the laundry back. But it had to happen secretly, because Mother never took any more than the payment they'd agreed. She was so darn stubborn.

When she did not have to help her mother, Halgard often played with Ulric. It was a bit boring, because he always wanted to play the same thing: she was the beautiful princess carried off by a monster that wanted to eat her for its breakfast with bread and cheese, and he was the hero who rescued her and killed the monster. Afterward, they often went to see Asla, and then there was really something to eat. That by itself was enough to make her play the silly game with Ulric every time.

The day before, Ulric had let her touch the magical dagger, the one he'd been given by the elven prince. She thought it must have been the same elf who had spoken to her up on the Hartungscliff. His voice had been strange. The whole time he talked with her, Halgard had thought he was going to start singing at any moment. His hair had been wonderful to touch, as soft as a cat's, only much longer. He smelled nice, too. Nothing like the other men who sometimes kidded her and who usually smelled of mead or sweat or onions.

The girl came out of her thoughts with a jolt. Something was missing and had been for quite a while: the sound of her mother rubbing laundry on the rock.

"Mother?"

"Silence!" came a hiss beside her. Her mother's voice was full of fear. Halgard listened. She could hear much better than anyone else in the village. She held her breath. There was the whispering of the little waves feeling their way up the gravel and receding again, and the sound of the wind sweeping across the fjord rustling through the branches of the trees along the shore. She heard her heart beating and the soft hum of her blood. And . . . yes, there was something else. A creaking, wooden sound and regular splashing. There was a boat out on the water, but it was still a long way off. If it was still foggy, then Mother would hardly be able to see it.

"Is it the boat?" she asked softly.

"No, it's . . ." Her mother's clothes rustled. "Get up! Run! It's seen us! It's coming!" Her mother grabbed her by the arm and jerked her up. "Run!"

Halgard stumbled to her feet. She couldn't run, and Mother knew it! When she ran, she lost her orientation and fell over.

"The path's in front of you. Straight ahead." Her mother's breath was coming in gasps. "Along the shore. We have to get to the priest! He's the only one who can help us. Quickly! There's nothing in the way. Come on!"

They were on the path, and again her footsteps smacked in the mud, but now it seemed to want to hold on to her. And it was so horribly smooth. She slipped and was just able to stop herself from falling, her arms swinging wildly. There was no sound behind them. Nothing could move so silently. "What are we running from?"

"The animal! Quick. Please, Halgard, don't stop! It came out of the water. Its teeth . . . run! By all the gods, run!"

Halgard toiled along as well as she could. Her mother described the path for her, staying close behind although she could easily have overtaken her.

Halgard bumped against a stone, and this time she could not stop herself from falling. She fell flat onto the soft path. Cold mud spattered her face. She began to cry. She couldn't run!

"Up! Up with you, my little one."

Halgard was hauled back onto her feet. She felt her mother's breath on her face. "You run now to Gundar. You go to Gundar as fast as you can, and you get him. It isn't far to his hut. I'll slow down the animal."

"What is it?" Halgard asked, sobbing.

"It's as big as a horse, but it has teeth like a wolf. And it looks like fog. Go now! Quickly! Keep straight on until you feel the shadow of the willow, then go left. You know the way. The willow is only twenty steps ahead."

"Why don't I hear it?"

"Because it's like the fog!" Mother's voice sounded like she was holding back tears. "Don't ask any more. Run now. Please! It's almost on us."

Halgard went on as fast as she could. The wind from the fjord cut through her wet clothes. Her whole body shivered. She listened anxiously for any sound. When she reached the willow, she heard a soft cry. "Mother?"

Halgard could not see the tree, but she could feel that it was close by. It felt as if even darker shadows filled the darkness that always surrounded her. She heard the thin branches whipping against each other in the wind.

She went to the left. Suddenly, there was no more mud. She had lost the path. She hastily turned around and went back a short way, but she could not find the path. If only the sun were there! The light on her face would help her get her bearings.

The wind had stopped. Now she could not even hear the branches of the willow. She could not be far from Gundar's house. She screamed his name, hoping he was already awake. She knew the old man liked to sleep very late.

For a moment, she thought about going on, but she knew she would only get more lost. If she was a long way from the priest's house, then he would not be able to hear her anymore. No, it was better just to stay where she was and shout.

Suddenly, the air around her grew colder. She felt no wind on her face. Something pushed into her chest. Her ribs felt like ice, like the bones of her fingers after she'd been wringing laundry for too long.

Very softly, Halgard heard the creaking of a door.

She was shivering so much that she was no longer able to stand. She could not shout anymore either. Her teeth chattered as loudly as the bone rattle her father had once given her.

"Halgard? Is that you?" she heard the warm voice of the priest say. *Yes, warm like the summer,* the girl thought. *Like the summer.*

She heard footsteps in the wet grass.

"Halgard? By the gods!"

THE GODSWHIP

W hat could it have been? No creature from my world would do something like that to a child." Asla spoke softly, but the whisper took none
of the anger from her words.

"I don't know of any being in my world either—" Yilvina's voice broke. "I
don't know what it was. I really don't."

Tears stood in the priest's eyes. When he had found Halgard in the wet
grass, he only recognized her by the brooch on her shawl.

By all the gods, what had they done to deserve such a judgment? In
moments like these, he found himself doubting Luth's wisdom. Hadn't the
girl been punished enough? She'd lost her father. She was blind. And now
this. Her face was as withered as an old woman's. Dark age spots marred her
cheeks and forehead, and her hair had turned snowy white. Gundar lowered
the curtain in front of the bed. The girl was sleeping soundly, and he was glad
he did not have to look her in the face anymore. *No child should look like that,*
he thought, filled with anger. Who could do something like that to a little girl?

Halgard did not yet know what had happened to her. She had been too
tired. She had, however, been surprised at how hoarse her voice sounded, as
if it wasn't hers at all. Gundar swallowed hard when he thought of the lies he
had whispered into Halgard's ears. He had not found the courage to tell her
the truth, nor did she know that her mother was dead.

The Luth priest went to the table that stood close to the fire pit and
slumped onto a stool beside it. Asla set a bowl of steaming fish broth in front
of him, but he pushed it away. He could not eat now.

If only he had held his tongue the day before! Then the girl would not
have had her youth stolen from her, and Alfeid, her mother, would still live.

"It must have been a ghost," said Yilvina. "There were no tracks. None on
the muddy path and none in the grass. It kills without spilling blood."

Gundar looked at the grain of the wooden tabletop. Yes, that had occurred
to him, too. But where would a ghost come from? He had even taken three
books from his library in his search for counsel but had found nothing that
could explain the incidents in the village. Only in the *Book of Omens* had he

found a few lines about ghosts. Apparently, they appeared when someone died before they had been able to bring some important matter to a close while they lived. Usually, it came down to revenge or love.

Sometimes, a ghost was sent back by the gods to haunt the living, but there had been no crime that the gods would have to punish. If a sin against the gods had been committed that deserved a punishment like this, then he as the priest would have known about it. It could not have remained hidden from him!

No one in the village had died in the late summer, so there was no one who could have become a ghost. Yet ever since this creature had begun spreading its wickedness, death had been a constant guest in Firnstayn.

So we must have angered the gods, Gundar thought. But how? Because they had opened the gateway to the elven world? It was clear that their problems had begun only after Alfadas and his army had departed. Was that a coincidence? Had something perhaps come back through the gateway?

"Are there ghosts in Albenmark?" Gundar asked.

"No," Yilvina replied firmly. She had returned to her place on the stool beside the unconscious queen. She had been standing guard in that same place for weeks, like a never-tiring watchdog, ready to give her life for Emerelle. In a house occupied by no more than a mother with two children and a seriously injured man who would probably never leave his bed again, her behavior seemed to the priest to be grossly exaggerated.

"The Alben, our distant ancestors, drove out all the beings of the darkness," Yilvina said. "The Devanthar and the Yingiz are either dead or banished forever into the darkness between the worlds."

Asla had joined Gundar at the table. She was tearing a fresh linen cloth into strips.

"What are those? Demons? I'm just a fisherman's daughter," Asla said with slight irritation. "You have to explain names like those for me."

"Of course. My apologies." Yilvina stood up, went to the fire pit, and poked at the embers with a stick.

For a moment, it seemed to Gundar that the elf did not want to say any more. When she did speak, however, she did so tentatively, her words faltering. She seemed to be weighing each word with care. Was she afraid she might bring the old terrors back to life by speaking about them?

"The Devanthar hated all forms of order. Whenever something was completed, they had to destroy it to make room for something new. For them, order meant everything coming to a standstill. I can explain it no better than that, for the Alben destroyed the Devanthar a very long time ago.

"It was the Alben who created all the worlds and races that we know today. To protect their creation, they had to destroy the Devanthar. The war between them was so catastrophic that one of the worlds actually broke apart. For many of the Alben, the horrors of the war wounded their souls deeply, and they began to abandon Albenmark forever or withdraw to a life of solitude. They sought out places like Albentop, where they meditated for centuries in isolation.

"With the Yingiz, things took a different course. The Yingiz were beings of pure malice, able to take pleasure only in the suffering of others. They were banished to the darkness between the worlds."

"That's it!" Gundar cried. The enemy finally had a name. "One of those creatures of the dark must have come through the gateway to our world."

"Out of the question." Yilvina broke the stick in two and tossed the pieces into the fire. "The Alben surrounded the gateways and the paths through the void with powerful protective spells. No Yingiz has ever returned. Nobody even remembers anymore what they look like. It has to be something else that has laid siege to the village. Are there no ghosts here in the Other World?"

Gundar nodded uncertainly. "There are, though I have never seen one."

"We can safely say that nothing of flesh and blood attacked Halgard. I would have found tracks. It must have been a ghost," the elf woman insisted. "Believe me. I'm an experienced huntress."

Ole rolled and groaned in his bed. There it was again . . . that smell, the odor of an open grave. Gundar took a twig of pine and tossed it onto the fire. The dry needles crackled and flared. Pleasantly scented white smoke spread.

It was pointless to talk to elves. She would never accept that the killer might have something to do with her or the queen.

Asla stood and looked across at Gundar, a silent plea for help in her eyes. She gathered the strips of linen and went to Ole's bed.

The priest picked up the earthenware bottle on the table and filled his cup. He drank the apple liquor in one draft. It burned his throat, and tears sprang to his eyes. Then he went over to Asla. When she pulled aside the blanket covering the sleeping niche and bed, he felt nauseous. The sharp odor of decay rose to meet him.

Ole's eyes were wide open, but he saw neither Asla nor the priest. His eyeballs were rolled up so that only the whites were visible. Cold sweat prickled his forehead.

Asla dabbed her uncle's ravaged face with a cloth. Ole did not blink once. Then she threw back the blanket. The bandages covering the stumps of his legs were soaked with a brown secretion. Asla took a knife and began to cut through the linen strips. With the tips of her fingers, she picked away what she could, trying to touch her uncle as little as possible.

"Blue sparks . . . ," Ole murmured, and began to giggle.

"Easy, Uncle. Easy." Asla stroked his forehead.

"The godswhip . . ." The dog breeder let out a deep sigh. "Gods . . ."

Asla looked at Gundar. "Now."

The priest leaned forward and pressed Ole onto the bed with both hands. At the same time, Asla jerked the bandages off. The fabric stuck to the open wounds. Ole screamed like an animal and tried to rear up. Dark pus dripped from the putrid flesh.

Gundar could only breathe shallowly through his mouth. The stink robbed him of breath. He had to look away and had trouble keeping his nausea in check.

Asla worked quickly, washing the wounds with spirits. Her uncle lay very still now. He had fallen unconscious. Like thin branches, two bones protruded from the ragged flesh of his thighs. The skin there was unnaturally white, and the blood vessels stood out as inflamed red lines tracing upward to his loins.

Asla wrapped fresh linen around the stumps. Dark fluid soaked through the cloth.

The priest looked at Asla's face. He concentrated on the fine lines around her eyes. She was still beautiful. Her golden hair hung in a heavy braid over her shoulder. Gundar understood well that Kalf could not simply forget her.

Asla changed the dressings on the stumps of Ole's wrists as well. Her uncle still lay unconscious. What had he meant when he spoke of a "godswhip"?

Gundar kept his eyes fixed on Asla's face. Tiny droplets of sweat formed on her forehead and dampened her eyebrows. Finally, she finished her work. She wiped one hand nervously across her brow. Then she bundled the soiled bandages together and threw them into the fire and laid a few more pine twigs over the top.

Gundar stood and poured himself another cup of liquor. His tongue felt like it was covered with fur. He had an unpleasant taste in his mouth, as if he had been drinking brackish water.

"Give me some of that, too?" Asla asked.

She was standing bent over a bucket, scrubbing herself with a brush. When she sat at the table, her hands glowed red.

"Didn't Kalf bring one of Ole's whips with him?"

"Two," said Asla flatly. "They lay where he found my uncle."

"Can I see them?"

"They're just dog whips. Horrible things with spikes in them. You know what they're like."

"Please."

"I'm tired." She pointed to an iron-banded chest. "They're over there. What do you want with them?"

Instead of answering, the priest crossed to the chest. Yilvina watched him with curiosity. The two whips lay on top of a patched blue child's dress. With care, the priest let one of the long leather bands glide through his fingers. Just recently, he saw, new pieces of iron had been woven into the whip with pale leather strands. Gundar inspected the metal spikes, one after the other. The pieces of iron that had been in the whip originally were covered only with a fine layer of surface rust. If he rubbed them, the metal gleamed silvery again immediately. But the newly added iron pieces looked very different. The rust had eaten into them deeply.

Gundar looked closely at the tip of a knife bound into the whip—on its cutting edge, the metal had peeled away in layers. Now, it looked as if it was stepped, as if the knife had once been put together from many thin layers of iron. The priest found rings of chain mail, nails, a piece from a horse harness. On all of them, the surface was eaten away and rough. Wind and weather had gnawed at those pieces of iron for a long time. He recalled a brief conversation he'd had not long before with Ole. The dog breeder had told him that he'd been on a pilgrimage and that now, with Luth's help, he was going to teach his dogs the meaning of obedience. Gundar had not taken him seriously at the time.

The priest straightened up quickly and pushed the whip into his belt.

"Well?" said Asla.

"He sinned against the gods! Yilvina was right. The beast is not from Albenmark or the void. I should have known. The corpses themselves scream out who sent this punishment. They scream it!"

PURSUED

Gundar had left the fjord behind him long ago. He was making his way up the mountain, following the same path that Mandred and his elven friends had taken when they had gone after the manboar. The old priest hoped that he would not have to go as far as the Luth's cave. Ole was a lazy bastard— he certainly would not have climbed all the way to the pass to commit his sin!

Gundar stopped abruptly and looked around. He sensed that he was being followed; he narrowed his eyes and peered into the driving snow. "There's nothing out there," he said aloud to himself. It felt good, hearing his own voice in the silence of the mountains. "There's no danger. I'm a man of religion." He spoke the last words somewhat louder. Not to impress anyone who might be following him, but just to hear his own voice. He was not a man for the wilderness. He felt most at home with a watertight roof close by and the prospect of at least two warm meals a day.

Kalf had offered to go with him, but Gundar wanted to be alone. He had to come to terms with himself. How could it have taken so long for him to recognize such a clear, unambiguous sign? All the victims but Ole had aged with unnatural speed. Alfeid, the washerwoman . . . she had been a young woman, yet when they had found her, her body had been as emaciated as a crone's who had far outlived her due. And Halgard . . . Gundar did not like to think of the young girl. It was no mercy that she still lived, a child in an old woman's body. How could Luth be so cruel? The weaver of fate had sent a ghostly executioner that had coiled the threads of destiny of its victims and wiped out their lives in an instant. Those deaths were meant as a sign!

Gundar began to move faster. He should have realized sooner what was going on, but the events of recent weeks had blinded him. Too much had happened. The elven queen seeking refuge; Horsa, the king of the Fjordlands, visiting the village not once but twice; the departure through the elven gate; the army.

Ole, fool that he was, had stolen from the ironbeards and had called down Luth's wrath on the village by doing so. Gundar thought of his own departure from the village. He had made the villagers swear not to leave their houses and had scrawled protective symbols with chalk and soot on their doorsteps. Luth could not punish them all just because one had strayed!

Puffing and panting, he continued up the path, the snow crunching softly underfoot. It was a pleasant, calming sound. Water seeped through the seams of his boots. He should have oiled them better, he knew: his feet were already soaked. Not much farther and he would reach Wehrberghof. He could spend the night there, but he would have to take better care of his boots the next day.

Gundar stopped again. Were those steps he heard behind him? The snow was falling more heavily now. He saw nothing but swirling white.

The storm was bringing the day to an early end. Gundar cursed. If he lost the trail or missed the farm, then he would be in serious trouble. His feet would freeze inside his wet boots. He should have accepted Kalf's offer.

Again, he looked back. Was that an outline there in the whiteness? No. He went on, accelerating his steps. But someone was staring at him! He could feel it clearly! He passed one hand carefully over the leather pouch hanging at his belt. "I'm returning what is yours, Luth," he whispered. "Please be patient for another day. Everyone in the village has given something of iron to sacrifice to you. Forgive them! They cannot be held to account for Ole's deeds."

Halgard entered Gundar's thoughts again. The memory made him angry. How could Luth have done that? What did the blind girl have to do with Ole? Gundar had been his god's loyal servant for almost forty years, but the previous night, for the first time, he had begun to doubt. A god that would send an avenger to ravage his village so indiscriminately . . . that was not the Luth of whose wisdom he had spent all these decades preaching. There was no visible pattern in the horrors that had befallen them, none that the priest could see, at least. They were simply cruel.

Steps! Gundar had heard them very clearly this time. But what did he expect? He cursed Luth, if only in his mind, though he knew an unspoken curse would not go unobserved by the weaver of fate. The priest turned around.

"Send him, then, your assassin!" he shouted into the wind-whipped snow. He planted his hands on his hips. "Come on! Put an end to it! I'll stand here and wait."

What was he doing? Had he lost his mind? "Let me return the stolen iron," he said in a placating voice. "Then take me as a sacrifice if you want. I'm as much to blame as Ole. Spare my village."

A horse whinnied close by. Wehrberghof. Was he already so close? Gundar moved on. Was it a sign from Luth? Did the god want to show him the way to the farm? Gundar bore left and paced on with more confidence.

After a short distance, the outline of a hill appeared through the snow. Gundar was all too aware that he would have walked past the hill entirely if had not heard the whinnying and changed course. The Wehrberg, on which Thorfinn's farm lay, was surrounded by three rings of half-collapsed earthen walls. There had probably been a settlement there a long time ago, but now only the large farm, Wehrberghof, huddled in the lee just below the crown of the hill.

Gundar followed the old path that led between the earthen walls. He smelled smoke. The thought of a fire and a bowl of warm porridge made the priest's heart beat faster.

In the swirling snow, the longhouse's gable looked raven-black. It was finished with two carved dragon's heads, their jaws opened wide. The back of the house had been dug partly into the hillside. The stable and the house proper were united under a single long roof with a thin wooden wall separating them. The thick earthen walls and the warmth that radiated from the fire pit to the stable kept the animals safe from even the hardest frost.

Gundar knocked at the heavy wooden door. Nothing stirred. The wind had freshened again. The priest pushed the door open. *Strange,* he thought, *that it had not been barred for the night.* He stepped into the tiny entryway. A heavy woolen curtain separated it from the rest of the house. An oil lamp burned on a stool.

"Thorfinn? Audhild?" He could not remember the names of their three children. The family did not come to the village often enough for that. Gundar was sure, though, that he'd recall the names as soon as he saw the youngsters again.

No answer. Maybe they were in the stable and hadn't heard him. He closed the door and used the scraper leaning on the stool to scratch the crusted snow from his boots. Then, humming softly to himself, he knocked the snow from his clothes.

Finally, he pushed the curtain aside and stepped into the parlor. It was pleasantly warm, and fresh rushes had been strewn on the floor. A fire glowed in a fire pit with a stone surround in the center of the parlor. Over it hung a heavy copper kettle from an iron hook. Whatever was in the pot smelled burned. He heard a soft blubbering noise and saw five wooden bowls on the table. A clay cup lay on its side at on one end of the table, and a pool of wine shimmered like blood on the wood. There was no one in sight.

"Thorfinn? Audhild?" Again, he received no answer. But even in the stable they would have been able to hear him. Gundar stepped over to the fire, picked up a rag, and lifted the kettle aside. Millet gruel. He stirred it. Black clumps rose to the surface. What was going on here? Was that a sound? Gundar looked up to the ceiling. Heavy black beams supported the roof. For a fleeting moment, he thought he saw something white, but in the wavering red light from the fire pit, it was impossible to say if anything was really there.

He shook his head. There would be a very simple explanation for everything. And what was supposed to be among the roof beams, anyway?

"Thorfinn? Audhild?" Maybe they were outside with the children, chasing a goat that had wandered off. The priest looked toward the door that joined the parlor to the stable. It stood slightly ajar.

Gundar returned to the entryway and fetched the oil lamp. Holding it in his outstretched arm, he entered the stable. It was pitch-black inside. He saw a few feathers in the light cast by the lamp. Some dirty straw. An overturned bucket.

The priest took another step. Brown branches? He lifted the lamp higher. The corpse of a horse lay in the center of the stable, its legs no more than skin and bone. Gundar could see every rib of its shriveled body. He swallowed. *Please. Not here, Luth,* he thought despairingly. *I beg you!*

Protruding from behind a chest-high wooden wall, he saw the sole of a boot. His heart pounding, Gundar stepped over the horse. Thorfinn! His thin face was frozen in a mask of horror. Audhild, his wife, lay beside him. Her skirts had slipped up as she had tried to crawl away from something. Her legs reminded him of driftwood sticks washed up on the shore of the fjord.

Thorfinn still held a wooden hayfork in his hand. He seemed to have tried—uselessly—to hold something at bay. "Not the children," Gundar whispered, and he moved on, into the back section of the stable.

The flame of the oil lamp flickered. The priest felt a breath of air on his face, icy cold. He moved around several dead birds lying on the floor and found two goat carcasses as well. All of them had retreated to the very rear of the stable. Then he discovered Thorfinn's elder son. The tow-haired lad had been twelve summers old. Gundar recalled his name now: Finn. He was half lying, half sitting, his back against the door that led outside. His hands were still pressed back against the gray wood. The door was slightly open, and snow was blowing in through the gap.

Gundar kneeled beside the boy. He pushed against the door, testing it. It barely moved an inch. He raised the lamp and looked out through the narrow opening. A snowdrift had sealed the door. The snow outside was as high as Gundar's waist. A strong man could not have opened that door.

Finn's eyes gazed into the darkness. Gundar tried to lower the boy's eyelids, wanting to escape his stare, but the dried skin tore.

Where were the others? *Aesa,* he thought. *That was the daughter. And Tofi, the youngest.* Finn was facing toward the sled. Gundar gulped. He was afraid of what he would find. Knees trembling, he crossed to the other side. A colorful horse blanket lay over a bench, an indistinct outline beneath it.

He snatched the blanket back. Harness and tack were on the bench, but nothing more. Maybe the children had escaped. "Aesa! Tofi! It's me, Gundar, the priest from Firnstayn. You don't have to be afraid anymore."

Gundar listened into the darkness. The wind outside howled beneath the gables. Wood clattered. The priest turned in fright. Something was in the stable!

"Who's there?"

Another gust wailed through the roof. Very softly, he heard a husky sound. A whisper!

The stable was so cold that Gundar's breath fogged in front of his mouth. The hand that held the lamp shook, and shadows danced over the stable walls.

Softly, he began to pray. Step by step, he moved back through the room. The hayfork. It had slipped from Thorfinn's hands. Someone must have bumped against it.

"In the name of the weaver of fate, show yourself!"

The whisper came again. Right at his feet! Thorfinn's mouth twitched. His lips were dried and pulled back so far that Gundar could see the farmer's yellow teeth. Hoarse sounds escaped his throat. Thorfinn's sky-blue eyes were fixed on Gundar.

"Chi . . ."

Gundar leaned down, trying to hear better.

"Children . . . the light . . . I see . . ."

"Save your strength, Thorfinn. I'll bring you to the fire," Gundar said, and he tried to lift the farmer.

Thorfinn's hand shot forward, closing around Gundar's left wrist. The skin was as thin as finely shaved vellum. Gundar could distinctly feel the bones in the farmer's fingers. It felt as if a hand from a grave had grabbed hold of him. He tried to push the claw away, but Thorfinn summoned all his strength to hold on.

"Life strings . . . eats . . . wolfhorse."

"A wolfhorse?"

"Door . . . it goes through . . . just . . . through . . ."

"Where are the children?"

A shudder went through the man's drained body. "Just through . . ." A single tear trickled down Thorfinn's cheek. His features softened. He seemed to have found his peace. "They're waiting."

"I'll take you down to the village," Gundar whispered helplessly.

A rattle came from deep in the dying man's chest. His hand released its grip. His eyes lost their shine.

"May the gods light your way through the darkness. May they open their halls to you and welcome you to their eternal feast, for you were a true servant always, and your soul is—"

Thorfinn reared up. The unspeakable horror had reappeared on his face, as if, on his journey into eternal night, he had once again encountered the terror that had come to haunt Wehrberghof. The farmer tried desperately to say something. His debilitated body tensed, then suddenly slumped. Thorfinn's life-light went out once and for all.

There was a puff of air, and the small flame from the oil lamp wavered and smoked and began to shrink. In a moment, it was little more than a spark. Gundar tried to shield it from the draft with his hands. Carefully, he set it on the floor. A red glow shone through the doorway that led back to the parlor.

Gundar kneeled and prayed fervently that the flame would not go out completely. It was only a few steps to the door, but the darkness was like a cavern with no end. Not even as a child had he been so afraid of the dark. He was sure the wolfhorse was lurking inside it, and that as soon as it was completely dark, it would come for him. Only the dying flame of the lamp still protected him.

Gundar tried to fight his fear. *The beast must be gone by now,* he told himself, *or it would have attacked me long ago.* But it could not be far away. He thought of the burned gruel. It could not have been more than half an hour since the family had fled the parlor for the stable. Gundar looked around fearfully in the darkness. Was it still here?

The snowstorm eased. The small flame on its wick did not waver anymore. Slowly, it grew stronger. The circle of light it cast in the darkness grew with every heartbeat. And then Gundar saw them—the other two children! Aesa had her arms wrapped around Tofi protectively. They had crept beneath the large sled to hide.

Tofi had his head pressed into Aesa's shoulder. They were gone. Tears sprang to the priest's eyes, and he wept silently. Helpless, he balled one hand into a fist and bit into it. Why were there gods at all if they let something like this happen?

Was that a sound? The soft crunch of footsteps in the snow? Had the assassin returned?

"Come into the parlor!" the priest bellowed in his fury. "I'm waiting for you!"

Hardly were the words out of his mouth than he regretted them. What had he done? With trembling fingers, he fumbled for the knife at his belt. It had a narrow blade, barely as long as his hand. All his life, he had only ever used a knife to slice meat and gut fish. He had never been in a fight in his life—he was a priest! His job was to stop senseless fights from happening!

He pulled himself together. If the beast was coming for him, he wanted at least to see it in the light. He looked at the dead children one last time. Hiding would be pointless.

He went into the parlor, turned, and barred the door to the stable. Then he threw pieces of firewood onto the coals until a bright flame shot up.

Sounds came from the entryway. Something was tinkering around behind the heavy woolen curtain that separated the parlor from the small space.

Gundar raised his knife protectively over his chest. To finally see the beast . . . maybe there would be some relief in that, at least? The curtain parted. A small figure dressed in white stepped into the parlor. Gundar's eyes were blurred with tears. He blinked.

It was Ulric!

"What are you doing here?" Gundar lowered the knife.

"I . . . I came to help you. I . . . You won't send me away now, will you?" Alfadas's son spoke quickly and avoided looking the priest in the eye. "It's already dark outside. I can't go back to the village tonight! I wanted to spend the night in the stable so you wouldn't notice me. But I guess you heard my steps, didn't you?"

Gundar slumped onto the heavy wooden bench beside the table. "Why did you follow me?"

"I'm going to fight the monster with you!" the boy said ardently. "When we've killed it, Halgard will get better. That's how it always is, isn't it? When the heroes kill the monster, everything is better again."

Gundar felt a lump rising in his throat. What was he supposed to tell the boy? That things for Halgard would never get better? Maybe miracles could only happen if someone believed in them. What had happened to the girl, after all, had also been a miracle, although of the most terrible kind. "Does your mother know you're here?"

Ulric shook his head. "She never would have let me go. But I had to come." The boy was wearing a thick coat made from white leather. It had a hood and was lined with sheepskin. His boots, too, were pale leather. No wonder he'd been able to hide so well in the snow.

Ulric unbuttoned the coat. At his belt, he wore a long dagger. "That's my magic sword," he declared proudly. "The elves forged it. We'll be able to beat any monster with that, Gundar. You know, Halgard is my princess. I've always protected her. In the village, they say you went out to deliver us from evil. I'll be by your side. I'll fight with you."

The priest looked at the boy in disbelief. Every word he said was spoken earnestly. He truly believed that he could save Halgard. But could he take

Ulric with him? What would happen if they actually encountered the beast? And yet, couldn't that happen in the village just as easily? And if he took Ulric back to Firnstayn, would he find the courage to go out again, now that he knew for certain that the creature was also up here?

Ulric was looking at him. He could not send the boy back. "Be my companion on this quest." Gundar was surprised at the emotion in his voice. The boy had opened a door to a world that had long been closed to him, one in which the belief that, in the end, everything would work out had not been extinguished by years of bitter experience.

The pieces of firewood that Gundar had thrown onto the fire were already half burned. Darkness was returning to the parlor when they took their places side by side at the long table. The priest ladled two bowls of millet gruel for them from the kettle and found some stale bread.

"Where are Thorfinn and his family?" Ulric asked abruptly, dunking his bread in the gruel.

Gundar sighed deeply. Could he tell him the truth? Wouldn't a lie only slam shut the door that the boy had just opened for him? "They're gone," he finally said evasively.

"Where? They can't stay outside in the storm."

"They're dead, Ulric. A wolfhorse, a . . . ghostly thing . . . was here. The very same that almost killed Halgard."

The boy placed his chunk of bread back on the table.

"It killed them all?" he asked very quietly. "The children too?"

Gundar nodded. "Yes, also the children." He pushed his bowl of gruel away. That was that for dinner. He couldn't eat now.

"Where are they?"

Ulric slid over, and Gundar finally laid his arm around the boy's shoulders and drew him close. "They're out in the stables. We can't bury them now. I'll send others up when we get back to the village."

"Do they all look like Alfeid?"

"Yes."

"It's good that Halgard couldn't see her mother like that. She looked so . . ." Ulric suddenly began to sob.

Gundar embraced the boy tightly. He was close to tears himself.

After a while, they pushed the table and the bench aside. They spread their coats on the rush-covered floor, close to the fireplace. They could not sleep in the beds of the dead. To do so felt wrong.

They lay beside one another in silence and listened to the crackling of the fire and the storm.

"Do you see it too?" Ulric whispered. "Up there, all the way in the corner. It's sitting up in the beams, watching us." His voice was trembling. "Is that it? The wolfhorse?"

Gundar squinted. There really was something white up there. A head? Thorfinn's words came back to him. *It goes through . . . just through . . .* Was the beast sitting on the roof? Had it pushed its head down through the shingles to watch them? Gundar blinked, but he could not see the thing clearly. He threw back his coat, jumped to his feet, and threw a handful of kindling onto the coals. An eternity seemed to pass before bright flames leaped.

Ulric had his dagger in his hand, ready to strike in a heartbeat. The boy seemed to know no fear. Then, suddenly, he burst into laughter. "It's a chicken!"

Gundar squinted at the ceiling again. Ulric was right! There was no apparition. A frightened chicken had pushed itself up against the slope of the roof right at the end of a roof beam. It must have escaped from the stable through the door he'd found ajar. Gundar began to laugh along with the boy. It was liberating. Perhaps they really could win, and everything would be good again when they found the desecrated ironman and had pleaded forgiveness for Ole's crime.

They lay down again, and Ulric soon fell asleep. Gundar propped himself on his elbow and looked at the boy. Ulric was smiling.

The old priest stretched and rolled himself in his coat. Did he smile in his own sleep sometimes? *What a foolish idea,* he thought wearily. And who was supposed to watch him when he slept anyway?

All that remained of the fire was a matte glow. Something moved in the darkness behind the table. A spider with a body the size of a pig was looking at them. Its jaws clicked softly. No, it spoke: "At the spider under the rainbow lies a gift for you."

FRIENDSHIP AND DEAD FISH

Ollowain had reached the large lake in the center of the Skyhall. He looked up at the Mahdan Falah. Where was she? It made no difference who he asked. All he got were evasions and shrugs. But she was not far away; she had not left Phylangan—he could feel that she was close by. Sometimes he even dreamed of her.

No. That was nonsense. He had no magical talent. How was he supposed to "feel" that she was close by? It was wishful thinking. He simply did not want to admit the truth: she had betrayed him. She had stolen the Albenstone and absconded with it.

Ollowain suspected, though, that the truth of the matter lay elsewhere. He gazed up at the bridge again. He would give anything to be standing up there with her, looking deep into her eyes, feeling the soft pressure of her hands. In his heart, he felt that she had not broken faith with him. Landoran knew where she was. She'd let him talk her into some foolish business or other, hoping that the old scoundrel would help her. If only she'd come straight to him, Ollowain, without sending Lysilla ahead.

Ollowain moved his fingertips over the snow-white lotus flowers that grew along the shore. Their heady scent lay over the water, and the air was oppressively hot. Lyndwyn had been right, of course. He would never have let her get close to him by herself. She had been forced to blindfold him so he would follow the voice of his heart. What a fool he'd been.

Hoofbeats caught Ollowain's ear, and he saw Orimedes come trotting down the path to the shore. He carried a wineskin over his shoulder and held two heavy silver goblets in his hands. "I have to tell you, White Knight, that you are not the easiest elf to find. Can you help me knock off this wine? This, at least, is not destined to end up as loot for a troll."

"So you also think the trolls will win?"

The centaur raised his eyebrows. "You don't? The question is not whether the trolls will win. That part is beyond doubt. The only question is how long we can hold on." He raised the wineskin. "Which is why we should polish off this wine."

"Maybe you and your men should leave Phylangan? You still have time. What sense is there in dying in a hopeless fight?"

Orimedes opened the wineskin and filled the silver goblets. "You're staying, too."

"These are my people. I don't have a choice. And . . ." He thought of Lyndwyn. He would not abandon her. The Albenstone could not be allowed to fall into the trolls' hands. He had to stay close to the sorceress.

"And?" Orimedes repeated, handing him one of the goblets of wine. "I hope you will do me the honor of drinking with a barbarian like me."

Ollowain took the proffered cup. "You're not a—"

The centaur clanged his goblet against Ollowain's. Wine slopped, splashing over Ollowain's sleeve, but it pearled off without leaving the slightest mark. "Don't tell me what I am or am not, elf. I know perfectly well what you think of me and those like me. You can't abide anyone who's relieved himself in your queen's ballroom." The centaur grinned broadly. "I can understand that, and I'm sorry I did, really. What can I say? Some things are stronger than I am." Suddenly, he grew serious. "I've come to say thank you. If not for you, I would have died in Vahan Calyd."

The swordmaster waved it off. "We both did our duty for the queen, no more."

"You know, you talk some rubbish. You were prepared to sacrifice your life when we climbed out of the cisterns—and you put Emerelle's life in my hands, ill-bred barbarian that I am. I know enough elves to know that most would have chosen a very different course. They would have sent me and my men against the trolls, not entrusted us with the queen. That was one of the proudest moments of my life. Now let's drink to that."

Orimedes raised the goblet to his lips, and Ollowain did the same. The wine was mellow; the aroma of the grapes had held up well, and the liquid contained a touch of honey and wild berries. "It would be a shame for wine like this to disappear down a troll's gullet," Ollowain said.

Orimedes nodded with satisfaction. "A crying shame. About the humans . . . what do you think of them? I mean, the thing with the ships is pure madness. I know you raised Alfadas, but his plan, well, I would never have come up with an idea like that, not even staggering drunk."

Ollowain thought back to the quarrel that had unfolded in the council of war, and how, in the end, Alfadas had won out. "The good thing about his plan is that it's *so* insane that the trolls will never know what's coming their way."

The centaur laughed, and droplets of wine sprayed Ollowain in the face. "No dog would think that one of the fleas on its back had made up its mind to kill it. And even if the dog did, would it be worried? No!"

Ollowain took a good swig of the wine and held it in his mouth, savoring its taste and aroma. Orimedes's objections were justified. But if Alfadas's plan worked, then things might never go as far as a siege. The attempt was worth it.

"Come. Drain your cup!" the centaur encouraged him. "This wine doesn't go to your head."

But maybe it can help one forget. Ollowain glanced up at the bridge, then he placed both hands around the bowl of the goblet and drank.

Orimedes gave him a friendly cuff and grinned conspiratorially. "I have an admission to make. I've hoodwinked you. I know my race has a reputation as a band of drunken louts, and maybe there's some truth in it, but there's a method to our drinking bouts. Fixed rules. When two men share a wineskin, then from that day forth, they're friends and no longer strangers." The centaur leaned forward and threw his arms around Ollowain, taking him completely by surprise. "Now that's behind us, know that you can confide in me. And know also that I would bite off my own tongue before I betrayed any secret of yours."

Ollowain looked at the centaur prince in confusion. "What are you talking about?"

"I might be a barbarian, but I'm not blind. You're not the same man I left at the Albenstar in Windland. Something's on your mind, so spit it out! Drinking and talking helps. Trust me. Take it from a notorious tippler and gabbler," Orimedes said, refilling both goblets.

Ollowain had to smile. Maybe his new friend was telling the truth. And what difference did it make if he wasn't? The days for all of them were numbered.

"It's Lyndwyn. She . . . she used our escape to steal the Albenstone from Emerelle. And she . . . it's . . ." He tried desperately to find the right words to describe what he had not yet managed to explain even to himself.

"Odious witch!" Orimedes snarled. "The moment I saw her, I knew she could not be trusted."

"I'm in love with her."

Orimedes choked on his wine. He coughed and gasped for air. A long, embarrassed silence followed. "Well," he finally said. "Sometimes it takes a witch to turn your head, doesn't it? Have you already . . . you know?" He gestured obscenely.

"Yes," said Ollowain curtly. "And we quarreled. I haven't seen her since." He told the centaur the full story, and found, in fact, that it really did help to talk about Lyndwyn. He was able to sense the truth behind all the disappointments, and he felt a pain he could not put into words. "I try to forget her, but she has touched my heart. I . . ."

Orimedes laid one hand gently on his shoulder. "I fear you are irretrievable, my friend." He smiled understandingly. "You're in love. Find her. That's all you can still do."

"But where?" Ollowain said in despair.

"Landoran will know."

Ollowain thought of his youth, of the dismay in his father's eyes when young Ollowain was not able to work magic, no matter how hard he tried. He was not the son that the prince of the Normirga had wished for, and Landoran had made that very clear to him. He would never help him! "Phylangan is concealing something from us. Something is going on that the Normirga are not talking about. And my father has drawn Lyndwyn into it."

The centaur stroked his beard thoughtfully. "My men have explored partway through the mountain. We ought to know what we're defending, after all," he said apologetically.

"One should also know where the wine is stored."

Orimedes laughed loudly. "We are truly kindred souls! There is a large stairway that descends from the front of the Skyhall. If you follow it down, you reach a place where three guards stand on duty. If you can get past them, I suspect you'll find what you're looking for."

"You think they're holding Lyndwyn captive? That's not possible, Orimedes. She is a sorceress, and she possesses an Albenstone. No one on this mountain could hold her against her will."

"And if she's down there because she wants to be?" the centaur conjectured. "She—"

Orimedes suddenly stood stock-still.

"What is it?" Ollowain said.

The centaur's mouth gaped as he looked out onto the lake. As if in a trance, he lifted his arm and pointed out at the water. "The fish. Look."

Eerily pale fish bodies were floating up from the dark depths of the lake. They bobbed lifelessly, their white bellies up on the gentle swell. Soon there were hundreds of them.

"What's going on?" Orimedes retreated a little from the shore, as if he feared he might share the fishes' fate. "The lake! It must be poisoned. More and more are coming up. Everything is dead!"

Ollowain gazed out at the green water. It was almost the color of Lyndwyn's eyes, those marvelous green orbs sprinkled with gold.

The centaur shook him. "What's going on?"

"Lyndwyn." Ollowain blinked. The spell was broken. "Stay here. Make sure no one drinks from the lake."

THE SPIDER UNDER THE RAINBOW

Gundar kneeled in the snow before the figure of the god. Ole had really done it! This was where the dog breeder's pilgrimage had ended in a moment of madness.

The priest ran his fingers over the rough surface of the wood. The sculptor had hewn the likeness of Luth from a thick oak trunk. Its head and bulging eyebrows were carved well and quite detailed, but from the shoulders down, the artist had only vaguely suggested the form of a body. Most of that had long disappeared beneath an armor of rusted iron pieces all jammed together in the wood: nails, pieces of broken blades, rings, a chunk of flattened iron, a horseshoe. A dozen or more of these idols stood at intervals along the trail that led over the pass. Every traveler going that way sacrificed a bit of old iron to them and asked the weaver of fate for protection on the way over the mountains. Over the centuries, the statues had become dressed in a suit of iron and rust that had earned them the name "ironbeards."

Ulric picked up the hammer with the stone head that lay on a flat rock beside the statue. Summoning up his strength, he drove a nail into the idol's foot.

Gundar was still looking at the gaps picked into the statue's rusty coat. What had gotten into Ole, robbing a god?

"Will Luth protect us?" Ulric asked, returning the hammer to its place.

"Your uncle made the weaver of fate angry," the priest replied grimly. "Let's pray that we can make him merciful again."

"But we're bringing everything back. Won't that make things right?"

Gundar sighed. "Perhaps." He opened the leather pouch that contained the rusty iron pieces that Ole had woven into the tails of his whip. Then he took the hammer and tried carefully to drive them back into the wood.

"Gundar?" Ulric rubbed his hands together for warmth. They were red from the cold. "If I stab my magical dagger into the ironbeard, will Luth make Halgard well again?"

The priest paused in his work and looked up at the sky. How could he possibly answer that? "The dagger is a great treasure, isn't it?"

The boy nodded.

"And you would sacrifice it for Halgard?"

"If Luth would make her well again."

"It is not the way of Luth to steal from us. I am quite sure that Luth has heard what you would be willing to give up, and he knows that you speak with a pure heart. Keep the dagger. It was Luth who knotted the thread of your life so that you would meet the elves' swordmaster and so that Ollowain would give you that gift. That also means the dagger is a gift to you from Luth. One does not return a gift to its giver. That would be an insult to the god."

"I didn't want to hurt his feelings," said Ulric remorsefully. "Sometimes it's very hard to understand the gods. I'm glad you're here and can explain what they want."

Gundar swallowed. "Yes," he said softly. He thought of the number of times he himself had doubted. He found the child's trust in him both comforting and a burden. He could not let Ulric down and hoped against hope that the wolfhorse would simply vanish as it had come.

The priest stared into the statue's great eyes, and the god returned his gaze, unperturbed. Luth had sent him the dream the night before. Spiders watched over the god's golden palace and sometimes helped him weave the threads of fate as well.

"I told you about my dream, Ulric. Look for a rainbow for me. Luth will send it to us as a sign when he has made his peace with us."

The boy looked up doubtfully at the radiant blue winter sky. There was not a cloud in sight. It was far too cold for any rain to fall, so where was a rainbow supposed to come from? Gundar was acutely aware that they were waiting for a miracle.

The priest returned to his labors, doing his best to force the purloined bits of iron back into the wood without breaking them. He had also brought along a small crucible of sticky fir tree resin. He used it whenever a piece seemed too fragile to risk hitting with the hammer.

Progress was slow. From the corner of his eye, he saw Ulric exploring the narrow defile that the mountain path rose through. The boy looked among the leafless bushes and searched for clues in the snow and rocks.

When Gundar was done with the stolen iron, he opened his second bag. Every resident of Firnstayn had given him a small gift to take along for Luth. He hammered on tirelessly, only occasionally checking on the boy.

Suddenly, a shrill cry made him jump. "There it is!" Ulric was jumping around like a young goat leaving the stable for the first time after a long winter. "The weaver of fate has sent us a sign! Come quickly, Gundar! Here's the rainbow. And I can see the spider, too!"

Gundar saw a colorful spot of light glittering on the gray rock wall opposite the ironbeard. Astonished, incredulous, he stood up. His old bones creaked, and his knees ached as he hobbled over to the boy.

"Look, Gundar! There on the rock. You have to look closely, just beneath the rainbow!"

The priest blinked and rubbed his eyes. Then he stepped closer to the rough rock wall. His fingers traced the weak lines, as if demanding physical proof of the unclear image he saw. A spider had been carved in the rock. It was almost weathered away and no bigger than the palm of his hand. Above the spider stood a crooked patch of light that shimmered in all the colors of the rainbow. "The spider beneath the rainbow," he whispered. His heart leaped. It was a sign from his god! How could he ever have doubted Luth? The god had accepted their sacrifice.

The priest looked up toward the pass. The sun was already low among the mountains. A sparkling icicle dangling from a branch caught his eye. Was that causing the rainbow? What difference did it make? Luth had given him a sign. That was all that mattered.

"Let me clear the snow," Ulric said excitedly. "What gift do you think he's hidden here?"

Gundar spread his arms wide, smiling. "How should I know?" He looked up blissfully at the sky as Ulric dug. A gift from Luth! The weaver of fate honored him beyond measure.

"I can't go any deeper." Ulric had shoveled the snow aside with his bare hands but had come to a layer of brown leaves encased in ice.

"His gift to us may have been here a very long time. It might have been covered up by falling leaves over the years. Maybe it's actually buried in the earth? Do you think you could make a fire here to thaw out the earth?"

"I don't have a flint or tinder," said the boy sadly.

"But I do. You find a little dead grass and some dry twigs. Maybe a thick branch we can use to dig with." Gundar looked up at the sky again. The sun was indeed very low. They would not make it back down to Wehrberghof before nightfall. If they wanted to get their hands on their treasure today, then they would have to spend the night right there. With the sky so brilliantly clear, it would be very cold. The priest pointed to a patch of fir trees surrounded by thick brush. "Let's make ourselves a camp for the night. We'll be sheltered from the wind, and there's a big rock that will reflect the heat of the fire. But first things first: we need to have a good supply of firewood to get us through the night. Then we can continue. Can you find us a pile of wood, Ulric? I still have a few of the offerings to knock into the ironbeard."

Ulric nodded enthusiastically and ran off.

Two hours later, they used sticks to push the hot coals aside. Ulric had gotten carried away and had built a fire they could have used to grill an ox. The dead leaves in the ice had burned to ash. Gundar was apprehensive. It had occurred to him too late that, should Luth's gift be something that could burn, it would be lost to the flames.

Ulric stabbed his digging stick into the ground with all his strength. It took some pushing and twisting to get the rubble and humus to move. The priest held up a torch to give the boy some light, while Ulric stabbed and dug at the earth until he was kneeling in a shallow excavation. Several times he came across larger stones, and Gundar helped him lever those free.

"There's a gap!"

"Can I see?" The priest leaned forward as far as he could. Alfadas's son had revealed a finger-wide crack at the base of the rock wall. Beside it stood a pile of fist-sized stones. "Those stones look strange, don't they? As if someone stacked them on purpose."

Ulric pulled a thin branch from the remains of their fire and pushed it into the gap in the rock. "It goes down a long way. Maybe we've found a treasure cave?"

Gundar had to smile. While he had no real idea of what Luth might have given them, he certainly did not believe it would be a treasure cave. He pushed the digging stick into the gap behind the stacked stones; with a quick pull, he levered them aside.

Ulric eagerly tossed the rocks out of the shallow pit he'd dug. The deeper they went, the wider the gap became. Finally, it was wide enough for Ulric to put his arm inside. He lay flat on his belly and fished around with his fingers inside the hiding place. "There's something slimy down there."

"Can you pull it up?"

"It's heavy. I can't get a good grip on it. It keeps slipping out of my fingers." Ulric stood up again. His white cloak was covered in mud and grime.

They dug deeper in silence for a while until the opening was big enough for Gundar to get his arm inside. His fingers touched something cold and slippery. A smell of decay rose from the hole. When the priest finally was able to get a good hold on the mysterious treasure, it took all his strength to lift it out.

Luth's gift was wrapped in moldy leather. Something inside the wrapping clinked softly when Gundar laid his discovery on the ground. The leather had apparently been oiled very carefully at some point in the past. In a few places there was no mold, and the leather still gleamed as if wet.

"Don't you want to open it?" asked Ulric impatiently.

Gundar shook his head. He thought he knew what he would find inside the leather, but he had no idea what he, as a priest, could possibly use it for.

Apparently, Luth was sending him to war. But against whom? Could it be that the wolfhorse had not been sent by the weaver of fate at all?

"Let's go over to our camp and add some wood to the fire. We'll want to look at our treasure in the light."

THE LOG OF THE ICE GLIDER
ROSEWRATH

First day, morning: *The council of war convened long before dawn. An ill omen overshadowed the day of our departure from the Snow Harbor of Phylangan. All the fish in the Skyhall lake are dead. There is no explanation, just as there is none for the dead kobolds found three days ago. An invisible enemy seems to have slipped into the fortress.*

Afternoon: *The* Rosewrath *still smells of fresh paint. Like the* Willowwind *and the* Grampus, *our glider was painted white to make it harder to see against the ice. The human, Duke Alfadas, has come aboard: he is to lead our small squad. His first officer is a man with only half a nose. Apart from myself, there are only seven elves on board. It is similar on the other ships. By order of the duke, many alterations have been made. Heavy, winch-drawn crossbows have been mounted to the railings, and long steel blades have been set close together, side by side, along the hull. The blades have been fashioned from the steel runners of other boats. The humans on board are an irreverent, unwashed lot. Though my only official role with the fleet is as a windsinger, I cannot deny myself the opportunity to keep a logbook, as I have done in happier times.*

Evening: *The fleet departed the Snow Harbor at dusk. It was hard for me to go. Shaleen fears that I will not return. I have asked her to get away from Phylangan on the next ice glider that leaves the Sky Harbor. Impending disaster hangs over the fortress like an all-smothering shadow.*

Second day, morning: The gliders are making good headway. We hope by midday to have reached the hills where we last saw the troll army.

Afternoon: The trolls are nowhere to be seen. Alfadas has sent three small ice gliders to scout ahead. Our flotilla is moving slowly in an easterly direction.

Evening: One of the small ice gliders has not returned. The humans are on edge. They are all but willing a fight to happen. I have proposed to Alfadas that I go out at dawn with my falcon, Snowwing, to search for the missing boat.

Third day, morning: I have found the wreck of the ice glider. The boat seems to have sailed at high speed onto rough terrain. Inconceivable! There are traces of blood on the snow, but no bodies to be seen.

Afternoon: We have discovered one of the trolls' scouts. After a chase of more than a mile over the ice, Lysilla, in command of the Willowwind, disembarks and kills the troll with obscene ease. I don't know if I should admire her as a mistress of the sword or despise her as the murderer of a hopelessly deficient opponent. The fleet continues to hold its eastward course. Alfadas decides not to send out the small gliders again. Instead, he asks me to fly ahead with my falcon.

Evening: I have discovered two more of the trolls' scouts, but we have managed to avoid them. The wind is blowing steadily from the northwest. We are making good headway.

Fourth day, morning: Alfadas asks me to fly east with Snowwing as far as Whale Bay. We are no longer very far from Rosecarn.

Late afternoon: The trolls have landed in Whale Bay. Their army is marching up the valley toward Rosecarn in a column that stretches from horizon to horizon. I am to fly out again to try to find out where their king is. I have a bad feeling.

As recorded by Fenryl, Count of Rosecarn

Windsinger aboard the *Rosewrath*

Year of the Return 786

COUNCIL OF WAR

Orgrim looked out at the endless column moving up the Swelm Valley. Pride filled his heart. They were like an avalanche, an unstoppable wave of flesh and blood. Nothing could stand in their way.

A shrill scream made him turn. Birga was pinning a strip of skin to a shield the size of a door that she had rammed into the snow in front of her victim. The human warrior she was interrogating was naked and tied to a second shield. The shaman had already peeled broad strips from the skin of his chest and both thighs. She was working quickly and approaching her task differently than she did with the elves. Breaking the will of a human required no great skill.

Branbeard and the troll dukes were gathered around the shaman. They watched her work, as if mesmerized. Skanga was also there, sitting close by on a bundle of old animal hides. Her eyes were closed, but Orgrim knew her well enough to know that she was not asleep.

"Well? What's he saying?" Branbeard asked. "Where are they from?"

The shaman was talking insistently to the human warrior in a strange language that sounded like angry whispers. Sporadically, the warrior said something in reply. They were such pathetic creatures! So far, they had only been able to capture two humans alive, and the first of those had died under light questioning. They had saved the second to interrogate him in the presence of the king. Orgrim knew that Branbeard put a lot of store in such spectacles.

"The man says he comes from a large town called Honnigsvald. He says it's surrounded by a strong earthen wall."

"Honnigsvald?" The king spoke the word slowly, as if savoring the strange taste of it on his tongue as he would a good piece of meat. "Where is that?"

"In the Fjordlands. An old king reigns there."

Branbeard waved one hand in annoyance. "I know the Fjordlands. In my youth, I went out hunting in the mountains north of that kingdom. The people there believe they can keep us away from the passes by setting up wooden statues with bits of iron stuck all over them." He sniffed noisily and spat. "Idiots! We left them alone for decades, and this is how they repay us.

Honnigsvald will burn, and you can skin that old king and send his hide back to me! They'll be sorry they sent their miserable soldiers to join the elven swarm." He stepped close to the tied man and looked at him face to face. "You hear me, you gutless little shitter? I'll burn the town that gave birth to you. I'll have every miserable hut put to the torch. The snow in your hometown will vanish under the ashes. You humans will suffer the same fate as all who help the Normirga!" He sucked in air, then spat a gob of mucus into the open wound above the human's heart. "Tiresome little lice!" Branbeard placed one large gray hand over the human's face, which disappeared completely beneath it.

"My king, it is not wise—" Orgrim objected.

"Shut up, you cocky washout! Don't talk to me about wisdom!"

The human let out a shrill scream. His skull creaked. The veins in Branbeard's arm stood out, and his muscles bulged. The king trembled with the effort. Blood spurted. With a satisfied smile, he stepped back and wiped his bloody hand casually on his breeches while he regarded the now-headless cadaver.

"You can crush 'em like lice." Dumgar, the Duke of Mordrock, grinned. "I'd wager a hundred of us could wipe out a human kingdom."

"The lice I've had between my fingers put up a better fight," murmured Branbeard, and his dukes laughed.

Orgrim thought of the human host with their long spears. These bootlickers had no idea, and their warriors would pay for their leaders' stupidity and arrogance with blood!

"You've reminded me of something, Dumgar!" Branbeard turned to Orgrim. "My friend, the ship sinker, has once again brought shame on our worthy army. As I've heard it, the coward barricaded himself on a hill and made no move to pursue these thin-skulls and their elven friends when they fled."

Orgrim could not believe his ears! He had done the reasonable thing, and he had inflicted a bloody defeat on their enemies when they had tried to storm the hill. *They* were the cowards forced to run from the field of battle! But, oh, how the old bastard could twist the truth.

"Orgrim! I relieve you of your command as pack leader!"

Orgrim's hand moved to the heavy war hammer in his belt. Time to put an end to this foolishness.

"One could look at things very differently, you know," came Skanga's voice then, very low. "With the sole exception of Kingstor, the elves have abandoned all their fortresses. One might go so far as to say that Orgrim conquered the Snaiwamark with only two hundred and fifty warriors. No troll has ever wrung a more impressive victory over the Normirga."

"Keep your nose out of the business of war, woman!" Branbeard flared. "I know why you're protecting the whelp. You were seen, old woman. Try to tell me you didn't spend a night alone with him in a cave after Vahan Calyd." The king laughed salaciously. "Was he so good that you still need to stick up for him every chance you get?" Branbeard looked around for approval, but none of his dukes dared to laugh at Skanga.

"Great rulers use their head for thinking, Branbeard, not the little thing dangling between their legs. Ever since that blow to your head, it's like every time you sniff, you spit out a little bit more of your brain. Throughout this campaign, Orgrim's the one who's clinched the greatest victories for you. Would anyone here disagree?" Skanga looked at the gathered dukes, one by one. None took it upon himself to contradict her. "Orgrim was the first one here. He occupied the Wolfpit, whether he had to fight for it or not. His mere presence was enough to frighten the elves so much that they abandoned all their fortresses but Kingstor. And what does he get for it? Your friend Dumgar of Mordrock will take over as ruler of the Wolfpit alongside his precious Mordrock because, by rebirth, he has the right to reclaim his old territory. And what reward goes to the troll who made all this possible? That you demote him from pack leader? Lummox! Send in your dukes, and you'll turn Kingstor into another massacre, just like your vain and pointless campaign against Reilimee!" She pointed down to the marching troops. "You lost almost four thousand men there. And which of your warriors was the first to stand on the walls of Reilimee?" Again, she peered into the faces of those around Branbeard. "Did I see one of your dukes up there?"

Orgrim smiled. He removed his hand from his hammer. It may be that he would never win the coveted title of duke, but with Skanga as his ally, he felt stronger than the king's entire council of war.

"Women have never had any insight into the needs of a military campaign," Branbeard objected weakly. "Nevertheless, because I honor you deeply, great shaman, I will continue to suffer your presence on my council. Orgrim, I rescind my order. Let's move to how long it will take our warriors to march to Kingstor."

Orgrim turned away and looked down on the broad valley again. He'd seen a number of enormous forms among the marching trolls. Mammoths! Such beasts were rare indeed in the world of humans, but in the old stories of the Snaiwamark, it was said that great herds of mammoths had once lived there, and wooly rhinoceroses, too.

Now the world of those stories was rising around them again. Orgrim was happy. As unjustly as Branbeard treated him, he was playing his part in something great, in taking back their old homeland. He and his warriors had been the first to set foot in this legendary land. For that reason alone, he himself would one day be a figure of legend, regardless of Branbeard's intrigues. When they brought the females from their fortresses in the Other World, many of them would want to lie with him. He would father many whelps!

He watched with satisfaction as the game-summoners led the mammoths up the final steep section of the path. He had always admired those hunters and scouts born with the special talent of being able to link their minds to those of wild animals, to call them and force them to bow to their will. A pack that had a game-summoner among its numbers would never go hungry!

The Maurawan hated the game-summoners. As far as Orgrim knew, no elves had the summoners' gift. They believed hunters had to chase their prey for hours or even days and could not accept that a hunt could be so much simpler. In former times, the Maurawan had come out of their forests for the sole reason of tracking down the game-summoners and killing them, apparently because they also summoned game from the Maurawan's forests. They would not dare come near an army this size, however. They had nowhere to conceal themselves here as they did in the woods, no opportunity to put an arrow through your head from an ambush. If they did try it, they would never escape the rightful fury of hundreds of enraged trolls.

The first mammoths reached the high plain. They were laden with packs of food, weapons, firewood, and all kinds of equipment. Some also hauled massive sleds.

Orgrim noted that more of the elves' weapons of war had been transported there. As soon as they reached Kingstor, the mammoths would be slaughtered. Once they had completed their task of bringing their heavy loads to the icy plain, their final duty would be to fill the bellies of thousands of hungry trolls.

On some of the packs crouched kobolds wrapped in thick furs and blankets. They were good for the work that required small, deft fingers. In the fortresses, too, they would make useful servants.

The past is returning to life, Orgrim thought cheerfully. Then he rubbed his arms, suddenly cold. Something had changed. There was an unnatural chill, one that cut to the bone, an iciness that had nothing to do with winter.

He turned in alarm. Branbeard had paused in the middle of an endless monologue about the attack on Kingstor. Even Birga seemed uneasy. Only Skanga had closed her eyes again, pretending to be asleep.

Without warning, from the ice by the feet of the king, the ghostly head of an animal appeared. Branbeard jumped back in fright, stumbling. Dumgar swung his club at the creature as it rose from the ice, but his fearsome weapon simply passed through the apparition without effect.

Now Orgrim recognized what was standing before them. While all the dukes—and even Birga—moved back in alarm, he remained calm, though his heart beat as wildly as a war drum at the sight of the supernatural beast.

"I welcome you, Prince Shahondin," he heard Skanga's soft voice say. "Have you brought me the news that will make you flesh and blood again?"

"I bring news that will save many trolls their *flesh and blood,"* the elven prince replied. Shahondin's voice sounded inside Orgrim's head. He pressed one hand to his forehead. How was that damned elf, or whatever he was now, inside his mind? The rest of the king's council seemed similarly dismayed.

"It is the only way our friend can talk to us," Skanga explained. "Speak, Shahondin."

The elf described in great detail the defenses of Phylangan and the troops it housed. When he was finished, the room was deathly silent. Even Branbeard seemed to realize the losses an attack on Kingstor would mean.

With a shudder, Orgrim recalled the bloodbath atop the walls of Reilimee. Now they were planning to charge up a narrow valley covered by dozens of elven catapults and several hundred snipers armed with crossbows and would have to bash in a gate that had been built to withstand even mighty trolls.

"We need battering rams that mammoths can carry," said Branbeard. "With those, we can get through even the gates of Kingstor."

"But the only place for logs that big is the forests of the Slanga Mountains," Dumgar pointed out. "The Maurawan will be on us like wild hornets."

"Afraid of a few stings?" Branbeard asked disdainfully. "Maybe Skanga is right. Maybe I should reconsider giving you back your old fortresses."

"Can't you open the gates from inside?" said Mandrag, addressing Shahondin directly.

The elven prince moved across to the elder troll and stopped in front of him. Suddenly, his head darted forward, into Mandrag's body, then back out again just as quickly. The old troll groaned and clutched at his heart. His lips had turned blue, and his legs trembled.

"*I can touch nothing solid,*" the eerie voice said in Orgrim's head. "*As long as I am trapped in this form, I will be no help at all in opening the gates. I pass through the chains and levers, that's all. Were I, however, to have my body back, that would change.*"

"I'm not about to let you haggle with me," Skanga countered sharply. "You know what you owe me. You have no other way!"

"Give me five hundred warriors, and *I* will open the gates of Kingstor from inside for you, Branbeard," Orgrim said. He had listened closely to the elf's descriptions and was surprised at the weaknesses the fortress obviously had.

"*You want to go in through the Albenstar?*" Shahondin asked. "*It lies atop a bridge that ends over an abyss. The other end is protected by a heavily fortified tower. There is no way through there.*"

"Five hundred fighters, my king," Orgrim requested. "If you're lucky, you'll be rid of me forever. And if I open the doors, you make me a duke."

Branbeard kneaded his chin thoughtfully. A smile suddenly appeared on his face.

"Good. I'll accept your offer! Open the gates of Kingstor for me, and you'll get what you so desire."

"You are sending your men to a certain death." The ghostly prince stepped close to Orgrim, and an icy draft wafted over him. *"The smell of death is already on you."*

"That's the stink of the enemies I've killed." Orgrim turned to Skanga. "I need you to lead me and my men safely along the Albenpaths. And you, elf, will answer all my questions. I need to know the fortress inside and out. I will choose my men tonight." He looked up to the sky. The dusk had stained the horizon a bloody red. High above their heads, a solitary snow-white falcon circled.

BREATH OF ICE

Asla stood in the entrance of the longhouse, her hands on her hips. When Ulric came home, he'd get a hiding he would not forget as long as he lived! And Kalf, too—the fisherman had better not show his face at the house, at least for the next few days.

"Be merciful with him, Firn," she whispered. Snow had begun to fall again at sundown. Ulric and Gundar were three days overdue. Kalf was certain they had found refuge from the weather at Wehrberghof. The snowstorm had raged for two days; anyone caught in it unprepared in the mountains would have died a miserable death.

Asla's fingers clawed into the fabric of her dress. She'd give Alfadas a good thrashing, too, as soon as he returned. He was the one who'd put ideas into the boy's head in the first place.

Five days before, Asla had asked Kalf to go in search of her son. The fisherman had tracked the boy in the direction of the pass in the mountains and had seen him reach Wehrberghof, where Gundar's tracks also led. But instead of bringing Ulric back, Kalf had returned alone, explaining that it was important for the boy to go through this adventure by himself.

Asla sighed deeply. Men! They were all mad! Ulric was seven years old. He had no business traipsing around alone in the mountains, and he knew it perfectly well.

Yilvina came to her side and peered into the dusk.

"Do you see him?" Asla asked.

"No. But the priest will look after your son. He is a sensible man."

There are no sensible men, Asla thought angrily, and she turned back into the longhouse. After a few breaths of the fresh air outside, she found the atmosphere inside the longhouse oppressive. The smoke from the fire stung her eyes and made her teary. A heavy curtain separated the boot room from the main parlor; she pulled it closed behind her.

Ole stank. Not even the smoke could cover the smell of rotting flesh anymore. He had a high fever and seldom woke, and in the brief moments when he returned to his senses, all he did was whimper in pain and curse an elk that had betrayed him. Nothing could save him now.

Asla checked on Kadlin. The little girl lay in her bed in the alcove, the straw doll that Yilvina had made for her pressed to her chest. Asla observed the elf woman from the corner of her eye. Yilvina was completely motionless, as if carved from wood rather than of flesh and blood. There was something unearthly about her. Being around her made Asla feel plump and ungainly. And ugly. If only Emerelle would wake! The queen would be sure to insist that they return to Albenmark as quickly as they could.

Blood raised his heavy head and snuffled softly. She had let the dog back into the house again when the storm had gathered three days earlier. Now he was tethered to one of the upright beams near the entrance with a heavy leash. The dog had not tried to chew through the thick hemp rope—Asla believed he was too grateful to her for being allowed back into the warm parlor to do that. Still, the dog looked often to the bed where Ole lay. He seemed to be waiting for his tormenter to die.

Suddenly, Blood pricked up his ears. He stood up and stared at the heavy curtain that concealed the boot room.

The door creaked and swung open, and Asla was instantly back on her feet, too. "Ulric?"

A stubbled face pushed past the curtain. Erek, her father. Blood lay down again.

"I was fed up with staring at the roof at home," he said. He rubbed his chilled red hands together, stepped into the parlor, and hung his threadbare fur coat from a hook by the fireplace. "Would you have a bowl of soup for an old man?" With a sigh, he slumped onto a chair at the table, then stared unwaveringly in Yilvina's direction. "Nothing warms old bones as much as the sight of a pretty girl. You still haven't told me if you've got a beau waiting for you back home. Now, I know I'm not the prettiest man in the village anymore, but I've got a brace of experience under my belt." He grinned mischievously. "Believe me, that makes up for a lot."

"Father!" Asla set a bowl of millet gruel on the table in front of him. Deep down, she liked it when he baited the aloof elf woman shamelessly the way he did, but it was not something she could decently tolerate under her own roof. "What would Mother say if she could hear you now?"

Erek cupped his red hands around the soup bowl. "Your mother liked it when I got up to my tricks." He nodded in Yilvina's direction. "And I do believe my pretty girlfriend down there likes it, too. She's not once protested, at least."

Nor did she now, and a feeling of shame suddenly overcame Asla. The queen and her bodyguard might not be the kind of guests she would wish to have, but the laws of hospitality applied to them as they did to anybody else. It was unforgivable for her father to pester strangers who had come in search of sanctuary beneath her roof.

"That will do, Erek." She spoke softly but insistently. "Leave her in peace, or you'll force me to show you the door."

Her father looked up in surprise. Had he thought he was doing her a favor, perhaps? She should have said something to him before today.

Outside, the horses whinnied. Before the first snows had come, they had managed to erect no more than a shoddy stable to the rear of the longhouse. What had Alfadas been thinking? She was not prepared for getting four enormous horses through the winter. She had had to buy food for them from all over the village. And why? Only once had she harnessed them to the large wagon and gone out for a short ride, and for that hour of fun, she was paying every day with extra work. *If only that good-for-nothing were here,* she thought. *Then I'd send him out to the stable in the storm.* Her eyes grew moist. *If only he were here . . .*

Blood jumped to his feet again. Snarling, he was staring now at the back wall of the house. The horses whinnied again. A thunderclap—no, it sounded as if one of the horses had kicked the stable wall with its heavy hooves. What was going on out there? Asla reached for her cape.

Kadlin pushed the curtain over her bed aside. Icy air poured into the parlor. Blood began to bark as if he'd gone mad and jerked desperately at the rope that tied him.

"Mama . . ." The little girl began to cry. Her face was red with cold. Had she scratched another hole in the moss and loam they used to fill the gaps between the heavy beams of the longhouse? Asla leaned down and picked her daughter up. She was as cold as if she'd been standing out in the snowstorm in her nightgown. Asla's breath fogged in front of her as she lifted Kadlin from her bed.

Despite Blood's barking, she heard a sudden hiss.

Yilvina had both swords drawn. "Stand back, human!"

Now Halgard began to whimper softly in her bed. Erek went to the ancient little girl and picked her up in his arms.

With the tip of one of her swords, Yilvina pushed the curtain over Kadlin's bed all the way back. The fabric crunched a little: the woolen fabric was covered with frost on the inside. Her sleeping niche was empty.

"What's going on?" Asla rubbed Kadlin's hands to warm them. The girl's lips were dark from the cold. She carried Kadlin to the fire pit, where the logs glowed a deep, dark red.

Yilvina looked around warily, her drawn swords ready in her hands. She turned slowly on the spot. What was she waiting for? There was no one there. The only way in or out of the house led through the small boot room.

Blood had stopped barking. The fur on his neck stood on end, and his ears were alert. His tail, however, was turned firmly between his hind legs. Suddenly, the coals in the fire grew darker. Something white pushed up through the pieces of blackened wood. For a moment, Asla thought it was just thick smoke—then she saw the beast's head. Blood howled and tore at his lead.

Asla backed away from the fire pit with Kadlin. A wolfish head as big as a horse's skull rose from the coals. Pale light swirled around it. Its teeth were like daggers. The emerging monster grew larger and larger, and as it rose, the matte glow of the coals faded and died. The room darkened, and an icy chill spread.

Yilvina was on it like a striking falcon. She whirled around the ghostly form, her blades blurring to streaks of sparkling light. They sliced through the beast again and again, but it showed not the slightest reaction.

The ghostly jaws snapped at her, and she dodged, somersaulting backward. She landed close beside Blood, and with a slash, she cut the rope that held the hound in place.

Snarling, Blood stalked toward the apparition. His steps were stiff as he fought against his own fear.

The beast had now lifted itself completely clear of the fire. It stood as high as a horse but was scrawny and gaunt, as if wasted away. Asla snatched the heavy wooden ladle from the table. Even with that meager weapon, she felt a little better, although she had seen for herself how useless Yilvina's swords had been. The elf had retreated to the bed where her queen was sleeping.

A low sound made Asla turn. With the stump of an arm, Ole pushed back the curtain covering his bed. His face was eerily pale, and his eyes gleamed with fever. "The elk cow!" He tried to sit up, groaning. He flailed the stumps of his arms, as if feeling for something beside him. "Take the godswhip. Drive it away!" His last words were a shrill scream as he searched frantically for the whip. He could not see the thongs that still lay beside the fire pit, where Gundar had recovered the stolen sacrifices to the ironbeards, cutting them out of the braided leather. There was no godswhip anymore.

The creature turned toward Ole. It drew back its lips, making it look as if it wore a hungry smile. With surprising speed, it was at Ole's bedside. Its head darted downward into his breast.

Asla heard a low sound, like the rustling of parchment. For a moment, she thought she saw something golden. Blood had stopped in his tracks.

Asla signaled to Erek to follow her. Cautiously, she crept toward the boot room. Her father had understood. He held one hand over Halgard's mouth to stop the blind young girl from blurting anything aloud.

The creature turned, lightning fast. Blood leaped at it but simply glided through the spectral form. The ghost-wolf moved swiftly, blocking their only exit.

Yilvina attacked again, but again her blades cut uselessly through the body of the beast.

A voice forced its way into Asla's thoughts. It spoke sluggishly, the words as heavy and slow as dripping wax. *"I seek the light. It shines especially brightly there in your belly. Stand still. It does not hurt."*

Asla wanted to raise the ladle in defense, but it was as if she was paralyzed. Kadlin began to cry again and pressed close to her mother.

The ghost-wolf slowly advanced. Blood moved between it and Asla. With a casual thrust of its jaws, the creature snapped at the dog. Blood recoiled but could not escape; he let out a yowl and collapsed.

The creature's breath was so cold that Asla heard her hair crackle. The ghost-wolf was only one step away.

INTO THE DEPTHS

W e cannot let you pass."
Ollowain took a step back and eyed the three sentries with disdain. The two men and the woman wore only light linen armor. They radiated the self-assurance of capable fighters.

"You know who I am?" he asked.

"The son of the prince," the woman replied.

"The commander of all troops in Phylangan," the swordmaster barked. "You are to report to the Snow Harbor, where you will be assigned something more useful than guarding a stairway in the belly of a mountain."

"Forgive me, swordmaster, but we belong to the personal bodyguard of your father, Landoran. We answer to him alone."

Ollowain clapped his hands. Hoofbeats and barely audible footsteps sounded from higher up the spiral stairway. Orimedes and several of his centaur fighters appeared on the broad landing. "This is the prince of Windland," Ollowain said flatly. "I call upon him to witness the fact that, in a fortress making preparations for a siege, you have refused my direct order." The footsteps on the stairs could now be heard more clearly.

"Swordmaster!" The elf woman balled her right hand to a fist and stretched her fingers. Then she laid her hand on the pommel of her sword. "You cannot reprimand us for following orders. We are at the command of your father, no one else."

Ollowain turned to the centaur prince. "For me, refusing an order from the military commander of Phylangan is mutiny. Would you be so kind as to inform these three of the resolutions passed by the war council? They seem to be having some difficulty understanding me."

Orimedes eyed the three elves contemptuously. "If you ask me, you've wasted too many words on them already. You should make short work of them, like with the mutineers on the Woodmer. I will back you before the war council, if such details should even warrant discussion."

A troop of ten kobolds with heavy windlass crossbows arrived at the landing. They arranged themselves in two rows on the lower steps. The stocks of their heavy bows scraped on the gray stone. The steel windlasses creaked as the kobolds wound back the limbs of their weapons.

The woman, who had so far led the guards' side of the debate, licked her lips nervously. "You cannot simply—"

"Oh, he can," Orimedes interrupted her. "And it won't be the first time."

The kobolds loaded bolts onto their crossbows. A few of them looked doubtfully toward Ollowain. This game could not go on much longer.

"What lies at the end of this stairway?" Ollowain asked icily.

The guards looked uneasily from one to another. Finally, one of the men replied. "The Hall of Fire. We are not to let anyone down there. Those are Landoran's orders."

It was oppressively hot on the landing. The stairs led down through solid rock, into the heart of the mountain. Ollowain felt a single droplet of sweat form on his brow and wiped it away with the back of his hand. "I'll offer you this: you let me pass, and I will see this Hall of Fire with my own eyes and decide for myself if it is important enough to warrant occupying the time of experienced soldiers who are otherwise needed for the outer defenses. Until I return, you are merely under arrest. My escort will guard you." He turned to the kobolds and snapped, "Bolts back in the quivers!"

With obvious relief, the crossbow-carrying kobolds obeyed. The sentries exhaled with relief as well. "You would not have ordered them to shoot, would you?" the elf woman asked.

"Why not?" Ollowain raised one eyebrow. Once, he'd spent weeks practicing the expression until he was happy that he could use it to convey everything from patronizing surprise to barely controlled anger. "Do you think the Normirga—the race for whom I count as next to nothing—are so dear to me that I would abstain from spilling their blood if the discipline of this fortress required it?"

The elf woman did not flinch from his gaze. She seemed to be waiting for a smile to take the harshness out of his words. With every passing heartbeat, she grew more uneasy.

"Clear the way!" Ollowain ordered.

The two men obeyed.

"What is the name of the oldest of your clan?" Ollowain growled at the woman.

"Senwyn."

"Senwyn from the clan of Farangel?"

"Yes. He is—"

"I know who he is, girl. He fought under my command at the Shalyn Falah in the last troll war. An exemplary warrior. I never had to explain to him that, in war, obedience is the father of victory."

The elf woman lowered her eyes and let him pass.

Ollowain's temper shifted between anger and disappointment as he descended the stairs. It was not the first time that he had commanded an army faced with a hopeless battle. But any final chance of victory, small as it may be, would vanish if intrigues were spun behind his back, and he could not rely on the unconditional trust of every defender. But what else could he expect from his father? Distrust and disappointments only, for apart from the blood they shared, nothing bound them.

Ollowain had learned a great deal about the fortress from Phylangan's kobolds. He pieced together the answers to many apparently harmless questions as he might the tiles of a mosaic. Seen together, they formed a terrifying picture. Almost two-thirds of the fortress's battle-capable inhabitants had disappeared, although they did not seem to have abandoned the mountain. Moreover, many kobolds had been ordered to attend to some mysterious duty deep in the belly of the mountain. So far, none had returned to talk about it.

The deeper the swordmaster went, the hotter it became. The air was heavy with the odor of hot stone. It was a dry heat, very different from the warmth of the Skyhall, which was insufferably humid.

Ollowain encountered no more sentries, nor did any corridors open onto the spiral stairway. At regular intervals he found semicircular landings with stone benches to rest on. On the landings, beautiful frescoes depicted mountain landscapes and expanses of fair-weather clouds. Some of the pictures were so perfectly done that, with a fleeting glance, an observer might think they were looking out onto a valley through an opening in the rock. The pictures helped you forget that you were deep underground.

Large barinstones set in the walls lit the stairs in a soft blue-white light, like sunlight on a hazy morning. In several places, Ollowain heard the rush of water inside the walls. He recalled the stories told by Gondoran, the holde who had led them through the cisterns of Vahan Calyd. The Normirga, far in the past, had created a magical pump there, like a stone heart, and it kept the water beneath the city in constant motion. Here, apparently, a similar miracle-machine was at work, hidden inside the walls.

The stairs finally came to an end in a huge cavern. Red columns, their irregular surfaces reminiscent of bark, rose to capitals from which curving supports spread like branches and ended finally in a crown of golden leaves. The hall was a forest of stone and gold. From where he emerged, the sword-master could see no walls marking the limits of the artificial forest. Somewhere ahead, he heard the echo of shuffling footsteps. He tried to follow the sound, but every few seconds, it seemed to come from a different direction.

Unsteady red light flickered between the columns, and hot fog drifted through the stone forest. The swordmaster came to a marble fountain, where streams of boiling water sprayed from stylized golden flowers. Ollowain's clothes were soaked in sweat and clung to his skin.

He moved past the fountain quickly. Now, in the distance, he saw a group of white-robed elves. Exhausted, heads down, they moved through the forest like apparitions. Not one of them noticed Ollowain.

He stepped behind a column and stayed out of sight until the elves were gone. Then he set off in the direction from which they had come. Soon, he found himself surrounded by clouds of hot steam. All around him hissed fountains. The vapors burned his face, and the heat grew even more unbearable. Finally, he came to a wall; he followed it until he reached a high arched doorway framed with ornamental golden flowers.

Passing through the doorway, he found himself on a terrace that looked out over a cavern perhaps two hundred paces across. The walls and ceiling were natural black basalt devoid of any decoration. Only the floor of the cave had been smoothed. Tiles of red stone had been set into the basalt and formed a pattern of swirling flames dancing around a large golden disk situated in the center of the floor. On the disk crouched a white-robed figure with raven-black hair. She held both hands pressed to the golden disk and had her head lowered, and although Ollowain could not see her face, his heart told him that he had found Lyndwyn.

Other elves were on their knees all around the sorceress—there must have been well over a hundred. All wore white, as Lyndwyn did. They had positioned themselves on the red tiles, especially where the tongues of flame overlapped. With their hands pressed to the stone and their heads down, they seemed to be in a state of deep meditation. Ollowain sensed the enormous magical powers at work in there. There was a tension in the air that he knew from a brewing thunderstorm, before the first lightning flashed.

Close to the floor, the air became a glassy blur that danced in the heat. Kobolds hurried among the kneeling elves, dabbing at their faces with wet sponges.

Wide benches were set into the cave walls on all sides. On the benches, here and there, sat elves ready to take the place of exhausted sorcerers. They refreshed themselves with fruit and drinks brought by the kobolds in ice-cooled carafes.

Ollowain's mouth was as dry as dust. Why had the Normirga built a cavern dominated by such an unnatural heat? What was going on down here?

Suddenly, one of the elves below tipped his head back. His mouth opened wide as if to scream, but no sound escaped his lips. A pale flame shot from his throat, and he seemed to gleam from the inside, like a red lantern. The fiery glow grew brighter and brighter. Flames now rose from his eyes as well. The elf collapsed. His white robe caught fire, and fine flakes of ash rose with the hot air to the ceiling of the cave. Then the ghastly spectacle was over. Nothing remained of the elf but ash swirling in the air.

No one in the cavern seemed to take any particular notice of the incident. The elves on their knees had not so much as turned their heads in the dying man's direction.

A young sorceress with long blond hair rose from among those waiting on the benches and took the dead man's place. She dropped to her knees and lowered her head, resigning herself to her fate.

"I see you have found your way to the Hall of Fire after all," said a familiar voice behind Ollowain. He did not have to turn around to know who was there. Landoran stepped up beside him and looked down at the gathering of those doomed to die.

"What is going on here?" Ollowain asked, deeply upset at what he had witnessed.

"They are fighting for Phylangan, as your troops above us will soon be doing from the tunnels."

Ollowain squeezed his eyes closed and shook his head. The image of the burning elf would not leave him. He'd seen other men burn . . . and suddenly the terrible images from Vahan Calyd returned. The vortex of flames . . . what was going on? Again, he was surrounded by fire.

"You have to leave this place, my boy."

For the first time, Landoran addressed him in a way that sounded paternal and lacked disdain. *My boy!*

"Come." The prince of the Normirga took him gently by the shoulder. "Come. I will explain everything, but you have to leave here. In this place you cannot win, swordmaster."

Lyndwyn! She still had her head lowered. If only she would look up and see him. But no one in the cavern looked up. All their attention was focused on the floor beneath their knees.

"We'll talk, my son."

"But Lyndwyn . . . she can't . . ." Again he saw in his mind the burning elf.

"She cannot leave. If she were to go, it would be like tearing the keystone out of an archway. Everything would fall apart. Lyndwyn and the Albenstone cannot leave this place!"

VAHELMIN IS YOUR NAME!

Gundar gasped for air. His heart felt like it was about to burst from his chest. He was an old man! He couldn't do this! That damned storm had trapped them at Wehrberghof for two days. Two days shut in with all those bodies, two days in which he'd been haunted by a dream the moment he closed his eyes. In it, he saw Firnstayn as if he were a bird flying over the village, and he landed on the gable of the jarl's longhouse. The sun had just set behind the mountains. From between the wooden roof shingles, a spider crawled. It grew and grew, and spoke to him: "You have to tell him: 'Vahelmin is your name!' You have to tell him that he must take your light if he ever wants to become again what he once was. 'Vahelmin is your name!' Don't forget it. And don't be late!"

Gundar blinked the snow out of his eyes. He trudged past his own hut. What a responsibility Luth had burdened him with. Him! An old man, not a warrior!

There was a second dream, too. One in which he'd left Ulric behind in the snow. *You have to do it,* a voice had whispered in his head. *Give up the boy's life. You have to.*

That nightmare had almost become a reality. Ulric had stumbled. It had happened on the final section of the pass trail. The boy had sprained his ankle and hadn't been able to go on. Gundar had begged and pleaded, and Ulric had tried pluckily, but there was just no way he could continue. For the first time in his life, the old priest had yelled at a child, but he could not bring himself to leave Ulric behind. Dark clouds had been gathering over the mountains in the north. The next storm was already on them, and they were still two hours from Firnstayn, plus two more if he'd sent help back immediately. That was too long to leave a child stranded on a snowy hillside. They'd left Wehrberghof before sunrise as it was and had made the descent as fast as they could.

Ulric was sweating inside his coat just as much as Gundar was. Abandoning the boy in the middle of all that snow, leaving him for four hours . . . it would have meant certain death.

Now Gundar held on to Ulric tightly. The old priest staggered. The only thing that drove him on was the anger that came from his refusal to accept that fate. He closed his eyes and pushed on. Up the final hill. Fifty steps. The boy was light, certainly much lighter than the gift of Luth they had dragged from the gap in the rock. It was the gift that was robbing him of breath. Everything hurt. His breath came in quick, despairing pants, like the gasps of a hunting dog chasing its quarry until it can go no farther.

Gundar had to smile. It pleased him to imagine himself as Luth's hunting dog. But a hunting dog at the end of its rope . . . and what was it again that the voice in the dream had said?

"Vahelmin is your name."

"What's the matter?" Ulric asked. "Who do you mean?"

Gundar leaned his head against the door of the longhouse. He'd made it up the hill! Admittedly, he could not remember *how* he'd made it to the top, but he was there. Still wheezing, he set the boy on his feet.

Relieved of the boy now, Gundar tried to breathe in with relief, but an iron clamp had wrapped around his heart. The god's gift was crushing him, but he could not give up now.

"Please, Luth," he managed to mutter. "Please, give me strength."

Gundar pushed the door open. He was met by a stuffy warmth and the smell of a beechwood fire. He pushed the heavy curtain of the boot room aside and almost fell. His fingers clawed at the coarse fabric. There it was! The monster! It was standing in front of Asla, who had a wooden ladle in her hand and looked as if she were going to swing it at the apparition.

"Vahelmin is your name!" Gundar croaked.

The dreadful beast turned to him. Its head really did have something wolf-like to it. The monster stared at him for the blink of an eye, and beneath its stare, Gundar felt a trembling in him that went down to the marrow of his bones. This was the darkness given form. The evil!

The wolfhorse turned away again. It snapped at Asla's belly.

"Vahelmin is your name!" The curtain slid through Gundar's fingers. His knees gave way. "You have to take my light if you want to go back to what you once were. Remember! Vahelmin is your name!" the priest wheezed with his final breath.

Ulric pushed past him. He held the elven dagger in both hands and hobbled into the parlor.

The wolfhorse turned. With a leap, it crossed the room. Its body glided through Ulric's, and the boy fell to the floor. Gundar spread his arms wide. He looked into the beast's gaping maw. Its daggerlike teeth sank into his chest. The iron band around his heart burst. Cold penetrated every part of him. The hair of his beard crackled, and a blue light engulfed him. Then there was a strange smell in the air, as if a thunderstorm had passed. The blue light was gone, and the ghost had vanished with it.

Gundar looked up at the ceiling of the boot room. He must have fallen backward, but he could not remember hitting the floor.

Asla's face appeared above him. She really was a beautiful woman. The priest no longer felt exhausted. Now the elf woman was by him, too. If he were a younger man . . . she was opening his doublet!

Someone pushed a blanket under his neck. His head tilted backward, and he lost sight of the elf. No . . . suddenly she was above him again. Their lips touched. He'd never dared dream of such a thing—being kissed by an elf woman! It must be her way of showing her gratitude for him saving her queen. That horrible wolfhorse would surely have killed everyone in the longhouse.

"What is that?" *That was Asla's voice,* Gundar thought. "He's got a rusty old chain mail shirt on. Erek, help me. We have to get it off him."

The elf woman leaned over him closely again. She held one cheek very close to his mouth. Then she straightened up a little and gazed at him with her beautiful dark eyes.

"He's not breathing." The elf spoke the words in such a pretty singsong way. Gundar felt like smiling, but he was too tired. What lovely eyes she had! And the pupils, black as charcoal. They looked as if they could swallow him up. Yes. Things were getting dark now. Was he falling? No. There was a light. A longhouse made of gold. What a magnificent hall it was! The great winged doors stood wide open. Gundar heard the joyful sounds of voices and feasting from inside. The smell of roasting meat filled his nose, and his mouth watered. He hadn't had a decent meal for far too long!

It would be good to take his place at the table, to eat, and then rest awhile.

THE TAMED FIRE

Landoran led Ollowain back through the stone forest to the stairway. The prince would probably have liked to put the Hall of Fire farther behind them, but at the bottom of the stairs, Ollowain stopped.

"Enough." No word had passed between them until then. What had begun with eloquent silence, and with the feeling that his father really had Ollowain's well-being most in mind when he led him away from the kneeling sorcerers, slowly grew into the same oppressive wordlessness that had existed between them ever since the mysterious death of his mother. "What is going on back there?"

His father seemed even more exhausted than usual. He slumped onto a stone bench, leaned back against the wall, and crossed his arms over his chest. "Why do you think, in your childhood, you never had to use a spell to protect yourself from the cold in the rock fortresses of Carandamon? Deep below the ice flows liquid fire. And as long as our people have lived in this land of eternal ice, we have used the power that hidden fire gives us. We create geysers and catch the boiling water in a network of pipes that lie concealed behind the rock walls. In the larger caverns, we erected hollow columns, and in this way, we made the warmth of the inner earth radiate even into the last corners of our fortresses. But fire is fickle. It is not unlike living with a cat. She'll gift you cozy moments, maybe even lull you into believing you understand her and can predict how she'll behave. And then, when you think you feel safe around her, she'll suddenly sink her teeth into your skin or slash you with her claws, and you can't understand why she did it. The fire deep below us is the same. It has warmed us for centuries. Now it wants to burn us to ash."

"I know better than most of our race what it feels like to freeze," Ollowain replied angrily. "And I knew even as a child where the heat in the walls of Carandamon's fortresses came from. You don't have to explain it to me, Father. I once lived here in Phylangan, too. What makes Phylangan any different from the others? The Hall of Fire . . . there's nothing like that in any of the other fortresses."

"The stone forest is part of an old volcano. Deep beneath our feet is an enormous cave filled with lava. It is under pressure, and the liquid rock is forcing its way upward through an underground vent." Landoran sighed. "The entire mountain is riven by a network of cracks and gaps, not to mention all the pipes we ourselves have created in the rock to be able to use the heat from below. Now gases are coming up. Boiling water is starting to erupt from the pillars in the Skyhall, and sulfur has risen into the lake and poisoned everything in it. But all that is just the beginning. Beneath our feet, a force is building that could blow this mountain apart."

Ollowain listened to his father with growing dread. This was far beyond his most horrific imaginings. His father's weary calm irritated him to the point of fury. How could he just sit there, exhausted, but so obviously smug? They had to evacuate Phylangan while there was still time! "When do we start moving the troops out through the Sky Harbor?"

"You want to give up?" Landoran looked up at him in disbelief. "You want to hand the most magnificent of all our rock castles over to its destruction? We've been in a similar situation before, twice in fact. Each time, we had to battle the fire, and each time, we made it through. We'll survive this time, too."

"Like that sorcerer I just watched burn."

"Sacrifices must be made," the prince replied flatly. "As a soldier, that should come as no surprise to you. Or have you never sent troops to certain death in battle for no other reason than to buy time and finally win a glorious victory?"

Ollowain wondered just how much his father knew about him. The question was no coincidence. "I, at least, would not call a victory won like that glorious."

"Don't give me that, boy! If you really thought that way, you would never have dedicated yourself heart and soul to the art of war. A man who leads an army into battle knows the price of victory. The sorcerer who burned to death down there had a name: Taenor. His talents were mediocre at best. And as we saw, he did not pass into the moonlight, which means he will be reborn, maybe into a body in which he can develop greater powers. What else does a death like that mean if not the gift of a new beginning?"

"And what of the kobolds, the centaurs, and the humans? None of them can hope for a new life. You're gambling with fire, and they are your stake. How can you do that?"

Landoran smiled with disdain. "I have forced no one to fight for us here. They came, and I accepted their offer of help with gratitude. I did. I'll even admit that I have to rely on them because our own people are not strong enough to fight down here and from the walls at the same time."

"You have to tell them the truth," Ollowain insisted.

"Why? They can't change anything that is going on down here. If they know about this, it will only weaken those who are already vacillating. I'm keeping it from them for their own protection."

"Then at least the war council should know."

"A gathering in which your human friend has surrounded himself with men like that fellow with half a nose? No, Ollowain. It's bad enough that we have to rely on the humans' help. We're not about to start sharing our secrets with them as well. That man—Lambi's his name, isn't it?—he will tell his men. In two days, everyone will know, and panic will break out. Breathe a word about what's happening in the Hall of Fire, and Phylangan will fall before the first troll is standing at our gates."

Ollowain let out a heavy sigh. His father's misgivings were not easily dismissed. "It is not right to lie to one's allies," he said quietly.

"But we are not lying to anyone." Landoran had adopted an encouraging, fatherly tone, as if he were talking to a child. "We're concealing something, yes, but what of it? Do you know everything about the soldiers who fight for you? That is the leader's burden. We see further than most of those who serve us. We have a deeper understanding of the world, of everything going on around us. To protect those we lead, we cannot share all our knowledge with them. Besides, nobody gives away all their secrets."

Ollowain clenched his fist in anger. "What difference do the secrets of one random human make to me? They are not threatening my life! You cannot compare these things."

"Don't come to me with your chivalrous tripe!" Landoran snapped. "But honor among allies aside, I actually agree with you. We should not compare ourselves with humans. Alfadas and his fighters will never understand us. Don't get me wrong—I do not reproach them for that. I'll go further and say that it would be a mistake on my part if I were to demand an understanding of which they are simply incapable. So I am not about to pester them with explanations about things that, at best, they would find uncanny. I don't even know how to explain to *you* what is going on in the Hall of Fire, considering that you have never managed to cast a spell in your life."

"I was expecting that. Every time we talk, we always come to this." Ollowain turned away and stepped onto the landing at the base of the stairs. Every argument with his father led to the point where Landoran found fault with him for being unable to work magic. His father was one step away from including him in his musings about humans and all the other simple beings that would never sip from the spring of true wisdom.

"Don't run off, you mule. You call yourself a warrior, don't you, sword-master? Then face the truth! How would you explain daylight to a blind man?" the prince shouted angrily at his back. "One has to engage in certain experiences because they cannot be put into words. Or would you be able to explain to me what binds you and Lyndwyn? I can see into your heart, my son. Please, don't walk away now."

Ollowain stopped on the first step.

"I don't know how I am supposed to make something comprehensible to you that you have never experienced," Landoran said. He was on his feet now. He supported himself against the wall with one hand, as if he might collapse at any moment. For the first time, Ollowain saw his father marked by age. He was too weak to hide it anymore.

"I would never reproach you if I were unable to understand what you say, Father. What separates us, though, is that you have never even tried."

"All right . . . magic, then . . . it begins with a descent into a deep meditative state. You try to leave your prison of flesh and blood behind you and to find inside that part of you that is immortal. And if you can do that, it is like a rebirth. You feel as if you are moving out of your body, and you see yourself from outside. Petty needs like hunger and thirst no longer plague you, nor do you still have a body dictating endless obligations to you to make up for all its shortcomings. A feeling of overwhelming freedom comes over you. And then you hear the singing of the world. And you feel it, too, as strange as that may sound when I talk about a song. You become aware of the power of the magic that permeates everything. Freed from your body, you are able to work the purest magic because you can be one with this mysterious power, you can be in harmony with it. From the outside, one sees your crouching figure, and that is all. One who has never opened the inner eye, the magical eye, is unable to see whether you have departed from your body." Landoran had grown even paler than usual as he spoke. His words came in broken bursts but with great passion.

"When you are down in the Hall of Fire, you hear a voice call you the instant you leave your body. It issues no command, and yet the voice is impossible to resist. It draws you down, down where the eternal fire burns deep beneath these mountains. Suddenly, you are part of something huge—the elation, fears, and memories of love of a hundred lives wash over you. You're confused at first, but everything suddenly falls into place. You are part of a great choir. What makes you who you are shrinks to a tiny spark of memory that all but fades away when confronted by this immense melody to which you now belong.

"Lyndwyn directs this choir. She leads every voice to its place. I have never before met an elf who has attained such mastery of the arts of sorcery so young. And the Albenstone multiplies her power. Everyone, even the most powerful magic weavers, submits to her because we sense that it is right to do so. Even I have submitted completely to her wisdom, and I sing her song when I take my place in the Hall of Fire. Together, we cool boiling stone and channel away the pressure that has built up. But the power we are confronting cannot be measured against anything you already know."

Ollowain thought of Taenor, the elf who had burned to death. What his father had just described sounded so harmonious and peaceful, but he had seen with his own eyes that the reality was something else. Landoran, once again, was not telling him the full truth. "What can kill you if all you are doing is singing a song?" he asked cynically.

"It's the fear. You leave your body, and while you may have left your flesh and blood behind, you can still tire. It is a spiritual exhaustion. And then there's the fire. You take it inside yourself to understand it better. You have to merge with it to be able to suppress it. But if fear seizes you and you return to your body suddenly, then you will burn from the inside out because you carry part of the fire back with you. When we return to our bodies consciously, the process is very slow. We have to unshackle ourselves from the great song, which makes us very sad. And then we have to find the spark of memory again, the tiny flare that makes us who we are as individual beings. When we become conscious of the brightness in which our own light burns, we can once again become one with our body. But if we rush the return, and if the flame in which our souls burn is still too hot, then it will destroy our bodies. That is what happened to Taenor. It must be said, though, that this happens less frequently since Lyndwyn began directing the great song."

"What does 'less frequently' mean? How many fatalities have there been?"

"When I sang the great song, we had two or three . . . losses every day. With Lyndwyn, it's usually only one, sometimes none at all. She looks after the magic weavers' choir very well indeed."

Ollowain peered intently at his father. Was he telling the truth? His face was an emotionless mask. The only thing he could read there was his father's endless weariness. "And one of the singers happens to die at precisely the moment I appear? What a strange coincidence."

Anger flashed in Landoran's eyes, although he otherwise remained calm. "It was no coincidence. There is a very strong connection between you and Lyndwyn. I told you that we share our emotions when the magic weavers join in the great song. I have sensed what she feels for you, how deeply she longs to be loved by you, and how she fears your scorn. Lyndwyn is exceptionally sensitive. She noticed that you entered the Hall of Fire. That was one reason I did not want you to come down here. Your presence distracts her."

"You're as much the master wordsmith as ever," said Ollowain. "Now you assume that I am to blame for Taenor's death. How the truth can be twisted."

"I am not assuming anything. If one of us is making assumptions, then it is you, to keep your peace of mind. I call things what they are, and it is noteworthy that a singer died in the brief space of time in which you were standing on the terrace. It may have been because of you. It may also have been a coincidence. I have learned to live with the sacrifices our great task demands. Only you can find your own peace. Hate me for what I say—that seems to be a feeling with which you are well acquainted. I don't care anymore."

"You never cared, Father. Don't start fooling yourself now. You're like this land, a block of ice. And your cold will kill or drive out anyone who can't protect themselves from it with magic."

Landoran had leaned back again and closed his eyes. "Don't think that you can understand what goes on inside me. I know the name of every magic-singer, man and woman, who has ever died in the Hall of Fire. I can tell you the name of everyone who lost their lives the last two times we battled the fire. In a fertile year, three children are born here in Phylangan. Our victories over the fire are wiping out my people. Don't think for a moment that leaves me unmoved."

"Then why not simply give Phylangan up?"

"If we do that, all those who lost their lives fighting the fire will have done so in vain. We will win this time, too. With Lyndwyn and the Albenstone, we are stronger than ever." The prince had closed his eyes again and did not open them now. His voice was flat, as if he were reciting a litany he'd been through so many times that its words were worn out and meaningless.

"I will not sacrifice our people to your limitless ambition," Ollowain said. "From this moment on, I will be watching very closely what goes on in the Hall of Fire. I will abandon Phylangan and take all its defenders to the high plains of Carandamon the moment I see that Lyndwyn is losing the battle with the fire. And I'll save her and the Albenstone from you, too."

Landoran opened his eyes. "It has been clear to me all along that you would betray the Normirga. You've been away from your race too long to still be able to understand us. I'll be ready for your treason, Ollowain. Fear the day!"

DANCE OF THE BLADES

The faerylight was starting to fade from the night sky as the three large ice gliders slowly picked up speed. Alfadas had impressed his plan on Ragni and Lysilla one more time, and they had only just returned to their ships. Alfadas did not want to start an open battle—they were on a raid, no more. For the next few days, he did not want the trolls to feel safe for a single moment as they marched across the ice.

The duke's thoughts turned to his quarrel with Landoran, and his mood darkened. Hiding behind the walls of Phylangan was a mistake. Until the hour of their departure, he had tried to convince the closed-minded prince that they should hazard a broader attack with the ice gliders. There were so many ships just standing around inside the Snow Harbor. If they were refitted as he had done with the *Rosewrath*, the *Willowwind*, and the *Grampus*, then the elves and their allies would not have to sit in the fortress and wait to see what the trolls did. He hated waiting!

Alfadas smiled. His soldiers thought of him as a man of patience and composure. How little they really knew him.

The duke grasped one of the handgrips on the railing, and the wind cut into his face. With every heartbeat, their speed increased. The gods were well-disposed toward them that morning. Firn in particular, the god of winter. He had given them a clear sky and a steady west wind. That was all they needed to fight an enemy a hundred times their size.

Ice sprayed beneath the sharp runners. An occasional jolt went through the heavy ship as it crushed a larger clump of ice. Close behind it followed the *Willowwind* and the *Grampus*, all three under full sail. The masts creaked softly with the pressure of the wind, and ice cracked off and fell from the oiled ropes as they pulled tight.

The deck trembled lightly over the slightly uneven surface of the ice. Alfadas loved the speed. The fear he had felt on his first brief journey was long forgotten now. Flying as fast as a falcon over the ice intoxicated him.

Everyone on board was at their post, ready for the fray. Ten heavy wind-lass crossbows were mounted on the railings on both sides, and a rotating catapult stood in the bow, already loaded. The men along the rails had slung broad leather belts slung around their waists to save them from being knocked off their feet in the heat of battle. Kobolds, humans, and elves were spoiling for the fight. There was not a fighter aboard who did not have faith in Alfadas's idea or that they would return victorious.

Fenryl stood beside Alfadas at the helm. The elven count peered at the shimmering ice ahead, his eyes narrowed to slits. It was time to put on the snow masks. In the east, the sun was no more than a narrow strip of silver on the horizon, but soon it would blind them.

Alfadas turned his face out of the rush of air and looked to Lambi and Veleif, who were standing with him on the quarterdeck. The war jarl understood what Alfadas wanted without him having to utter a word. He unwound the leather strip with its eye slits from his belt and fitted it over his eyes. Then, in a thunderous voice, he bawled, "Snow masks on, you dozy shits, or I'll come and rip open your asses and make you eat whatever I find inside for breakfast."

"He can't be serious!" exclaimed Fenryl, who had come to learn a few words of their language. "I must say, it is hardly the time for breakfast."

Alfadas knotted the straps of his snow mask behind his head. "He was speaking metaphorically," he replied in the count's language. "The jarl likes to paint somewhat colorful pictures."

"He doesn't really strike one as—"

"Enemy in sight!" shouted Mag from the foretop.

Now Alfadas also saw the thin black line along the horizon. "All stations ready!" he called calmly.

The shooters set bolts atop their crossbows. Two elves manned a heavy lever in the front, ready to release their secret weapon when the moment came. Alfadas suddenly felt uneasy. Had he really thought everything through? Or was he leading three ships to certain destruction?

The line along the horizon took shape with surprising rapidity. Alfadas could now make out a marching formation and a camp area. Fenryl corrected their course slightly, steering for the camp.

Alfadas glanced back over his shoulder. The *Willowwind* and the *Grampus* followed their maneuver.

Three hundred paces to the camp. Alfadas stepped to the railing and secured himself with a strap attached there.

"Right, boys," Lambi bawled over the whistling wind, "prick up your ears, clamp your balls, and never give up!"

A hundred paces! Most of the trolls simply stood and stared in astonishment at the approaching gliders. They had no idea of the danger they were in.

Alfadas gave the signal with his right hand. The elves on the foredeck turned the heavy lever over. With a sharp clacking sound, long steel runners shot out on both sides of the hull, but these runners were never intended to touch the ice. Jutting out at right angles, they stood like huge scythes ready to reap a bloody harvest.

The crossbows began to fire, and the windlasses clattered, drawing back the steel laths for reloading. Several trolls reacted now, hurling clubs and stone axes at the approaching ship.

A light jolt ran through the ship, and blood sprayed along the side. Alfadas looked back at the mutilated bodies behind them on the ice. Slightly offset and mounted in three rows, the blades had taken their victims at the level of the knees, the midriff, and just below the head. The various sections of the trolls were now spread across the ice over a distance of ten paces.

The ship jumped again. Alfadas watched as Lysilla turned the *Willowwind* onto a particularly murderous course. With the port blades, she rammed the front of a marching column. Severed body parts went flying on both sides, but she had to swerve clear after just a few paces because the glider was in danger of losing too much momentum. The *Willowwind*'s hull dripped blood, and it had sprayed into the faces of the crossbowmen along the railing. Only Lysilla stood in flawless white on the quarterdeck, calling out her orders in a clear voice.

The *Rosewrath* leaped forward. Its runners shrieked as it flew across a dip in the ice. For a long heartbeat, the glider soared into the air. Alfadas clenched his teeth and held tightly to the railing. Then came the landing, and the duke was flung against the ship's side. His legs gave way, and only the leather belt prevented him from falling to the deck.

"Keep your eyes open, you sleepy bastards!" Lambi snarled. He rubbed his bruised ribs and muttered a quiet curse. One of the crossbows had been torn from its mount. A kobold hung halfway over the railing, held by the leather belt.

"There!" Fenryl cried. "That's it." He pointed to a place close to the edge of the cliff where two huge wooden shields had been rammed into the snow.

From one of them hung something like pale strips of cloth. "That's where their leaders were gathered yesterday."

Alfadas cursed. He could see no one there now who looked as if they might be of importance. Fenryl had described the commanders of the trolls in great detail the day before. They were gone.

With a frustrated sigh, Alfadas looked out over the enormous camp that stretched for several miles from the top of the path that led down into the valley. He had hoped to decapitate the troll army—literally—by killing their leader in the very heart of their camp. It would have taken the enemy weeks, maybe months, to recover from such a strike, and they would have won the time they needed to forge a wider alliance among the remaining races of Albenmark. They might even have ended the war at a stroke.

"Can you see the pack sleds?" Alfadas shouted, trying to be heard over the loud noise.

Fenryl took the time he needed to survey the confused battlefield. All around were piles of supplies, war loot, and various plunder that the army had brought with it. The count guided the heavy glider between the lethal obstructions with a sure hand. If a piece of wood or something else jammed in the ice glider's runners and slowed it down, the trolls might take it into their heads to board the *Rosewrath*. Speed was their best protection.

Alfadas looked out apprehensively at the trolls swarming on every side. There were thousands of them. Despite the stiff breeze, the glider was losing speed—too many carcasses were caught in its scythe-like blades. It was time to go. They had not achieved what they wanted to, but the trolls would remember their visit for a long time to come.

"Over there," Fenryl said, and he pointed to a low hill, on the brow of which stood a number of sleds. A group of trolls was in the process of throwing back the tarpaulins covering the loads the sleds carried. "That's where they are. The catapults!"

"Will we make it up the slope?" Alfadas asked, although he already knew the answer.

"We'd lose too much momentum. Don't even consider it! We'd stop directly in front of the catapults."

"Who taught these filthballs to use artillery?" Lambi growled.

Alfadas could see the trolls on the hilltop preparing the catapults for battle—at least some of this horde was terrifyingly disciplined. "Turn off! Hoist the red pennant!" he called down to the main deck.

A kobold opened the chest lashed securely to the mainmast. He rummaged among the various flags until he finally found the red pennant.

The first shot left a round hole in the mainsail. Alfadas swore and turned back to the hill. Would the troll in charge of those catapults confound him at every turn?

"We can't afford too many of those," Fenryl called from the helm. "Every hole in the sails slows us down."

"I'm aware of that," Alfadas snapped back. The last thing he needed now was a lecture. He glanced back at the hill. So near, and yet unattainable. "Course west-southwest. We're breaking off the attack."

The runners scraped on the ice. Fine crystals sprayed over the deck as the ship tipped worryingly to one side. Alfadas clenched the railing. For a moment, the glider was sailing on only one runner. The kobold at the flag chest rolled across the deck and slammed into the bulwark. Swearing, he got to his feet. He shook his head, dazed—and suddenly disappeared. A jagged hole now gaped where he'd been standing at the bulwark.

"I fear that Norgrimm is wiping his ass with our signal pennant!" Lambi shouted angrily. "I can't stand the gods' jokes!"

"Hold our course!" Alfadas ordered Fenryl. "The others will follow us even without a signal."

Balls of stone whirred around the *Rosewrath*. "Looks to me like they struggle to hit anything faster than a company of spearmen," Lambi mocked.

Alfadas saw several trolls die beneath the murderous projectiles. *They'll stop shooting soon,* he thought with grim satisfaction. Lysilla was following them, but Ragni was taking a different course. His glider was losing speed, and now he made a risky turn. The jarl was waving to his crew with both arms. Then he went to the helm.

All was chaos aboard the *Grampus*. The men in the masts slid down ropes to the main deck. Everyone seemed to be trying to get to the quarterdeck. And then they started to jump. Alfadas could not believe what he was seeing. Elves, kobolds, and humans were abandoning the safety of the ship in the middle of the enemy camp, leaping from the stern to avoid the lethal sickles along the hull.

"Bring us around!" the duke shouted angrily.

Fenryl had seen what was happening aboard the *Grampus*. He swung the helm around, but the ice glider could not turn quickly. The sails luffed and flapped in the wind, and the *Rosewrath* lost speed dangerously.

Lambi jammed his sword into the throat of a troll that tried to climb over the railing. "Give our boys on the ice some cover!" he bellowed at the crossbowmen. "And show me you can reload faster than your gouty grandmothers!"

Alfadas's mind raced. Going back to rescue the stranded was tantamount to suicide, but he could not simply leave them to these man-eaters. "Pull the sickles back to the hull!" he ordered. Then: "Ropes at the ready to pull our comrades aboard!"

Several soldiers immediately manned the big capstan at the bow. Slowly, the deadly blades were hauled back into place along the sides of the hull. They were connected to tension winches and could be redeployed in a heartbeat, but resetting them took great strength.

Victory cries sounded among the trolls as they swarmed toward the men exposed on the ice, while Ragni steered the *Grampus* toward the cliff. His ship had picked up speed again. The trolls he was racing toward threw themselves onto the ice to avoid the deadly blades.

The situation of the men on the ice, however, was growing more and more desperate. They were surrounded by trolls and defending themselves doggedly.

"Slow us down!" Alfadas shouted at Fenryl.

The elf looked at him doubtfully but followed the order. If they were too fast, it would be all but impossible to grab hold of a rescue line. But if they were too slow, the swarming trolls would try to board the *Rosewrath*.

Alfadas reached for one of the rescue lines. He wrapped it around his waist and made sure it was securely tied to the railing. If he balanced on one of the curved struts that supported the runners, then at least he was not damned to being only a spectator to the massacre of his men. Besides, it was easier to grab hold of an outstretched hand than it was to snatch a rope twisting like a snake on the ice.

Suddenly, Lambi was beside him. "You're not doing this alone!" He, too, had a rope around his waist. "I'd rather go down with you than have to tell your wife you perished because you decided to go dancing on a glider's runner in the heat of battle. I wish I'd never met you, you maniac!" A smile took the edge off Lambi's words, then he went over the rail first. Alfadas followed close behind.

The *Rosewrath*'s blades lay snug against the sides of the glider. Alfadas looked down at the steel runners slicing across the ice with a menacing hum. They were no wider than the blade of a sword. Curved wooden struts as broad as his hand connected the runners to the hull. The duke moved hand over hand along the railing a short distance, then lowered himself onto one of the struts. He wrapped his legs around the wood and hooked his feet together to keep a better grip. *I hope Asla never hears about this one,* he thought. He checked the fit of the safety line around his waist.

The *Rosewrath* had lost most of her speed and now moved no faster than a running man. They were heading straight for a knot of trolls.

"Hey-ho, you oversized shiteaters," Jarl Lambi bawled at them. "Here comes Lambi to stroke your asses for you." Like Alfadas, he sat astride one of the struts. He leaned forward a long way and waved his left hand at the trolls.

A naked troll fighter carrying a war hammer came running toward the ice glider from the side. He had his eyes fixed on Alfadas. The troll easily kept up with the glider and was moving in. He swung his war hammer in a circle over his head.

Alfadas knew very well how little room he had to duck the swing if he did not want to fall from where he was sitting. He glanced down at the steel runners hissing over the ice. They were red with frozen blood. Falling would not be a good idea.

Suddenly, the troll's head jerked backward as he ran at full stride. A dark crossbow bolt jutted from his forehead, just above the bridge of his nose.

Veleif leaned over the side of the ship. "I've ordered the crossbowmen to cover you and Lambi. We'll . . ." The skald's words were lost in a din of screams and bellowing as the *Rosewrath* shot into the knot of trolls. Even though the blades had been retracted, the glider's hull knocked many of the enemy to the ice. Alfadas saw the razor-sharp runners separate one of the warriors from his legs.

He ducked beneath a swung axe, which buried itself in the wooden side of the glider and was torn from the troll's hand. Warm blood sprayed from the runner, hitting Alfadas in the face. Blinking, he tried to see what was going on ahead of them. A small remnant of survivors still stood together, back to back. The trolls had withdrawn a short distance, keeping a safe distance between them and the ice glider's runners.

A shadow shot past the *Rosewrath*. The *Willowwind* had also returned to rescue the survivors but was going a lot faster. Lysilla and two other elves that Alfadas did not know had secured themselves with ropes and, with both legs, pushed themselves out at an angle from the side of the ship. Lysilla gave her companions the protection of her two whirling swords. With an effortless swing, she knocked a flying spear out of the air, then stabbed through the eye of a troll lunging for her. Then they were through to the survivors.

Strong hands reached out. Lysilla dropped her swords and pulled a wounded elf aboard.

Alfadas turned away. He had his own work to do and could not afford to miss the moment. Above him, he heard the sharp clacking of the crossbows with which his crew kept the trolls at bay.

Among the survivors now running toward them with outstretched hands, Alfadas saw, was Egil, the king's son. The young man was supporting two wounded comrades.

Then Alfadas was reaching for hands, pulling the fleeing fighters to him, helping them get a grip on the ropes hanging from the sides of the glider. Like drowning men, they clung to Alfadas. Some were dragged along the ice by the glider.

Although the ship was moving slowly, it was still too fast for the wounded. Alfadas saw men screaming helplessly, their arms raised. Limping, even crawling, they tried desperately to get to the *Rosewrath*.

Egil helped his two comrades grab hold of ropes. Then he dropped back, racing back over the ice. He was not injured. He grabbed hold of another one of the wounded and with a heave managed to get the man onto his shoulders. He began to run.

Lambi waved at him. "Drop him, you idiot! You'll never make it."

The trolls had begun hurling chunks of ice at the ships. A dark-haired elf on the ice was hit in the back. The impact sent him staggering into

Alfadas's arms, where he coughed warm blood into the duke's face. Alfadas pushed the elf higher, and hands came over the railing and hauled him aboard.

Meanwhile, Egil ran. He ran as fast as his legs would carry him, and Norgrimm himself seemed to be holding his shielding hands over him, for no spear or hurled chunk of ice hit him. Slowly, he was catching up.

Alfadas leaned out as far as he could. There were only inches between them. Egil stretched his right hand forward. Their fingertips touched. His face contorted with the effort, he grasped Alfadas's wrist. "Take him!" he gasped, and he pushed Alfadas's hand up until it could take hold of the injured man's belt. "I'll still make it."

Alfadas swore. He hauled the man in by his belt and threw himself back at the same time. A chunk of ice shattered against the hull above him, and cold shards struck his neck. He quickly tied the end of a rope around the injured man's belt and he was heaved on board.

Egil had fallen back a little. His breath was coming hard, his face red with the effort.

"Come on, man. You can make it!" Alfadas shouted back at him.

Again, their fingertips touched. Alfadas stretched desperately. Egil was at the end of his strength. Their hands lost one another. Alfadas threw himself forward, trusting in the safety line to hold him. If he could get hold of Egil, they would be pulled up together.

Their hands locked. Alfadas fell on the ice and tumbled between the runners as he took Egil down with him. Alfadas turned over, hanging on desperately to the king's son. He looked up and saw the troll axe still buried in the hull. Above it dangled a frayed rope, flying in the wind.

The ice glider's hull slipped past overhead. With the desperation of fear, Alfadas lunged with his left hand for one of the horizontal crossbars that supported the glider's hull. His fingers closed around the ice-caked wood. Half kneeling and half lying, he was dragged across the ice. With his right hand, he still held on to Egil.

"Reach for my belt!" he shouted. "I need both hands, or I can't hold on!" Slowly, his fingers were slipping from the round wooden crossbar.

Alfadas's muscles were at the breaking point. He tried to pull Egil closer so that he could more easily reach his sword belt.

Something touched Alfadas's shoulder lightly. White forms glided past. Uneven ice! A chunk of ice scraped across Alfadas's knee, and he growled in pain. He could not do any more! The crossbar he was holding onto was too thick to get his hand all the way around.

Egil looked up at him. With his left hand, he was holding tightly to Alfadas's trousers. The young soldier smiled. "It was right to come here with you, Duke. Save yourself." With that, he let go.

"No!" Alfadas screamed. But it was useless. He could not save Egil now.

Trembling with pain and exhaustion, Alfadas reached up for the crossbar with his other hand. Looking back between the struts, he saw Egil get to his feet once the ship had passed completely over him. The king's son drew his sword. A troll with a war hammer came running toward him. Egil strode toward the troll, then disappeared from Alfadas's view.

Hand over hand, Alfadas edged along the crossbar toward the side of the glider. If he managed to get back on deck, he would order the ship to turn. Maybe Egil could hold on long enough. He could not simply leave him behind.

Alfadas hooked his heels over the crossbar. Blocks of ice hissed by beneath him. Every second, the ship was picking up speed. Alfadas looked toward the bow. It was only a matter of time before he was torn from beneath the glider. He looked around desperately for a way to escape. The only route led up and over the wooden braces that connected the steel runners with the hull, but wide beams beneath the ship separated the crossbars from the braces on the sides.

Alfadas stiffened his back and stretched forward. For a moment, he hung with his head down, with only one heel still hooked over the crossbar. Far behind him, he saw Egil fall on the ice. The troll struck. It was over.

Exhausted, Alfadas managed to grab the brace. With the last of his strength, he pulled himself across. One of the crossbowmen spotted him. Hands reached down and pulled him back on board.

Lambi smiled at him. "I knew you were stuck to this boat like a flea to a dog's ass. You gave us all a hell of scare, you bastard." He offered Alfadas his hand. "Stand up and see what Ragni's up to, the son of a whore."

Still dazed, Alfadas stood at the railing. The *Grampus* was racing at full speed down the pass, ploughing a bloody path through the column of trolls marching toward the high plateau. There was no way for them to avoid the glider. Suddenly, the *Grampus* rammed a large supply sled, tilted to one side, and rolled over, smashing its masts. But the heavy wooden hull still slid onward.

"Never has one man killed so many trolls," said Veleif reverentially.

"He sacrificed his crew for the privilege. He's no hero to me," Alfadas said.

"In battle, don't you sacrifice men for victory with every order you give?" Veleif asked. "Did Ragni do anything that you do not?"

Alfadas did not know what to say to that. Weak and worn out, he turned away. They'd managed to rescue seven men. "How many made it onto the *Willowwind*?"

Lambi shrugged. "Only three or four, I think. More than seventy stayed on the ice. Who was that fellow bringing in the wounded? I've seen his face before, but I don't remember where."

"You'd find him at King Horsa's court."

The jarl frowned. Then his jaw dropped. "That wasn't . . ."

"It was. Egil Horsason. I wish I'd given him command of the *Grampus*. He would not have sacrificed his men for his own renown. Maybe, one day, he would have been a great king." Alfadas waved to Fenryl at the helm. "Take us back to Phylangan."

"You've led us to a great victory today," said Lambi, in an unusually somber tone. "And you've prepared a place at Norgrimm's banquet for Egil. The boy I saw today . . . there wasn't much he had in common with the swaggering little fucker Horsa's son used to be."

TWO HEARTS

A sla stared into the deep grave dug into the frozen earth. For half the night she had listened to the sound of the pickaxes battling away at the rock-hard soil. Isleif, a tall, dark-haired farmer from an outlying farm, carried Ole's body down from the longhouse. In Isleif's thatch of hair, the first silver strands were starting to show. He was a friend of her father, Erek, and the only one outside the family to turn up to Ole's final farewell. No one from the village had come to give the dog breeder an escort of honor. Only Asla, the children, and Erek stood beside the open grave.

Ole's corpse was thin and gaunt. He did not weigh heavily in Isleif's arms. The stake jutting from Ole's chest stood out brightly. They had come at dawn, the worried ones, the ones who feared that Ole, because of the terrifying nature of his death, would find no rest. They had brought the stake with them. It had been whittled from pale ash. Ignoring Erek's objections, they had driven the wooden stake into his brother's breast—where once his heart had been, if he had ever had one. The moment they did it, Blood let out an unearthly howl. Asla was sure that this alone would keep the villagers whispering for the rest of the winter.

Isleif climbed down cautiously into the grave, Ole's body pressed to his own, like a mother carrying a large baby in her arms. Even in death, Ole looked to be in agony. *No one will ever know what he did,* Asla thought. No one would ever know why the gods had punished him and the village so cruelly, but all agreed that he had been responsible for the appearance of the enormous phantom wolf. The killings had begun immediately after he'd been found so horribly mutilated in the woods.

Asla held Kadlin on her arm. The little girl played with her hair. She wore her thin blue linen dress, the one her father loved so much, over warm woolen clothes. It was the same dress she had worn when she had learned to walk. Asla thought with longing of the warm summer days when she and Alfadas had gone down to the pebbled shore and watched the little girl together as she tottered over the stones. What would the next summer bring? Would she ever see her husband again? She looked at Ulric. The boy had his lips pressed in a thin line. He looked very serious, no longer like a child.

Isleif laid Ole's body carefully in the bottom of the grave. A fine sprinkling of snow, thin as the flour on a baker's table, lay in the hole. The big farmer turned the body so that the face lay in the muck. He looked up apologetically. "It's how they wanted it," he said softly.

"I know," said Erek, his voice hoarse.

Asla sighed. That was how they buried someone they were afraid might become a revenant. If he woke in his grave and tried to dig his way back to the world of the living, he would only go deeper into the earth. While a stake of ash in the heart was indeed said to be enough to keep a dead man in his grave forever, for the village elders it was not certain enough.

Asla thought back to the time when she was still a little girl and Ole had given her a brown-and-white pup. As a child, she had loved her uncle. He had not always been as he'd become in the last few years. Maybe if he had found a wife . . . *Loneliness eats away a heart,* she thought bitterly. She knew that only too well! She had already spent so many nights alone in her bed. The smell of Alfadas that made her believe he was still lying next to her when she rolled herself up in her blanket was slowly fading. Soon it would disappear from her life completely.

Isleif pulled himself out of the grave. One by one, he took the heavy rocks that had been carted to the graveside and dropped them onto Ole's body, and although he tried to be careful, Asla heard Ole's bones crack as the stones came to rest on his corpse. *Could they do any more to make sure my uncle never leaves this hole?* she wondered. She looked to her father. Erek had shed no tears for his younger brother, but the old fisherman's lips trembled as he saw the companion of his childhood slowly disappear beneath the stones. Her father had always felt responsible for Ole, had always stood up for him when, yet again, there was trouble on his account in the village. He'd even defended him when he knew full well that Ole was as guilty as sin. Asla ran her fingers through Ulric's blond hair. Would he one day stand up for his younger sister as unconditionally? Asla's hand left his head and fell to her navel. *And what about this one?* she thought. *Will Ulric be its protector too?*

Beside the pile of freshly dug earth stood a plain stone, and her eyes turned now to that. Erek had almost broken his back the day before getting it up from the shore to the longhouse, then spent half the night scratching at it with an old nail, carving a dog's head into the surface. He did not want his brother's final resting place to be forgotten.

"Mother, when are we going to Gundar?" Ulric asked softly.

Asla looked at Erek. He nodded. She was released from her final duty to Ole.

Downcast, she went with the children to the grave of the priest. She was deep in Gundar's debt, and she would never have the chance to repay him, or even thank him. He had saved Ulric. The boy had told her how Gundar carried him all the way back to the village. Asla knew the effort had taxed the old man's powers far beyond their limit.

The low mound of the priest's grave was surrounded by thin branches spiked into the earth. The villagers had chosen the straightest branches they could find and had decorated them with strips of fabric that fluttered gently in the wind. Everyone who had come to Gundar's grave to pay their last respects had tied a piece of cloth to a branch. There was not yet a stone to mark where he lay. Maybe he had not wanted one? Or maybe someone was still chiseling away at a beautiful marker for Gundar's final abode and had not yet finished his work.

Asla kneeled to say a silent prayer for the old priest. The day before, when he'd been laid to rest, she had not been able to come. With men like Ole—men who could not be trusted to stay in their grave—the obligation to sit vigil was strictly observed, and nobody had been willing to relieve her of the burden. Not even her father. Erek had been far too shaken to count on. Unreliable corpses like Ole's were laid out in the center of the main room of the house. A large candle was pushed between their folded hands, and for a day and a night, the body was not left unattended for a moment. The villagers wanted to be certain Ole did not move again, and Asla, as a result, had been unable to attend the priest's funeral.

Her only consolation was that, because his body had lain in her house, she had helped prepare him for burial. She had peeled the heavy chain mail from his portly body. Then they had dressed him in his best robes and had combed his hair and beard with care.

Ulric took the strip of cloth that he'd wound around his belt. It was two fingers wide, the decorative border from his best tunic. He'd insisted on giving it to Gundar. Tears ran down his cheeks as he tied the fabric to one of the long branches. But he did not sob.

Kadlin played in the snow while Asla tied a strip of her thin summer dress to a branch for her. Feeling chilled, Asla pulled her bulky red cloak closer around her shoulders. Alfadas had brought it back for her from one of his raids; apparently, it had once belonged to a king's daughter. The coat was made of heavy wool dyed a deep red. There were no knots in the fabric, and Asla had often wondered how one could spin wool so fine. She had cut her own offering to Gundar from the coat.

"I hope you have found a place at a good table with plenty to eat and drink," she said dejectedly. "There is so much more I would have liked to say to you. You brought my son back to me. As long as I live, I will never forget that."

Suddenly, someone in pale-brown boots was standing beside Asla. She had not heard any footsteps in the snow. Had she been so lost in her thoughts? She looked up—beside her stood Yilvina.

"Do you think I would be allowed to decorate his grave, as well?" she asked in that strange accent that invariably gave her words a melodic under-tone. "He saved my life." Her face betrayed no expression as she spoke.

What does she feel? Asla wondered. Shame? Shame, because of all possible saviors, it had taken a human to rescue her and the queen from the monster? Or gratitude?

"I think Gundar would be happy to know that you, too, will remember him fondly."

"I know that," the elf woman replied.

Her self-assured reply irritated Asla.

"My concern is that the people of your village may take it badly if I honor him according to your custom."

"I can't speak for the others," Asla replied coolly. "But it is no slight to me if you pay your respects to Gundar."

Yilvina tilted her head. For a while, she looked at the grave, lost in her own thoughts. Finally, she drew her dagger, sliced a strip of cloth from her cloak and knotted it to one of the branches. "I was very close to him when he died."

Asla thought of the kiss the elf woman had given the dying priest. Yilvina's behavior had struck her as strange, but not wrong. She had not understood exactly what was happening, but she had sensed that the elf woman was fighting to save his life.

"The walls of his heart were as thin as vellum. His god must have held a protective hand over him, because he really should not have lived as long as he did. A heavy meal or a walk along the fjord could have killed him. He was very fond of your boy, but carrying Ulric did not cause his death. Nor did the ghost-dog's bite. His time had come. He went in peace."

Asla bit down on her lip. She wanted to say something, but it was as if a lump had caught in her throat, choking her voice. How did she know how Asla had reproached herself? Until now, she had thought that Yilvina cared for nothing but the well-being of her queen. She always seemed so cold and aloof. And yet she had seen with perfect clarity what was weighing on Asla's heart.

Yilvina reached for Ulric's hand. "Let us go up to the house. Gundar would prefer us to remember him over good food than by freezing at his grave."

STONY DAYS

A lmost more unbearable than the battles to come was the waiting. Eleven days passed before the trolls mustered before Phylangan, days of confidence and excitement. We knew how strong our fortress was. Any attempt to take the Snow Harbor in a straight charge would have meant a massacre. Almost all our forces were deployed to the positions inside the mountains that flank the valley. Every embrasure was manned. The tower at the end of the Mahdan Falah had also been completed. Anyone daring to set foot in Phylangan through the Albenstar would be met by a hundred arrows. The exposed narrow bridge made it all but impossible to miss one's target.

Although our commander, Ollowain, was quietly confident, many were worried. "Will the trolls surprise us, as they did before?" some asked nervously, covertly. The apprehension in the air only evaporated when the great black worm of their army appeared on the horizon. I had seen their army once before, at Rosecarn, but I was shocked at their sheer numbers. They stretched across the horizon like a dark stain, and how they had changed was terrifying to see. They were disciplined. They set up a decent, well-organized camp. Of course, compared to an elven army on the march, they were nothing, but they certainly made a more orderly impression than did our allies, the centaurs.

The trolls took their time. They allowed themselves a full two days to prepare their assault. Only years later did I understand that this was one of their weapons: their self-assured calm and the waiting we had to do. Centuries of exile had changed them very much.

When I think back on the long days before the attack, however, I remember nothing more clearly than the terror perpetrated in Phylangan by an evil spirit. It seemed to be everywhere and left a trail of death behind it. One day, we found seven dead in one of the kobolds' bowmaking workrooms. The next day, five humans died in their beds in the lazaret. I will never forget the sight of two centaurs in particular. They had probably wanted no more than to sleep off the night's drunkenness. It horrified me to see what the specter had done to their big frames, normally so bursting with strength.

The signs of its killings were unmistakable. It seemed to melt the flesh from its victims' bones. When found, there was little left but bleached, fragile skin stretched over sinew and bone. Their hair had turned gray or white, and sometimes, when they had seen their killer before they died, an inexpressible horror was etched into their faces.

Of particular note was the fact that the ghost never murdered an elf. Our allies were quick to realize this, too. In those times of restless waiting, it drove a wedge between us.

They found many names for the invisible assassin. The kobolds called it "the cold light," the centaurs "frostbreath," and the humans "deathbringer." It made no difference how many sentries we set, it came and went as it liked. Soon, our defenders were more scared of the ghost than of the trolls, and they longed for the day when the attack would begin. Then, they hoped, the killings of that immaterial terror would come to an end. How foolish it was to imagine that the enemy would give up one weapon just because it had a second!

In those stony days of fear, days spent trapped within the fortress walls waiting for our doom, the council of war was in almost constant session. Now, with the benefit of distance, I am filled with sadness and incomprehension when I think of the things upon which we could not agree. For days, we squabbled about whether the humans should be allowed to bury their dead in the Skyhall. Landoran argued against it vehemently. He did not want that wondrous place to be soiled with the cadavers of humans, nor that the trees there should take their sustenance from decaying bodies.

The argument grew so bitter that the human prince, Alfadas, went so far as to threaten to leave. He and his fighters, he said, no longer felt it right to contaminate the pristine fields of Phylangan with their presence. Orimedes had taken Alfadas's side; he also threatened the pact between us, saying that if the humans abandoned the fortress, then the centaurs would also go. In the end, Landoran had to accept the demand, not least because his own son, our commander Ollowain, also supported the humans.

When I think now of what Landoran must certainly have known then about the days still to come, our bickering feels petty and mean, and I am overcome with deep shame. At the time, despite my debt to the humans, I took the side of the prince of the Normirga. For me, as for Landoran, the idea of corpses rotting in the most beautiful of all our halls was unbearable.

As bitter as these memories may be, I recall with a smile one particular incident in those far-off days. Ollowain and Landoran were at each other's throats again, this time about sending off the women and children through the Sky Harbor, when a small gray-haired figure entered the council hall. It was a holde, in the traditional dress of his race. Wearing only a loincloth and a circlet inlaid with gold, he seemed out of place, maybe even ridiculous, there in the lavish council chamber, all gold and marble. Everyone fell silent and stared at the newcomer. Only Landoran rose from his seat, went to the holde, and, to our amazement, bowed before him.

"I greet you, Gondoran of the Bragan clan, master of waters in Vahan Calyd."

Ollowain and Orimedes, as it turned out, also knew the holde, but he had kept his true rank concealed from them. Landoran offered the master of waters a seat in the war council, but the holde replied, none too subtly, that as far as he could see, Phylangan did not need another fighter. Instead, he asked for plans of the cisterns, waterways, and hidden springs. In his opinion, he said, the stone heart of the fortress was sick, and he wanted to do everything in his power to heal it. He could better serve Phylangan like that than he could with a sword in his hand. At the time, I smiled at the holde's request. Landoran willingly acceded to his wishes and allowed him to borrow the Stoneformer's Eye, one of our most precious artifacts. It was a ruby set in a gold circlet. When worn, the stone rested in the center of the wearer's forehead and gave them the power to form rock as if shaping soft clay.

After his visit to the council chamber, I never saw Gondoran again. Later, though, he would show all of us that he was not some eccentric fool, but that the heart of a warrior beat in his breast. Thus did Gondoran of the Bragan clan become a mirror of my own arrogance, and the memory of him warns me not to confuse external appearance with the quality contained within.

When the trolls finally drew closer to Phylangan, it was one of my duties to serve the stone garden as a scout. Once, I flew over their camp with Snowwing. They had brought a large amount of wood with them, and they used it to fashion crude protective walls and covers for three huge battering rams. The trolls seemed to know exactly what to expect when they charged up the wide pass to the Snow Harbor. Let them prepare, I thought, filled with hubris. Wood might protect them from arrows, but I knew how many catapults we had trained on the valley and also what awaited the trolls besides arrows and artillery, against which their wooden walls would not help.

As I turned to fly back, I sensed a dark power. It planted the seeds of despondency and thoughts of impending death. I had felt it before, at the Swelm Valley, but here it was far stronger. The trolls' shamans were working blood magic.

Back then, I sensed very clearly that they were casting spells that made a mockery of all the powers of nature, spells suffused with deep maliciousness. And I sensed their confidence. They were certain they would defeat us.

From *The Eye of the Falcon*, page 783

The Memoirs of Fenryl,

Count of Rosecarn

KNIFE IN THE HEART

Orgrim shouldered the goat leather sack containing the heavy iron rods. He'd had to rely on the help of the kobold slaves to forge them, and even through the leather sack, the metal caused an uncomfortable tingling on his skin.

A chill wind swept across the ice, and in the sky the green winterlight rippled in broad belts. He had five hundred warriors at his command, a fighting force that at any other time only a duke would lead. *My days as pack leader are numbered,* he thought confidently. If he were victorious this time, Branbeard would have no choice but to grant him the title of duke. The bloodbath that the three ice gliders had left behind when they had carved a path through the troll army had only served to reinforce his resolve: he would dare, and he would win! And Skanga's ghost-dog had given him all the information he needed.

Orgrim eyed the solid wooden wall with its two wheels. Three long shafts allowed the contraption to be pushed forward and also served to support the barrier the moment they were set down. Right and left of the wall, shields as big as doors could be folded down to extend the heavy barrier downward. Skanga's ghost-dog had sworn there were no catapults where they intended to launch their attack. Victory or defeat hung on whether that son of an elven bitch was telling the truth.

The pack leader looked at Brud. The wound in his chest had healed well. The scout had suffered a deep gash in the ice glider attack, and the falcon on his chest looked as if someone had cut its throat. Brud had been furious beyond measure at the mutilating wound and had talked day and night ever since about how he could hide the scar with other decorative scars to give the falcon back its dignity.

Brud carried a heavy roll of rope over his left shoulder. Half of the trolls were similarly equipped. Boltan, Orgrim's artillery master, joined them and spoke.

"Skanga says she's ready."

Orgrim inhaled deeply. The shaman was standing beside the black stone column that jutted skyward there. It projected straight out of the ice and marked the large Albenstar that lay close to the needle of rock.

"Are you afraid?" Orgrim asked softly.

The artillery master smiled nervously. "I won't be once we get over there. I'm not scared of the elves. But the way there . . ."

"Only cowards are afraid," taunted Gran, who was standing behind them and had heard the exchange.

"Can you really be brave if you've never had to get over your fear?" Boltan snapped back angrily.

Gran's forehead furrowed. "Are you calling me a coward?"

"No, a blockhead!"

"Enough!" Orgrim hissed. Then he raised his arm and gave Skanga the agreed sign. Almost simultaneously, an arch of shimmering light grew from the ice. "You know what you have to do?" Orgrim asked, fixing Boltan's eyes with his own.

Boltan nodded once. "I'm to sing the song of King Slangaman, all the verses. We follow then, and only then, five at a time."

"We need the time over there. You know how little room there is where we come out."

Boltan grasped his wrist in a warrior's grip. "Good luck, Pack Leader. With a victory this time, they'll soon be singing the song of Duke Orgrim."

"Let's hope Skanga's cur hasn't been lying to us." The pack leader turned away and grabbed the center shaft behind the wooden wall. Several warriors rushed to help him. Brud and Gran were at his side.

With an uneasy feeling, he pushed the heavy construction slowly toward the gate of light. Skanga clambered over the thick shafts to join him.

"I'll lead you," she said in her creaking voice. She stroked Orgrim's forehead with her thin fingers. Her touch was like a dead branch scratching over his skin. "When you've won, Pack Leader, we shall talk. There's something you need to know." Her blind eyes looked up to him. "You have to win today!"

"What do you want?"

The shaman shook her head. "First, you win. Then I'll talk with the king and you! Forward, now!"

Orgrim obeyed in silence. His hands were wet with sweat. He was not afraid of battle, but he, too, feared the path through the void.

"Let go and stay behind me," he ordered the warriors on his left and right. Then he gritted his teeth and leaned his shoulder against the protective wooden barrier. Behind him, Gran grabbed hold of the shaft and helped push forward. The path through the nothingness was narrow, and the wooden wall would project beyond the sides of it. Anything that was not on the path could be attacked. That was why they had lost so many ships when they had come back to Albenmark.

Flickering light danced on the surface of the wood. The north wind blew against Orgrim's shoulder. Then he took the step. He stood in darkness. There was no wind anymore. At his feet was the golden path. The pack leader could see no more than the bit of the path that lay directly before him. But he sensed the shadows that lurked beyond the light. He felt their hungry eyes on him.

Keep moving, he mentally ordered himself. *Just don't take your eyes off the path.* A piercing scream sounded behind him and was cut off abruptly. *Don't leave the path!*

His shoulder pressed against the wall. His head tilted, he stared at the path. Skanga would protect them! They just had to keep going straight ahead. Something tore at the barrier, as if a gust of wind had caught it, but there was no wind there.

Orgrim pushed ahead with all his strength. *Don't give in!* Suddenly, white stone glowed beneath his feet, and a humid heat washed over him. The pack leader looked up. Far above him stretched a strangely transparent cave roof the color of the summer sky. Thick clouds drifted up there. The Sky Cave!

Jubilant cries sounded from behind Orgrim as more and more of the first fifty warriors stepped through the gateway. The cave was breathtaking. Skanga's cur had told Orgrim about it, about its scale and magnificence, but all the words in the world would not have been enough to prepare him for what he now saw. It was a wonder to behold, and at the same time false, warped. Like everything the elves did! The pack leader knew that he was in the heart of a mountain, but it felt as if he were looking out over a wide valley. The elves had robbed the cavern of its majestic gloom. Everything around him was wrong! Caves should not look like that—the elves had robbed the mountain of its heart, had hollowed it out like worms eating into an apple. This mountain had once been Kingstor, the rock fortress of the troll king. How could it ever be that again after what the elves had done to it? How could a mountain with neither heart nor dignity be the throne of a ruler?

Angrily, Orgrim tore his eyes away from the spectacular sight. The elves would pay. He would crush them underfoot like worms!

Signal horns were blaring. The dance began. "Man the shafts!" Orgrim ordered, and he gave his own place to a young warrior. The polished stone of the Mahdan Falah was treacherously smooth, and the sides of the bridge had no rails. Only an elf could come up with that kind of nonsense! Orgrim moved with care along the narrow walkway over the abyss. The wooden wall projected a good way beyond the bridge on both sides. The pack leader released a catch, and a large wooden shield creaked down on one side of the wall, dropping past the side of the bridge. On the other side, Brud released a second shield.

An arrow fell almost vertically from overhead and smashed against the bridge close beside Orgrim. The wooden wall protected them from any direct shot from the tower at the end of the bridge. A defender could only hit one of his warriors by shooting upward at a sharp angle and letting the arrow fall along an even steeper path once it had reached the zenith of its flight. But the pack leader had prepared for that, too.

"Shield bearers to the shafts!" he ordered calmly. "Cover your comrades."

Warriors moved forward, carrying long wooden shields over their heads so that they covered not only themselves but also the fighters pushing the shafts. Orgrim hurried back to the center of the wall of wood.

Arrows bored into the shields with muffled thuds. He looked back along the bridge and smiled. He had not yet lost a man on the Mahdan Falah, and all the first-wave fighters were now assembled behind him on the bridge. Skanga waved once, then disappeared through the gateway of light. Boltan would soon appear with more warriors. There was no time to lose.

Orgrim opened a small hatch in the wall and peered ahead to the tower that rose at the end of the bridge. Behind the battlements, he saw the elves' helmets, sparkling silver. They fired salvo after salvo toward the roof of the cave, but they could not see what was going on behind the wooden wall.

The pack leader estimated the distance to the gateway behind him. He must not advance too far—the Albenstar, from which reinforcements would soon arrive, had to stay out of the archers' line of sight. They'd moved perhaps twenty paces forward. That would have to do!

"Halt!" he ordered. "Drop the shafts!" The pack leader slipped the goat leather sack from his shoulders. The iron bars clanged softly. Orgrim was now level with one of the massive pillars that supported the bridge. This was where he needed to be. He kneeled. He and his warriors had practiced what was to follow dozens of times.

"Stanchion holders to your posts!"

Three warriors broke from the group of trolls and kneeled beside Orgrim.

The pack leader wrapped heavy strips of leather around his hands. Then he reached into the sack and took out the first iron bar. One end was as sharp as a thorn. The kobolds had assured him that they had used a special process to harden the tips. Would it be enough?

"Hammer bearers, to me! Shield bearers, cover us!"

Gran came to Orgrim's side. The giant troll pulled a heavy war hammer out of his belt and hefted it in his hand. Others joined them until there were two trolls with hammers beside each of those kneeling. The shields scraped as they closed over their heads to form a protective roof.

Orgrim held his iron bar with both hands. Carefully, he positioned the sharpened tip on the polished stone. Everything came down to this moment! If they did not succeed in pounding the iron bars into the bridge, their assault would fail.

A cry made Orgrim look up. One of his warriors had fallen, a black-feathered arrow jutting from one leg. The falling arrows rattled like hail onto the roof of interlocked shields. An occasional lucky shot was bound to get through.

The pack leader looked up to Gran. "Get started. And if you smash my fingers, I'll have you thrown off the bridge!"

The giant grinned. "You still need your hands. Maybe today will be the day when you finally kill almost as many elves as me. It would spoil the whole battle for me if you couldn't fight."

"Shut up and hammer!" Orgrim snarled.

The heavy stone hammerhead came down on the iron rod. The iron vibrated between Orgrim's fingers. Gran and the other warrior quickly fell into a rhythm, taking turns striking the end of the iron spike. At first, the point found no grip on the polished stone of the bridge. Again and again, the hammers came down. Orgrim's arms ached, and he was holding the bar so tightly that his fingers were numb.

Then, finally, a tiny flake of stone splintered away. "Stop!" he ordered. Then he set the tip of the iron rod in the fine crack in the surface. "Continue!"

The hammers took up their rhythm again. From the corner of his eye, Orgrim could see one of the other spikes already boring slowly into the stone of the bridge. It would work!

The work went on, unbearably slowly. The elves had stopped shooting at them. Maybe they would try a direct attack from the tower in an attempt to push the wooden wall from the bridge?

"Man the shafts again!" Orgrim ordered without looking up from the iron bar. As long as his warriors held against them, the puny elves would never be able to move the wall.

Orgrim could let go of his bar now. It had been driven more than a hand's width deep into the stonework. Deep enough to carry the load? The pack leader looked back to the Albenstar. How long would it be until Boltan sent the first warriors through? The short stretch of bridge they possessed was already full.

"Stop!" The hammers stopped in midswing. Orgrim grabbed hold of the spike and pushed against it with all his strength. It didn't move.

"Let me try!" Gran kneeled. His face contorted as his naked fingers closed around the iron. The muscles in his mighty arms tensed. Nothing! The spike didn't move.

"I'd hang on that," the giant said, looking at Orgrim.

"The ropes!" Orgrim ordered. Rolls of heavy rope, each woven from thongs of leather, were tossed onto the stone beside him. They were easy to grip, and loops had been tied into the ends of each. The pack leader laid one of the loops over the iron spike. He looked up to Gran. "Only four ropes for each rod, and no more than two warriors at once on a rope. They won't hold more than that. Drop the ropes left and right of the bridge so we don't get in each other's way on the way down."

Gran peered over the edge of the bridge. "Let me go first. It could be dangerous down below. You can't defend yourself if you're hanging on a rope."

"Which is why *I'm* going first. Good prospects for you to become duke in my place if anything happens to me." The pack leader pushed his war hammer into a leather loop on his back to keep it out of the way as he descended.

The giant gave him a lopsided grin. "You're right. After you."

Orgrim slung the rope around his hips, then let himself slide backward from the side of the bridge, his feet pressed against the bridge pylon. The side panels of the wooden wall protected him from elven arrows. He still had the leather wraps around his hands. Pushing away from the stone pylon with his feet, he glided into the depths. Thick fog beneath him drifted over the hillsides of the Skyhall. *It is unbearably hot, even worse than in Vahan Calyd,* Orgrim thought. But the Normirga had left Vahan Calyd only to return here. Maybe they'd liked sweltering in the mangroves? Who knew what went on in the heads of elves?

When he entered the fog, Orgrim slowed his descent. Despite the leather strips, his hands burned. Warm water settled on his bare skin and rolled off. The air smelled of rotten eggs.

He stopped for a moment and looked down. Something was wrong. The stench . . . it was not like the elves to allow something like that, not at all. Somewhere in the cloudy gloom, he heard a gurgling sound.

At least no archers would be able to see him in that musty vapor, Orgrim thought as he continued his slide down the rope. Moments later, he had firm ground under his feet again. Beside him was a bush, its leaves drooping. What was going on here?

The fog could be dangerous to them. He had to find the entrance to the broad tunnel that stretched for five miles through the belly of the mountain. It connected the two harbors, and whoever commanded that tunnel, he knew, also ruled Kingstor. From there, connecting passages linked to all the other caverns, and anyone trying to leave the fortress had to do it through that tunnel. Orgrim smiled, sure of victory. They would think that he was trying to get to the Snow Harbor to open the gates for the attackers. But he knew better and had very different plans in mind. Plans he had not shared even with the king or Skanga. With a little luck, they would defeat the elves in their magnificent fortress in a single day.

Beside him, another troll came sliding down a rope. Soon, there would be five hundred of them in the heart of the elven fortress. Who could hope to stop them then?

RETURNING FIRE

Ollowain peered down along the route that led through the pass. He was standing in a casemate a hundred paces above the Snow Harbor. The large chamber, buried deep inside the rock, had been constructed from the start to serve as the command post for any defense of the pass. In raised alcoves along its eastern wall stood catapults, their firing lines trained on the pass trail below. Several heavy crossbows were also there, set up on wooden carriages and ready to loose their bolts on an enemy in the pass. In the center of the room stood a large map table on which plans of the fortress had been rolled out. Crystal carafes of apple wine, swords, and daggers weighted the ends of the maps to stop them from rolling up. Several crystal glasses, half-filled with water or diluted apple wine, also stood on the table. A second, smaller table held a platter of cold meat and fragrant fresh bread.

The swordmaster stood in the central defensive alcove. Along its sides stood pyramids of heavy stone balls, and bundles of crossbow bolts leaned against the wall. From this wall, just behind Ollowain, projected four golden tubes, their funnel-shaped mouths stoppered with wooden plugs.

From the embrasure where he stood, Ollowain had a good view over the entire valley. Four similar casemates were built into the cliff wall beneath him, like the levels of a defensive tower.

The catapults were firing stone after stone at the advancing trolls. There were so many that the pass was black with them, and they were paying a terrible price, targeted unrelentingly by the casemates above the harbor and by the defenses inside the long mountain flanks on both sides. Hundreds of warriors must have perished already. And they had no way to get back at the elves, humans, and kobolds, protected as they were behind the narrow embrasures.

Almost all the troll fighters carried massive wooden shields. They formed columns and tried to protect themselves from the projectiles and arrows flying from every side. But it was a deceptive security, for the columns made easy targets for the catapults. Again and again, their stone ammunition carved bloody furrows through the marching columns.

Some of the trolls had hung thick bundles of brushwood on themselves, relying on that strange armor to stop an arrow, but it only made them a natural target for the archers shooting flaming arrows.

The most forbidding weapons that the trolls had brought with them, however, were three huge battering rams. They had been fitted with protective roofs on which thick, grass-filled leather pads had been attached. Most of the stone projectiles simply bounced uselessly off the padding, and flaming arrows were just as ineffective on the ice-crusted leather.

Their kobold slaves built those for them, Ollowain thought in annoyance. The trolls never would have come up with something like that themselves.

The first of the battering rams had made it to the gates of the Snow Harbor, and when the ram pounded against the great gold door for the first time, it sounded like an enormous gong. Ollowain saw the glasses on the map table tremble. The sound went deep into one's belly, but for a noise created by trolls, it sounded strangely solemn.

The swordmaster leaned far out of the embrasure to get a better look at what was going on at the gate directly below. Another low, loud beat of the gong rang. Slowly, the trolls were bringing their second ram into position.

"Can they break through the gate?" asked Alfadas, worried. He was watching the trolls from the embrasure beside Ollowain's.

"The gate is made of solid gold and is as thick as your underarm is long. I don't think they'll be able to destroy it. The vibrations they create won't loosen any hinges either. Opening the gate means pulling the wings sideways into the rock with chains. Still, gold is relatively soft. They might be able to buckle it enough where the wings come together to open a gap and slip through. But only one at a time, maybe two side by side at most. On the other side, we have five catapults waiting and two hundred kobolds with heavy crossbows. If the trolls can't attack on a wide front, then they will never make it past our little comrades in arms."

The second battering ram began to hammer the fortress gate. Ollowain felt the floor beneath his feet shudder. *The trolls must have huge tree trunks beneath those roofs,* he thought. Had they been fool enough to take the wood they needed from the forests of the Maurawan?

The swordmaster stepped back from the embrasure and went to the four golden tubes set side by side in the wall. He removed the walnut plug from the nearest tube. A small gold chain prevented the stopper from falling. "Is the oil ready?" he called loudly into the tube. Then he leaned forward and listened.

"Oil is boiling, Commander," came a tinny reply.

"Then close the embrasures. Relay the order to the other casemates!"

Ollowain left the speaking tubes and returned to his perch above the gate. Below, on the ice, the trolls were pulling their third battering ram into position. Ollowain gestured to Lysilla to attend to the speaking tubes. The thumping of the rams merged into a steady beat. Ollowain signaled to Lysilla, swinging one hand down.

"Now!"

"How many vats?" she said.

"All twenty!"

"Close the embrasures," he ordered the catapult crews.

Ollowain looked down a final time. Fans of scalding oil spewed from the mouths of wide, flat tubes mounted beneath the lowest casemate. Hundreds of guttural screams sounded from the trolls, and the oil flowed in streams across the ice. Ollowain shut the wooden hatch that covered the embrasure.

There was a loud hiss, and a sudden light flared through the fine cracks in the wooden shutters. A heavy, oily odor penetrated the casemate, followed closely by the stink of burned flesh. Ollowain fought the urge to vomit. Beneath him at that moment, hundreds of trolls were dying on the ice, and he had ordered their deaths. Not one within twenty paces of the fortress gate would survive. With the smallest flame, the hot oil transformed in a heartbeat into a fireball. The swordmaster remembered the fires of that night in Vahan Calyd. The flames that the trolls had brought with them to Albenmark had now returned to them.

He went back to the speaking tube. "No back-burning through the funnels?"

"No, Commander. It's hot in the casemate, but there have been no mishaps."

"Then refill the vats."

The swordmaster pressed the stopper into the speaking tube and returned to the embrasure. When he opened the shutter, thick black smoke hid any view of what was going on immediately below, and a foul smell filled his nostrils. Farther away, he saw figures still on fire, screaming and writhing in the snow. Streams of fire stretched as far as a hundred paces down the glacier. Countless trolls were fleeing in panic, but too many still remained.

Ollowain could see them trying to pull the burning battering rams back from the gate with long hooks. Would they be ready to negotiate peace after such a defeat? After this attack, it had to be clear even to their bullheaded king that he could never conquer Phylangan. Two or three more assaults like that, and his army would start to fall apart, perhaps even rebel against him. The stone garden was the strongest fortress in the north. Nothing could defeat it.

Alfadas was standing at one of the embrasures and looking down, his face a mask of stone. *What is going on inside him?* the swordmaster asked himself.

Lysilla smiled halfheartedly. "That looks like the end of this troll war."

Ollowain, however, found it strange that more and more trolls were pushing back toward the gate. And with all their formidable strength, others were hauling the battering rams away. Maybe the soldiers in the first casemate could see better what was going on? He went to the speaking tubes.

"What is happening at the gate?"

Instead of an answer, all he heard was a metallic scraping.

"Report!" Ollowain shouted, angry at the apparent lapse in discipline. Someone always had to be at the speaking tubes in battle!

He cleared his throat. Everyone in the chamber had their eyes on him. "I request an immediate report about the situation at the Snow Harbor gate," he said with pointed composure.

Suddenly, a piercing scream sounded from the speaking tube. There was another scraping noise, and then a deep voice snarled: "Come out of the pipe, little elf, so Gran can eat you!"

Ollowain inhaled sharply. How was that possible? How had the trolls penetrated the fortress? And where else were they? He had to act but at the same time needed to keep a cool head, needed to think.

"Lysilla, relay an order to the other casemates—all fighters are to meet at the north stairway of the third casemate. They are to withdraw all crews on the catapults and crossbows."

He crossed to the map table. Had the trolls actually managed to get into the Snow Harbor? They could penetrate the casemates from there. But how had they made it through the gate in the first place?

"Commander!" Count Fenryl appeared at the entrance of the north stairway. His left arm hung limply, and his white linen armor was soiled with blood. "They're in the fortress. They're coming from the Skyhall. Hundreds of them!"

"Where are they?"

The count joined him at the map table.

"Here in the main tunnel and in the systems that run parallel to it. The only place they haven't attacked yet is the Snow Harbor itself." He pointed to one room. "They've occupied the north winch room, and I fear they are also on the other side, in the south chamber."

Ollowain shook his head in disbelief. "From the Skyhall? How could they overcome the tower at the Mahdan Falah so quickly?"

He looked at the plans in front of him again. Then he understood what was going on.

Whoever was leading the attack must have had a spy inside the fortress. The trolls were armed with intimate knowledge of Phylangan's weak points. The winch rooms not only allowed the gates of the Snow Harbor to be opened—anyone wanting to enter the defensive positions along the two mountain flanks that overlooked the pass along the glacier had to pass through those chambers. If the trolls managed to occupy and hold those positions, then two-thirds of all Phylangan's defenders were trapped in the outer defenses. They could certainly still fire at any attacker coming up the glacier, but they could not leave their positions, because there was only one way out: through the winch rooms! To make matters even worse, of course, those chambers also allowed the harbor gates to be opened. The army outside would storm the fortress. If they did not act quickly, Phylangan was lost!

Ollowain reached for his sword belt, which lay on the map table.

"Come with me, immediately," he said to Alfadas. "Lysilla, seal the south door to this casemate, and make sure the south doors of the lower casemates are also sealed. We cannot let the enemy attack us from behind here, too."

As he raced down the winding staircase, the swordmaster tried to picture the fortress plans in his mind. There were many tunnels that led to the Skyhall from the east, but only one opened into the enormous hall from the west: the central tunnel that went straight through the mountain from Sky Harbor to Snow Harbor.

The stairway wound downward in an endless spiral, and Ollowain's thoughts were turning in spirals, too, circling around how the trolls were able to break through as quickly as they had and how he might save at least part of Phylangan. As things stood, they could no longer hold the eastern part of Phylangan. But a new defensive line could be established beyond the Skyhall. First things first, though. They had to try to stop as many troops as possible from being cut off and surrounded by the trolls.

Battling the giants in the narrow tunnels would be suicidal. They had every advantage. As big as they were, a single troll would be enough to block one of the smaller tunnels, and in such a small space, an elf would have little chance of evading the powerful blows of their clubs.

On the landing to the third casemate, he was joined by Silwyna. Several archers accompanied the Maurawan.

"How does it look?" Ollowain asked.

She laughed bitterly. "How is the weather outside? Is it a good day to die?"

"Where are the trolls?"

"They've taken the second casemate. We just managed to escape them, then they went back down. I think they're focusing their attack on the Snow Harbor now."

Ollowain looked up the stairs and saw Lysilla. He waved to her. "You come with me."

He had a plan now. At first, only the two of them would attack. There was not enough room on the stairway for more fighters. He wished he had Yilvina with him now. He knew he could rely on her swords.

Alfadas looked at him expectantly. Taking the human with them would mean throwing his life away. But he had to have a task. Ollowain could not risk offending their allies now.

"Alfadas, you and your men cover our backs. Make sure all doors are closed behind us!"

Alfadas nodded.

Ollowain drew his sword. It had served him truly in countless battles, and no battle had been more desperate than the one they now faced.

Lysilla stepped up beside him. Her white hair accentuated the scornful gleam in her blood-red eyes. "Would it be untoward of me to invite you for a glass of good apple wine this evening?"

Ollowain smiled. "Only if you are speculating on my not coming and your drinking it alone to my memory."

The swordmaster trotted deftly down the stairs. They encountered only one troll, taking him utterly by surprise. Ollowain leaped at him feetfirst. His blade slashed forward and sliced through the warrior's throat. Then he somersaulted over the falling troll and landed a little uncertainly on the stairs.

"The next one is mine!" said Lysilla with a cold laugh, overtaking him.

Ollowain let her go ahead. He gathered himself, forcing himself to breathe deeply and evenly. This time, he was prepared for the clash—things were different than in Vahan Calyd, when he'd fought the trolls at the fountains in the park.

They found both lower casemates abandoned by the trolls. Deeper down, they heard screams and sounds of battle. Ollowain led them through a short passage that curved to the north. Then, abruptly, they were standing in the entrance to the winch room.

The winch room could only be called a room, however, when compared to the vast expanse of the Skyhall itself, for it was enormous in its own right, with a high vaulted ceiling. The wall opposite them was occupied entirely by heavy golden chain-blocks threaded through with chain links as thick as Ollowain's arm. A row of large barinstones in the ceiling bathed the hall in a pale-blue light. There, too, huge gold chains hung in wide curves.

Dead bodies sprawled everywhere. The defenders seemed to have been taken completely by surprise—not a single troll lay among the corpses.

Nearly two dozen of the gray-skinned monsters were positioned in a semicircle in front of a portal at the eastern end of the hall—the portal, Ollowain knew, that led to the outer defenses. Grunting, growling, joking, the trolls were playing a deadly game, toying with the few elven fighters still alive who were desperately trying to break through.

Ollowain took everything in at a glance. He could hardly believe his luck: the chamber seemed built for his style of fighting. But there were two more doors to consider. Behind one was a passage that led down to the Snow

Harbor, and from the other ran a tunnel deep into the heart of the mountain. If the trolls got reinforcements from there, then their battle against the giants would be hopeless.

Lysilla was waiting for Ollowain at the entrance to the winch room.

"Do you still insist on leading the next attack?" he asked her. More than twenty trolls stood between them and the portal.

"I was only waiting for you to catch up. Just watch me, old man." With catlike grace, she dashed across the hall. Ollowain thought she was going to simply cut down the first enemy without warning when she suddenly shouted a surprisingly vulgar insult in the trolls' own language.

The swordmaster hurried to her side. After their easy victory, the trolls clearly did not see the two elves as much of a threat. Only three of their number broke from the group at the portal.

The first died with a slashed throat before he had a chance to raise his war hammer. Lysilla tried to crush the second's knee, but her strike missed its target and left only a bloody gouge on the troll's shin that did not slow him down. She ducked beneath a swing, then Ollowain was with her. His blade pierced the lunging attacker through the gut.

With a light turn, the swordmaster freed his blade and leaped among the trolls blocking the portal. Too close together to use their weapons properly, they were all but at the mercy of Ollowain's attacks.

The fighters beyond the portal found new courage then and charged forward in a fierce counterattack. The trolls' line broke.

As if electrified, Ollowain gave himself over to completely to the dance of his blade. He sprang, thrust, and somersaulted to safety, only to attack again the next moment. Once, he leaped up to the ceiling and, ducked low, ran across the heavy chain links suspended there to cut off a fleeing troll trying to make it to the Snow Harbor for reinforcements.

When the defenders from the casemate came charging into the winch room, the trolls' fate was sealed. Ollowain ordered the entrance to the Snow Harbor sealed and all troops to abandon the northern outworks, and he checked personally to make sure that all the outposts were empty.

Looking down through the embrasure at a catapult position, he saw that half of the harbor gate stood open. The large battering rams were still burning but had been dragged partway down the pass to stop them from blocking the massive entrance.

Thousands of trolls were swarming into the mountain, and there was no longer any hope of breaking through to the second winch room.

Enervated, Ollowain ordered a retreat beyond the Skyhall. The trolls, on the first day, had managed to overthrow the fortress's most powerful bulwarks, and more than half of the defenders were dead or cut off. Phylangan seemed lost, and the fight had hardly begun.

THE PRINCE OF THE NIGHTCRAGS

S kanga stepped over a kobold that even in death still grasped a comically tiny sword. The air in the immense cavern beyond the golden entrance smelled agreeably of roasting meat. She looked over the ice ships tied up inside and shuddered when she recognized the two that had reaped such a bloody harvest among the trolls. Angry, she peered back beyond the gates, where hundreds of charred bodies lay on the ice. She saw death far more clearly now than she ever had before losing her sight many centuries earlier. Now, she watched the life-lights of the dying slowly fade. Sometimes, the glimmer of life did not leave the dead immediately, but none ever burned beyond the following dusk.

The cavern she was in and the pass outside were crowded with the fading lights. Her race had paid a terrible price for their assault on the golden gate. Now Skanga understood why the elves had not attacked a second time with their ice ships. Emerelle's brood had put their trust in the impregnability of their fortress, believing they could defend it with practically no losses of their own.

The shaman smiled with pride. Many had fought that day, but the battle had ultimately been decided by a single troll. And she knew he had survived.

Behind her, she heard Branbeard's voice. He was lavishing praise on his warriors. The king sat atop a barrel, and when he saw Skanga, he called her over. He was in the middle of his usual crowd of fools and lickspittles. *If Branbeard one day decides to add a few warriors to his retinue who are not dumber than he is,* she thought, *then he might become a great king.*

Beside the barrel that Branbeard had turned into a throne lay a growing pile of elven heads, with warriors bringing in new ones all the time. Some had tied several heads together by their long hair. Branbeard found praise for each of his fighters.

"What foolishness is this?" Skanga asked.

"We're counting our victory," replied Dumgar in the king's place. "They say the Normirga number three to four thousand. Well, we have more than two hundred of them right here and more to come. Some elves die before you can cut off their heads. Emerelle's race will die out! This pile of heads is like an hourglass." Dumgar grinned with self-satisfaction at the comparison, but Skanga doubted that the Duke of Mordrock had thought of it himself. She turned to the king.

"We need to talk. Alone!"

Branbeard sniffed and spat green phlegm on the pile of heads. Then he dismissed his ring of sycophants with a cursory wave.

"What do you want, Skanga?" His good mood had clearly flown.

"You know who he is?"

"I knew it in Reilimee when he put forward his strange proposal for storming the harbor walls. Trolls don't fight like that. Boarding ramps in the mastheads, walls of wood hung between the yards . . . in the past, we beat the elves with the power in our arms."

Skanga sighed. Branbeard ought to know better. One before him had also gone down such untrodden paths. "Who he is, after today, can no longer be kept a secret. That should be clear to you. Others will remember. Earlier victories, battles that are now legend—"

"I know!" Branbeard slapped one hand against his disfigured forehead. "My head might look like a chunk of meat, but I can still think. I'll give him his damned dukedom!"

"Why are you so afraid of him?"

"Isn't it obvious? You're usually so insightful, Skanga. I'm thinking ahead. What will become of Orgrim once he's the prince? There's nothing else to achieve—except to become the king."

The shaman sighed. What a fool Branbeard was. Perhaps it would be better if he died in battle. "You know our laws. As Orgrim is born to be prince of the Nightcrags, you will always be reborn our king. Even if Orgrim murders you, his rule will not last, and he may never use the title of king for himself. He can't raise a finger against you, and he knows it."

Branbeard suddenly seemed weary. "Look at how he wins battles. He is so different. Maybe one day he will find a way to send me into the darkness. He's the only troll I would not put that past." Branbeard looked at Skanga intently. "The only one apart from you, perhaps. Lately, I've been getting the impression that your interest in Orgrim weighs heavier than your interest in me, your king."

"Why do you think that might be?" Skanga asked sharply. "You needed Orgrim to win this battle. I had to protect him from your folly because his death would have meant your failure today, here at the very gates of Kingstor. Now you don't need him anymore. Make him prince and send him to the Nightcrags. Give him some trifling task. For a long time, he'll be satisfied. He'll waste his strength on the females he can now have." Skanga knew well that she would never be able to anticipate Orgrim's behavior. He was too unpredictable even to say what would be on his mind a single moon from now. She had to observe him much more than she had. But Branbeard had to believe that he himself was not under threat.

"How long have you known him to be the reborn duke?" the king abruptly asked.

"Since the first time I touched him. You know that when an old soul returns as flesh and blood, it cannot stay hidden from me." Skanga kept her answer deliberately vague. Branbeard should not suspect that she only knew with certainty in Vahan Calyd.

"Any reason I shouldn't get our great commander off my back now?"

Skanga turned her milky eyes on the king. She saw the burning ambition inside him. He would give anything to be like Orgrim but at the same time knew he would never be Orgrim's equal. After today's victory, he could no longer risk just killing him. "What do you have in mind?"

"The men love a big speech after a bloody battle." Branbeard pushed himself off his barrel and moved out into the massive cavern.

Skanga followed. Branbeard was not the brightest, but he had a nose for power. She was curious how he would act toward Orgrim.

They found the pack leader at the golden gate. His arms folded over his chest, he gazed out over the corpse-strewn pass. He seemed tense, angry.

"Step before your king, Orgrim!" Branbeard bellowed. All around him turned and looked. The trolls picking through the dead for valuables paused in their work. Warriors carrying the wounded into the safety of the cavern stopped where they stood. Even a troop of captured kobolds glanced around nervously.

"Did you think you could hide what you carry within you from your king?"

Skanga saw Orgrim tense. After this victory, he was not about to swallow another rebuke from Branbeard.

"Come and kneel before Skanga. She will reach for your soul. All should hear what she finds in you!" Branbeard sniffed and spat.

Skanga smiled inwardly. The king was playing his part well. Breathless anticipation hung in the air on all sides. Orgrim seemed suddenly unsettled but obeyed the king's order and kneeled in front of Skanga. She laid her hands on his head. Yes, it was clear which soul inhabited his body.

"Is it as I suspect?" the king asked.

Everyone in the cavern held their breath. Skanga decided to play the king's game. After the carnage before the gate, Branbeard could well use this moment of melodrama to restore his standing in the eyes of his army. "It is, sire. His soul rebels against being your warrior."

Orgrim looked up at her, shocked. She knew precisely that she had laid bare his most private thoughts with her words.

"Your deeds have betrayed you, Orgrim!" the king thundered.

Skanga sensed that the young pack leader would not resign himself to his fate without a fight. Branbeard had better not push too far!

"Rise, Orgrim. You have been recognized." The king strode toward the perplexed pack leader with outstretched arms. "I welcome you at my side, prince of the Nightcrags. It is good to have found you again after so long."

Jubilant cries rang throughout the hall. The prince of the Nightcrags was the most renowned of their past commanders, hero of numerous legends, although a shadow hung over him. It was said that an elven warrior pursued him with unrelenting hatred. In his last incarnation, the prince was murdered in his own rooms inside his fortress. But perhaps that had been no more than royal intrigue, said some.

"At our feast this evening, you shall sit at my side," Branbeard declared jovially. He had one arm slung across Orgrim's shoulders, as if they had always been the best of friends.

"I have big plans for you, Commander." Branbeard had raised his voice again so that those around them could hear him well. "Now that Kingstor is all but ours, we will avenge ourselves against all who helped our enemy! Your task will be to go to the humans, Orgrim. Skanga will lead you to the Nightcrags tomorrow, and from there you will travel to the Fjordlands and raze every human hut you see. They will learn what it means to challenge the trolls!"

Branbeard's announcement of a new field campaign was met with widespread exultation. Orgrim seemed at once relieved and a little stunned.

"Can I still assemble my troops tonight?"

"Of course, Prince, of course!" Branbeard clapped him on the shoulder. "Time enough for that after the feast. You're to take twenty of your best men with you. Pick your warriors from the bodyguards protecting the women in the Nightcrags. You're to cross the mountains and descend on the Fjordlands from the north. I'm sending my good friend Dumgar with five hundred warriors from the south. He'll burn the king's city and march up the fjord to meet your troops. Be a good adviser to him. He's sometimes a little . . . at a loss."

Orgrim looked at Branbeard in disbelief. "Twenty warriors? That's all? And I'm not in command but there to advise Dumgar?"

The king smiled and nodded. "Yes. That's how it will be. Without a head as capable as yours beside him, Dumgar would be doomed to fail. You're my best field commander. I have faith that your victories together will be as glorious as our victory here today."

Skanga withdrew. Branbeard had taken her by surprise. He had accepted the inevitable. Orgrim had achieved his goal. Finally, he was a duke. And at the same time, he could hardly have been punished worse. If Dumgar were successful, all the acclaim would be his. But if he were to fail, Branbeard would point the finger of blame at Orgrim.

She moved away, toward the ice ships. She would seek out a quiet place among them and sleep awhile. She supported herself heavily on her walking stick. After any victory, she felt the burden of her centuries with a special clarity. It had been a long time since she had been able to celebrate a victory feast; she preferred to retire instead.

Let the whelps have their celebration, these youngsters who knew nothing about enduring the breath of time, and who never would.

The shaman started. Beneath her feet, she felt the ice shudder very slightly. There was something down below, deep in the mountain.

Shahondin had been unable to find a way down. *The Normirga are renowned for their skill with magic, but not a single sorcerer fought in the battle,* Skanga thought uneasily. Where were they? What was going on inside the mountain? She chided herself. This battle was not yet won. Maybe the elves had wanted them to enter the mountain?

Again, she felt the light trembling underfoot. She had to find out what was going on down there.

OF FORGOTTEN HEROES

B uilt to last centuries, lost in days." Many today speak thus of Phylangan. But those who do are mainly proud young warriors who were not there in the days when the city fell. They have no idea of the lonely courage of those who fought with all their might against the inevitable.

Ollowain, the keeper of the Shalyn Falah, is remembered. He was always to be found where the blades sang their lethal chorus. His calm humor gave strength to those whose sentry duty seemed endless.

But there were so many others whose names today resound on nobody's lips.

There was Gondoran, the holde, and the master of waters from far-off Vahan Calyd, a friend of Prince Orimedes, who fought a solitary battle in the darkness and yet remained unknown though he gave the stone garden its final victory.

Forgotten, too, is that human of honorable blood and rude tongue who, with his men, demolished tunnels and filled passageways with stones to deny the trolls a way to reach the Sky Harbor. And though they were so exhausted they could hardly raise their picks, not one of the humans shied from the fray when the superior enemy broke through yet again. No one will ever know where they found their courage, for the only recompense they could expect were the scars they carried on their mortal bodies.

There were four large gold gates in the wide tunnel that led beyond the Skyhall to the remaining harbor. The tunnel had been built so that even the largest of our ice gliders, with its masts lowered, could pass through the mountain from one harbor to the other. Today, the final battles fought in Phylangan are named after those gates. They were the Gate of the Garden, which opened to the Skyhall; the Lily Gate at the necropolis, where those who had failed to find their way into the moonlight rested, enclosed in ice; the Old Gate, close to Landoran's royal palace; and the Sky Gate, the last stronghold before the remaining harbor.

Each of the gates cost the trolls a day to destroy with battering rams and axes. And when they had broken through a gate, each step of the path ahead had to be paid for with blood.

The defenders fought from behind hastily built barricades or slipped away through narrow tunnels only to reappear through concealed drop-gates and *surprise the attackers on their flanks. They drove the burning hulls of ice gliders down the sloping tunnel toward the trolls, and sent flames and smoke at them with enormous bellows brought from the forges in the blacksmiths' halls.*

For twenty-two days they fought, those warriors. They had been given a week at best. Then the trolls at last destroyed the Sky Gate.

A counterattack by riders, led by Orimedes and his centaurs, pushed the surprised enemy back a final time. But we all knew that the time had come to abandon the stone garden. The survivors drew lots to decide who would stay behind to buy a few precious hours for the rest to get away. A white stone meant a place on the last ice glider to leave the fortress. A black stone meant death.

From *The Eye of the Falcon*, page 912

The Memoirs of Fenryl,

Count of Rosecarn

GOLD AND STONES

"Don't judge me by the nose, Dalla," Lambi said, and he reached down and patted the flap of his trousers. "Everything down here's still in perfect working order."

The king's mistress knotted the bandage around Lambi's head. Then she looked at him with her sky-blue eyes. Lambi had never had much time for red-haired women. They brought a man nothing but trouble, it was said.

He thought of the stone he carried in his pocket. Whatever trouble he brought on himself, it would not last long. He grinned.

"So how about it? You and me? I reckon we've got time enough before we have to march."

Dalla laid her hand on his chest, where his heart lay. "I know that everything in here's in good order, Lambi. That is the only thing that interests me about a man."

The jarl could hardly believe his luck. "Then should we? I know a place. It's just—"

She shook her head. "I have to tend to the wounded. You know that."

"You've just wounded my heart. It'll kill me, too, if you don't treat it right away."

Dalla laughed, then stood up. "May Luth spin you a long thread."

"I'm never in luck with redheads," Lambi murmured, loud enough for Dalla to hear. "They always run off."

She shook her head, and her red locks danced around her shoulders. "Maybe you just ask at the wrong time." She gave him a captivating smile, then she walked out through the wide harbor gate and climbed onto one of the ice gliders where the wounded were convalescing.

Lambi's hand played with the stone in his pocket. He would not have the chance to find the right time to ask, not now. "'Twas just a redhead," he grumbled. "Should have tried my luck with a blond." Then he crossed the hall to the sled with the red tarpaulin. It was the last one they had loaded that morning. Ragnar, one of his men, sat on the driver's seat. In his old life, Ragnar had been a tree feller, but as long as Lambi could remember, Ragnar had never missed an opportunity to get into a fight. His scarred face and broad nose, broken numerous times, told more than all the stories.

"Don't even think about taking off, you old whoremonger. With what's on that sled, you could buy every house of pleasure in Gonthabu and screw away the rest of your life for free."

Ragnar smiled conspiratorially. "That's why we chose you to be jarl, Lambi. You always have the best ideas. I'd never have come up with this one."

From the corner of his eye, Lambi saw Alfadas hurrying toward the sled. That was all he needed! As much as he liked Alfadas, there were things that the elvenjarl would never understand, and things he didn't have to know about in the first place.

"Take off, Ragnar!"

"But—"

"Drive, damn it, if your jarl orders you to!"

Alfadas was waving his arms at them.

"Get going. Right now," Lambi hissed, then turned to Alfadas, waved back, and smiled.

"But he wants me to stay," Ragnar objected.

"And *I* want you to leave, you cretinous oaf!"

Ragnar put down the reins. "The duke's saved my hide twice. If he wants something from me, you can shove your orders up your ass!"

Too late. Alfadas was at the sled. Lambi could see that he knew.

The duke turned back the tarpaulin. He ran his hand over the gold as if that was the only way he could believe what he was looking at. "So it's true," he said softly. When he looked at Lambi, he had infinite disappointment in his eyes.

Lambi would have understood if Alfadas had started yelling at him, or even better, if he had punched him in the face. He was used to things like that. But the look in his eyes . . . he could not bear that. He looked away, ashamed of himself.

But I'm in the right, he thought angrily. "It's one of the goddamned doors," he finally said. "If you have gold doors, you shouldn't be surprised if one of 'em goes missing occasionally."

"They're our allies. Our hosts."

"Yeah. And we're the nice kind of guests who stick out our necks for them, and what do we get for it? Almost half the men who came here to Albenmark with you are dead, and they *still* adore you. Alfadas, who lies in the muck with us. Alfadas, who saves our hides when we're up to our necks in shit. Alfadas this. Alfadas that! I'm sick of it!"

"So you decided to rob the Normirga of a few of their doors? What are you trying to tell me?" the duke said harshly.

"What I have to say to you is not meant for Ragnar's ears. Come with me!" Lambi pulled Alfadas away with him to an empty dock. He'd been stewing for weeks, and it was high time to clear the air.

"You blind 'em with your fame, but in reality you don't give a sweet shit about them. You're the elvenjarl, the duke, guest at the tables of kings. They love you! And here you are, slogging through the mud and muck with 'em, risking your skin for 'em, and because such a fine gentleman as yourself does all that for 'em, they feel more important. Then your skald comes and writes pretty verses that turn all of them who've died into heroes. But truth be told: they don't matter to you at all!"

"You're drunk, Lambi. You know I do anything and everything for my men."

Lambi laughed angrily. "Of course you do! And I also know what you don't do. You never think how things will be for 'em when they get home again. Do you think a hero's saga is going to fill a belly? Back in the Fjordlands, a few moons from now, they'll be the same scum of the earth they were when they landed in your army. What are you going to do about that, Duke?"

Alfadas looked at him, deeply hurt. Now it was his turn to avoid the other's eyes.

"You're not even thinking about going back, are you? You've decided you're going to perish here. That's up to you. But don't expect your men to do the same. Fine, call me a thief because I've pinched a few golden doors from passages nobody ever uses. We only took 'em off walls where nobody's going to fight. In a few hours, the whole mountain's going to belong to the trolls anyway, and then nobody's going to miss the doors anymore. I don't know who told you what we got up to while you were fighting beside the elves and they had us breaking rocks. Frankly, I don't care. Everybody knew it. I've seen to it that everyone who makes it home to the Fjordlands goes back rich."

Alfadas raised his hands in surrender. "Enough. I've understood, Jarl. Maybe I really am looking for death, but I shouldn't take you and the others down with me." He took a white stone from his pocket. "My stone. Take it. I saw what you drew. You can go back."

Lambi slapped the stone out of his hand. "D'you think I'm not good enough to die here with all the hero volunteers? When it comes to dying, we're all the same, you . . . you puffed-up—"

Alfadas's punch came completely without warning. Lambi would never have thought the wiry son of a bitch could hit so hard. The fist to the gut was followed by a hook to his chin.

"Come and get the jarl, Ragnar." The duke looked sad, the goddamned bastard!

Lambi shook his head, dazed. He could not believe that two punches could incapacitate him so badly. *Must be the head wound,* he thought. He felt hands lift him up. Ragnar laid him on the sled and wrapped a blanket around his shoulders.

"Sorry." Alfadas was at his side, pressing the white stone into his fist. "You're right, Lambi. I'm no longer the right leader for you. Until now, it was good to have a duke who protected his men in battle whenever he could. Now they need a man to get them home in one piece. A man like you."

Lambi tried to get up but immediately collapsed again. He felt as sick as if he'd spent an entire night on cheap wine. "You can't—"

Alfadas gave Ragnar a sign. "Drive! Take him to Dalla. She should take another look at his head."

With a jerk, the sled began to move. Through the blanket, Lambi felt the cold gold of the stolen door.

Alfadas remained behind, in the center of the harbor hall. He drew his sword and raised it in salute. "Good-bye, Lambi. May Luth spin you a long thread."

A high-pitched horn sounded from the last gate. The trolls were returning. Alfadas turned away and took his place among the host of the lost.

WATER, AT LEAST

Sweat trickled from Gondoran's face and neck. He smoothed the wall of the tunnel, then wiped his hand nervously across his forehead. The heavy circlet pressed uncomfortably into his skin.

Although the master of waters was wearing thick felt boots, he felt as if the soles of his feet were standing in an open fire. He was far too close! The air was stuffy down there, the small lantern dangling overhead woefully inadequate. Certain death lurked a few fingerbreadths below his feet. *What better place from which to fight the trolls?* he thought grimly. Right now, he would much rather be galloping across the wide plains of Windland on Orimedes's back or taking part in one of the centaurs' drinking orgies. He had not been able to say good-bye to Orimedes.

He stooped forward inside the narrow pipe, which rose above him almost vertically through the rock. His fingers prodded at the hot floor. *The white pumice should shield me from the heat better than this,* he thought. *I must be very close now.* He had to be careful. He opened his mind to the power of the Stoneformer's Eye. Then he swept a little of the pumice aside. The floor vibrated beneath his fingers, and somewhere far above, a crunching sound emanated from the rock. Dust and small splinters of stone rained down. Since morning, low tremors had been shaking the mountain every few heartbeats.

I must be mad, Gondoran thought. No one crept through a narrow water pipe inside a mountain when a tremor could—would!—happen at any moment. But these hours of life were not really his. By rights, he should not have survived the caress of the prickly shroud. He should be lying with his dead comrades in the mangrove swamps of Vahan Calyd. No prince should ever abandon his people, but staying would have meant betraying his queen.

Gondoran was certain that the only reason he had survived was because he still had something important to do, something to see through to its end, and when he'd seen the fountains of steam shooting from the high pillars of the Skyhall, he knew immediately where his task lay. Even with a weapon in his hand, he would be of little use in battle against the trolls. He was a poor shot with a crossbow, and the trolls would have laughed at the stones in his sling. But he knew something about water, in all its forms.

"Hurry up, Gondoran!" Coming through the narrow pipe, the young elf woman's voice sounded fractured and harsh. Fahlyn had been assisting him ever since the war council had allowed him to enter the system of pipes inside the mountain.

It required some courage to crawl through the narrow tunnels while the mountain quaked. Fahlyn was extraordinarily brave. Gondoran had not understood what Ollowain had against her. He would not accept her among the defenders of Phylangan, although she was part of his father's bodyguard and was no doubt a good fighter. She was one of the ancient Farangel clan.

The holde recalled his childhood, the wonderful days spent with his uncle. The old man had often talked for hours as they poled their way through the peaceful darkness of the cisterns of Vahan Calyd. His stories had been about the Normirga, and how, in their years as refugees, they had lived with the holdes. When those elves from the far north came, the mangrove swamps had been a place that none but the holdes, among the races of the Albenkin, truly knew or appreciated. It was the Normirga who had wrested that magnificent city from the dark coastal swamp—the city where, every twenty-eight years, the Albenkin came as pilgrims from every corner of their world to witness Emerelle, most eminent of the Normirga, once again being chosen as their queen.

Since the days in which the foundations of Vahan Calyd had been laid, the Farangel clan had been close allies of the holdes. From the Farangel had come many of those who built the canals and cisterns. Gondoran was proud, after all these centuries, to be the first master of waters to work with the Farangel again. *The circle closes,* he thought.

Together, he and Fahlyn had studied the plans of the hidden waterways. They both knew Landoran's secret, knew what was happening deep beneath their feet. They had used some of the large main pipes to channel scalding fumes out to the mountain flanks, thus saving the Skyhall from filling with boiling steam. Their work had also eased the work of the magic weavers in the Hall of Fire because they had been able to relieve some of the pressure that was building up constantly inside the rock.

Again, Gondoran ran his hand over his sweaty brow. He knew what the defenders above him were going through. Sometimes, he heard far-off echoes of battle, although there at the bottom of the riser, he was almost a mile from the Skyhall. The evening before, until late in the night, while the defenders had been engaged in a desperate battle farther south, he had worked at the pale rock of the final section of the main connecting tunnel. He had softened the stone, then pushed his long rod up through it until it reached the large pipe hidden above. Days before, he had isolated the pipe from the water network and connected it instead to other pipes that led deep into the earth. Now the hour had come for him to fight! He had pushed more than a hundred holes through the stone that connected to the main pipe.

The rock quaked around him. A shower of stone fragments rattled down through the riser.

"Come, Gondoran! It's time," Fahlyn called from far above. Faintly, he heard the echo of the single blast from a horn.

The holde reached for the safety rope and jerked on it. Fahlyn would believe that he had begun his ascent. "Go ahead to the well shaft. I'll join you soon," he shouted back.

He was sorry that their work together had to end with a lie, but today was the day on which his hourglass ran out. The time he had borrowed was due for repayment. The holde blew out the flame of the lantern. He was glad he'd survived the shroud. Looking at the situation most generously, at least it was his element that killed him. For the master of waters, that was only right.

He leaned forward. The power of the ruby flowed in his hands. The pumice beneath his feet softened. He reached for the long staff leaning beside him. For a heartbeat, he waited and listened. Then he heard it. Three blasts of a horn. The signal he'd agreed with Ollowain.

Gondoran stabbed the staff downward, thrusting it through the soft stone. Searing steam rose to meet him.

THE OTHER SIDE OF CHILDHOOD

Ollowain touched his wounded cheek. Blood ran down his neck. He was getting tired. The day before, the blow would not have grazed him. He thought of the enormous troll with his club studded with splinters of obsidian. The bastard had almost knocked his head off, but he'd managed to duck clear just in time.

Two hundred paces away, the trolls gathered behind the protection offered by their large wooden shields. One more charge, and they would be victorious. Ollowain mustered those still standing, the final line of defense, among them: Alfadas, Mag, and two more humans. One kobold, whose name he did not know, was leaning, exhausted, on his crossbow. Beside him stood Silwyna. She had set a new arrow on her bowstring and was waiting for a gap to appear in the trolls' wall of shields. One of the swordsmen from Landoran's bodyguard also remained. They were too few to continue the fight.

The swordmaster looked at the long row of openings in the wall of the tunnel. The time had come to accept Gondoran's offer. Against all likelihood, they had managed to repel two attacks by the trolls, but they did not have anything to stop a third—except for the holde!

The last of those escaping would be far out on the ice of the high plain by now. The trolls would not catch up with them. At least, not today. Ollowain took the silver horn from his belt and put it to his lips. Three long blasts were his valediction to Phylangan.

"What was that?" Alfadas asked tiredly. "An invitation to the trolls?"

"No. A call to our last ally." He turned to the others. "Retreat! Back to the Sky Harbor. Run as fast as you can. Our friend will unleash the dragon's breath."

Before anyone could ask, a distant, ominous whistling could be heard. Ollowain jumped down from the barricade. "Run!" he ordered. "Take the small ice gliders left behind."

The whistling turned into a snarling hiss. His companions ran. The sword-master snatched up the kobold and threw him over his shoulder. He would apologize later for the discourtesy.

The trolls broke out in roars of triumph. Ollowain heard the heavy stamping of their feet.

"What's going on, Commander?" the kobold asked fearfully.

Ollowain did not have the breath to answer. His companions were a short distance ahead of him. Silwyna looked back, and he saw her eyes widen. The snarl reached the tunnel. Ollowain did not look back. Shrill screams rang in his ears, screams of death.

The kobold shrieked, "Run! Run! The dragon's breath is catching up."

Ollowain leaped over the twisted remnants of the Sky Gate. "Stay left," he shouted. "Run to the docks! Do not run straight ahead!"

Beyond the door, he turned to the side and ran around the white-painted wall of the cave. The screams behind him had ceased, and the only sound now was the menacing hiss. A thick white jet of steam exploded through the destruction of the Sky Gate. His father's bodyguard was caught by it and let out a short-lived scream. Only then did Ollowain realize he had called his warning in the language of the humans.

The others had escaped. They were running toward the ice gliders tied up at the docks.

Slowly, the steam spread in the expanse of the Sky Harbor. The floor of the harbor hall was covered in ice, and the breath of winter entered through the wide door that opened on the far side onto the high plain of Carandamon.

Ollowain put the kobold down. The little warrior's beard was covered with fine silver droplets of water. An uncomfortably warm blast struck Ollowain's face and burned on his wounded cheek.

"Thank you, Commander, for ignoring all protocol and throwing me over your shoulder like a sack of flour."

Ollowain smiled tiredly. "Who knows how many times your crossbow saved my life? You owe me nothing."

The kobold shook his head defiantly. "I owe you a life, Commander. You can call in the debt anytime you want. My name is Murgim. You'll find me—"

"On one of the gliders!" Ollowain said, interrupting the kobold. A thick fog engulfed them. The little fighter blurred to a vague outline. "Stay close to the wall, then you can't miss the docks."

"Aren't you coming with us, Commander?" Murgim called after him.

Ollowain felt his way back along the wall. The rock was slippery with warm condensation. He was not a commander anymore, Ollowain thought, and despite their defeat, he felt an endless sense of relief. Phylangan was lost. He had fought to the very end, but the fortress could not be saved. Now he would do what he should have done long before.

He found the stairway he'd descended once before and ran down into the depths of the mountain. There were no guards to stop him now. The stone forest was deserted, and the fountain among the columns had ceased to spray. The ground beneath his feet vibrated constantly. It was like walking on ice about to break up beneath the spring sun.

A hot, trembling stream of air flowed from the entrance to the Hall of Fire like liquid glass. The stream drove flurries of large flakes of ash before it that danced madly like black butterflies. Ollowain's throat was bone dry. Sweat poured from his face and back and burned in his wounds. The air smelled of stone dust, and something bitter coated his tongue.

The hot air scorched his cheeks as he stepped into the hall. There were less than fifty Normirga still there, crouching on the floor. The benches along the wall were empty. They had no reserves left in their battle with the mountain.

Ollowain moved cautiously between magic weavers to the center of the hall. No one took any notice of him.

Lyndwyn still kneeled on the golden disk. She looked as if she had not moved an inch in all the weeks she'd been there. Her face was pale, her features silent and grave. The first strands of silver shimmered in her black hair.

The swordmaster kneeled before her. He laid his hands gently on her shoulders.

"Do you hear me?" he asked softly.

Lyndwyn's face showed no reaction. Her eyes stared without seeing.

"It's over." He stroked her silvering hair tenderly. "We did all we could, and now we have to go."

Lyndwyn did not hear him. Ollowain thought of what his father had told him about the chorus of the magic weavers. What would happen if he broke the keystone out of its arch, if he simply took the woman he loved away? Would she perish in flames if she woke from her trance too quickly? He did not know. But he knew what would happen if he just stayed there at her side. The trolls would come. Flush with victory, they would murder them all.

Ollowain lifted the sorceress gently in his arms. He carried her protectively, pressed close to his chest.

The spell was broken! All the magic weavers looked up. A young woman close to Ollowain burst into flames.

"Traitor!" A slim figure rose from among the sorcerers. His father.

Ollowain did not stop. Unwavering, he moved toward the entrance that led to the stone forest.

"We could still have beaten the mountain," his father shouted accusingly. "You've made all our sacrifice worth nothing."

The swordmaster said nothing. He had bowed to his father's insanity for far too long.

"I curse you, my son! I curse you! Take her! It won't help you. Lyndwyn knows where she belongs. You cannot possess her again. Even now, she is trying to banish the disharmony from the great song. You! You will never lie with her again. That is my curse!"

Ollowain tried to close his mind to the words. His father had no power over him anymore. His magic was bound up in the song.

The magic weavers lowered their heads again, and silence fell over the Hall of Fire. Even the distant rumbling had fallen silent. Only the sound of his own footsteps accompanied the swordmaster.

With Lyndwyn in his arms, he crossed the stone forest. The ground was vibrating more intensely now. Fine dust drizzled from the golden branches that curved along the arches of the ceiling. Ollowain kissed her and whispered endearments, but she woke no more than did Emerelle.

Desolately, he carried Lyndwyn up the long stairway. He knew he would not be able to make it back to the Sky Harbor. No ice glider would be waiting there for them. The trolls would have overrun the harbor long ago. Still, he turned to the west. And then the distant rumbling returned. The ground beneath his feet bucked, and a fretwork of fine cracks appeared along the passage.

Ollowain began to run. Here and there, he heard heavy footfalls and the guttural shouts of trolls. Finally, he reached a stairway that wound its way upward along the glowing face of the cliff, high above the lake in the Skyhall. The broad marble steps were strewn with rubble, and hot air swirled around him as he sped upward, the cliff rising on one side, dropping away on the other.

Far below him stretched the Skyhall. Many of its trees were burning. Where the lake had once been, fountains of liquid fire now sprayed from beneath. Hundreds of trolls were fleeing across the Mahdan Falah to a golden arch of light rising at its end.

Higher and higher shot the fire fountains in the lake. For himself and Lyndwyn, Ollowain knew, there was only one chance: the portal before which, as a boy, he had so often stood, but through which he had never been allowed to pass.

The marble steps rocked. Ollowain looked back. A section of the stairway had broken away, and far below, the Mahdan Falah was descending toward the fiery lake. Two of its monumental pylons had cracked and failed.

Slowly, as if bowing in farewell, the white bridge leaned down toward the fire. The trolls slipped by the dozen from its smooth stone until, finally, it was empty. Flawless. It had shaken off the intruders and shone now like freshly fallen snow.

"You'll die with us, little elf!" A dust-covered troll with a long bloody graze on his forehead was climbing the stairs after him.

Ollowain began to run. His legs hurt, and his strength was almost at an end. Closer and closer came the heavy slapping of the troll's bare feet on the marble.

At the end of the stairs was a small grotto. Stalactites shimmered inside it, oily black. There had once been a crystal-clear pool inside the grotto, but now a wide crack gaped in the cave floor. The water had disappeared.

Ollowain's breath came in pants. The air was filled with fine, stony dust that burned his eyes and parched his mouth. Every breath was agony. Just a few more steps to the forbidden door. Half blinded, he forced himself onward. Once he locked the door behind them, they would be saved.

Finally, he reached the concealed corner beyond which the door lay. It was gone, smashed out of the rock!

The troll was close behind him. Gently, Ollowain laid Lyndwyn on a wide bench carved from the rock and bedded her head on dusty silk cushions. Then he turned and drew his sword.

The troll, too, seemed exhausted. He glowered at Ollowain from red-rimmed eyes. "Wretched elves! You couldn't just let us have it, could you? You'd rather destroy Kingstor than lose it to us." Swinging his axe wide, the troll attacked.

The swordmaster tried to duck clear, but at the last second, the troll changed the direction of his swing. The broad blade of the stone axe missed Ollowain's shoulder by a hair. He slipped on rubble, but, half sprawling, he managed to jump clear of his enemy.

"Then I'll kill your woman first," the troll grumbled, clomping toward the bench where Lyndwyn lay.

Ollowain tried to shout, but only a croak escaped his raw throat. He leaped forward. His sword sliced into the troll's arm.

"Nasty little man."

The troll's elbow caught Ollowain in the chest. He was thrown off his feet and fell back hard against a rock.

His enemy was after him instantly. Dazed, the swordmaster threw himself to one side. Too slow! This time the troll's axe did not miss his shoulder! His chain mail tunic gave way. He felt bone splinter, and bright sparks shot before his eyes.

The troll leaned down to lift him, and Ollowain swung his sword up. The troll jumped back, straightening quickly to avoid the blade. There was a crunch. Too tired to attack again, the swordmaster waited for the final blow to fall.

But the troll did not move. Blood poured from beneath his chin.

Ollowain blinked. *So the mountain beat you after all,* he thought. The point of a stalactite jutted from the troll's chin—the stone spike had pierced his skull cleanly as he jumped up.

Ollowain pulled himself to his feet and staggered over to Lyndwyn. She still lay in a trance. Ollowain's left arm hung uselessly. He felt nothing in it. Blood flowed darkly from the jagged wound.

With a groan, he tore a broad strip of cloth from his tattered tunic and stuffed it into the wound. He pushed his sword into his belt and lifted Lyndwyn with his good arm. Just a few more steps.

A massive jolt ran through the mountain. Stalactites broke from the cave ceiling and clattered to the floor. The dead troll slipped from the stone spike impaling him.

Ollowain crossed the threshold that had been forbidden to him for so long. Whoever took that step moved beyond their childhood. Blinking, he looked around inside the narrow stone chamber. He knew it only from stories he'd heard. Two sleds with high-curved runners stood on the floor of the chamber before a tunnel mouth. Here, in solemn procession, were led those who were to face their final test.

Ollowain lifted Lyndwyn in front of him onto the first of the sleds. Then he pushed off with a foot. Steel grated over stone. The sled tilted forward in the tunnel.

The swordmaster jammed his feet behind the runners, and the sled raced down the tunnel toward a spot of light that rapidly grew bigger. Then they were surrounded by brilliant, blinding light. The sled made a jump and came down hard on a steep ice field.

Wind burned against Ollowain's cheek. He could hardly see a thing. Desperately, he held on to Lyndwyn and did what he could to steer the sled. The most treacherous rocks, he knew, had been removed from this part of the mountainside. All he had to do was keep the sled on course. If they kept going more or less straight, they would be carried many miles out into open country. The trial by ice began with this sled run. Young elves whose magical powers were thought strong enough to protect them from the cold and defy the elements began their journeys here. If they made it back across glaciers and crevasses to the Skyhall on the other side of the mountain on their own, then from that day forward, they were seen as adults among the Normirga.

Ollowain let his chin fall onto his chest. Lyndwyn's hair whipped into his face. It smelled of stone dust. The bright slope blurred before his eyes. Then there was just light, the grinding of the runners, and the song of the wind above the cliffs.

BENEATH THE TREE OF ASH

She danced on the warm wind. Far below her were flames that waned and vanished when her gaze met them. Voices murmured in her head, whispering to her, telling her to smother the flames, but try as she might, the fire stayed. And yes, it grew stronger. The flames came higher, and now her dress was burning. Someone tore it from her body. A shadowy figure. Strong arms embraced her. The fire moved far away. Cold breath grazed her cheeks.

Lyndwyn blinked. She was lying in snow. Something menacing was close by. She hardly dared to breathe. How did she get there? She remembered the Hall of Fire, the magic weavers' chorus . . . and the one night with Ollowain.

Something translucent glided past. Snuffling, ravenous. Lyndwyn sensed the Albenstone against her breast. Nothing could defeat her. She stretched and sat up. Snow fell from her dress. She found herself on a mountainside. Close beside her, the runner of a sled jutted from a snowdrift.

When she became aware of a distant rumbling, she looked up. She was at the foot of a mountain. Miles away towered a dark-gray column of billowing smoke, its top spreading like the crown of a tree, a deep-red glow flickering along its base. The wind dragged the smoke westward. Points of light shot upward through the smoke, only to tumble to earth again in long arcs. Where they landed on the mountainside, bright steam flew skyward. The summit had changed. It looked wider, and the snow had vanished beneath a layer of gray ash. Lyndwyn saw a stream of red spilling down the southern slope of the mountain, and she felt the earth tremble beneath her several times.

She recalled the choir. She sensed that all her singers were silenced now, forever.

How did she get there? She looked around. Farther down the slope lay a figure, doubled over, half buried in the snow. On unsteady legs, she made her way down. Her knees hurt with every step she took.

The long blond hair. The white tunic! Lyndwyn began to run, stumbled in the deep snow, pulled herself up, and tried again. It was Ollowain. He had come for her.

With trembling hands, she held his face, felt his cheeks like ice. One shoulder had suffered a deep wound. She laid a hand on his forehead, closed her eyes, felt her way into his body. His heart beat weakly, yet steadily, but he had lost a lot of blood. His left collarbone was shattered, his shoulder blade cleft, and one rib broken.

She gave him, her beloved, warmth, more than the amulet around his neck could. Then she reached for the Albenstone's power. With the strength of her mind, she healed the bones and rejoined ruined muscle. But she could not replace all the blood he had lost.

His heartbeat was stronger now. He lay in a deep sleep. Lyndwyn put his head on her lap.

"Ah. How moving it is to witness the bloom of young love."

Lyndwyn started—the voice was inside her head.

"It is me, Granddaughter. Shahondin. No need to fear."

"Where are you?" Lyndwyn looked around in surprise. Apart from herself and Ollowain, there was no one to be seen on the expanse of mountainside.

"Promise me you won't be frightened." The voice sounded immeasurably sad now. *"The trolls took me prisoner. They have done something terrible to me, my girl. I am not the grandfather you knew before."*

"Prove you're my grandfather! Tell me something only he could know."

"Wise girl. Why should you trust a stranger's voice? You were always clever. Do you remember in the pavilion by the sea, how we first composed the bird of light? The moon stood low over the bay when you made the bird fly for the very first time. You were still a little girl. Your first attempt, admittedly, was a little unbirdlike. Its wings were like sheets of parchment, and its head was just a ball."

Lyndwyn could only smile. Yes, she remembered that first bird. She had been very young, just a child. Afterward, Shahondin had taught her how important it was to look at things very closely, for the form of nothing that lived was random. "Show yourself, Grandfather."

"Please, child, do not let yourself be swayed by how I look. The trolls have treated me monstrously. But I sense the power that surrounds you. It is a power that can change everything. You can bring me back."

Lyndwyn had steeled herself for anything imaginable, but the thing that now rose from the snow was something no one could truly prepare themselves for. The huge ghostly dog with its blood-red eyes had nothing in common with her grandfather beyond his memories.

"Don't be scared, my child. Touch my spirit. Feel that it is me!"

The creature opened itself to her, and what Lyndwyn found inside it was familiar, even the darkness in Shahondin's soul. That was the only part—his dark side—that he kept shielded from her, and though she knew it was there, it was not a part she ever wanted to look into.

"Summon me back. Remember the man I was. With the power of your thoughts, you can return to me everything the trolls stole. Think about the grandfather with whom you spent so many hours studying. Use the Albenstone! It has the power to bring me back."

Lyndwyn focused her mind on those distant days in Arkadien, on the trips they took together, she and her strict but learned grandfather. She thought of the way he furrowed his brow when she had not been able to follow his reasoning, and of his laugh, as clear as a bell, when her spell casting proved too unskilled. His laughter had vanished over the years, and there came a time when she found secrets of her own that were forever hidden from him.

The magic weaver sensed the Albenstone warm against her breast. In her mind, she created a spark of bright light, and she made it dance just as she had when she created the bird of light in Vahan Calyd. At first, its contours were ill-defined. Then she wove thread on thread, tearing away at the essence of the ghost-dog. Lyndwyn finally stole away its life-light and wove it into the newly fashioned form of her grandfather.

When she had completed her work, the light paled. Shahondin stood before her, naked in the snow. He lifted his hands and ran them over his body disbelievingly. "A miracle!" His voice sounded strange, deeper, and the words were as slurred as if spoken by a drunkard. "It seems I'll have to learn how to speak again." He reached out toward her with one hand. "What power! Now give me the Albenstone. We'll use it to drive out the trolls."

She took a step backward. The deep, demanding voice sounded unearthly. Something had gone wrong with her spell, it seemed.

"You will not defy your own grandfather! The stone! We wanted it in Vahan Calyd, or have you forgotten? It belongs in the hands of a real magic weaver, not those of a girl. You—" Suddenly, he clutched at his chest. Something inside him had begun to move. His ribs pushed forward, curving outward. Beneath the skin of his belly appeared something like a face pressed against thin silk fabric.

Shahondin screamed. He pressed both hands to his stomach. There was blood on his lips. Something dark was pushing its way out of his body. His ribs made a creaking, tearing sound, bending apart, shredding muscle and skin. A dark dog's head covered with gleaming black scales pushed its way out of his middle. Shahondin collapsed in the snow. Paws with long talons emerged, tearing apart the body Lyndwyn had created.

An icy chill emanated from the dog-thing, so cold it would make even winter shiver.

"Don't be afraid, my child."

Again she heard the voice inside her head. It sounded lecherous now, and false.

"An accident. A small mishap, no more. Your spell was imperfect, like it was with the first bird you created. Give me the stone. We can change that. We can change everything."

Lyndwyn shouted a word of power. A flaming magic circle flared on the snow. She'd let herself be deceived. Whatever it was that had been born from her grandfather's body, it was no longer Shahondin. This creature was not meant to be!

She thought of her dance above the fire. The dream. The choir of magic. She thought of the heat. She had woven her thoughts of the heat into the body she'd created.

The dog's head lifted, leaning back.

"You can't—"

She closed herself off from the voice inside her. She carried the Albenstone! *I can master any spell, any magic,* she thought angrily.

The black creature seemed to want to crawl back into Shahondin's ruined body. It whined like a pup, then abruptly began to glow from the inside out, like a dark silk lantern with a candle burning inside it. Flames shot from its snout. The body that Lyndwyn had created disappeared in a blinding flash. All that remained were a few flakes of ash, carried down the mountainside on the wind.

Exhausted, she sank into the snow. Had that creature really been her grandfather? It had known so much about her, but it was not the Shahondin with which she had spent her childhood. She watched the flakes of ash drift away. Far down the mountain, something moved. Trolls. They must have seen the light.

Lyndwyn looked to where her beloved still lay. It would be hours yet before he awoke, and even then, he would be too weak. She did not have the strength to carry him, and there was nowhere to hide. Two hours, perhaps. Then the trolls would be there. Unless . . .

Sadly, she leaned down to Ollowain and kissed him lightly on the lips. "You came to save me from the fire, my white knight. Now I will save you." She pressed the Albenstone into his right hand. She had created a body for her grandfather and destroyed it again, and now her powers were at their lowest ebb. But there was another way to save the man she loved.

She stood up. A final, melancholy look to Ollowain and then she turned away, toward the trolls.

MY NAME IS BIRGA

Lyndwyn was tied to a large shield that had been half buried in the snow. A leather sling was wrapped tightly around her neck, and her arms and legs were spread wide and bound with straps. The shield stank of blood and excrement. One of her eyes was swollen closed, and yet, so far, she had gotten off lightly. So far.

Spread out on the snow close to the shield lay a light-colored hide, and strewn across it were small knives of all kinds, primitive blades of bone and flint. Dark stains betrayed their purpose.

A second shield was rammed into the snow opposite Lyndwyn. The masked shaman stood beside it, talking in adamant tones to a bent old woman who supported herself on a stick.

"I am telling you, Skanga, she's different from the others they've brought me. I sense her power when I touch her. If she were not exhausted, three simple scouts would never have been able to bring her in." The troll woman in the repulsive mask looked across at Lyndwyn, who was certain that the shaman intended her to hear every word.

The ancient hag was not letting herself be swayed by the shaman's words, however. Lyndwyn realized that it was the old woman who had the final say.

"You go today, Birga. At dusk. Soon, Orgrim will reach a village close to a large Albenstar, so you can join him easily. He needs you at his side. He can't be allowed to do anything stupid when he meets with that overbearing bastard from Mordrock. You will watch him for me!"

The troll woman with the mask snorted. "Orgrim has looked after himself well enough so far."

"Don't misunderstand me, Birga. I am not asking you to go. I expect you to."

"But this elf"—the shaman pointed at Lyndwyn—"she matters, I'm sure of it. It would be wise not to rush things with her. She can—"

"Then see to it that you get your answers before sunset. With Kingstor lost forever and the pass to Carandamon blocked, there isn't much your little elf could tell us that matters. Perhaps . . ." The older troll shrugged. "Do what you want with her, but do it quickly." With that, she left.

The shaman muttered something to herself that Lyndwyn did not understand. Then she went to the hide on which the knives lay. Bending down, she chose a dark stone blade with a slight curve.

"Are you thirsty?" the troll asked abruptly.

"No." Lyndwyn had no interest in finding out what she might be offered to drink.

"I'm sorry that everything has to happen so quickly. I apologize for that." The giant woman straightened up. She stroked Lyndwyn's face with her bandaged hands. The stained rags reeked of decay. "Pretty skin. You elves have the most perfect skin of all. So very soft . . ."

The shaman was standing close enough for Lyndwyn to feel her breath on her face. She stank of sour milk.

"I know that you are a powerful magic weaver. For now, somehow, you're spent, but you will soon recover. Maybe I should tear your tongue out and blind you to protect myself." The troll woman leaned forward and sniffed at her. Lyndwyn wished she could see behind the mask to read her face.

"Very good, little elf. You're starting to smell like fear. Tell me, how did you get out on that mountainside?"

"Magic."

"I don't believe you. You don't look foolish enough to conjure yourself onto the wrong side of a mountain. Your kind always tries to lie to me at the start, but I'll make it easier for you to choose the path of truth." She reached for Lyndwyn's right hand and spread her little finger apart from the others.

Lyndwyn bucked and tried to pull free, but she could not fight the troll's strength.

"My name is Birga. Conversation tends to improve when those who talk know each other's name. Will you tell me yours?"

"Lyndwyn."

"That's pretty." The shaman raised the knife. "I'm going to hurt you a little now. It's not a big thing. I would just like you to be better able to imagine everything else I could do to you." Carefully, she sliced the skin of Lyndwyn's little finger with the knife. As she did so, she took care that Lyndwyn could see clearly everything she was doing. The blade moved from the pad of the finger all the way to where the finger sprouted from the palm, where the shaman made a second cut that encircled the base of the finger like a thin, bloody ring.

Lyndwyn felt ill. "I did not get onto the mountainside with magic." She could reveal that much. It was no secret.

"Oh, I know that." The shaman's voice was friendly. "We'll talk more about that soon. Give me just a moment." She pushed the narrow stone blade carefully beneath Lyndwyn's skin and began to loosen the skin from the flesh of the finger beneath.

Lyndwyn writhed, but it was impossible to break free of the troll woman's iron grip.

"Don't squirm so, little one." With a tug, she pulled off the skin covering Lyndwyn's little finger. "Look at your tendons and muscles. You can see them so clearly, and it's hardly bleeding at all. It takes a lot of practice to do such neat work." The shaman picked up a bone knife and impaled the small strip of skin to the shield standing in the snow opposite, so that Lyndwyn had a good view of it.

Nausea washed over Lyndwyn. Her finger burned as if it were being held in a flame. She could not bring herself to look at it. *You can get through this,* she berated herself mentally. *You can save Ollowain if you do!*

Birga caressed Lyndwyn's face with one bandaged hand. A little fresh blood shimmered on the ragged cloth. "You have no idea what a boon your skin is. Just to look at you elves . . . one can never tell if you count your age in decades or in centuries." She sighed. "You wanted to tell me something about the mountainside?"

Lyndwyn said now that she had escaped the mountain through a tunnel. How else could Ollowain have gotten out onto the mountainside with her?

The shaman nodded, satisfied. "Let's move on, shall we? Tell me what kind of magic weaver you are. There's something different about you."

Lyndwyn wondered if she had the courage to bite off her own tongue. She could not breathe a word about the Albenstone, whatever Birga did to her.

"I can already see that things are getting more difficult." Birga looked to the wooden shield to which the skin of Lyndwyn's finger was pinned. Then she reached up to her mask. "Do you know that this was made from the face of a whore who tried to deceive my king? She was a very pretty woman. Pretty and stupid!" Again, she stroked Lyndwyn's face. "You are pretty, too. Are you also stupid?"

"I helped the magic weavers of the Normirga keep the fire beneath the mountain in check," Lyndwyn blurted.

The troll woman laughed. "Well, that wasn't so hard to admit, was it? Now you shall know a secret about me." She lifted the mask so that Lyndwyn could see her face. The merciless winter light revealed a mass of shapeless flesh that reminded her of molten wax—no, more of a dripping candle. Were they warts? Fleshy growths, rows of lumps and bulges covered in gray skin. They rose from Birga's eyelids, turning her nose into a formless clump, and even her lips were lumpy and uneven. In places, the growths grew on other swellings, making parts of her face look unnaturally swollen and thick. Some of the lumps seemed to have tied themselves off and now held on only by the thinnest threads of skin. Birga stroked Lyndwyn's cheek. "You have been beautiful your entire life. You will never appreciate what it means to look like this." She stretched the mask back over her face. "Now, let's discuss your queen. Do you know where she's run off to?"

"I am not Normirga," Lyndwyn replied evasively.

"Ah. I can see we're starting to touch on hidden truths." Birga took her knife and sliced Lyndwyn's dress open from neckline to waist. She pushed the fabric back almost tenderly. "There's something fragile about you, my pretty thing. It may be that you have not lain with men very often. We have that in common." She probed the soft flesh of Lyndwyn's breasts with her fingers, and ran her hands over the arching ribs and down to her navel.

"One finger is easy enough to hide, Lyndwyn. It may even increase your fascination—the elf who always wears one glove. What other parts do you think you'll be able to hide from the gaze of men? Or would you perhaps like to tell me something about the queen?"

Cold sweat prickled Lyndwyn's face. "I am not Normirga," she repeated.

"Well, yes. You said that already."

Birga raised the knife.

LIKE A TALE FROM CHILDHOOD DAYS

Asla peered into Isleif's frost-reddened face. He was feverish, and his breath stank of liquor. He'd been found at the gate of the palisade that protected Firnstayn.

The gate was locked at sundown every day. But early that evening, smoke had been spotted rising far to the north, and a sentry had therefore been stationed at the gate.

Isleif was half frozen and as weak as a child when they brought him in. Delirious, he'd been speaking brokenly about monsters from the mountains. Now, wrapped in blankets, he crouched by Asla's fire. Her house was the biggest in the village, so it seemed the reasonable place to go. Almost all the village's inhabitants were crowded around him.

"Giants, they are . . . bigger than cave bears . . . ," the farmer stammered. "They burned my farmhouse down." He looked at Asla. "Have you any more to drink? You know . . . to warm the soul."

"He's already drunk," someone murmured behind Asla. "Everyone knows he drinks like a leaky bucket. He probably knocked a candle over and burned his house down by himself, and now he's telling stories."

"I seen what I seen!" Isleif rose unsteadily to his feet. "They're as big as cave bears!"

"Maybe a cave bear really has come down from the mountains?" said Kalf. "Sometimes they wake up in midwinter."

"There were lots of 'em . . . a whole herd . . . ," the farmer persisted, then hiccupped. "Asla, where's the grog?"

"You've had enough!" she said sharply. "Did the giants follow you?"

The farmer shrugged. "Don't know . . . just a little sip, Asla. A teeny, tiny . . . for the soul!"

Erek crouched beside his friend and stretched one arm across Isleif's shoulders. "You have to sleep now, old fellow. We'll go up to your farm tomorrow and see what's what."

"No! Not back to the giants!" Isleif protested vehemently. "Not to the giants. I seen what they did to Fang. One wallop with a club . . . he was a big dog, you know. I seen him tear a wolf apart more than once. One of Ole's best bloodhounds. But one wallop, then they ripped his legs off. He was still alive." Isleif began to sob. "Such a good dog, he was. I'm not going back!"

"That's enough! I'm not listening to this old drunk anymore," Asla's aunt Svenja said as she reached for her cloak and went to the door. "We all know he spends half his time drunk."

"But what if he's right?" Asla asked.

"With this rubbish? Giants appear out of nowhere and burn down his farmhouse. Asla, really. They're stories for children. There are no giants. Not unless you're blind drunk."

Murmurs of assent rumbled through the crowd.

Asla could understand her neighbors' skepticism. Isleif's words, in fact, reminded her of a tale she knew from her own childhood, one that she had heard more often than anyone else from her father, because he'd been part of it. The story of Mandred and the manboar—the monster that came down from the mountains. Then, too, a man had come to the village and warned them about the monster. And no one had believed him.

"We should send someone to Isleif's farm to see what's happened, someone we all trust." She looked at Kalf.

The big fisherman nodded. "Yes. It would be sensible. Maybe I can round up his animals, too, if the stable hasn't burned."

"Don't go, boy!" Isleif cried. "They'll slaughter you like they did my dog. My good boy . . ."

Silence fell over the big room. The farmer sat by the fire and buried his face in his hands.

"We have to send messengers out to the other farms," Asla said. "And we have to be ready to leave the village. We could be in Honnigsvald in two days if there's no storm. We need sleds!"

Iwein, who owned more livestock in the village than anyone else, stepped forward. He was a corpulent, red-haired man and notorious for his volatile temper.

"Your husband's not here, Asla, and you've got the elves in your house. I can understand that you're afraid. But you're going too far. There's no reason to get so worked up. Let's suppose the worst case: a few wandering bandits have attacked Isleif's farm and burned it down. They'd never dare to come here to the village. There are too many of us for them to be any danger."

"And if it's really giants? Or trolls?" Asla persisted.

Iwein's face flushed red. "That's just stupid prattle. Giants don't exist, and the trolls have never come this far south." Suddenly, his tone brightened, and he smiled broadly. "Besides, all the trolls are in Albenmark, at war with the elves."

Asla looked around at her neighbors. She could see in their faces that they were ready to brand her a madwoman. They would mock her to the end of her days if Isleif had really just imagined everything. And she could certainly believe that, as drunk as he was, he'd managed to accidentally set his own house on fire. But the dog . . . that wasn't the kind of thing you made up.

"Some of you are old enough to have known my father-in-law, Mandred. You know the story of the manboar, and maybe you remember the night the elven queen came to take my husband away." Asla pointed to the alcove where Emerelle lay. Yilvina stood in front of it, her arms crossed. So far, she had only listened in silence.

"You yourselves have been part of things that people in Honnigsvald stopped believing long ago," Asla went on. "Do you think I'd drag my children out into a winter's night for nothing? Kalf will go and see what's happened. If we're in danger, he'll light the signal fire on the Hartungscliff. I can't order you, but I can advise you, and I'll accept being called a madwoman from this night forward. But I advise you to be ready to leave at a moment's notice. I'll personally make sure that the big sled is harnessed. I'd rather spend one night nervous and be mocked for it later than see a fire on the cliff and not be ready."

"I think she's right," said Kalf.

Asla could have hugged him. Now Svenja nodded, too. The mood was starting to shift.

"All right, then," Iwein muttered. "We'll get ready. Let's throw some provisions together and grease our boots."

"That's not the end of it," said Asla. "Your sons have been grown men for years, Iwein. It's easy for you to talk. But I need a warm place for my Kadlin. I have to be able to change her diapers. Out on the frozen fjord, a wet diaper would mean her death."

Iwein threw his hands over his head. "Have you lost your senses, woman? What do you have in mind? Putting your house on runners? How do you see this 'warm place' of yours?"

She rapped her knuckles on top of the trestle table. "Just like you said, Iwein. A hut on runners. A tarpaulin over the wagon bed will keep the wind off, but not the cold. It's not enough. No, we knock together a cabin from tabletops, doors, and boards, and we put a brazier inside it. A warm place for the children, the old, and the worn out."

Iwein shook his head. "I wouldn't like to be in your skin when your husband sees what you've done to that pretty wagon of his. And all because of a drunkard. We'll be up the whole night, and tomorrow we'll find out the trolls were just the wanderings of a lonely old man's mind. You'll see, Asla."

ALFADAS'S STAIRCASE

The signal fire blazed brightly! As the flames shot high into the sky, Kalf could see, in the distant village, the big wagon being hauled out onto the ice of the fjord. Behind it followed tiny figures. Hand-pulled wooden sleds and a herd of sheep pressed closed together all but disappeared against the white winter landscape.

Good that Asla sent me to Isleif's farm, Kalf thought. After the meeting with Isleif and the others, she had quietly told Kalf that she might benefit from a warm cabin herself, then confided in him that before long she would have a third child to look after.

Kalf had come across the trolls in the forest. Harsh voices and a throaty laugh had given warning enough, and he'd found a hiding place in a tangle of blackberry. Through the snow-covered vines, he'd gotten a good look at them. They were truly huge, a good three paces from sole to scalp! Most of them, despite the cold, were all but naked, with furs wrapped around their loins and little more. One of them carried the remains of Isleif's dog over his shoulder. Their weapons betrayed that they were no hunting party—they were armed with axes and stone daggers, and only one or two carried a bow or spear. They were raiders!

One of the trolls, bigger than the rest, his fat belly decorated with bloody handprints, came so close to Kalf's hiding place that the fisherman could have reached out and touched him. Kalf said a silent prayer of thanks to Luth that the trolls had not brought dogs with them, or he would not have gone unnoticed.

The band of warriors was following Isleif's footprints through the snow. The prints would lead the trolls straight to Firnstayn, and Kalf found himself wishing they'd surprised the old drunkard in bed. Perhaps then they would not have found the village.

Asla's big sled was now almost half a mile out on the fjord. The last stragglers were still leaving the village. Had anyone refused to leave their hut on that icy night just because of a story and a fire? Kalf hoped not. After he'd seen the trolls, any doubt he may once have harbored about the terrible tales told of them vanished. So that was what man-eaters looked like!

One last time, he stretched his bare hands toward the flames. Then he pulled his heavy, fur-lined mittens back on. He avoided crossing the stone circle that crowned the steep cliff. Instead, following the goat track that led alongside it, he hurried back toward the gentle slope that led downward behind the Hartungscliff. And there they were! Three giant figures stamping through the deep snow, following his own tracks.

Kalf swallowed. He should not have stayed by the fire so long. Its bright glow must have been visible far into the forest. He'd all but called out to the man-eaters to come and get him, and they'd certainly welcome having a fire already burning to roast him on!

Kalf looked to the stone circle where Mandred had saved himself all those years before. A miracle had happened, and he'd passed through to Albenmark. But Kalf did not want to go there. Asla could not lose him, too. It was bad enough that Alfadas was off in the distant elven realms instead of there in the Fjordlands, standing by those who mattered most.

The trolls were approaching fast. They could see there was no other trail that led down from the cliff. Kalf retreated.

The cliff fell sharply toward the fjord. Alfadas had gone up there often in his first summer. Back then, he'd spoken every second day about how his life might have been different if his father had had another way out: a second path down from the cliff. And at some point, he'd begun to build it. Although "path" was too generous. As far as Kalf knew, no one but Alfadas had ever used the route, and even the jarl had only ever tried it when the weather was good. Never in midwinter or at night.

The fisherman looked around at the edge of the cliff. The trolls were now so close that he could hear them grunting to each other. Where was the damned descent?

Finally, hidden beneath the snow, he found a rusty hook. A rope black with grime and mold hung from it.

The first troll reached the edge of the stone circle. With a guttural bellow, he pointed at Kalf.

Kalf pulled off the mittens, gripped the rope, and lowered himself over the edge of the cliff—better to die in a fall than be eaten by trolls!

The rope was frozen. The frost sliced into Kalf's naked fingers. The lower he went, the more alarmingly the rope creaked. And then it ran out, in the middle of the cliff! He looked around desperately. Snow lay on the rock ledges, and in places, the stone was covered by a layer of clear ice.

Some distance to one side, Kalf spied a bent iron hook. There was a narrow rock ledge there, above which a rope had been attached to act as a handrail. Kalf stretched out and was just able to grab hold of the hook.

A crash made him look up. The trolls were hurling rocks down the cliff. With the strength of desperation, Kalf pulled himself onto the rock ledge, where an overhang protected him from the treacherous attack. He worked his way along, both hands clenching the rope. The ledge grew a little wider.

Beneath the overhang, he found a natural niche in the rock. Charcoal and blackened sticks lay on the alcove floor—apparently, Alfadas had camped there one time. Twining patterns were drawn in charcoal on the rock. The jarl was a strange man. It would never have occurred to Kalf to camp in the middle of an inaccessible rock wall.

He looked out toward the fjord. The train of refugees had left the village a good distance behind them. They would make it. *Good that Asla was so prudent,* he thought.

No more rocks had been thrown from the cliff above, and Kalf looked up cautiously from his hiding place. The trolls were nowhere in sight. He crept carefully out along the rock ledge a short distance. Nothing happened. The man-eaters seemed to have given up the hunt—he would live!

His fears eased, he sought out the rest of Alfadas's staircase. Using the ice hooks, narrow ladders, and ropes, he worked his way down the cliff until he finally reached a field of boulders and scree that gave way to coniferous forest farther down.

One careful step at a time, he made his way down the scree, which was covered by a layer of snow. He was halfway down when the loose stones underfoot began to slip. Arms flailing for something to hold, he stumbled, fell backward, and slid down the steep slope on his back. He hit a concealed stone and tumbled over; then one ankle collided hard with a rock. He was sliding fast toward the fir trees. In the cold starlight, he could clearly see the dead branches jutting from the trunks like daggers.

He jammed his feet into the snow, jumped, and went flying through the air. There was a hard jolt. Kalf pressed his eyes closed. He was lying in a snowdrift. Dazed, he looked around. He was no more than five steps from the edge of the forest. He tested his limbs one by one. His right ankle felt sprained, and every bone hurt, but at least nothing was broken.

Groaning, he got to his feet and limped into the forest. If he didn't stop, he'd reach the refugees on the ice in two hours.

DARK OMENS AND A HERO'S DEATH

*A*fter his son abandoned him, the king was haunted by bad dreams. He was found on many occasions in his banquet hall in the dead of night, dressed only in a tunic. The ruler, who possessed a bear's strength even in his latter days, had wilted in a matter of weeks.

It was a time of dark omens. The market hall in Gonthabu, which had taken three years to build and was the first large stone building in the royal city, collapsed when the first snows piled on its roof. One afternoon, a shadow appeared on the surface of the sun. It was just a tiny speck, but it was to remain four days.

In the night that followed the first bad winter storm, Horsa sent for his scribe to take down his testament. He summoned the oldest priest from the Luth temple as well. To all in his royal court, Horsa seemed that day to have regained his strength. He drank strong wine until midday. In the evening, word of the trolls reached him. They had appeared on the coast and burned down a fishing village and were now moving along the fjord toward the royal seat in Gonthabu.

Immediately, Horsa dispatched messengers to the four winds and gathered his army before the city gates. In three days, seven hundred men answered the call to arms. By horse and by sled, they came through the deep snow, while those who had already lost hope left the royal city in droves.

They assembled beneath the banner of the red eagle, the king at their heart. The thunder of their hooves on the ice was heard far inland as the old king rode into his final battle. But what can human might do to quell the dark wrath of trolls? Even the bravest of the kingdom's brave warriors perished. The battle was too one-sided, lost before the first sword was drawn. Horsa Starkshield fell as he saved the life of his young banner bearer, Jarl Oswin. With his dying breath, he ordered the young man to gather those still alive and withdraw from the ice, to battle to victory another day.

"We need the jarl of Firnstayn" were the last words spoken by Horsa of the strong shield.

The Life of Horsa Starkshield (33–35)

As recorded by Eginhard von Daluf

THE SHED SKIN

Ollowain found the camp on the mountainside deserted. Lyndwyn's tracks stopped abruptly at a trampled patch of snow.

He did not know how long he had slept on the mountain. The Arkadien must have used magic on him: his wounds had healed, but he still felt weak. When he found the Albenstone in his hand, he had been shocked beyond words. He had called out for Lyndwyn, then had followed her tracks, which led him straight to the trolls. He had understood what must have happened and had quickly hidden the Albenstone to prevent any risk of its being found on him. Then he had gone in search of Lyndwyn.

It had taken him almost a day to reach the trolls' camp, and all that was left was a broad, flattened snowfield. Here and there, he found piles of rags and rubbish in the snow, and loot from Phylangan that the looter had decided was no longer important enough to lug any farther. The army had turned to the east, toward the old mountain fortresses. Kingstor, Phylangan, for which both sides had fought so remorselessly, had been won and lost in the same hour. A red glow pulsed over the far summit, and a pall of smoke still lingered.

For a while, Ollowain wandered aimlessly through the camp, then made up his mind to follow the trolls eastward. He would find Lyndwyn, although the many bones that lay where the trolls had made their fires told him how senseless his search would be. But Lyndwyn would live until he found proof of her death, and even then, there was hope. One day, she would be reborn. He only had to wait.

His way led him past frozen kobolds, the tusks of a mammoth, and shields that tired warriors had simply abandoned in the snow.

"Ollowain." The voice was a mere whisper, lost on the wind. The swordmaster stopped in his tracks. It was impossible to say from where the low cry had come. Then he saw the movement. A torn cape fluttered in the wind. From beneath it stretched a hand. The four fingers closed and opened—a wave!

"Lyndwyn?"

He hurried to the hunched figure. She was huddled in the lee of a troll shield to which strips of silk and a pale mask had been pinned with knives of bone.

She had drawn the cape close around her body. As he approached, she lifted her hands to cover her face, but he recognized her long, dark hair immediately.

"Lyndwyn!" He fell to his knees with relief. She'd survived. He could hardly believe his luck—everything would be good again!

"I did not . . . betray her. The queen." She spoke so softly and hesitantly that her voice was barely intelligible.

"I know," Ollowain said. "Forgive me for not believing you from the start."

Lyndwyn's body trembled; he could not say whether it came from sobbing or from despairing laughter. He tried to take her gently in his arms, but she recoiled at the slightest touch.

"Forgive me. I can't. I have to leave you now. My power is fading . . . the mesh of my last spell is unraveling. I knew you would come. I wanted to see into your eyes one last time, my wondrous white knight. Now go and save our queen. You have already saved me."

A silver light engulfed the trembling figure.

"No, please! Don't go . . . I . . ."

"I will wait for you." Her voice sounded as if it came from far away. Then she was gone. Lyndwyn had found her way into the moonlight. She had fulfilled her destiny in Albenmark.

The tattered cape lay in the snow. Ollowain picked it up and held it to him. In the final moment, he had seen Lyndwyn's face. He turned to the shield. What he had taken to be a mask had vanished. He remembered what he had said to the Arkadien so long ago: *You would have to shed your skin to make me trust you.*

The swordmaster buried his face in the ragged cape.

THE RAMPARTS OF HONNIGSVALD

The wood's so rotten, I could poke my thumb into it if it wasn't frozen. You can't stay here!" the ferryman said beseechingly. "No one is safe behind these walls."

Asla sighed. For two terrible days on the ice, the thought of the town with its earthen ramparts topped by palisades had given her the strength she needed to keep going. Now they had been in Honnigsvald not even half a day, and all hope had vanished again. Kodran, the ferryman, had come to Asla late in the afternoon. He said he was a friend of her husband and had not let himself be dissuaded until she finally agreed to climb the defensive walls with him.

Asla looked at Kalf, his face a mosaic of scabs from his fall. She had thanked the gods a thousand times that the fisherman had made it down the Hartungscliff as unscathed as he had. It was a miracle.

Kalf took his fisherman's knife from his boot and scratched at the wood. He swore softly. "Kodran's right. I reckon the trolls, as big as they are, must be as strong as bears. This rotten palisade won't stop them. We have to keep going."

Asla kicked angrily at one of the tree trunks that formed the palisade. She'd felt so safe there in the big town. To add injury to this insult of a palisade, now her foot hurt—she was no troll, after all.

"We can't move on as we are," she said dispiritedly. "We need more sleds." She looked to the tall ferryman. "Take me to the man who talked my husband into buying the wagon."

"I don't think he'll help us," Kodran said hesitantly. "We'd do better to just get out of town than get caught up with Sigvald. He's a crafty profiteer."

"Then let him make his profit! We have no choice. There are too many old people and children with us, and there's—" Asla stopped herself and cleared her throat. She had almost mentioned the queen. Emerelle lay on the big wagon, but no one in Honnigsvald needed to know that. "Take me to this Sigvald. Right now!"

Kodran acceded and led her through the overflowing streets to the shore of the fjord. The town was filled with refugees. The column of smoke that rose above Firnstayn had been seen for many miles around. Fishermen and farmers had fled to the deceptive safety of the town with their families and their livestock. Asla cursed silently. She had to warn these people! But first, she had to talk to Sigvald.

The wagon maker was at work in his factory as if all the turmoil in the town meant nothing to him. He had ice-gray hair combed back from his face and greased smooth. Asla noted how he eyed her red mantle as he decided that she was probably a wealthy woman. "What can I do for you?"

"How many sleds do you have?"

The question seemed to make the man uneasy. "What kind of sled did the lady have in mind?"

"I have in mind to take every sled you have."

The wagon maker cleared his throat. Then he looked to Kodran and Kalf, who had accompanied Asla. Neither smiled.

"That will be rather expensive," Sigvald finally said, vacillating.

"I have a chest full of silver on my wagon. My husband is Duke Alfadas, so I am not a needy woman. The silver will be yours if you can prepare the sleds by midnight. As many as possible need to have wooden cabs on them, strong enough to stand up to a storm." Asla nodded toward Kalf. "This man will stay here and advise you on what the sleds will need. Get me more than five, and I'll rent them from you for a thousand silver coins each. Once we're safe, you'll get the sleds back and can keep the silver. But we leave at midnight, not a minute later! And you'll come with us to repair any damage along the way."

"My sleds are solid! There won't be any damage."

Asla raised her eyebrows. "Then tell me: to whom am I supposed to pay the money for the wagons? If you stay here, you won't survive to get it. There is a band of trolls marching on Honnigsvald, and the ramparts of this town won't stop them."

The wagon maker smiled. "Trolls. Dear lady, there are no trolls in this land. There are only plunderers."

Asla had faced this kind of derision at least a dozen times that day. She was sick of it.

"Ask Kalf what your plunderers look like. He's met them. But maybe you should think a little further. Do you think I'd pay a fortune to flee a big town if there were really just a few robbers coming down the fjord?" With that, Asla turned on her heel and left.

RETURN TO THE ICE

L isten to me!" Asla raised her hands imploringly. She was standing on a barrel at the end of the fish market. The square in front of her was filled with people. Although it was already late at night, there was little rest for the inhabitants of Honnigsvald. Refugees were still coming in from the ice.

Sigvald, in the end, had taken her words seriously. He had come at midnight with nine sleds, which now stood at the north end of the market square, ready to depart.

"We've built cabins so the children will be safe from the cold. Come with me. I am going to Gonthabu. King Horsa will be able to protect us. If you stay in Honnigsvald, you will have no chance! The trolls will break through the town walls as if they're made of sticks." Asla tensed her shoulders. She had donned the chain mail tunic in which Gundar had died. Now it was starting to weigh heavily on her and seemed not to be helping at all—she had hoped that Luth might be just a little closer if she herself wore his gift to the priest, and had prayed to the god that her words would be able to persuade the people. But few of those gathered were even listening to what she had to say.

A troop of armed men led by a gaunt, bald-headed man pushed their way through the crowd. His name was Godlip, and he was the jarl of Honnigsvald. His men dragged Asla down from the barrel.

"For all my respect for your husband, woman, I will no longer have you stirring up strife. You are banned from the town. Take anyone who wants to follow you and go, but don't try to set foot in Honnigsvald again." The jarl climbed up onto the barrel himself. "Don't listen to this demented creature! Look at her, wearing mail like a soldier. And she wants to lead you over the ice? In midwinter? Gonthabu is days away. Who here thinks they'll make it alive? But Honnigsvald is overcrowded, so I'm not going to stop you if you want to go. We may have only a few soldiers, but we have no shortage of volunteers, and I sent a messenger to the king this morning. If we can hold out for a little while, the king will come to us, and no one has to die on the ice." The jarl garnered murmurs of agreement. He pointed at Asla. "You, woman, are banished. There's no place for you here anymore. You've dragged the name of this town through the mud—now leave!"

Asla wanted to fight back, but Erek took her arm and pulled her away with him. "Forget these blowhards," he said angrily. "We know you're right. We've already lost too much time."

They pushed their way through a chorus of boos and catcalls to the big wagon. Ulric was sitting on the driver's seat. "Why was that man so mad at you, Mother?"

"Because he's stupid!" Erek replied for her. "Leave your mother in peace now."

"But we have to get Halgard! She's not here."

"I just saw her on the wagon that Kalf's driving," said Asla. "Don't worry about her."

Ulric stood up to jump down. "I'll go and get her."

"You stay here," said Erek, pulling him back down on the seat. "Listen to your mother. You'd only get lost in the crowd."

"I'll see to Halgard." Asla smiled tiredly at her son. "We won't leave anyone behind." With that, she set off toward the end of the caravan, but she had hardly gone a dozen steps before she found herself surrounded by Godlip's men. "We're here to see to it that you leave town, woman," said their leader gruffly. "Now!" He grabbed hold of her and dragged her along with him.

Asla waved to Kalf. "Drive! Get everyone moving." Her thoughts raced. Had she thought of everything? They'd bought food, blankets, and furs; coal for the braziers in the cabs built onto the wagons; and even strong spirits, medicine, and bandages. Asla had to smile. What would Alfadas say? Everything he'd collected on his campaigns in recent years, all his treasures, had gone into the caravan. In a single afternoon, she had made him a poor man.

Godlip's soldiers cleared a path for them, making sure they got out of town quickly. Only a few had listened to Asla and joined those leaving, and it was a convoy of fourteen sleds that moved out onto the ice, heading south. Livestock was driven along beside the wagons, and many of those fleeing on foot pulled small, hand-drawn sleds.

Asla sat on the driver's seat beside Kalf and peered along the column of people ahead. More than four hundred had put their faith in her, she estimated. If only she had more wagons!

They rounded a tongue of land on which a scanty grove of birch trees grew. Beyond it, the fjord stretched southward, framed by steep rocky outcrops. Faerylight meandered across the starry sky, dousing the winter landscape in mysterious green shadows.

Asla rubbed her hands together for warmth. She felt most of all like leaning against Kalf. It felt good to be close to him. Whatever happened, he was a boulder of calm and confidence. But she would have to make do with sitting beside him on the driver's seat. As a married woman, she could go no closer.

A scream abruptly tore through the peace of the night.

"Trolls!" A man that Asla did not know pointed back toward the birch grove. Five giant figures came running out onto the ice, heading straight for the column of wagons.

Kalf stood and reached for the whip attached to the side of the seat. Their wagon was far back in the column. Just ahead of them, Erek steered the big wagon that Alfadas had brought to the village.

The men and women walking beside the sleds began to run. Someone handed a small child up to Asla. She held the child in her arms and looked back. The trolls were rapidly gaining ground.

Kalf cracked the whip over the heads of the horses, but it didn't help. As hard as the horses pulled, the trolls were closing in. Asla could clearly make out their faces now and could see that they carried light spears. A man fell on the ice, and a troll stabbed him in the back in passing.

The column had broken up, and the lighter sleds were pulling clear. Asla heard her father curse and beat at the horses. Many of the refugees tried desperately to hold on to the sleds. Asla saw a young woman fall beneath the runners of a wagon. She was left behind on the ice, her legs crushed.

The trolls hurled their spears. The night was filled with panting, the cracking of whips, the shouts of the wagon drivers, and the scraping of runners on the ice. Those on foot had no breath to spare to cry out.

The trolls' attack ended as suddenly as it had begun. They gave up the chase, then gathered the dead and injured from the ice and retreated.

"Hunters," said Kalf. "We must be like a herd of reindeer to them. They kill only as many as they can eat. For now, at least."

Asla looked at the fisherman in surprise. His words had come as coldly as if it really had just been a few reindeer that were killed.

"Those were people who'd put their trust in me," she cried. "Not animals to be slaughtered!"

Kalf laid one hand on her arm. "I know. But we have to understand them if we want to escape them."

"Stop!" Asla climbed down from the driver's seat. She went back to check on those who had not been fast enough. "Get the wagons together again," she ordered Kalf, more sharply than she really wanted to.

It took more than an hour to reassemble the convoy. Asla helped where she could and listened patiently to the protests of those who complained bitterly that the wagons had abandoned them. Blood trotted beside her, and if anyone in their anger grew too loud, the big black dog silenced them with a glare and a low growl.

The first silver was gleaming over the mountains when Asla gathered with Yilvina, Kalf, Sigvald, and a few other men at the head of the column to talk about when they could risk a brief stop to rest. She still wore the chain mail tunic. She felt as if she had a burning stick inside her back instead of a spine. She was exhausted and wanted only to withdraw to the cabin on her wagon when a rider appeared on the fjord ahead.

When he reached the convoy, he headed straight for the small gathering. He was a young man, his beard and brows covered in white ice crystals. "Where are you going?" he asked.

"We are running away from trolls, believe it or not," replied Sigvald sardonically.

"That much is clear," the rider replied. "But you're going the wrong way. They are coming from the south, an army, just two days' march from here. There are two more columns of refugees not far ahead of you. You have to go north! To the south is nothing but death."

Asla felt as if someone had punched her in the stomach. No! It could not be! The men conferred briefly, then the rider went quickly on his way, hoping to make it unscathed past the trolls camped in the birch grove and bring the news to the jarl of Honnigsvald.

Everyone stared at Asla as if they expected her find a solution on the spot. "Well, what now?" she said tiredly. "Any suggestions?"

Yilvina, silent until now, spoke up. "We have to get off the fjord, into the mountains. Maybe we'll find a safe place there. The trolls are using the fjord like a military road. They make good progress on the ice, and with all the towns and villages, they don't need to carry provisions."

"How are we supposed to get into the mountains with the sleds?" Kalf said. "We would have to leave them behind, and half a day later, we would also have to leave the weakest of us behind."

"On the fjord, everyone dies," the elf replied matter-of-factly.

"Let's have no illusions," said Sigvald heatedly. "She speaks the truth. But I know a place that could serve as a refuge for us, one we could even defend—Sunhill. It's a mountain village not far from here. We can reach it from an arm of the fjord and avoid the troll army altogether. Sunhill lies along a pass that is not too steep for the sleds. Besides, the pass is fortified with two well-built wooden palisades. Reindeer migrate through the pass in spring and autumn, and the Sunhillers use the trail like a giant pen for the herds. They cull a few animals, then let the rest of the herd move on. The palisades are kept in good order—the village survives because the palisades are strong."

It sounded like a godsend. Asla ordered Sigvald to the front of the convoy to lead them to the remote branch of the fjord. Scouts were sent out to watch for other refugees on the ice and for scattered soldiers from Horsa's army. They would take anyone they could save with them.

When everything had been talked through, she returned to her own big wagon. She pulled herself up tiredly onto the driver's seat. Her father sat there, hunched over—he must have fallen asleep.

Asla stretched. The winter sun felt warm on her face. No one would say a word if she nodded off at Erek's side and leaned against *his* shoulder. She nudged him gently. "Hey, wake up. We'll be moving again soon."

Erek didn't move.

"Wake up." She shook him by the shoulder, then saw the blood. His hands, his trousers, the reins he held—everything was soaked with blood.

"Wake up!" she pleaded, although she already knew that Erek could not hear her anymore.

Someone pulled her down from the driver's seat. Kalf! He held her tightly. Yilvina climbed up to Erek and examined him.

Asla resisted Kalf's embrace, but he was stronger than she was. He held her tightly to his chest.

"A spear pierced his side." Yilvina looked at Asla. There was no emotion on the elf woman's face, although she had taken her evening meal at the same table as Erek for weeks. "He pulled the spear out. The wound is deep and did not stop bleeding. He kept the sled on its line, and at some point, when the column was moving more slowly again, he would have fallen asleep. The horses just followed the team ahead of them."

Asla was too exhausted to cry. She heard the elf's words and yet still could not comprehend what had happened. Erek had always been there for her. Never had he been more than a few miles away. He'd grown old, but he was not frail. At least, not in her eyes.

"We have to bury him," she finally said.

"We can't," said Kalf softly. "The hunters might still be after us. We can't stop. Not yet. And carrying a corpse is bad luck. You know that."

"So you just want to leave him on the ice?" she asked, her voice breaking. "You've known him your whole life, and now you want to leave him behind to feed the trolls!"

"No." Kalf still held her tightly in his arms. "He once told me that he would like to end his days at the bottom of the fjord like King Osaberg. He felt it was the right grave for a fisherman."

Asla swallowed. Erek had spoken to her about the same thing. When he was dead, he wanted to go back to the fish that had nourished him throughout his life. She also knew that they could not wait. "Let me go," she said quietly. "I'll get the children from the wagon. They should be able to say good-bye to their grandfather."

Blood trotted beside her as she went to the rear of the sled. Her hands trembling, she opened the hatch. Stuffy air flowed from inside. A handful of charcoal chunks glowed dully in the brazier. Her aunt Svenja was sitting on the platform inside with several children, and the elven queen lay on the floor on a makeshift bed of furs.

Svenja squinted against the bright morning light. "What's the matter?"

Asla began to say something, but no words came. She saw Kadlin, sleeping peacefully in her aunt's arms. But Ulric was not there.

"Where's my son?"

"Isn't he with Erek?"

Asla's legs gave way. She had to hold on to the wagon to stay upright. She felt like she was going to vomit. She thought of all the turmoil in Honnigsvald. Ulric had still been sitting on the driver's seat beside Erek. And then . . . she had not checked on him the whole night. He was . . . Asla looked to the north. Smoke was rising into the sky.

"Where is Halgard?" she asked in despair. "Kalf! Halgard's in the back of your wagon, isn't she?"

The fisherman hurried back. Every sled was searched. But neither Halgard nor Ulric could be found.

Blood prodded at her with his nose as if wanting to console her. Asla's hands gripped the thick skin at the dog's neck. She brought her face very close to the dog's ears. She knew that she could not go back, although there was nothing in the world she wanted more. The trolls would catch her, and that would not help Ulric. And she had to think of Kadlin, too.

"Go back," she whispered to the dog. "Go back and find Ulric. You can find him."

"I'll go with him," said an oddly melodic voice. "I'll return in two days if all goes well."

Asla looked up at Yilvina. For the first time, the elf woman's face did not seem carved from stone.

NEW CHALLENGES

Boltan wandered along the shore among the milling humans. They avoided him respectfully and ducked low if he even came close to one of them. What pathetic little creatures they were! He did not know which one to choose. Not one of them looked good enough for the prince's table.

Boltan was feeling especially proud because Orgrim had made him his cook. That made him their second most important man, after the duke himself. It was an important office with many new challenges. He had to keep the lists of those eating and all their provisions up to date. And he had to please his duke's palate.

Orgrim was in a bad mood. Dumgar was on the march and would soon unite with Orgrim's troop. Then the ruler of Mordrock would be in charge.

For today, Boltan had nothing in mind but to cheer his commander up. Nothing took your mind off your worries like a delicious meal, after all. A few days earlier, Brud had told him about a special way to prepare jackrabbits. You broke open their abdomen and removed the intestines, stomach, and gallbladder. Then you smothered them with clay until they looked like big gray lumps. You put the lumps in the coals in a fire pit. Sealed inside the clay, the meat would stew in its own juices, and it tasted wonderfully tender when you took it out of the fire and broke open the gray crust. The skin and hair stuck to the clay, and you could start eating right away.

Boltan had found some good clay that morning beneath a fireplace by the shore and had been thinking about trying out Brud's method of preparing meat ever since. He would take a small human. One of the pups.

He wandered on aimlessly. He wanted something special. Finally, he settled on a young female with white hair. She was a little skinny, but none of the others had hair like hers. She also seemed strangely clumsy, and only when he was standing in front of her did Boltan realize that she could not see. Surely that would not affect how she tasted.

He reached down to her, but another pup jumped up and pushed himself protectively between Boltan and the female. The little human held a sparkling dagger in his hand and behaved as if he wanted to challenge Boltan to single combat, as soldiers sometimes did.

Boltan could not help himself. He burst out laughing. At the same moment, the little human jumped forward and stabbed him in the leg. The elven blade burned like fire. Angrily, Boltan disarmed the youngster, then pinned him under his arm and carried him to the fireplace he'd prepared. He threw the dagger on a pile of bones.

The pup was small but already had a warrior's heart. He would be sure to tickle Orgrim's palate.

FAREWELL

We pulled back as far as Eagle Peak, the next fortress after Phylangan. The journey took four days, and in that time, we could see a cloud of ash rising above the lost mountain. At night the sky was red, reflecting the blood of the earth. At times, I felt as if the land itself had brought an end to the war. The only pass between Carandamon and the Snaiwamark was now sealed, and the fortress for which so many races had fought so doggedly was gone. As bitter as the loss of Phylangan was for the Normirga, the humans seemed in equal measure relieved. I had promised Alfadas that I would release them from their service in their homeland. Emerelle would then be brought back from the duke's village. There would be no peace with the trolls in the foreseeable future, but hostilities would at least pause for a little while. Both sides were exhausted. If the trolls wanted to attack Carandamon, they would have to take a long detour across the Windland or once again tread the net of Albenpaths.

We arranged a feast in Eagle Peak to say farewell to our brothers-in-arms. They were to take sleds and horses with them, and each man was also given a gift when we asked them to return the golden amulets. I knew what they had taken from Phylangan, though the soldier with the missing nose and foul mouth believed I had noticed nothing. Let them keep their loot! Phylangan is gone. No one cares about its gold anymore.

Our feast was drawing to a close when a pale figure appeared at the arched entrance to the Silver Hall. Ollowain, whom we had thought dead, had returned, although there was little enough of the living still in him. His hair was white as frost, his eyes were sunk deep in their sockets, and instead of his cloak he had wrapped a dirty woolen blanket around his shoulders.

He never told me how he escaped the mountain. Most of the time, he was silent. I believe that even his foster son, Alfadas, never discovered what had happened to him.

Ollowain wanted to accompany the humans to the Fjordlands. When the time to depart came, he was once again the flawless white knight. But it was a facade. He still did not speak, and his eyes were abysses.

From *The Eye of the Falcon*, page 903

The Memoirs of Fenryl,

Count of Rosecarn

HOME

Alfadas's world greeted him with a slap in the face. An icy wind whistled over the Hartungscliff, driving fine ice crystals with it. The storm tugged at his cloak, and he almost slipped on the ice-caked stone underfoot. It was night, and only a few clouds sped across the sky. The moon was three-quarters full and washed the snow-covered land in ghostly light.

Behind him, more and more men crowded through the gateway. They were too exhausted to celebrate, but their faces showed relief. Few of them had believed they would ever see the Fjordlands again. After the fall of Phylangan, nature had separated the enemy armies. The trolls were reluctant to attack through the network of Albenpaths, and the elves were too weakened. Between them lay an entire mountain range.

Now the time had come to get Emerelle back. She would be the one to make the difference in the war, if she were awake.

The wind eased. Alfadas stepped cautiously to the edge of the cliff. A cloud now covered the moon, and both the fjord and Firnstayn lay in darkness. He could not make out the village at all, and not a single light burned. But it was the middle of the night, and anyone leaving a shutter open in this cold would be a fool. Alfadas envisioned himself entering the smoky warmth of his longhouse: Ulric would leap into his arms, Kadlin would cling to his knees, and Asla would say something pert about him coming at such a late hour. And yet, he would see the love so radiant in her eyes.

He sighed deeply. It made no difference how King Horsa welcomed him, he was relieved to be back. Everything would work out. Alfadas smiled. When he rode to the royal court at the head of his veterans, Horsa would think twice about an unfriendly reception.

He looked across to the low quarrystone wall close to the edge of the cliff. It served as a windbreak for the signal fire, which was kindled if someone needed help or as a warning if anything threatened the village. Alfadas thought of the story his father Mandred had told him. Terribly injured, pursued by the manboar, and close to death, he had dragged himself up the hill. All he wanted was to light the fire to warn his village. He knew he could not make it back down the Hartungscliff and that the creature after him would tear him apart.

Mandred had focused all his remaining strength on getting to the top of the cliff, only to find in his exhaustion that a rockfall had knocked the woodpile over the cliff. In that hour of deepest despair, the magical gateway in the stone circle had opened. Mandred made it through to Albenmark, despite being unconscious. He never knew what had taken him across to the world of elves and centaurs, although sometimes he asserted that it had been a tree: Atta Aikhjarto, an ancient, souled oak. And sometimes, when Mandred was very drunk, he mumbled that he would say thank you to Atta. He wanted to feast with the oak. Alfadas smiled at the memory. When his father said "feast," he really meant get drunk. Had he ever made good on his mad plan? And where was Mandred now? It would be good to have him at his side. Alfadas's smile vanished. It had always been that way with his father. When he needed him, he was not there.

He looked across to Ollowain, who was standing close to the gateway. Since Lyndwyn's death, Ollowain had seemed somehow stooped, though in the eyes of others he stood as upright as ever. His face looked like it was chiseled from stone. The swordmaster stood by the gateway that had opened over the Albenstar and watched the men as they stepped from the nothingness.

I have always been able to rely on him, Alfadas thought sadly. How little had he ever given his foster father in return? He had tried to approach Ollowain about Lyndwyn, but the swordmaster had not opened up. It was not yet the right time.

Would he ever see Ollowain again? The swordmaster had come to take Emerelle back to Albenmark. Once they were down in the village, he would not leave her side again. Did clinging to his duty to the queen dull his pain?

Silwyna came through the gateway. Alfadas turned away and went to the windbreak at the cliff edge. He had been avoiding her ever since the night on the ice, when she had told him so much. They could not become close again. His home was down below. His children were waiting for him. And Asla . . . things would never be the same with her as they had been with Silwyna. He had chosen her to close the wound that Silwyna had opened in him. Now he knew that the wound would never close. Unless . . . He looked back toward Silwyna. She turned in his direction, as if she had felt his gaze as a physical touch. There it was again, the bond that had existed since that night on the ice, as if all the bitter years between had never been.

He could not give in to his desire! Asla had always been loyal to him. He could not betray her. He liked her. He had missed her sharp tongue. She would probably throw some bitter recrimination at him, then throw her arms around him.

No, he would never leave Asla. Not her, and not the children. Silwyna and Melvyn were strong enough to lead a life without him. His love for the elf was like an ocean—endless and extraordinarily beautiful. It showed a new face a thousand times a day and yet was filled with hidden depths and ravaged by sudden storms.

His love for Asla was different, like a crystal-clear stream that had its source among the cliffs by the coast and babbled and bubbled as it rushed along. It was refreshing and without secrets. He knew the spring from which the stream came, and he knew where it disappeared into the sea. Its course was clear and fixed. Alfadas swallowed. He would return to Asla. His heart was filled with love for her, though that love would never be able to erase his need for the ocean.

Silwyna nodded to him. She had been looking directly at him. Again, Alfadas felt as if she could read on his face every thought that passed through his mind. He must not look at her! With every glance they shared, the bond that connected them grew stronger. It was not right. He turned away abruptly and walked the few steps to the stone wall. His future lay below, on the fjord.

The moon was already low in the sky. Soon, the small village would awaken. If he hurried, he could perhaps kneel beside Kadlin's bed when she opened her eyes. He remembered fondly the radiant face with which she had so often sweetened the start of a day. Unlike Ulric, she was not yet able to hide her feelings. Sometimes, her moods were as changeable as a spring breeze, and her little face was the mirror of her soul. She was pure and untainted. Still.

Filled with yearning, he gazed into the darkness. Ulric would certainly have pestered Yilvina into giving him sword-fighting lessons. When the biting frost-wind blew from the north and the snow drifted halfway up to the gables, then you were trapped inside the longhouse. Those were days of cozy, comfortable tedium. The thought made Alfadas smile. He hoped that Ulric had not secretly been testing the blade of his elven dagger on the benches, the table, or the legs of the chairs.

Half-burned pieces of wood littered the snow behind the stone wall. Like scrawled runes on fresh parchment, they told a story. For a heartbeat, Alfadas stared at the meager remains of the wood that had once been stacked in layers behind the wall, before he understood what he was looking at. Someone had been there. Someone had warned Firnstayn of impending danger! The signal fire had been lit and had burned, but worse still was that no one had come back up the Hartungscliff to rebuild it.

Alfadas squinted into the darkness. Dark clouds still hid the moon.

What had happened here? Plagued by misgivings, he went to Ollowain and described the situation to him, then asked him to lead the men down to the fjord.

"Do you really think it's wise to go ahead alone? You don't know what's lurking down there."

"Wise or not, I cannot wait. My family is down there!" Without letting himself get trapped in talk, he turned and hurried off. He knew that Ollowain's objection was right; the elf was always right.

He began to run. The first section of the descent was very steep, the path treacherous. Sometimes he went knee-deep through the hard-crusted snow, and then it would carry his weight for a few steps.

He slipped, arms flailing, trying to keep his balance. In vain. He pitched headlong into the snow. He picked himself up immediately and ran on, not even bothering to knock the snow out of his clothes.

The trail down felt endless. When he finally reached the fjord, he was soaked with sweat and breathing hard. The cold ate through his clothes. He looked out across the frozen inlet. If he changed course and traveled across the ice, he would cut hours off the time it took him to get to the village. He moved forward cautiously before breaking into a run again. His lungs burned, and his heart hurt with every beat. But his fear hounded him on.

When the clouds parted and the moon appeared, Alfadas saw, in the distance, the collapsed pier. The remains rose darkly from the snow and ice. Beyond it, he could not see a single straight gable. He should have been able to see Kalf's hut and the crooked boathouse. Erek's little house, too, with the wooden weathervane on its roof, had been close to the shore. Now it was gone . . . as was the longhouse on the hill a little apart from the village.

Alfadas wanted to scream, but his voice failed him. His breath came in gasps. He sank forward as if someone had struck him in the back of his knees with a club. All the strength drained from his limbs. His eyes wandered over the irregular heaps of snow where houses had once stood. The cold moonlight showed everything now with merciless clarity: blackened roof beams projecting from the snow like the ribs from enormous carcasses. Fallen walls.

Cold ate into the duke's bones. A light breeze was blowing across the fjord, and fine ice crystals grazed Alfadas's cheek. Groaning like an old man, he struggled back to his feet. *They're just burned houses,* he reminded himself. Firnstayn no longer existed. But his family . . . perhaps they had fled. The signal fire on the Hartungscliff had been set alight, after all, so someone had warned the village.

He looked up to the hill on which his longhouse had once stood. He would find the answer there. Fear and hope found a balance again. Yes, up there he would find the answer.

He trudged up the gentle slope of the shore. He detoured past Kalf's hut; among the ruins, he saw the curved struts of a fish trap. Broken fishing rods lay strewn in the snow. Winter was playing a capricious game. In places along the collapsed timber walls, the drifts were higher than his head. Elsewhere, the covering of snow was as thin as a linen sheet and barely hid the things scattered on the ground.

Alfadas passed Svenja's hut. His foot banged against a small soot-covered copper kettle, which rolled away with a light clang. The duke was afraid to climb the hill, afraid of the certainty he might find there. As long as he wandered through the village, he could hope.

He found no bodies in the destroyed houses. Slowly, his courage grew. They had been warned in time! But who in the name of Luth had attacked Firnstayn? Who waged war in the dead of winter? As far as he could tell, the attackers had not been after loot but had put the houses and all that was inside them to the torch, caring only about destruction. What was the point of a war like that?

He looked to the hill again. He could not put it off forever. Only there would he find an answer to his most urgent question: Had Asla and the children escaped?

With a heavy heart, he turned up the little hill. He'd climbed it countless times before, and just as many times Asla had stood between the doorposts, waiting for him, or Ulric had come running through the open door to meet him, squealing with joy, to leap into his arms and almost knock him off his feet.

Now, only the scarred face of the moon stood between the blackened doorposts, and only silence welcomed Alfadas. Tentatively, he stepped inside the ruins that had once been his home. The main roof beam dominated the rubble, surrounded by charred rafters and smashed furniture. The fire had not been able to destroy the beam. Alfadas recalled how they had felled the enormous oak tree in a patch of ancient forest on the other side of the fjord. Hauling it down to the shore had been arduous work, and from there, they had towed it across the fjord with boats. Only when they got it to the top of the hill had they carved from the ancient trunk the beam that would one day carry the longhouse roof.

Alfadas, his mind drifting, ran his fingers over the wood. In places, the charred surface broke away, but nowhere had the fire burned to the heart of the beam. He could still make out most of the twining patterns that he had carved into the wood, the winter three years before.

He eyes roamed over snow and ash. Nothing else had withstood the fire as well as the main beam had. Of the alcoves where the family slept, only outlines remained.

Alfadas drew his sword and poked around among the burned pots and pans. They still lay where Asla had once had her fire. Beneath an upturned bench, he found the wooden horse he had carved for Ulric. The legs and mane were gone. Only the body and part of the head had survived.

Alfadas wiped the blade of his weapon clean and returned it to its sheath. There were no charred bodies. Asla and the children had not been there when the house burned. Strangely, though, that certainty did not give him the relief he had hoped for.

Close to a fallen rafter, he saw one of Asla's chests. It was blackened on all sides but had not broken apart. He went to it. With some effort, he managed to get the lid open. On top lay a small blue dress. Tears came to Alfadas's eyes. Awkwardly, with frost-reddened fingers, he lifted the dress out. Kadlin had often worn it toward the end of the summer in which she had learned to walk. Alfadas stroked the fine fabric tenderly. He found a dark bloodstain and remembered the day that Kadlin had grazed her knee on the stones along the shore. At the time, the little girl had hardly cried at all. She had simply got up again and kept going, chasing after all the miracles that only children on a deserted pebble beach can find. Alfadas recalled the fuss Asla had made because the bloodstain would not simply wash out of the blue linen. Grazed knees were unavoidable, of course. But only a good-for-nothing and a day-dreamer, in her opinion, would ever get it into his head to take his daughter down to a stony beach in her best dress.

Alfadas laid the dress back in the chest, then carefully closed the lid. He looked around one final time and left the ruins that now housed only the wind and memories. He climbed down the hill at the back of the house and went to the graveyard. When he saw all the new stones, the fear that had briefly retreated to a hidden corner of his soul leaped out at him again.

He hurried from stone to stone and wiped the snow aside. Most of the new stones were unmarked. On one, he found the image of an animal's head. It had been scratched only roughly into the stone, with little skill, probably a dog's or a wolf's head. Did Ole lie there?

On the final stone, he found a spider, carved with great care. The herald animal of the weaver of fate. The keeper of the threads. Sticks decorated with colorful strips of cloth had been jammed into the earth around the grave.

Sadly, Alfadas crouched beside the snow-covered hill. "Gundar, old friend. Couldn't the banquets in Firnstayn fill you up anymore?" He tore a strip from his cloak and knotted it to one of the sticks. "I'll miss arguing with you about the gods. Maybe you would have ended up converting me after all." He murmured a quiet prayer and wished the priest a good journey through the darkness. Then he stood up and looked over the freshly dug graves. Were Asla and the children here, too?

No, most certainly not! At least Asla's gravestone would have been marked with a sign of some sort. Maybe an ear of wheat to recall her straw-blond hair or an oak tree as a symbol of her quiet strength. She would never have been buried beneath an unmarked stone. Unless the situation the survivors found themselves in had left them no more time.

"You won't find her there," said a quiet voice.

Alfadas turned around in surprise. He peered into the darkness but only gradually made out Silwyna. In her white hunting clothes, she blended into the snowy landscape. "I found tracks. The snow had covered them. Runners cut deep grooves in the ice, and I also saw the marks left by large horseshoes. She escaped with the sled." Silwyna pointed southward, along the fjord. "They were moving in the direction of Honnigsvald."

"Who destroyed the village?"

Instead of answering, Silwyna tossed something dark that landed at Alfadas's feet. Alfadas crouched. In the snow lay a chunk of coarsely chiseled flint. "Trolls?"

"Yes. It's from an axe blade. I found it wedged in a beam."

"When were they here?"

Silwyna shrugged. "Hard to say. The snow's covered everything. More than a week but less than a moon. I can't say how many there were either, but I'm sure there were more than just a hunting party passing through."

Alfadas looked around the field of ruins. "Why?"

"The queen. They must have discovered that Emerelle was here. Probably from one of your men that they caught in Phylangan. We should have thought of that sooner," she added quietly.

Alfadas nodded. Emerelle. Her presence in the Fjordlands would have been enough to draw the trolls to the village. So the war had now come home. He looked up to the Hartungscliff. A fiery snake was winding its way down the snow-covered slope. His men had lit torches. Two, maybe three hours, then they would be here in the village. A short rest, then he would lead them farther along the fjord. Honnigsvald, with its earth walls and wooden palisades, would not be able to hold out long against the trolls. A few days, a week at best. "Are you sure the attack here was more than a week ago?"

"Yes."

Alfadas looked out over the ice again. If he met his men on the other side and led them southward past the Hartungscliff, they would save at least an hour on the way to Honnigsvald. It was pathetically little when it came to making up for a week's lead or more, but maybe that one hour would make the difference.

"What are you planning?" Silwyna asked. She lightly moved across the ice to his side.

"To win a war," he replied bitterly. It was as if his sense of hopelessness had been blown away by the wind that swept the ice. He felt ashamed that he had not thought of Emerelle for even a heartbeat before Silwyna mentioned her. "Take Lysilla and go back to Albenmark. Find Orimedes and anyone else who can carry a sword. We may be too weak to defeat the trolls alone."

"I will ride to my people. I am sure some of the Maurawan will help us fight."

"You'd fight to save Emerelle? I thought you all hated the queen?"

"They would come for my sake and for your family."

Alfadas looked keenly into Silwyna's eyes. "*You* are worried about my family?" He was honestly surprised and not entirely sure if the elf woman's words had not been meant ironically.

"I am part of your family, Alfadas, and I always will be. I carried your child in me. For me, that is a stronger bond than any lightly spoken vows of loyalty."

"I thought none of your race knew about our child." Alfadas was confused. Had she lied to him? This sudden display of passion was not like her.

"Everyone knows that I loved you. That's enough. They will come if I ask them to help me for you and your human wife. They will help us because we love each other. Not one of them would leave the forest for the queen. Don't try to understand them. We think differently about love and loyalty than you humans do. One does not have to live under the same roof to belong together, not even in the same world. I will be back when you need me the most." With that, she broke into a light trot.

Alfadas was too weary to be able to go with her. He watched her run ahead until her pale form blurred into the distant winter terrain.

THE FIRST WALL

A big, knotted hand came down on the edge of the wooden parapet, and Kalf swung his axe. Twitching fingers fell at his feet. A shrill cry rang out, only to be swallowed by the din of battle.

The palisade shuddered under the furious pounding of the battering ram. Arrows buzzed like giant hornets from the nearby slopes. He'd seen some trolls take ten arrows or more before they breathed their accursed last.

Kalf ducked below the parapet as a salvo of hurled chunks of ice came flying. Most of the projectiles flew harmlessly over the parapet, but a few smashed against the edge of the palisade, sending shards spraying across the wall-walk. Asla swore.

Kalf saw her from the corner of his eye—a red furrow had opened up across her cheek. Dark blood dripped down her neck, and she pressed one hand to the wound. He'd done everything he could to keep her from being up there, but she simply refused to listen to him. And the last thing she would do was be intimidated by him. Maybe it was better that Alfadas had gotten her as his wife. Kalf smiled sadly. No, it was not better. She was exactly the woman he would have wanted beside him in his life.

Cautiously, the fisherman looked up and over the edge of the palisade. The wooden wall was four paces high, enough to be a serious obstacle to the gray-skinned bastards below. Still, they tried repeatedly to reach over the top of the wall to pull themselves up, even more when the defenders were forced to take cover from the salvos of ice.

There was another one! "Sigvald, by you!" Kalf screamed.

The wagon maker jumped to his feet and raised his axe, but a huge fist shot forward and sent him tumbling backward from the wall-walk. A heartbeat later, the troll was over the parapet. He let out a shrill victory cry, casually crushing with his club the farmer who'd had the bad luck to be crouching beside Sigvald.

"For Firnstayn!" Kalf cried, and jumped up. They had to finish the troll quickly. If the beast managed to clear a section of the wall-walk and two or three of his comrades pulled themselves up, the palisade was lost.

One of Horsa's soldiers attacked the troll, his slash opening a gaping wound in the troll's granite-colored hide. But the giant barely took notice of the injury. His club swung down. Instinctively, the soldier jerked his shield upward. Kalf gritted his teeth. He'd tried to impress on the men a hundred times or more: duck or jump out of the way. If you have to, jump off the damned parapet, but never, ever try to parry a troll's attack. It was always the soldiers who let themselves be lured into making that mistake. They'd been drilled for a lifetime in fighting with a blade and a shield, and it was in their blood to parry an enemy's strike.

The troll's club destroyed the shield, the arm behind it, the helmet, and the soldier's skull. The man's blood sprayed as far as Asla. Her face turned as white as snow. Kalf pushed past her before she could do anything rash.

Below, at the foot of the palisade, men with long spears were already attacking. They stabbed at the troll and tried to distract him from the defenders on the wall-walk, and the many light wounds they were causing would weaken him. None of the archers on the slopes dared shoot, however. There was too much danger of hitting one of the defenders.

The troll leaned forward and swung his club in a wide arc. The spears he hit snapped like twigs, and the men holding them were thrown into disarray by the force of the blow.

The troll was straightening up again when Kalf leaped at him. He hit the troll in the side, feetfirst, and the beast grunted and threw up his arms. Both of them crashed from the walkway.

The men yelped and ran clear. Kalf landed in the snow, next to the monster—the impact knocked the wind out of him. Dazed and blinking, he saw the troll push himself to his feet. Kalf realized that jumping at him like that had probably not been his best idea.

Arrows flew into the snow around them, one missing Kalf by a hair's breadth. The fisherman cursed and wished that his archers included more hunters and soldiers than farmers. The last thing he needed was to die from a wayward arrow fired by one of his own men.

The monster's club came crashing down. Kalf rolled to one side. Then the troll lashed out with his foot—it was like getting kicked by a horse, and Kalf was thrown against the palisade. Stars sparkled before his eyes. Between the stars, he saw the leering scowl of the troll.

Kalf's left hand closed around a broken spear. *Imagine he's a fish. A very big, very ugly fish. You can kill him. You've never seen a fish you couldn't kill. Do it like you do with the big salmon when you ram your barbed spear into their eyes to pull them on board.* Kalf's thoughts were racing. *You can do it,* he told himself. But his hand was shaking.

Something silver flashed and hit the troll on the head, leaving a bloody graze. Kalf looked up and saw Asla's face. She was lying flat on the wall-walk and trying to hit the troll a second time. The beast's enormous club swung upward.

"No!" Kalf screamed. He pushed himself away from the palisade with all his strength. The spear struck the troll in the neck, just beneath the chin. Kalf felt how the iron spike of the weapon carved through the tough flesh. There was a sudden jolt as it penetrated more easily and another as the tip hit the top of the troll's skull.

The club dropped from the troll's hand. As if struck by lightning, he tipped over backward. The broken spear shaft was jerked out of Kalf's hands. From the wall-walk and the slopes came jubilant cries, but the fisherman had no eye for the men hailing him. All he saw was Asla. The troll had missed her, gods be praised.

But he could not stare at her like that, not in front of the men. She was the duke's wife. "You should have talked to him," Kalf called up to her. "Your tongue is deadlier than your sword."

Asla smiled. "I know. But these bastards are too dumb to understand me, so it doesn't help much. I think you've been lazing around in the snow long enough. Get back up here. We've got to defend this wall."

The men laughed. Asla's brash manner made them forget they were in an unwinnable fight. It was important for her to be standing up there. No man, neither soldier nor farmer, would abandon the wall as long as a woman stood her ground there and mocked the trolls. She was the rope that bound them all together. It was right that she was there, and yet Kalf was terrified for her. He could bear anything but watching her die.

The fisherman stretched his aching limbs. He looked with concern at the trunks that made up the palisade. They would not stand up to the trolls' assault much longer. It was time for them to pull back to the second wall, higher up the valley, even if their defenses there were not yet finished.

Kalf looked around for one of the leaders familiar with their plan. He saw Sigvald crouching in the snow close by, his face contorted with pain, one hand pressed against his hip. Kalf crouched beside the wagon maker. "Should I have them take you up to the village?"

"I'll survive," Sigvald growled. Then he smiled wryly. "A man would have to be a damn fool to let a troll talk him into a fistfight."

"It looked to me as if you wanted to find out what it's like to fly like a bird."

Sigvald pushed himself up to his feet. "The flying part was fine. But the landing . . . I need to work on that."

"Funny how everyone's in a mood for jokes."

Sigvald smiled. "When no one's looking, I cry in my sleep. But enough. What do you want me to do?"

"We have to abandon the palisade." Kalf pointed to the middle section of the wooden wall. Several of the trunks were already splitting lengthwise. Soon they would fail completely, and once the trolls broke through, any thought of an orderly retreat to the next defensive line would be impossible. They would be simply overrun.

The smile vanished from Sigvald's face. "So soon? I'd hoped we could hold out a little longer."

Kalf shrugged. "Luth has his own plans for us. I'm relying on you, Sigvald. See to it that our reserve is ready and waiting twenty paces behind the palisade. When we retreat, they could break through." He turned away, picked up a poleaxe from the snow, and climbed back up to the wall-walk.

The trolls had fallen back a short distance from the wall and were re-forming. Their leader seemed well aware of exactly how close they were to breaking through. Kalf gazed at their immense opponents. They looked like lumbering, ungainly creatures. Their arms were too long in relation to their torsos; their gray faces seemed somehow unfinished, with thick, swollen noses, wide bulges above the eyebrows, and heads devoid of hair. They looked as if they'd been crudely formed from clay and never completed, half-done sculptures on which the artist had yet to work out the finer details. With their sloping foreheads and wide mouths, they really did resemble fish.

And yet they were very different from how he'd always imagined trolls to be. Strong as bears, bloodthirsty man-eaters, all that was part of how he'd pictured them. But they were not stupid. They knew how to wage war, and it seemed very possible that their leader knew more about it than he did. A silly wooden palisade would not hold them for long, and each defensive line behind it was weaker still.

How much time did they have before the last line fell? He shuddered at the thought of what would happen then. The white torrent . . . at least that would buy the women and children another day.

Asla came to him. She laid one hand tenderly on his arm.

"Don't ever do that again," she said gently. "My heart stopped when I saw you fall from the wall."

Kalf avoided her eye. Her touch sent a pleasing shiver through him, but he could not let it show. No one there could know what he felt for the duke's wife.

"How would a life at your side have been, Kalf?" she asked, her voice low.

"Don't talk like that!" he whispered sharply. "Anyone might hear." Indeed, the nearest men were several paces distant, but he was still worried.

"Alfadas will never return from Albenmark."

"But he said—"

She stopped him with a shake of her head. "Pretty lies. I know him too well. The way he said good-bye . . . he left knowing that he would die in Albenmark. He tried so hard to hide his fear from me that it was impossible not to see it, although I tried. Don't you go, too, Kalf. I couldn't—" Her words were lost in the wild war cries of the trolls.

Kalf grasped the poleaxe tighter. A troll, one of the bigger ones, had begun to run toward his section of the wall. He was met by a hail of arrows, but they did not slow him down.

Thick black smoke rose along the length of the palisade. Sigvald had set fire to the bundles of brushwood soaked in seal oil. Up on the wall, they would have to endure the smoke and heat until the heavy trunks of the palisade caught fire and the flames were licking at the wall-walk. If they pulled back prematurely, the trolls could break through too easily. Then everything would have been in vain.

Kalf looked down at the charging troll. Kalf could see it in the way he ran: he was going to jump! The troll glared back fixedly at him. He would try to climb the palisade right where Kalf stood.

A ball of ice hissed past, close to Kalf's head. Farther back, he saw several trolls that had clearly set him as their target. They were already picking up new chunks of ice to throw. But he could not afford to duck! The only chance he had against the troll was when he reached for the parapet to pull himself up. For one or two heartbeats, the troll would be helpless.

A chunk of ice shattered against the palisade close beside Kalf, spraying smashed ice in his face. He blinked to clear his eyes and raised the pole-axe. When the troll jumped at the wall, the entire palisade shuddered with the impact. With his right hand, the troll reached over the wooden wall and pulled himself up until his head appeared in front of Kalf. He had a second pair of eyes tattooed on his forehead.

Kalf had missed the moment to strike at the troll's fingers. He changed his grip and stabbed at the troll's head with the long spike topping the weapon. His hands were trembling. He missed its eyes—but no, he had stabbed at the tattooed eyes. The iron spike glanced off the side of the troll's skull before the top corner of the curved blade struck home with all Kalf's strength behind it. The troll grunted. A second blade buried itself in the beast's shoulder—the troll lost its grip and fell back in the snow.

"I won't let them take you," said Asla with determination, flicking the blood from her sword with a twist of her wrist.

The smoke grew thicker all along the wall-walk. Kalf could feel the heat of the fire through the boards beneath his feet.

"Thank you," he said simply, and wished he had a silken tongue like Alfadas's, always able to find elegant words when needed.

A desperate cry made him look to the left. They'd started angling for humans again! Some of the trolls carried leather slings tied to strong ropes. They threw them over the palisade and tried to pull down the defenders—they'd lost more than a dozen already that way. Kalf had ordered the archers to focus mostly on the trolls with the leather slings, but there were too many of them, and the arrows did not stop them.

Kodran, the ferryman, went to the aid of the young man they'd snared. He raised his sword to cut through the rope but came too late. With a jerk, the poor man was hauled over the parapet.

Kalf watched in horror as the monsters fell on the young man. They tore him apart, stuffing bloody clumps of flesh greedily into their maws. Dark blood steamed in the snow.

Asla buried her face against Kalf's shoulder. "What did we do to the gods?" she asked. "Why is this happening?"

Kalf put one arm around her and embraced her tightly. In that moment, he didn't give a damn what the others thought.

Bright flames licked through the gaps between the boards of the wall-walk. The fire hissed and snapped like an angry beast, and Sigvald and his helpers were still piling new brushwood onto the flames.

The rhythm of the battering ram increased. The trolls had realized that the humans were on the verge of defeat, or at least delay. Another tried to scale the palisade, but Kodran chopped into his hand, and he fell.

The first of the defenders were already climbing down. "Asla," Kalf said in a low voice. "You have to stop them. They'll listen to you." He took his arm from around her. She looked up at him. Her lips were pressed into a thin line, as if she were struggling to smother a sudden pain. Then she swept a strand of hair from her face, squared her shoulders, and looked along the wall-walk. Almost half the defenders were already down the ladders or had simply jumped into the snow.

"Strange creatures, you men!" she shouted, rubbing her hands together. "Here I am, not freezing for the first time in two weeks, and you'd rather run off and hand this cozy spot over to the trolls. I don't understand you at all. As for me, I'm going to stay a while longer." She raised her sword and sidestepped a tongue of flame that shot up between the boards beside her.

Many of the retreating men stopped, shamed, and many who had already left the palisade turned and looked up at her. In her heavy mail tunic, her sword raised and surrounded by smoke and flames, she looked like one of Norgrimm's sword maidens, or even Svanlaug herself.

A chunk of ice grazed past Asla, knocking the helmet from her head. She stumbled. Kalf reached out to stop her from falling, but she pushed him away. She had already caught herself.

With a loud crack, one of the trunks of the palisade split. The trolls roared.

"Go down and make sure any of them that sticks his head through the breach gets a bloody nose," she ordered Kalf. Then she turned to the remaining men. "We all will die—maybe today, maybe tomorrow, maybe in fifty years. Luth alone knows when our hour will come. But we bear at least a little responsibility for how we tread our final path. Me? I'd rather burn here than let a troll beat me to death when I'm running away. But that's a choice you have to make for yourselves."

Kodran, who was already standing on a ladder, stepped back onto the wall-walk. "Asla's right. I'm not going to let the trolls spoil my chance to warm my rear up here." He trotted back to his place on the wall. Others followed.

The sound of splintering wood drowned out the din of the flames. Kalf hesitated a moment longer. Only when he felt sure that his apparent retreat would not cause the men's temper to swing against Asla did he spring from the wall-walk.

"Archers, to me!" he bellowed as loudly as he could.

The back of the palisade was blazing along its entire length. The trolls had breached the wall almost exactly in the middle and were now attacking it feverishly with their stone axes to widen the gap.

Several boys carrying bows and arrows came running; the oldest had seen perhaps fourteen summers. They were the last stand.

"Shoot into the breach!" Kalf ordered. "Sigvald! Bring in the last of the brushwood. Let's see what our friends think of a wall of fire behind the wall of wood."

The youngsters did their job well. With a few accurate shots, the trolls were driven back from the breach. The flames were flying high above the wall-walk now. The thick trunks that formed the defensive wall itself began to catch fire. The wall of flames would hold the trolls for hours.

Kalf looked up at the wall-walk with concern. A screaming man leaped down into the snow, beating at his burning trousers. Asla was still pacing back and forth along her section of the wall. She seemed calm, like a sentry on a balmy, peaceful summer night. Her face was black with soot.

The fisherman swore to himself. Could she allow herself no rest? She leaned over the parapet and peered down at the enemy. Finally, she waved to her men. "Down from here! Before the soles of your shoes fry!"

Even then, though, she waited until the others had abandoned the wall-walk. Flames blocked her route to the nearest ladder. Kalf began to run. She could not be allowed to jump. Not with a child in her belly!

Asla swung down from the back of the walk, landing hard. The heat of the fire had melted the snow close to the wall, and the ground underneath was stony. Asla got back to her feet, swaying a little.

Kalf grasped her under her arms, supporting her. Her face was as black as crow feathers, her beautiful blond hair singed by the flames.

"Let me go!" she hissed at him. "If you want me in your arms, then be in my hut tonight. I'll wait for you." She pulled herself free.

A hundred pairs of eyes were watching them. Suddenly, one man cried out, "Long live the duchess!"

More and more around him joined in his call. The exhausted fighters rushed to her and clapped her on her shoulders, then hoisted her on theirs. Louder and louder rang the cry, "Long live the duchess!"

Kalf felt a lump in his throat. He watched as she was carried away. He'd spent countless nights dreaming of lying with her. Now he was afraid of just that.

RUNNERS

Alfadas had ordered his men to set up camp outside Honnigsvald. They had completed the march from Firnstayn in a little more than a day. Almost half his warriors came from the town or close by. They had marched on despite the heavy snow and the murderous chill. Without the elven amulets, they found the winter more bitterly cold than they had before, but fear had spurred them onward.

Alfadas stood at the shore where Sigvald's workshop must once have been, although he was not completely certain. The town had lost its familiar face. Nothing known to him still stood—not a single wooden building had survived the conflagration.

A flat strip of iron jutted from the snow in front of him. Alfadas bent down and pushed the snow and half-charred wood aside. Just another barrel hoop. Alfadas sighed heavily. Then he straightened up and tried to orient himself. What had he seen on the other shore when he'd visited Sigvald's shop? How could he find the spot on which the long shed had stood? Was it here? Or had it really been a little farther along the shore?

For two hours, he searched but found no traces. Down by the harbor, no wagons or sleds appeared to have stood at all, nor did he find the remains of a burned wagon anywhere else, which meant that they had left the town. From Firnstayn, Honnigsvald was the nearest town of any size. Here was where you would run if enemies came from the mountains in the north. But Asla had no longer been there when Honnigsvald burned. He was certain of it.

He climbed the hill that dominated the center of town. He was searching for other traces now. Although Honnigsvald had not been a large settlement, he found it hard to get his bearings. Only the slightest outline remained of the broad road that had once led from the harbor to the banquet hall. All the narrow alleys had utterly vanished, buried beneath blackened roof beams, fallen walls, and smashed slate shingles. Over all of it, winter had laid its white linen.

Every time he saw a flat, bent piece of iron in the rubble, he was gripped by fear. Once, he'd been misled by the blade of a scythe. When he moved aside the heavy beam around it and saw for himself that no sled had stood there, he had not understood how he could have seen the runner of a sled in the scythe. The fear . . .

Dozens of other men picked their way through the town, just as he did. They were men who had stood up to all the horrors of the troll war in Albenmark, only to collapse now when they found the charred remnants of their huts. Mag, who had not shed a tear at the funeral of his brother Torad, wandered pale and distraught through the field of ruins, calling for Kodran.

Alfadas chewed at his lips until the metallic taste of blood filled his mouth. He could not lose control. He had to lead these men. They needed him now more than ever before. Tomorrow, before sunrise, they would march onward. They would hunt down the murderous beasts until the last troll was dead, the last troll that had come here to slaughter women and children, and then they—his mind went blank. He could not allow himself to think about what else they had done. It would destroy him! Asla was alive. She was smart. She would never have waited until the trolls made it to Honnigsvald. She had fled farther along the fjord.

Alfadas had covered less than half of the burned town, but no large wagon had been there. He did not want them to have been there—it could not be, and he could not even allow the idea!

Tears welled in his eyes. He went down to the fjord. What did it prove if he did not find the wagon? Asla and the children might still have been there. Maybe someone had stolen the wagon from them. Who knows what might have gone on inside the walls when the trolls attacked. The heavy wagon might have broken through the ice and would now lie hidden forever at the bottom of the fjord.

Alfadas wandered a short way out onto the frozen arm of the sea. It was a beautiful winter's day. A radiant blue sky covered the snowy land, and an icy wind blew from the northwest. The duke hardly felt it against his face. He felt as if he were dead.

His feet unconsciously led him southward. There, some distance from the earthen ramparts of the town, lay the abandoned camp of the trolls, close to the shore. That morning, Alfadas had told his men what they could expect to find there, but few had yet dared to visit the place. Lost and in silence, they had wandered among the snow-covered ruins, poked through the snow, and hoped to find nothing. Only then did they go down to the water's edge.

That was where the trolls had taken the survivors from the town. To all appearances, they had overrun Honnigsvald with their first assault.

Alfadas looked across to the dreadful mound beside which Lambi and Ollowain were standing. He knew what the snow, mercifully, covered there, and he did not join them. Nor did he return to the water's edge. The men who had no relatives in the area were carrying out their grim service there. If the frozen corpses could be moved, they had carried them down to the shore and laid them out. And from the hill of bones where Lambi and Ollowain stood watch, they recovered anything they could that might help identify the dead. Things that were unmistakable. Embroidered boots, a colorful scarf, a skirt on which small freshwater pearls had been sewn, dolls, armbands with distinctive markings, an amber necklace . . .

Alfadas had been with the men briefly that morning when they had begun their work. He had not been able to watch. They had cleared away a mountain of human bones. The gouges that the stone knives had left in the bones as the trolls trimmed them of flesh were clearly visible. Marrow bones had been smashed open and sucked clean. They had even broken open the skulls. They ate everything, the beasts. Alfadas thought of the delicate children's bones he'd seen strewn all around. His stomach tightened.

"Asla took the wagon. She was not here," he said to himself aloud. There was no trace of her, the children, or the wagon.

Again, he turned his eyes toward the shoreline. A man was there on his knees, doubled over—one who had found certainty. Alfadas knew he should go there, too, but he could not. Searching for a wagon in the town was one thing, but he could not bring himself to walk along the row of frozen bodies. Most were old people and young children, many about Kadlin's age. A wet bottom out there in the bitter chill was a death sentence. He swallowed hard. There was no doubt that Asla had fled across the ice with the children. But they had found no dead along the way to Honnigsvald. Whatever Asla had done, wherever she had gone, she had saved everyone, at least until they had reached the treacherous security of the town.

Ollowain had left his place at the hill of bones and was coming his way. Alfadas turned away. He acted as if he had not seen the elf. He trembled—he did not have the strength to run away. He did not want to talk about his duties as commander now. And he was dreadfully afraid that Ollowain was coming for another reason.

If not for the faint crunch of snow, he would not have heard Ollowain's approach. The elf could move as silently as a cat, and he knew that Alfadas had seen him coming. He wanted Alfadas to hear him.

"What is it?" the duke asked, without turning.

"I have to talk to you." The elf stepped in front of him, forcing Alfadas to look at him. Ollowain held something out of sight beneath his sweeping white cloak.

Alfadas exhaled. He could not take his eyes off the hidden hand. What was he hiding?

"Let's go into the woods." Ollowain pointed a short distance along the fjord, toward a sparse stand of birch trees. "I want to talk to you alone."

"We're alone here." Alfadas's voice shook, although he was trying as hard as he knew how to keep himself under control.

"No one should be watching us. You're the duke. They cannot be allowed to lose their faith in you. Not now."

"I'm just a man. They know that. A man like any one of them."

"No! You're the elvenjarl, a man like those in the old sagas, a hero who has never been defeated, a celebrated commander. That's what you are for them."

Ollowain turned away and moved off toward the birch grove.

"You know better than anyone else that I am just a human, my master. Those are stories, no more. You know all my weaknesses. You know what I truly am. The sagas are just tall tales invented by skalds like Veleif. None of them are true."

Ollowain did not reply. He simply walked on unperturbed toward the stand of birches.

Alfadas suppressed a desire to run after him. He knew that they were being observed from the shore. He could not afford to show a weakness like that! He strode along after the elf and had to force himself over and over not to break into a run. But try as he might, he could not catch up with Ollowain. The swordmaster only stopped when he reached a clearing in the middle of the grove.

"What are you hiding there?"

Ollowain turned. His face was a mask. He held a dagger in his hands. It was a long, sleek weapon, almost a short sword. The grip was carved from light whalebone and showed two rearing lions frozen in a deadly embrace. Fragments of turquoise had been set in the silver sheath. There were eighty-three altogether, Alfadas knew. Ulric had counted them.

"I know what you really are, human," said Ollowain gently. "Even if you don't want to believe it, there is a lot of truth in the stories. The men look up to you, more than ever in this hour of mourning. They will find their strength in you."

Alfadas took the silver dagger. "It lay among the bones?"

Ollowain nodded.

"Please, leave me alone," Alfadas said quietly.

A STRONG OAK AND A DECENT PIECE OF MEAT

It took a long time, but finally he appeared among the trees. Orgrim had been waiting for the scout for more than an hour. He immediately led Brud to Dumgar's fire.

"Well?" asked the Duke of Mordrock. "Did you find the path?"

Brud knocked the snow from his mantle as he and Orgrim sat. "There is no path. The wretched humans chose their site well. To reach the village, you have to go up the valley. There are two more walls, one at the top of the valley and one closer to the huts."

"How many humans?" Orgrim asked.

"Less than two hundred who can fight."

Dumgar jumped up from the fire. "Then we have two warriors to one puny human, and we can't even rip that many of them apart? Weak little pissants! What are you, warriors or lukewarm ratfarts?" The duke snatched up a few ribs that lay on a wooden board beside the fire and began to gnaw the scanty meat from the bones. Orgrim had seen the man they'd chosen for the meal—a skinny, sickly looking fellow with a pocked face. He'd whimpered like a whipped pup. *I'm not about to touch that meat,* Orgrim thought.

"Maybe it would boost the warriors' morale if they saw you fighting in the front line for once." Orgrim held Dumgar's glare. Orgrim loathed his commanding officer. The only lukewarm ratfart in that camp was him.

"I can read your mind, Orgrim. You'd love to see the humans kill me and hand you my command. But that's not going to happen. I'm too important. The army can't afford to lose me."

Orgrim ran his fingers over the scab that marked the fresh arrow wound on his shoulder. He'd been one of the warriors who'd tried to open the breach in the wall while Dumgar waited out of range on the hillside. "Let me reassure you, Commander. As long as you keep your distance from the battlefield, the greatest danger you face is choking on a rib."

Dumgar threw a bone into the fire. He gave Orgrim a sour smile. "Don't worry about that. I'm an experienced eater."

You're a pimple on the king's ass, Orgrim thought angrily, but he held his tongue. *One day I'll squeeze you dry.*

Dumgar turned to Birga. The shaman sat by herself, away from the fire. With a thin twig, she was marking a twisting pattern in the snow. "Are you certain that Emerelle is up in the humans' village?"

The shaman's stick stopped moving. The leather skin she wore over her face slipped to one side a little when she jerked her head around, but the motion was too quick to see anything of her face in the darkness. "Believe me, Dumgar, a man I interrogate is only too happy to give up his secrets to me. Emerelle is there!"

Dumgar licked his lips nervously. "I did not mean to doubt your knowledge. It would just be—how long will it take us to overrun the village?"

"I can't see into the future," she replied with irritation. "That damned golden-haired slut is always firing them up. I've been watching her for a long time. She's carrying a baby. The prisoners say she's the wife of the elvenjarl. She's the one we have to kill. Once she's dead, we'll finish the rest easily. But how fast that happens depends entirely on who's in charge the next time we attack." She looked to Orgrim. "I'm sure you would take a different approach than what we've tried so far. Or am I mistaken?"

Orgrim knew that he could not oppose Dumgar. The easiest way for him to reach his goal would be to kowtow to the Duke of Mordrock. "I think Dumgar has been taking the right approach, but we need to use more force. Our battering rams are too weak, and that comes from attacking too fast. We should leave the humans in peace for a day. Even if we don't attack, they'll be so afraid of us that they'll just sit there and stew, and we can use that time to find a big oak. A huge tree, that's what we need! Then we carve it into the kind of battering ram only trolls can lift. We'll break through the humans' next palisade in one rush."

"That's exactly what I had in mind," Dumgar asserted. "You just spoke up before I could, Orgrim. I give you permission to work out the details of my idea. But hurry it up. You know we've only got enough food to last a few more days. We have to take the village to get more meat."

"Of course." Orgrim stood up. "I'll take care of everything immediately." Relieved to be able to leave the duke's fire, he withdrew. Brud followed him.

"Are you going to kiss his feet next?" the scout asked in a low voice. "Slice open his belly and strangle the bastard with his own entrails. The maggot hasn't earned the right to be in command here."

"Let him do what he wants. I'm sure he'll find a way to dig his own grave."

"But how many good warriors is he going to take with him? You can't be indifferent to that."

"Have you tried Boltan's new dish? Meat baked in clay—delectable! Come to my fire and be my guest."

"You owe me an answer," Brud persisted. "He didn't listen to you when you advised him to send the captured humans back to their huts to get their warm furs. And what happened? They froze to death on the ice, and now we're almost out of food. What else does he have to do before you save us from him? If you don't have the guts for it, then I'll go and cut his throat myself."

"Then you might as well kill me while you're at it. If anything happens to Dumgar and there's even the slightest whiff that I might be behind his death, Branbeard will have me executed. The king's just waiting for it! That's why he gave the fool command in the first place. Branbeard was sure I wouldn't be able to stomach Dumgar's idiot orders for long. But if I raise a hand against him, then I put myself at the king's mercy."

"I hate the power games you princes play!" Brud said, and spat in the snow. "As soon as this is over, I'm going off to the forest, and you won't see me again for a long, long time. Being around you and Dumgar is poison for my soul."

"Help me find a strong oak tomorrow, and I promise you we'll sweep the humans aside the day after. As soon as we've got Emerelle, we return to Albenmark. Maybe we'll be lucky, and Dumgar will lose his way on the path through the void."

"You have the talent of making everything you say sound so simple."

Orgrim laid one hand on the scout's shoulder. "It *is* so simple, Brud. Now forget your anger. Come and try a decent piece of meat."

THE FIRST TIME

Y ou know what to expect?"
     Asla watched Kalf as he turned his steady eyes from one to the next of
the three men and two women standing before him. He had selected them
personally, and it seemed that he had chosen well. Asla did not know the five,
but all were able to meet Kalf's gaze. They did not seem at all hesitant, let alone
afraid. If they were lucky and the scouts really did find the scattered remnants
of Horsa's army, and if they then returned to Sunhill in time, then perhaps
there was yet hope. *Too many "ifs,"* thought Asla gloomily. She should not
start fooling herself now. It was unlikely that anyone would survive the trolls
in the valley once the last palisade fell. *At least these five will not perish with
them,* Asla thought defiantly. One of the two young women was very pretty.
She had beautiful doe-like brown eyes, and around her neck hung an amber
pendant almost the same hue as her eyes. No doubt she could have her choice
of husband from many who courted her, if she managed to elude the trolls'
sentries. Another damned "if"!

"Separate," said Kalf. "Do not try to help each other if the trolls catch one
of you. And if you make it out of the valley, head in different directions. But
work your way mostly to the south. You're more likely to find what's left of
Horsa's army there. Don't come back if you find less than a thousand men.
You'll need at least that many to beat the trolls. If you search longer than five
days, again, don't come back. You won't find any of us left."

One of the men spoke up. "But the trolls haven't attacked for two days.
Maybe they're sick of the fighting?"

"Can you picture a wolf living peacefully among sheep? There are just as
few trolls that get sick of fighting! I don't know what's stopping them, but I do
know that they will attack again. Any other questions?"

Asla thought of the sleeping queen housed in a hut with her aunt Svenja
and Kadlin farther up in the village. As long as Emerelle was with them, the
trolls would never rest. It was smart of Kalf not to say it openly. Asla would
rather forfeit her own life than hand over the queen, but she was not at all
certain that everyone else felt that way.

She saw eagerness and fear on all five faces. Each of them wore a long sheepskin coat. The refugees and the inhabitants of Sunhill had donated the clothes, and now their emissaries were dressed head to foot in white. That improved their chances of making it through the trolls' lines alive. At least, Asla hoped it would. Again, she realized just how very little they knew about the trolls. Could they see well? In some of the legends, it was said that they turned to stone in sunlight. That had proven to be utterly untrue. Did they have a discriminating nose, like a hunting dog? Would they simply follow the scent of the scouts? How were you supposed to beat an enemy you hardly knew?

Kalf said his parting words, warmer now, to the scouts.

"May Luth have spun you all a long thread," said Asla solemnly.

The girl with the amber pendant embraced Asla and whispered in her ear, "Please don't let the village fall. My grandmother is here. She is the last of my clan I have left. I trust you, Duchess."

"We will fight well," said Asla, her voice unwavering. "And I put my trust in Luth and his mercy." She could not lie to the girl and simply tell her everything would work out well. Asla squeezed her tightly to her breast.

Kalf was standing in the doorway. All had been said. For a moment, the five clung to the security of the small hut, putting off their departure into uncertainty for a few more heartbeats. On the threshold between blackness and light, they did not want to take the step out into the dark, and yet they could stay no longer. It was the girl with the amber pendant who finally went out first. The others followed, and the small group quickly vanished among the dark trees.

The hut that Asla had chosen as her quarters lay close to the second palisade, concealed in a small patch of woods. From there, it was less than two hundred paces to the wooden wall that would decide their fate. They had, in fact, built a third barrier at the entrance to the village proper, but everyone knew it would not stop the trolls for long. Whoever fought there was doomed to die. What mattered was to hold the trolls back long enough to unleash the white flood.

"It's getting cold," said Asla calmly. Tomorrow they might all be dead, but she had made up her mind: that night she would find out what other road her life might have taken.

Kalf was still standing in the doorway, peering out into the forest, although the five young emissaries had long since disappeared into the woods. Was he afraid? Did he not want this to happen? A surge of doubt came over Asla. Had she been wrong about him all along?

Kalf cleared his throat. He opened his mouth, tried to say something, but did not find the words. Finally, he closed the door. He could not look her in the eye. "I've wanted you for so many years. But now . . . You were always the light in my life. I admired you from a distance, but won't a man burn if he reaches for the light? Is it right . . ."

For as long as Asla could remember, she had looked up to Kalf. Even as a small girl, she had decided that she would one day be his wife. His broad shoulders; his flowing blond hair; the self-confident calm he radiated—all these things had charmed her. He was so different from the other young men, who drank and boasted and thought themselves irresistible. His quiet ways had attracted her, and she had believed back then that he loved her in return. She had never doubted that, one day, they would dance around the stone together.

Asla thought about what Alfadas had told her about love among the elves. *They promise to separate before the first lie passes between them. They believe that when there is something they cannot discuss together, then it is time to let each other go.* Alfadas had come into her life like a storm. He had charmed her and changed the course of her fate. The hero from the land of the elves, the man who had known women of inexpressible beauty, had come to her, the fisherman's daughter, and had asked for her hand. Back then, she had felt as if she were in a faery-tale-come-true. How could she have said no? Years had passed before she understood that one could not live a faery tale. At the start, it had not bothered her when he stood beside the house and gazed up at the Hartungscliff, where the stone circle stood, the gateway to the Other World. Only slowly had she come to understand the yearning inside him. Beyond the stones lay something that separated them, although she had never been able to put it into words. Alfadas loved her and the children, Asla knew. He had always been a good man. He came to her with more warmth and affection than most of the other women in the village ever got from their husbands. His pretty words and his smile still managed to captivate her. He tried to fulfill her every wish, but the way he looked up to the Hartungscliff wounded her more deeply with each passing year. In that place was something that she could never give him. He never talked about it, and that only made things worse.

Again, his words about the love of elves ran through her mind. If she were an elf woman, then she would probably have separated from him long before. But she was Asla, the fisherman's daughter. She could not simply give up the man whose children she had borne. Nor did she want to!

If the elves had never come to Firnstayn, maybe she would have found the strength to live with his yearning. Now she knew what it was he craved. She had seen the women. They were so different. Not only their beauty was bewildering. They radiated a strength and pride that Asla had never seen in a human woman. Everything about them was perfect. They could walk along a muddy path without dirtying their feet. They could gut a fish, and still a pleasant scent clung to them, more pleasant than the perfume of the loveliest flowers Asla knew. What was she compared to them? A flower at the end of summer, at best, its petals wilting and brown-edged.

She had had to take all those women into her house and serve them, and not for a moment had Alfadas given a thought to how she felt about it. She might have been able to live with that if not for that one. Silwyna! There was something catlike about her, and the scent of the woods surrounded her. Silwyna had barely entered her house before withdrawing again. Alfadas had kept away from her, as well. But the *way* that he had avoided her, the way that he had not even exchanged a glance with her, betrayed him. Alfadas had loved that elf woman once, and his feelings for her were perhaps buried, but they were not extinguished. She was the one he was thinking of when he looked up to the Hartungscliff. Asla wished that she had never encountered her.

She thought of her husband's pledge of love, his last words before he stepped through the gateway into the alien world of the elves. He had promised to return to her. And because he had spoken so openly of his feelings for her, he had shown himself before the king and all the other men to be vulnerable. Men did not do such things. It was considered effeminate. *But he was not like all the other men*, Asla thought sadly. That was why she loved him. Even now.

She looked to Kalf. He was still standing uncertainly before the closed door, avoiding her eye. The years had carved their lines deeply into his face, and yet she found everything there that she had always been attracted to.

He was more mature, stronger, even when he could not find the courage to come to her and speak of his love. In that, he seemed as innocent as a raw youth. As far as Asla knew, Kalf had never had a woman he called his wife. Sometimes he'd go away to Honnigsvald for a few days to sell fish, or furs in winter. Maybe there were . . . but that would not be like him. Asla knew that if Kalf found a woman to whom his heart belonged, he would go to her. Her throat felt suddenly tight. She knew what it was. He'd found his woman, and that was why he'd stayed. For her.

She went to him and reached tenderly for his hand. "It is good that you are here. Knowing you have someone at your side gives you so much strength."

Finally, he looked into her face. His eyes were endlessly sad. "Yes" was all he said.

Asla resisted the urge to hug him. He was no little boy that she had to console. She wanted more from him. She wanted to lie in his arms, feel his love, and feel herself safe. If she hugged him now, then all that would be lost to her.

Asla sighed. She had to find another way. "I don't understand how some men can run around the whole day long in chain mail. It's crushing me! When I take it off, I feel so light, as if a puff of wind would be enough to blow me off to the stars." She loosened the broad belt that served to carry some of the weight of the mail shirt and let it fall to the floor. Then she raised her arms. "Now I know why soldiers usually wear their hair short." She smiled. "The rings catch in your hair. Let me wear this thing for one moon, and it will turn me into a bald woman. Please help me take it off."

Kalf's hands were strong. Carefully, he freed her from the heavy armor. Even through the mesh of rings, Asla felt his warmth. With the patience he needed when mending damaged nets, he freed her hair wherever it caught in the iron rings. Finally, he lifted the heavy load from her shoulders. It rattled to the floor.

Only then was Asla conscious of what she was wearing under the armor. A heavy, padded dress onto which she had sewn wide shoulder pads made from old rags. The grease she'd rubbed into the chain mail had left black spots and streaks on the already plain dress, and she herself could smell that she'd been wearing it for days. The upholstered dress was indispensable, because the mail shirt was ice cold and sucked the warmth out of her body if she didn't protect herself. But now, inside that shapeless garment, she felt like a

240

rancid sausage. Filthy and stinking, her hair unkempt, no man could desire her, though his trouser-flap was all but bursting open otherwise.

Kalf smiled. He stroked her hair smooth. She hardly dared to look up at him. Was he laughing at her? What was he thinking? Since the battle on the palisade, he'd been avoiding her. For two endless days. When he did not come to her the night after the battle, she'd felt like dirt, like a smutty whore. She never wanted to exchange so much as a word with Kalf again.

But her vow had not held for long. She could not bear being without him. He and Kadlin were all that gave her strength. She could not let herself think about Ulric at all. Yilvina had not returned, and that could only mean one thing.

Asla had ordered the five emissaries to her hut to see them off. She knew that Kalf would come with them. He had chosen them, and he could not simply let them go off without sharing a few final words. He was not the man for that. Of course, he might have waited for them at the palisade and spoken with them there, but Asla had prayed that he would take the opportunity to come to her hut. Like this, no one would find anything untoward in his being there.

Kalf stroked her cheek gently. "You are a beautiful woman."

She looked up at him angrily. How could he call her beautiful, the way she looked? Was he trying to mock her? The sadness was gone from his eyes. They were radiant. Asla's anger evaporated. He truly meant what he said.

She took his hand and placed it over her right breast. He let it happen. "We can't—"

"Why? Don't you want it?"

This time, he did not avoid her eye. "I've wanted it since the first time I saw you watching me secretly from the shore when I went out with my boat. On that day, I knew you were the woman Luth had chosen for me. No other."

She smiled sadly. Why had they never found their way to each other? What plan was the weaver of fate following with them? She would have to lead Kalf along the path of love. The idea that he had never lain with another woman excited her, and at the same time it filled her with melancholy.

"We can't . . . the people . . . ," he said, but he did not take his hand from her breast.

"Forget the people! Before the moon is full again, there may be no people left alive who know that you even entered this hut. We were meant for each other. We need to forget the years that have passed." Asla smiled coquettishly. "Imagine it's still that summer night when you crept after me to watch me bathe in the lake in the beech grove."

Kalf looked at her in surprise. "You knew about that?"

"I wanted it. The trail past your hut was not the shortest way to the beech grove." She reached for his weapon belt and unbuckled it.

Suddenly, Kalf grabbed her, pulled her to him awkwardly, and kissed her passionately. Asla gave herself over to him, even as she felt the child in her belly move. For a brief moment, she thought of Alfadas, but the thought did not make her feel guilty. What was happening then was right.

She sank into Kalf's arms. It felt as if she were drifting in warm water.

Gently, the fisherman laid her down on the bed of old blankets. He did not let go of her for a second. His wild kisses and the weight of his body robbed Asla of breath. His large, powerful hands ranged over her body, pushed beneath the padded dress. Clumsy, yet filled with craving.

"Undo the leather loops at the sides," she whispered.

She heard the worn fabric tear as he tugged at the dress. She felt for the loops, trying to help him. Their hands touched; their fingers locked together.

Suddenly, Kalf froze. Then he straightened up and listened.

Now Asla heard it, too. The long, wailing blast of a sentry's horn. The trolls! They were attacking the palisade.

With a leap, Kalf was on his feet. He reached for his weapon belt. Only when he reached the door did he stop. "I'll return." Then he disappeared into the night.

Asla saw a tiny spider scurrying across the rushes on the floor. Angrily, she stomped on the little creature, crushing it. "I curse you, Luth. Couldn't you have granted us just one hour? One hour in a lifetime? Was I asking too much?"

She reached for her sword. There was no time to get the chain mail on again. Asla ran out into the cold. She knew that neither she nor Kalf would ever return to this hut. Luth would never forgive her for cursing him. And she would never forgive the capricious god!

AWAKENING

S venja began to tremble when she heard the call of the horn. The trolls had never attacked them at night. At sunset, she had felt secure, at least for the night ahead. She pictured her niece Asla wearing that horrible chain mail tunic and climbing up onto the wall to be with the men. A woman should not stand in the middle of a battle line, least of all a woman expecting a child. What had they done to the gods for them to impose such trials on them?

She turned her attention to her obligations. She would stay with the children. Whatever happened, she would never leave them alone. A lot of the little ones could not even walk yet, and far too many children had died already. She looked across at the heavy pan beside the fire. A woman should not run around with a sword in her hand, but that did not mean she had to be defenseless.

"Sing another song," Loki begged. His father had died two days before, snatched off the wall by a troll with a rope. The boy had not cried. He was six. Old enough to understand.

"Fly, little bird . . . ," Svenja began, but her voice failed her. There were so many songs she did not like to sing anymore. In the past, she hadn't given a second thought to the words of children's songs. She'd sung them just as her mother had sung them for her. But things were different now.

"Don't stop," Loki urged her.

Kadlin, sleeping in Svenja's arms, squirmed restlessly. They had brought all the small children who were still alive to Svenja. There were only seventeen, mostly sleeping peacefully by the brick fire pit, like the queen. The elf woman made Svenja's flesh creep. She lay as if dead. She did not move, nor could Svenja hear her breathe. Her face was as white as the snow outside and had a cold beauty like the fjord on a winter's morning. Asla had told her that the queen was many hundreds of years old, but that could not be right. She had the face of a young lady who still dreamed about men because she didn't know any better. She had none of the scars that life left one with—the fine folds around the eyes from laughing or the deep grooves at the corners of the mouth that marked despair and disappointment.

"The song!" Loki complained. "Did you forget how it goes?"

Svenja smiled. "I did. I'll sing something else. The song of the golden king. That's much nicer, anyway." She took a deep breath. Kadlin flailed in her sleep and pressed her head against Svenja's breasts.

"So many little fishes swim
Along the bottom of the fjord . . ."

Svenja's voice faltered, and she began to tremble again. The elf woman! She had opened her eyes and was looking at her. What eyes! Now she believed that the queen had lived for hundreds of years.

"You do not need to fear me, mortal."

The elf spoke with a gentle, amiable voice. Someone with a voice like that was not to be feared, whatever her eyes might look like. The children were looking at the queen now, too. None of them seemed afraid of her. Loki even went over to her.

"Why were you asleep so long?" the boy asked.

"I was hurt and very tired." The queen looked around. Her eyes, to Svenja, were like two chasms, gulping down hungrily everything she saw.

"How did I get here? And what is your name?"

"I am Svenja." She wondered at how firm her own voice sounded. Her hands stopped shaking. A deep calm came over her. She told the queen about how the elves had come to Firnstayn, how the ghost-wolf had haunted them, and how it had finally been killed by Gundar. Then she told her about how the trolls had come and about their flight across the ice that had led them here, to Sunhill. As she was talking, Kadlin woke up. The little girl went to the queen as if she had known her all her life.

Emerelle stroked Kadlin's hair gently. "You're the daughter of Alfadas. I knew your father when he was as big as you are now."

"Papa gone," said Kadlin indistinctly.

A shudder ran down Svenja's spine. The little girl could not speak properly yet. What had the queen done to her? Svenja wanted to stand up and take Kadlin in her arms, but it was as if her legs were paralyzed.

"Ulric gone. Mama sad. Good you wake up." The little girl's voice was becoming clearer and clearer. Svenja had been looking after children for nearly thirty years, but she had never seen anything like this.

"Let Kadlin go," she said fearfully.

The little girl turned around to her. "I am well, Auntie. Don't worry."

Emerelle removed her hand from the young girl's hair. The war horn sounded again in the distance. "I am what the trolls want. I will go out and surrender to them. This is not a war for mortals. It should never have come here. I did not see it."

Svenja did not understand what the queen meant with her last words. She inhaled deeply. Suddenly, she felt filled with energy. She jumped to her feet and threw her arms around Kadlin.

Emerelle rose from her bed as if she had only rested for a few moments. Pale and dressed in only a thin nightdress, she looked like a ghost. She bowed momentarily to Svenja. "Thank you for watching over my bed for so many hours. You have a very lovely singing voice. It is a special gift. I hope you will sing the children happy songs again soon." With that, she opened the door, and winter's icy breath crept into the hut. "By the way, Kadlin likes you very much, Svenja. She wanted me to tell you that."

Svenja pressed the little girl to her tightly.

"Dada." Kadlin pointed to the door. A gust of wind hit the hut, rattling the wooden shingles. The door creaked and swung on its hinges.

"Shut winter out before Father Firn bites all our noses," Svenja ordered Loki. Then she eyed Kadlin suspiciously. The child seemed unchanged. "What did you talk about with the elf?"

Kadlin tilted her head to one side and smiled.

Svenja breathed a sigh of relief. The episode was over.

THE REFUGE

Blood ploughed a path for them through the deep snow. They had seen lights on the fjord some time before, and now moved deeper into the woods, out of sight from the ice. Ulric was very tired but was intent on not complaining. Halgard was still on her feet, although she sighed quietly with every step she took. Ulric looked back to Yilvina, who walked in silence. She kept her left hand pressed to her hip. Her makeshift bandage was drenched with blood. The wound had opened again, despite so much time passing since she had come to the trolls' camp to rescue him and Halgard.

Ulric's belly growled. They had hardly eaten anything for three days. Yilvina had dug up a few caches of nuts hidden by squirrels, but nuts alone could not fill you up. Yilvina had led them deep into the forest, far from the fjord. She did not think anyone would come looking for them back there.

Ulric knew enough stories about the hunt. He was sure he knew what the elf was thinking. She was like a she-wolf with its belly torn open by a wild boar. She knew that her strength was failing her, bit by bit, and now wanted only to rescue her young. That was why they had turned back toward the fjord. Yilvina hoped that they would find the refugees again. She wanted to get him and Halgard to safety. Then she would return to the woods to die.

The lights on the fjord had appeared just after sundown. They had been unable to make out the shadowy figures on the ice very well, but it had to be the trolls. They were heading south, looking for new victims.

Ulric had, in fact, expected Yilvina, as an elf, to be able to tell a guinea fowl from a snow hare from a mile away, but the elf told him she was so dizzy that she could barely see her own feet, and they had then decided to give the figures on the ice a wide berth.

If only I weren't so tired, thought Ulric in despair. It was good to have Blood forging a path through the snow for them. Ulric would not have found the strength for it. The moment he stepped off Blood's track, the snow was over his knees. He probably wouldn't even make it a mile. It was better to rely on the dog's strength.

Halgard held on to Blood's tail. Ulric had worried about that at first. He knew that dogs didn't like someone pulling on their tail, but Blood put up with it. Maybe he sensed that Halgard had no choice. Sometimes she even had to lean on him for support. Without Blood, their escape would have failed long ago.

The day before, they had stumbled onto a farm that had been plundered and burned, and Ulric had learned that it made no difference if you spent a night in four walls without a roof or among a few rocks that protected you from the wind.

He could see that Yilvina was gritting her teeth as she moved along. She was in great pain, he was sure of it. Dark blood seeped through her bandage, and every few steps a fat, red drop fell onto the snow. But with the track the dog was making, a few drops of blood made no difference. You would not have to be an experienced tracker to follow them—having eyes in your head would do. Even at night, the deep furrow through the snow was impossible to miss.

Yilvina looked back. She supported herself against a snow-covered birch trunk and squinted into the darkness. She shook her head angrily.

The boy started. Was that a sound? Ulric peered as hard as could but could not make out anything. After just a few paces, the dense tree trunks blurred with the night to become a dark, impenetrable wall. Was it footsteps crunching in the snow? Or was it just the sound of swaying branches? Who would be following them?

Ulric thought of the battle in the trolls' camp. Yilvina and Blood had appeared in the middle of the night. The elf woman had only wanted to take him and Halgard. She had no interest in the others at all. But that wasn't right! He had balked, and only then had others seen what was going on. In the cold and darkness, their only concern was for themselves. Most had been sleeping, though some lay stiffly, already frozen to death.

Ulric now knew how to tell the dead from the sleeping. With the dead, the snow did not melt in the fine line between their lips.

When he demanded that Yilvina save them all, the other prisoners had crowded her, wanting to be taken along. Then the guards had come, two trolls with stone axes. Yilvina had needed less time to kill them than his mother took to kill and gut a chicken. Ulric wished that he would one day be able to fight like that. Her movements had been faster than his eyes could follow.

When the trolls lay dead in the snow, Yilvina had picked up Halgard and him bodily, and that had caused an uproar among the prisoners. Anyone with the strength to go a few steps had tried to take advantage of the terrible confusion to escape. More guards came running, but Yilvina somehow managed to get both of them out.

They had already left the camp behind them when that one troll had suddenly appeared. A warrior, a giant even among trolls. He had decorated his naked belly with bloody handprints. He held a freshly carved club in his hand and had emerged from the woods, making straight for them.

Yilvina had dropped them in the snow and attacked the troll at a run. One of her blades struck home, and the wounded troll had bellowed like a rutting elk and fallen to his knees, one hand pressed to his crotch. Yilvina had tried to retreat, but the troll lashed out with a backhanded swing. He hit Yilvina with so much force that she flew several paces through the air and had trouble getting back on her feet. She had her left hand clenched at her side, and a thin strand of blood trickled from her nose and covered her lips. One of her swords was gone, lost somewhere in the snow. She staggered and called out to Halgard and him to run. But he was no coward! Luckily, the troll had not been able to get back onto his feet. When Yilvina saw that, she took the two of them and led them deep into the woods.

Several days had now passed, but the face of that one troll had haunted the boy in nightmares ever since. In the troll's eyes, Ulric had seen unbridled hatred, and he knew he would come after them as soon as his injuries allowed.

Ulric shook himself, as if he could simply shake the troll warrior out of his mind. He glanced back at Yilvina fearfully. She looked like Kadlin's ragged straw doll: crooked, her hair unkempt, somehow crushed. More and more, she had to stop and lean against a tree to catch her breath. She would not make it much farther, Ulric knew. Someone had to help her. Halgard, too, was at the end of her rope. She moved now less with her own strength and more because Blood was pulling her along. They urgently needed to find somewhere to camp, somewhere where there was dry wood and where they could light a fire. But no one could be allowed to see the firelight. Luth alone knew who else was creeping around in the dark. Maybe there really were trolls on their trail.

Ulric tried to remember what his father had told him about a good night-time camp, all the things you had to keep in mind. In this kind of cold, they should light a fire in the shelter of rocks, which would reflect the warmth. In winter, you could sit at a fire and still get frostbitten if you didn't choose your campsite carefully.

He looked around desperately. They were making their way down a gentle slope. Somewhere off to their left, there had to be a branch of the fjord. All around them were trees. There was no place here to camp. But Yilvina and Halgard would not make it much farther. He had to find a place for the night. He had to!

Ulric fought back tears. What should he do? If only he were a little bit older! Then he would pick Halgard up and just carry her, and he would come back and get Yilvina as soon as he'd found a place for the night. *It's always so much easier in the skalds' songs,* he thought angrily. *The heroes never have problems carrying their maidens in those.*

A faint shimmer among the trees distracted him. Blood stopped in his tracks as golden light poured like resin from a large tree. Suddenly, Ulric was standing before a familiar figure. Gundar! The priest smiled, spread his arms out wide, and came toward them. Blood greeted him with a friendly bark.

"What is it?" Halgard asked anxiously. "I can sense a light."

Yilvina moved up beside the children. She held her remaining sword ready to defend them.

"You won't need that, my pretty elf. You could not injure me, but you don't need to." As if to underscore his words, the priest walked through a tree.

"Are you a ghost?" Ulric asked suspiciously, putting one arm protectively around Halgard.

"First of all, I'm your friend. And you can take my word for it that I did not carry you all the way down that hillside to your mother's house to watch you freeze to death now." Gundar had stopped a few steps away from them.

Ulric felt a lump form in his throat. "You died for me, didn't you?" He bit down on his lips to hold back his tears.

"No." Gundar shook his head amiably. "I died because Luth had spun the thread of my life to its end. You are not to blame at all. It was the weaver of fate's decision." He blinked. "They must still talk about me a lot, don't they?"

Ulric nodded.

"I had a good death," the old man declared. Then he looked past them, up the slope of the hill. "The warp of your lives has broken from the weft. Luth has allowed me to return to rescue the tapestry he is weaving. You are being followed. A terrible enemy has picked up your trail. There is only one place where he is unable to kill you."

"I am protecting the children," Yilvina said, through clenched teeth.

Gundar looked sadly at her. "I do not have to tell you how you are faring, elf-maid. Trust me. I did save you, after all, when I faced the wolfhorse."

"I'll go with you," said Halgard softly. "I . . . I can see you." The blind girl was gazing steadfastly at where, between the trees, the apparition of the priest glowed.

"I'll come, too," Ulric decided. He was terribly worried about Halgard. His friend was shivering with exhaustion. He put his arms around her and embraced her tightly. "Do we have to go far?"

"Just down to the fjord. Come now."

Yilvina still seemed suspicious, but Ulric knew that following the priest was the right thing to do. He had known Gundar all his life, and the old man had never been anything but good to him. One could trust him always, even as a ghost.

Gundar led them some distance down the slope until they came to a broad swath of trees blown down by a storm. Dozens of them lay felled, like soldiers in battle. Some were snapped through the middle; others tipped from the ground, roots and all. They had fallen left and right and had formed an impenetrable thicket of dead wood.

Beneath a tree trunk gleamed two eyes, like polished pieces of gold. A low growl sounded, but a gesture from the priest was enough to silence whatever was lurking there under the trunk.

Ulric's hand went to his belt. He wished he still had the elven dagger.

Finally, they reached the shore of the fjord. There, too, were fallen trees, locked in the ice. Gundar glided through a trunk, and Ulric had to duck to follow him. The going was much harder for Halgard. She caught her hair in upturned roots, and it seemed to take an age before Ulric was able to free her again.

Something rolled down the slope. Stones and snow slammed onto the ice behind them.

"Quickly, now!" Gundar pressed them. "Or else it will all have been for nothing. It's not much farther."

Just beyond the broken trees, the side branch of the fjord ended before a steep rock wall. The ice cracked threateningly under their feet.

"Stop!" Yilvina cried. "It won't carry us. There must be an underwater spring that opens into the fjord here. The flow stops the ice from getting thick enough. If we keep going, it will break. What are we doing here, priest?"

Blood tilted his big head to one side and looked from Gundar to the elf, confused.

"That's just what I want," said the priest in all seriousness. "You're supposed to break through the ice." He pointed toward the sheer rock wall. "Over there is a cave. The entrance is hidden underwater, behind a rock overhang. It's the only way into the cave. You will survive in there. No one knows this place."

"Survive? A fall into cold water can kill you in a heartbeat, priest." Yilvina had her sword raised threateningly again. "Have you lost your senses? You say you love the boy. How can you expose him to such a danger?"

"I know the course of the threads of your destinies. The water will not kill you. There is some driftwood in the cave, enough to dry your clothes by a fire. The smoke can escape through a vent in the rock. You are well protected down below. If you stay out here, you will either die at the hands of your pursuer, or the cold will kill you."

"I trust Gundar," said Ulric, although the thought of the icy water made him feel queasy.

"I'm coming with you, wherever you go," said Halgard, reaching out for his hand. Her fingers were as cold as ice.

Ulric hesitated. With Halgard at his side, walking out on the thin ice was suddenly something very different. "And the cold water won't harm any of us?" he asked doubtfully.

"No. But you have to wait in the cave until they find you."

"I don't think anyone knows this place," Yilvina protested. "How are they supposed to find us?"

"I can't reveal your future to you," Gundar replied. His voice sounded very tired now. "It is one of the weaver of fate's ironclad rules. I've already told you far too much."

Ulric took a step forward. The ice cracked menacingly. He saw a network of fine cracks eat through the crust atop the water. He took a deep breath. He remembered the time his father had thrashed him with a leather strap because he had thrown a gold-rimmed drinking horn into the coals of the fire. He wished he was back again in the warm hall of his house on that afternoon. Anything would be better than being here. For the space of a heartbeat, he closed his eyes. If he wished it enough, then perhaps none of this would be happening. He would lie across his father's lap and take his well-deserved hiding.

"Ulric," he heard the priest's friendly voice say. Gundar was looking at him sadly from beneath his bushy eyebrows. "It has to be."

The boy took another deep breath. Then he took a determined step forward. Halgard held on to him tightly.

The sound of the breaking ice grew more ominous. Everything in Ulric fought against the next step.

"Don't do it," whispered the elf.

He moved his foot forward. Defiantly, he stepped onto the ice. He wanted to put it behind him. Water rose through the cracks, onto the surface of the ice. Suddenly, there was a loud crack, like splintering wood. With a jolt, Ulric was thrown off his feet. Halgard let out a high-pitched scream. Blood barked madly.

A merciless cold snatched at the boy. Now he screamed, too, as his heavy winter clothes sucked up their fill of water. As if by an invisible hand, he was pulled deeper. He made no attempt to hold on to the jagged break in the ice. Something sharp-edged banged against his cheek. With an effort, he still kept his head above water. He tried to see where Gundar was, but the priest had disappeared.

Yilvina had thrown herself flat on the ice and was trying to reach him with her outstretched hand. Halgard clung to him. Ulric's feet pedaled but could find no grip. Then he sank. The water closed over his head, and he held his breath. He opened his eyes, squinting. He felt as stiff as a frozen salmon.

Halgard was holding on to his arm with both hands. Where was Gundar? Something dark slipped through the water beside them. Blood! The dog had followed them. Ulric reached out for the big dog but could not get a grip on the wet fur. Suddenly, in front of them, a bright light glowed. Gundar was back!

You have to hold on to Ulric's belt, Halgard, so he can use his arms. Gundar's voice was in his head. Halgard obviously heard it, too, for she did what the priest told her.

Now paddle with your arms, boy, and come to me.

Ulric felt himself growing rigid with the cold. A burning pain began to spread inside him. He wanted to breathe.

Don't do that. Come to me now. You can do it!

Ulric moved his arms. Slowly, inch by inch, he found he could move toward the priest. He could feel Halgard writhing. Did the same fire burn in her?

Faster, Ulric.

Beside the priest, a dark hole gaped in the rock wall. The boy steered for it, but the water around him seemed to become more solid. The strength in his arms flagged. He hardly made any progress at all. The fire spread inside him—he had to get air! The cold water would still the flames.

Something jabbed into his back and pushed him forward. Blood! Ulric's head broke through the water's surface and he gasped for breath. The air eased the burning in his lungs and slowly made it subside.

Gundar appeared again. The light that played around the priest drove back the darkness. A smooth stone floor rose gradually from the water. Driftwood, bleached as bones, lay all around.

Gasping, paddling clumsily with his arms, Ulric splashed forward. Halgard's teeth were chattering so much that she could not talk. Her lips were dark from the cold.

With the last of his strength, Ulric pulled himself clear of the water. Blood sank his teeth into Halgard's coat and helped drag her up where it was dry.

"You have to collect the driftwood," said the priest. The voice was no longer in Ulric's head. "Hurry up, boy. I can't stay much longer. Then you have to get out of your clothes, or the fire won't warm you at all."

Trembling all over, Ulric picked up a few branches and layered them for a fire. There was not as much wood in the cave as he would have liked.

Gundar stretched one hand toward the pile of wood. He closed his eyes, and deep folds appeared on his forehead. Flames flared from inside the pile—tiny flames, but they licked hungrily along the thin branches. Ulric could see them gaining in strength, and as they brightened, the priest's apparition faded.

"I wish you luck," Gundar breathed, his voice drifting away as he became one with the blackening wood.

Blood shook himself, and a shower of water droplets sprayed onto the fire, extinguishing some of the flames.

"Get away!" Ulric cried. "Don't do that again." Quickly, he hunted along the water's edge for more thin branches. The fire was losing strength.

"Please, Luth, don't let it go out," he begged. "I promise I'll do what Mother says, always. But don't let it go out." He layered the small branches carefully around the last of the flame and held his breath for an anxious moment. Finally, the fire began to grow again. And now it burned stronger than before, one good flame licking along the bleached wood, growing as it moved, before it jumped across to the branches above it.

Halgard pressed a shivering kiss to Ulric's cheek. She tried to say something, but the chattering of her teeth smothered all words.

"You have to take your clothes off now," Ulric said uncertainly.

Awkwardly, Halgard pulled off her coat. The boy turned aside, embarrassed. He knew that it wasn't right to watch when a girl got undressed. He peeled off his own clothes until all he had left was a pair of woolen shorts. They clung to his loins like ice, even as he felt the warmth of the fire on his arms and chest.

Halgard had taken off her clothes and now crouched close to the flames. Her skin was wrinkled all over, and her arms and legs were like brittle branches. The line of fine bones down her spine stood out beneath the skin of her back, and her ribs showed down her side. She rubbed her hands under her arms.

Hesitantly, Ulric removed his shorts, too. Only then did it occur to him that Halgard could not see him at all. How could he have forgotten that? Relieved, he sat beside her, and Blood also lay beside the fire. The big dog, with an expression of annoyance, looked across at Ulric. Steam rose from Blood's fur. Then, with a deep sigh, he stretched, flailed his paws like a puppy, and rolled onto his back.

Something slid, jangling across the stone floor. Ulric and Blood both leaped to their feet. Halgard let out a sharp cry. "What is it? What's happening?" she cried fearfully.

Yilvina was trying to push herself out of the water. She had thrown her sword ashore. Ulric tried to help, but the slightly built elf woman was heavier than she looked. Only when Halgard came to his aid was he able to drag Yilvina up until she was lying in the dry part of the cave.

She said something in a language Ulric did not understand. Her eyes were aglow with fever.

"We have to undress her, too," said Halgard.

Working together, they pulled her chain mail tunic over her head. Halgard touched Yilvina's body lightly with her hands. "I've never felt cloth so soft," she said quietly. "She must be wearing wonderful clothes."

Ulric did not think there was anything particularly special about the padded jacket and shirt that the elf was wearing beneath the mail, but he did not say anything. He did not want to spoil Halgard's pleasure.

Pulling off Yilvina's boots was all but impossible. The leather wrapped her calves like a thick second skin. Ulric toiled at the boots while Halgard removed her last layer above: a delicate silk shirt.

The elf's clothes were soaked with blood. Yilvina groaned and doubled over in pain when they freed her from the shirt, which had stuck to the scabs of her wounds. A bone protruded sideways from her torso, and blood was now seeping again through the thick scab. Her entire chest and most of her belly were discolored red and blue. Her body looked strangely misshapen, and Ulric found something else confusing as he examined her terrible bruises. He had to look for a long time before he realized what it was. On the left side of her chest, no ribs stood out anymore. In disbelief, he ran his fingers over the damaged skin. Bones could not disappear like that! He felt something firm in the flesh, and it moved under his touch.

Yilvina groaned. She looked at Ulric, tears in her eyes.

"I'm sorry," he whispered.

Yilvina nodded weakly. Her lips were trembling. Ulric had to lean very close over her to hear what she was saying. "My sword . . . give it . . . to me."

"What does she want?" asked Halgard.

"Her sword."

"What use is it to her now?"

"You don't understand," said Ulric adamantly. "She's a warrior. She will feel better if she has her sword."

"I don't understand that at all," Halgard replied, her feelings hurt. "In fact, it sounds like complete nonsense to me."

Ulric did not reply. He did not want an argument now. Besides, Halgard usually won their arguments. She simply found the better words, and afterward he always felt like a complete idiot. Sometimes, after they'd fought, Halgard's words would still be going through his head even hours later. He laid out every possible response in his mind, but by then it was too late—they rarely argued about the same thing twice.

The boy looked around inside the cave. It was Yilvina's wish to have her sword, so there was nothing left to discuss!

Their hideout was not particularly big. Ulric could stand upright without banging his head, but only just. They were surrounded by gray rock that was veined with white and rust-colored lines. The cave was an irregular shape, with several niches into which the light of the fire barely penetrated at all.

Ulric saw the sword lying on the floor close to the rear wall of the cave. He went back to it tiredly. All he wanted was to stretch out by the fire and sleep.

The wavering firelight distorted his shadow grotesquely where it danced across the irregular walls. Ulric ducked lower. Just in front of him, the wall cut back. The water had eroded an elongated alcove into the rock. And inside it was . . . someone . . .

Ulric hastily grabbed for the sword. In the alcove lay a warrior in green armor, sound asleep!

"Is something wrong?" Halgard asked.

"Shh!" Ulric hissed. He strained to see into the niche in the wall. The sleeper did not move. Slowly, the boy's eyes adjusted to the darkness. The man wore a green winged helmet. His face was hidden behind wide cheek guards. A green breastplate reached the warrior's hips. His pale gauntlets held a magnificent sword with a broad blade. His breeches were tattered, the fabric decorated with a pattern Ulric had never seen, and the leather of his boots was shriveled and cracked.

Holding his breath, Ulric leaned in, trying to look at the man's face. He had never heard of a warrior with green armor, but someone like that would have caught people's attention.

He crept forward until he was as close to the alcove as he could get, then pushed his head inside. His heart was beating wildly. He must not touch the sleeper! Luth only knew what kind of fellow this was. He certainly did not come from the Fjordlands—no one there wore such strange armor.

Ulric turned his head. He had to support himself with one hand on the alcove ceiling to stop himself from losing his balance. Just a few inches more. Finally! His face was very pale—no! Shocked, Ulric jerked back, banging his head on the ceiling. He lost his balance and fell across the man's body. But the man would not awaken. Never again. The helmet concealed a skull.

Blood had jumped up and run to Ulric's side. Sniffing curiously, he pushed into the alcove beside Ulric, who had trouble pulling him out again. Halgard also came, feeling her way carefully over the cave floor. She made Ulric describe the dead man in detail.

Now Ulric discovered two holes in the side of the man's breastplate. In one was a rotted wooden shaft. On the roof of the alcove, something had been painted in brown, almost faded away now. A spider! The sign of Luth.

"And his armor is all green?" Halgard asked.

"Yes."

"Take a stone and scratch it."

What? What was this now? Only a girl could think of something like that.

"Do it for me?" Halgard urged him.

Ulric sighed. He was cold. He wanted to return to the fire. And he had to give Yilvina her sword. Carefully, he took the elven blade and scraped it across the breastplate.

"Well?" Halgard said.

Ulric squinted. "There's something golden underneath the green," he said in amazement.

"Bronze," the girl replied triumphantly. "I thought so."

"What?" Ulric was annoyed. Yet again, she'd made him look a fool.

"It's King Osaberg!" Halgard announced reverently.

"Never!" Ulric said. "Osaberg is lying at the bottom of the fjord. You don't know the story right."

257

But the girl was not about to let him put her off. "He must have made it into the cave, just like we did. He hid from his enemies in here. He just wanted to rest, but he was too badly injured, and he died."

"It's just some soldier," Ulric said truculently.

"No. Luth gave him a winged helmet, and the king of the kobolds gave him a sword with a blade that would never rust and never get dull."

Somehow, Ulric did not want to admit that Halgard was right. He had always imagined Osaberg as a big, strong warrior with long hair, lying stretched out on the bottom of the fjord, asleep. He was a hero waiting to return, not just a pile of bones in a cave. Ulric stood and went back to the fire. He laid Yilvina's sword close beside the sleeping elf. *Will she sleep here forever, too?* he wondered uneasily.

Blood followed him to the fire, and then Halgard. Her teeth were chattering again. She rubbed her hands over her skinny arms. "It *is* Osaberg," she murmured defiantly.

Blood growled.

You can't stand girls who have to be right all the time either, can you? Ulric thought, and he grinned.

The black dog rose to its feet. Its growls grew deeper and more menacing.

Wavelets splashed up the slope at the water's edge. Suddenly, a big, ungainly head rose from the water. Ulric recognized the face instantly. He had seen it again and again in his nightmares. It was the troll Yilvina had wounded so gravely days before.

JUST ONE WORD

K alf pulled himself up onto the wall-walk inside the second palisade. In the moonlight, the trolls were gathering just out of range of the archers, their outlines clear against the snow as they formed into a column.

Kalf looked along the wall-walk. A short distance away stood the wagon maker, Sigvald, supporting himself on the shaft of a poleaxe. He looked as if he barely had the strength to stay on his feet.

"Where are our archers?" Kalf called.

Sigvald pointed up to the cliff on the western end of the palisade. "Kodran sent them up there. He wanted fighters on the wall. No children."

Kalf nodded. He looked up to the edge of the cliff. Nothing moved. By foot, it took almost half an hour to get up there. He knew that Kodran was trying to save the children and young men, and sighed. The trolls had given themselves two days to prepare for their new attack. Maybe they still needed a little longer.

The second palisade, situated as it was at the top of the trail that led up the pass, was not as high as the wall they had already lost. It would be easier for the trolls to pull themselves up. The defenders had also had little time to reinforce the defenses with more tree trunks. The clash would be harder this time. But the men who stood along the wall-walk were also the better fighters. On the first palisade, those who had fallen were unskilled fighters or simply unlucky. The survivors were a harder breed to kill. And in the final reckoning, on the barricade close to the village, only the best would remain.

A low drone sounded. Below, the trolls on the pass trail began to move. They swarmed around something that lay in the snow. A drumbeat reverberated, a slow, sinister rhythm.

Kalf squinted his eyes to slits. What was going on down there? The troll warriors had formed into a column. The fisherman glanced up to the cliff-top—the archers had not yet arrived.

"So what are the bastards up to?" a familiar voice asked loudly. Asla! She was not supposed to be there. Kalf sighed. Trying to send her back would be a waste of time.

"I think the trolls are trying to impress us by holding hands, Duchess," Kodran called.

Laughter rang. Even Kalf had to smile. With Asla there, hope returned, and laughter with it. He did not know how she did it, but it was at least a little miraculous.

"What's become of your mail tunic, Duchess?" Sigvald asked.

"If I'm picking a fight with hand-holding trolls, I don't need chain mail. I could have brought a decent-sized wooden spoon and left my sword at home."

Below, a single command rang out. The trolls hoisted something between them. They weren't holding hands at all, but were carrying something, all of them, together! To the beat of the drum, the column of trolls began to move up the hill. Kalf refused to believe what he saw. This was the end—it could not be!

"That's a tree trunk they're carrying," Sigvald muttered. It had come from a tree that must have seen a hundred winters or more pass before the trolls had cut it down. The trunk was more than thirty paces long and as thick through as a wagon wheel was round.

The drumbeat down below slowly increased its tempo, and even though they were moving uphill, the trolls picked up their pace.

Kalf glanced up to the clifftop. Still no archers! Nothing would stop the trolls.

"Get off the palisade!" he bellowed. "Down, all of you!" He grabbed one man and pushed him down into the snow. "Back to the longspears!"

"What do you think—" Asla hissed furiously, but Kalf cut her off.

"We can't hold the wall. They'll break through on the first charge. Anyone up here when they do is dead. Get back to the village! I'll try to buy you a little time. Take the children and the old. Escape to the mountains, to the caves."

"You can't just—"

Kalf grabbed her and forced her to look down at the trolls. They were now no more than a hundred paces from the palisade. "See the trunk they're carrying? It's heavier than all the wood in this wall put together. What do you think is going to happen?"

Asla pushed his hands down. "I'm staying with you," she said firmly.

"Then you're letting the children die! Think of Kadlin. You have to flee. Fast!" He kissed her forehead. Then he lifted her down from the wall-walk.

"Go, go, down from here!" Most of the men followed his order. Only twenty steps more. The beat of the drum thrummed in Kalf's ears. He jumped, landing in the snow. "To the longspears. We counterattack when they break through!"

He stumbled ahead to where the spears jutted from the snow like a trellis. Most of the men simply kept running. Kalf could not blame them. He snatched up one of the weapons.

The trolls shouted a bloodcurdling battle cry. Their drum was pounding now faster than Kalf's heart. Waving his arms, he managed to gather some of those fleeing around him. Kodran was one, and a baker from Honnigsvald, men who had never wanted to be fighters. They clasped the longspears in their hands in desperate, hopeless fury.

Kalf was organizing the small group of the brave into a single line when, with an infernal crash, the battering ram smashed into the wall. The trunks forming the palisade folded like blades of grass—the trolls broke through with their first charge. Those at the front immediately pushed their way through the breach.

"Attack!" Kalf cried. Everything around him faded. All he saw was a troll warrior who had smeared wide stripes across his chest with soot. The troll stepped over a shattered tree trunk. Then arrows rained down on the trolls in the breach. Finally! But the salvos from the archers did not stop them. They could sense how close they were to victory.

"Attack!" Kalf cried, more and more desperately. "Attack!" He was screaming against his own fear.

His legs planted firmly in the snow, he rammed his spear into the charging troll's chest. The iron tip bore deep into the flesh, struck a rib, was deflected upward, and came out again close to the troll's neck.

The troll threw back his head and roared. The sudden movement snatched the spear shaft out of Kalf's grasp. He drew his sword, holding the long leather-wrapped grip in both hands.

His opponent snapped the shaft in two, lashing out furiously, trying to keep Kalf at a distance. The fisherman ducked under the blade of the stone axe. The troll threw up his left hand defensively, and Kalf's sword struck him between the fingers, slicing through bone and wrist as far as the troll's forearm.

Kalf's ears were filled with the troll's screams. His sword was stuck fast in the troll's arm, and the troll shook him aside like he was a small child. He fell in the snow. Heavy feet tramped past him as more and more of the enemy forced their way through the breach. He had no weapon left with which to fight them. Tears of rage blurred his sight as he pulled himself to his feet and began to run. He had to make it to the barricade. They might be able to hold the trolls there a little longer.

The feeble line of men that he'd led against the breach had been crushed. Most lay dead in the snow, and those still alive were running.

Stumbling, Kalf pressed onward. The trolls made better progress in the deep snow. A short distance ahead, he saw Asla. She tried to stop a few of the men and form a new defensive line, but there, in open terrain, it was hopeless, an act of desperation. They would be overrun in an instant.

Kalf bent down and snatched up the sword of one of the dead men, then hurried to Asla's side. It was all he could still do: to die at her side. Trying to run now would be in vain. The trolls would be on them well before they reached the final barricade.

The fisherman saw a troll grab Kodran by the hair and snatch him backward. The troll's foot crashed down on the ferryman's broad chest—it was like crushing a beetle. The ferryman spat blood and lay motionless where he fell.

Asla touched Kalf's arm gently. "You were always there," she said sadly. "I wish I had understood that earlier."

The troll that had killed the ferryman charged toward them, his huge club raised.

This is what death looks like, thought Kalf.

And then a strange word cut into the night. Not loud, but forceful. The troll lowered his club. As if spellbound, the fighters on both sides stopped in their tracks. A slight figure dressed in white appeared from the shadows of the woods. The elven queen was awake!

"Go back!" Asla cried. "Save the children!"

Emerelle came directly to her. "So you are Asla," she said, her voice warm. "I thank you for your hospitality."

Kalf noted that the trolls retreated a little, re-forming in small groups. All were looking at the queen. Some gesticulated wildly. The momentary peace crumbled.

"Go and save the children!" Asla begged her again.

"I will do that. Please forgive me. This war should never have been allowed to come to the human world. I did not see it . . . I . . . the trolls are here because of me. If I give myself up, the fighting will end."

"No! It can't end like that!" Asla said rebelliously. "So many have died for you. You can't just surrender to them now."

"It is the only way to protect the children. If I am captured, there is no reason to fight anymore. Farewell, Asla, and forgive me, if you can."

One of the troll warriors came to Emerelle. The moonlight gleamed on his bare head. The elf and the troll exchanged a few words, then the warrior signaled to his men to withdraw.

Tears of fury flowed down Asla's cheeks. Kalf wrapped one arm around her shoulders. "It's over."

"Nothing is over! What power does Emerelle have as a prisoner? How is she supposed to stop the trolls from attacking us again tomorrow? These beasts will eat all of us. They'll come back. She shouldn't have gone."

"But maybe—"

Asla freed herself from him. "No! Maybe isn't enough! My only surviving child is up there. I'm going to take Kadlin and anyone else who wants to go with me. We will use the time we have and flee deeper into the mountains."

"I won't go with you. My place is at the last barricade. If the trolls betray us, I'll hold them back there as long as possible. And if they really withdraw, then I'll come to the mountains and find you."

"I . . ." Asla bit her lip. "I'll wait for you."

"Luth will protect us," said Kalf with confidence. He trusted the weaver of fate. The god had always been merciful with him.

Asla lowered her eyes. "Perhaps," she said softly. Then she went up to the village.

WITHOUT HONOR

Barking madly, Blood bounded along the narrow strip of the waterline. The troll was too big to stand in the low cave and had to crawl out of the water on his hands and knees, pausing to swing a club studded with shards of stone in front of him. The way he crept along, trying to get to them, was grotesque. Grotesque, yet terrifying.

Ulric and Halgard had retreated all the way back to the niche in the wall where the soldier's body lay. The boy felt wretched. Yilvina had been awakened by the commotion and was groping for the sword that he had fetched for her. He could not simply leave her for the troll.

A swing of the club just missed Blood. The big dog tried to snap at the troll's throat, but the monster turned aside, and Blood's fangs sank into his shoulder. That was a mistake! With a grunt, the troll reached up for the dog. He propped himself on one hand, grabbed Blood with the other, and hurled the dog against the cave wall.

Ulric heard a crack. Blood's bark became a high, plaintive howl. The dog shook himself and tried to get back onto his feet, but one of his back legs kept folding strangely and would not hold him up.

Yilvina lunged forward, taking the troll by surprise. She took a two-handed swing at the arm on which the troll was propped, striking him just above the wrist. The silver steel sliced through flesh and bone, and the man-eater let out a bellow. With helpless rage, he jerked the stump of his arm upward. Dark blood pulsed in streams from the wound, spraying over the elf's face.

Blinded, she tried to crawl away, but the troll was able to grab hold of her leg. He pushed his mutilated arm into Yilvina's chest where the bone jutted through her skin. She twisted in pain. The sword slipped from her grasp.

Again, the troll struck at her wound, making strange grunting sounds as he did so. Yilvina did not move anymore, but the monster kept beating her.

Halgard was weeping and holding on tightly to Ulric. The boy felt for the sword in the alcove. When it comes to killing, he thought, he'd never seen anyone who acted with honor. No one observed the rules of chivalry that his father had taught him.

Finally, the troll stopped hitting Yilvina. He pulled a glowing branch from the fire and, wailing and wheezing, pressed it against the stump of his arm. The stink of oily flesh filled the cave.

Ulric got to his feet. The monster, still crouching close to the fire, was too occupied with his own pain to pay Ulric any attention.

"Troll!" said Ulric loudly. He was standing now directly in front of the warrior, who rocked back and forth in agony. Finally, the troll looked up at him.

"Die!" Ulric slashed the dead man's blade across the troll's throat. Then he jumped back. A deep gash opened on the troll's neck. He looked up at Ulric in disbelief. With his remaining hand, he snatched at his throat. He made a gurgling noise and tried to stand up but knocked his head hard against the ceiling of the cave. His mutilated arm tried to reach for the club beside the fire but could only prod helplessly at the weapon.

Again, his eyes fixed on Ulric. He did not dare to move his hand from his throat. Blood welled through his fingers.

The boy did not look away. He'd had to do it, he told himself, even though there was no honor in the act. The beast was a man-eater! They had to be killed, and it made no difference how.

Halgard sobbed quietly.

Ulric took her hand in his. "Everything will be all right. Everything will be all right." He stood and watched as the troll died, and felt dead himself. He felt nothing. No triumph, no anger, not even fear.

Slowly, the giant slumped forward. Ulric waited. He held the girl and stared at the troll. Only when the fire had burned down to dark coals did he dare approach the troll again. Blood hobbled over to him and sniffed at the body as Ulric, cautiously, pushed at it with one foot. The troll no longer moved.

Ulric sighed with relief. Then he gathered the rest of the branches and fanned the fire to life again. As the dancing flames forced the shadows back into the farthest corners, he kneeled beside Yilvina. Her breathing was shallow. He did not know how he could help the elf woman. A cut was something he could have bandaged. But this . . .

Finally, with Halgard's help, he pulled Yilvina close to the fire. Even together, though, they could not move the troll. He was as heavy as a block of stone. After several failed attempts, they sat on the other side of the fire, as far from the dead giant as possible.

Blood lay at Ulric's feet. He licked one of his back legs and whimpered softly.

"I'm hungry," said Halgard.

The boy still had the smell of burning troll flesh in his nose. He couldn't eat anything. He rummaged in Yilvina's leather hunting bag but found only a hard piece of cheese. He handed it to the girl.

"What about you?" Halgard asked.

"I'm not hungry."

Halgard put the cheese on the rocky floor in front of her. "Then we'll share it when you get hungry." Her blind eyes stared in his direction. With her snowy hair and withered skin, she looked unearthly.

For a long time, they listened in silence to the crackling of the fire. "This cave is a grave, isn't it?" the girl finally said. "King Osaberg and the dead troll, and Yilvina is dying."

"But we're still alive," replied Ulric heatedly.

"How much wood is left?"

"Enough to keep the fire going for a few more hours." He thought of the darkness that would then follow. The thought unsettled him. He wasn't scared of the dark. He just didn't like it.

"If we stay here, we'll starve to death. If we go back through the water, the winter cold will kill us," said Halgard calmly.

"We'll send Blood. He'll fetch help." Ulric scratched the thick fur of the dog's neck. "Right, Blood? You rest a little longer, and then you can go and find Mother or Kalf."

OF HONOR AND FULL BELLIES

Birga lifted the amber pendant from the neck of the dying woman in whose lidless eyes stood madness. The shaman had stripped the skin from her face, and still the young woman smiled at Orgrim. The duke turned away. He did not find it difficult to look on as prisoners were tortured. It's just the way things were. At some level, they were due some respect for it: they had an opportunity to redeem themselves for the shame of not having fought to the death. One who showed courage in the face of torture won back the goodwill of their forebears. And the woman had showed courage.

"What did she tell you?" Dumgar wanted to know.

Birga pointed to the other bodies. "No more than the others. It seems Emerelle has been hiding in the human world for many weeks."

The Duke of Mordrock poked at his teeth with a thin bone and spat on the ground. "Why didn't Skanga know that?"

The shaman pushed the woman's amber into a pocket tucked away among the folds of her dress, then wiped her bloody hands clean in the snow, taking her time. With every moment she delayed her answer, the silence grew more oppressive. Dumgar threw his toothpick away and began to toy nervously with a leather strap hanging from his loincloth. He wore no more than a fur wrapped around his hips. Like most of his warriors, he went barefoot in the snow.

"Well, Birga? Will you answer me?"

"Aren't the actions of Skanga and the king answer enough for you? Is that thick skull of yours nothing but bone? Haven't you understood what's happened? Who sent us here? Skanga and Branbeard. And who do we find? Emerelle. Do you really think she didn't know that the tyrant was here? Do you think it was just a coincidence, a trick of fate? She wanted us to catch Emerelle. This was meant to be your chance to win perpetual renown. That's why you're here, not just to burn a few run-down huts!"

The Duke of Mordrock wiped his hand over his forehead. "They should have told me what they wanted of me."

"Why? So you could march to war with the humans trembling with fear? Think of the feasts that followed your victories. Could you have celebrated like that, without a care in the world, if you'd known that the tyrant was here? Would you have gone after our enemies like a hungry wolf and never let them rest? You know the answer!"

Orgrim enjoyed watching the shaman toy with Dumgar, but he did not believe a word of it. If Skanga had really known where Emerelle was, then she would have sent him through the Albenstar on the mountain at the end of the fjord. Ten warriors would have been enough to capture the tyrant there.

Dumgar began to pace. "It isn't right, doing things like that." He looked to Emerelle. She was tied up, crouched in the lee of the destroyed palisade. "We should kill her right now. She's an evil that has to be wiped out. Can't you feel it? All she has in her head is our death!"

Birga laughed. "Have you been eating rabbit meat, Dumgar? Look at our little tyrant there. Her hands are tied to stop her from weaving any magic. Her mouth is gagged to keep her words of power stuck in her throat. And her eyes are blindfolded to stop even her glance from causing any trouble. What are you afraid of, Dumgar? All the tyrant has left are thoughts of revenge."

Renewed silence followed Birga's words. Orgrim observed the elven queen. She was so small, so fragile. It seemed unimaginable to him that she possessed such power. She had once had him murdered, and Orgrim had always believed that, if he were ever to meet her, the memories of that night on the Shalyn Falah and of all his previous lives would return. But the gateway to those faded days was sealed well, and maybe it was better that way. What did a tree care about the leaves of the year before?

"Don't you sense the evil that clings to her?" Dumgar murmured. He kneeled in the snow beside the tyrant. His hand groped for the stone knife at his belt.

"You know why Branbeard wants to have her alive," Orgrim said. "She has to walk out on the Shalyn Falah. She has to fly and embrace the depths, as we once did. What do you think Branbeard will do when he finds out you've killed the tyrant?"

Dumgar stood up. Anger flashed in his eyes. "Are you threatening me?"

Orgrim's hand slid as if by mere chance to the heavy war hammer at his belt. "On the contrary, Dumgar. I'm worried about you. I'm trying to imagine what Branbeard would do when he found out about the demise of the tyrant." He pictured himself bashing in the fool's skull. But no! He had to control himself. He only had to let Dumgar follow his own path. He was born to walk into trouble if no one got in his way.

Orgrim looked to the dead men tied to the shattered trunks of the palisade. "Maybe the king will give you the opportunity to redeem yourself as a warrior by handing you over to Birga. The pain will purify you, and when your soul clothes itself in flesh again, it will come back untainted."

Dumgar followed his gaze. He scratched his chin nervously. "All right. Then we'll take her back. Lead us to the nearest Albenstar, Birga! We're returning to the Snaiwamark."

"The nearest big star is close to the village that Orgrim destroyed," the shaman explained. "From there, we can return home safely. It will take us three or four days to get there—at least, if the weather doesn't turn."

Orgrim cursed silently. He knew what going back that way would mean.

"So we'll have to cross through ravaged lands," Dumgar said. "The supplies we have will only last us two more days. We need meat." He narrowed his eyes and looked at Orgrim.

"No!" the prince of the Nightcrags said resolutely. "I gave the tyrant my word."

"Then I hereby absolve you of your promise."

"You might rule this army, Dumgar, but you do not rule my honor. I swore to Emerelle that the humans would live if she surrendered to us, and I will stand by that."

"What do I care about your word when five hundred troll bellies are at stake? We will overrun the village and take enough provisions for the return journey. You are mad, Orgrim! Did the tyrant give a damn about the promises she'd made when she ordered you and me to be pushed from the bridge? You owe her nothing. Tomorrow morning, at first light, we bring this battle to an end. And I expect you to fight!"

"What the tyrant did back then is no concern of mine. My word is my word. It is as strong as granite."

Dumgar remained surprisingly calm. He even smiled. "So you rebel against my orders, Prince Orgrim. May I remind you that the king gave me overall command of this campaign? Branbeard will not be pleased to hear that a promise to Emerelle matters more to you than a full belly for his warriors. I'm looking forward to telling him all about it."

ON THUNDER SCARP

A fine wedge of silver gleamed along the horizon, far beyond the fjord. Sigvald slipped away from the column of refugees and concealed himself among the trees. No one took any notice. The march through the snow was draining, and no one raised their head.

From his hiding place, the wagon builder watched Asla march onward. What a woman! There were few women that men would listen to beyond their own four walls, but Sigvald had followed her gladly, and it grieved him now that he had to go behind her back. Ever since they had seen the night sky's red glow behind them after their flight from Honnigsvald, no one challenged Asla's decisions. She was what there had never been before: the duchess, the woman in command of the last remnants of the lost.

Sigvald turned away and tramped deeper into the woods. His route led him upward, to Thunder Scarp, where the big sled stood. It had been Asla's idea to take it up to the scarp. The wagon maker smiled, thinking of how he'd griped and grumbled when she told him about her plan! The duchess had no idea what it meant to haul a coach that heavy all the way up there.

Thunder Scarp was situated at an angle to and overlooking the path that the reindeer took when they descended to the fjord. When the last barricade fell and the defenders had fled upward along the reindeer trail, Asla wanted to use the large sled to trigger a landslide. A good plan! But the previous night, Kalf and the men who were to stay behind to defend the barricade had come up with something even better.

Sigvald had reached the edge of the forest. He looked out from the top of the steep slope that stretched down to the reindeer trail. Here and there, jagged outcrops raised their heads above the snow, but there were hardly any trees, not much that would hold the snow at all. Almost every winter, avalanches tumbled down from Thunder Scarp, and the village had been built a good way from it, on the other side of the mountain path.

The sun now stood like a great red ball above the mountains in the east. To the north, the sky was still dark. A storm was gathering there, but it would still be many hours before it reached the valley.

Up here on the scarp, a man could feel like a god, Sigvald thought. Everything was so far away, so tiny. The village huts lay below him like gravel stones among the trees, which looked like tufts of grass. The destroyed palisade at the entrance to the valley was no more than a twig, dark against the snow, and the trolls were like flies crawling over a white tablecloth. And like flies, he would crush them!

Sigvald felt a surge of pride as he eyed the sled that now stood just a few steps from the edge of the forest. He'd done a magnificent job with that wagon. The roughly hewn construction set up on top of the wagon bed bothered him a little, but that was not his handiwork.

Sigvald reached for the heavy rope that led from the front axle back to a strong fir tree. Fine ice crystals shimmered on the pale hemp. The wheels of the wagon had been removed, and it stood now on wide runners. As a sled, it was harder to steer. He looked down the slope. It seemed to him now that the rocky outcrops had multiplied. Had there always been so many?

He held on to the rope tightly and clambered down the short distance to his wagon. With care, he loosened the big stones that held the runners in place, freeing them from the crusted snow and cautiously moving them aside. The last thing he needed now was for one of those stones to go tumbling down the slope.

When the work was done, Sigvald climbed up to the driver's seat. He swept the snow from the bench, enjoying the feel of the smoothly polished wood beneath his fingers. A pity that he would build no more sleds, no more coaches. Just the day before, he'd come up with a way to make the struts that fixed the runners in place even better than they were.

He thought about the future his workshop might have had. This wagon would have made him famous! King Horsa had spent the night on it, and the elven queen herself, as well. Duke Alfadas had driven with it, and Duchess Asla had led the flight across the fjord aboard the same vehicle. Anyone who thought anything of himself would have to own a wagon built by Sigvald, the wagon maker of Honnigsvald. Such a pity . . .

Sigvald took the small hatchet from his belt. He swept the last of the snow from the seat and noticed a couple of stick figures scratched into the smooth wood. Presumably some high-spirited lad trying out his new knife. How irritating!

He laid the small axe beside the rope, which led over the driver's seat and down to the front axle. Then he rummaged in his pocket for the whetstone he'd brought with him.

With calm strokes, he honed the blade of the hatchet. One swing was all he wanted to use. He leaned forward a little. Asla had been right once again. Tiny dark points were crawling over the snow down in the valley: the trolls on the pass trail were storming up toward the barricade.

"Little flies," he murmured to himself. He reached inside his fur-lined vest and took out a flat silver bottle. He removed the cork with his teeth and raised the bottle in a toast to the valley. "Sorry I had to lie to you in the end, Kalf. It wouldn't do just to cut the rope. There are too many rocks on the slope, and the heavy sled might lose its way. Someone has to show it where to go."

Sigvald emptied the little bottle in a draft. There was really just one good swallow left inside anyway. Then he carefully stoppered it again and put it away inside his vest.

The weaver of fate is a god with a sense of humor, Sigvald thought, and he smiled. "Thank you for letting me end my life with a sled ride. What better death could a wagon builder ask for?" He reached for the hatchet beside him. A shame, a crying shame, that he'd now have to leave a notch in the seat himself.

THE WHITE TORRENT

Kalf gazed down at the trolls. The final barricade lay at the narrowest point of the reindeer trail, and the man-eaters were charging toward him in a tightly packed mob. With grim satisfaction, the fisherman raised his poleaxe. Only ten men had remained behind—his collaborators. He'd sent the rest of them away, up the path, despite their protests. Those who had stayed with him had lost everything already, men whose wives and children no longer lived, or who, like himself, had never married.

He stood stolidly on the bed of a sled. They'd hauled everything that could be moved to the reindeer trail—wagons, cupboards, and chests—to build this last line of defense. The fisherman knew that the trolls would overrun it almost instantly. But a few moments were enough. They did not have to hold out against the enemy longer than that.

Kalf's mouth was dry, but his hands were sweating. It was always that way before a battle began. A troll that had painted a spider in soot over his face had gotten ahead of the rest. *Luth will make you pay for that,* thought Kalf. The troll hurled a short throwing spear at him.

Kalf turned slightly to one side, and the spear shot past, missing him by a fingerbreadth. A blow shook the sled, almost knocking Kalf off his feet. The spear thrower had rammed his shoulder against the side of the heavy sled's bed, as if trying to simply flip it over.

Kalf was too busy keeping his balance to swing at the troll with his poleaxe. A chunk of hurled ice missed him by a good margin. More trolls reached the barricade. Wild war cries rang from a hundred throats. A quiet young man from the ranks of defenders was caught by a lasso and vanished into the mass with a scream.

High above them, a low rumble could be heard. One of the mountains had raised its voice, and, faced with its wrath, even the trolls recoiled. The man-eaters looked up, and Kalf savored the look of fear in their eyes. One of them bellowed something. Then the first of them broke and ran.

Kalf swung his poleaxe forward. The long spike disappeared into the eye of the troll that had reached him first. "Luth would like to have a word with you about spiders," he said.

The sled shuddered. Cornices of snow slid from the trees all around, as if the trees were shaking themselves free. In panic, the trolls tried to escape, pushing and elbowing each other on the narrow reindeer trail. Those who fell were trampled. A few tried to climb the cliffs on either side.

A deep peace came over Kalf. He pulled the spike from the skull of the dead troll and threw the weapon aside. He did not turn around. Since he had said good-bye to Asla the previous evening, he had accepted that he would die. The duchess had always been right when she had urged them to flee. She'd been right in Firnstayn and right in Honnigsvald. Why should she be mistaken now? And although he knew that, he had argued against her and stayed behind. Someone had to stay so that the rest could save themselves.

Kalf spread his arms wide. The cold breath of death engulfed him. The air was filled with fine ice crystals. He breathed in deeply. Then the avalanche struck. The white torrent engulfed him, sweeping him along with it.

Kalf paddled with his arms. He was enclosed in a muffled roar. Then it grew dark. Still, he struggled against the unstoppable force that had swept him up. Something slammed into his shoulder, and he felt himself spun around. A searing pain shot through his head. Then, suddenly, all was still.

The fisherman lay curled up like a sleeping child, held captive in a tight-fitting cloak of cold. The thunder of the avalanche still reverberated in his ears.

Kalf tried to stretch, but the snow held him tightly. The chill was already eating its way into his limbs. He pushed his feet against the snow underfoot, and his boots crunched into the caked powder. He tensed his shoulders, but his prison did not shift. Then he realized that he could not tell which way was up or down. Swept along by the avalanche, he'd tumbled again and again. In the darkness of his icy prison, he could not orient himself at all.

He pressed against the snow wall in various places and managed to expand a little the space in which he was trapped. The rumbling in his ears had diminished now, and in its place he could clearly hear his own gasping breath. He ran his hands over as much of himself as he could reach. Everything hurt, but nothing seemed to be broken, and the cold dampened the pain. His sword belt was gone, but he still had the fishing knife stuck in his boot. Carefully, he jabbed the blade into the ceiling of his tiny cave. With both hands, he moved the chunks of snow he loosened—he would dig his way to freedom.

A sound made him pause. The snow creaked. Someone passed by underneath him! Kalf laughed silently. Not underneath him, of course. He'd been digging in the wrong direction. With renewed strength, he went back to digging, working to turn himself around.

Soon, the snow was less compacted. He found he could push it aside with his hands, and finally he saw a spot of gray winter sky. Carefully, inch by inch, the fisherman pushed himself clear of his icy prison. The avalanche had dragged him several hundred paces with it. A little to his left lay a large clothes trunk. Farther down the slope, he saw trolls probing the snow with spear shafts, looking for the buried.

Watchful, Kalf pulled himself out into the open. His clothes were crusted with snow, his hair full of ice. Slowly, he crawled up the slope. A little more than a hundred paces away lay a dark forest of fir trees, untouched by the avalanche.

Now Kalf discovered a small group of trolls above him, moving higher up the slope. One of them must have stepped over his icy prison, showing him the right way to freedom. The group stopped and turned back.

He pressed his face into the snow and lay still, hardly breathing. Again he heard the creaking steps slowly coming nearer. They stopped, and he could clearly hear the trolls' voices. They seemed to be arguing about something. Finally, the heavy steps moved away again.

Kalf waited a moment longer. Then he pushed himself up and ran toward the woods. He stumbled, sprawled, stumbled again. Only when he was among the trees did he risk looking back. No one followed him. Had they not noticed him? Or did it simply not matter to them if one of the humans escaped?

His shoulder ached, and his head felt as if a coach horse had trampled on it. Exhausted, he made his way up the forested slope just off the reindeer trail, staying in the cover offered by the trees, afraid of running into trolls.

He pushed himself onward throughout the day. The sun had almost disappeared behind the treetops when he smelled a fire. He stopped in his tracks and peered ahead as far as he could see. A figure in a red cloak was leaning against a tree. The crimson sky of evening made her golden hair look like a crown of light. Asla!

At last, Kalf ventured out onto the path. He could move more easily now and hurried toward Asla. She cradled Kadlin in a sling of cloth at her breast.

"I knew you'd still come," she said, smiling.

The sight of her filled Kalf with renewed strength. She was so beautiful. None of the radiance that she'd had even as a young girl had faded. He wanted to take her in his arms then and there but was afraid of the others' prying eyes. "Do you have a camp in the woods?"

"There's a big hunters hut up there." Asla suddenly seemed reserved.

"Is something wrong?"

"I ordered the caravan of refugees to disband, and it has caused some quarreling. There are some camped up there who don't want to listen to me. But we can't go on as we have been. We don't have enough who can fight to face the trolls again. It would be like last night, after the palisade was stormed . . ." Her voice faltered. "I had to give the order! The trolls look at us as if we are livestock to be slaughtered. Now it's up to us to stop acting like cattle! Reindeer form huge herds because they're safer that way. The wolves weed out the weakest, the ones that don't have the strength to run with the herd. But no herd of reindeer was ever hunted by hundreds of wolves. It's not safe for us to move on as a group. If the trolls find us, they'll kill all of us. Only if we form smaller groups, if the herd separates into individual families again and each family goes its own way, will at least some of us make it."

Kalf nodded toward the pale column of smoke rising among the trees. "What about them?"

Asla's face hardened. "The weak and dispirited and those who can't leave them behind. They've decided to stay in the hunters hut and trust the mercy of the gods." Her voice turned husky now. "They . . . if we all went on together, we would have had to leave them behind anyway." Asla closed her arms around Kadlin, who snuggled close, asleep inside her sling. "The trolls will not get my little girl! Most of us who've escaped have decided that it's better to freeze in the woods than wait like cattle for the trolls to come."

"Where will you go?"

Asla pointed to the west. "They say there are caves at the far end of the valley. We can find refuge there."

Kalf looked to the clouds gathering slowly in the north. They had a few hours, no more. "How far is it to the end?"

"If we don't rest in the night, we should make it to the caves early in the morning."

Kalf held out his hand to her. "Then we should be on our way." She was right. Anything was better than waiting there.

ONE GOLDEN HAIR

Orgrim felt respect for the humans' courage. He never would have believed that the fragile little creatures were capable of inflicting such heavy losses on them.

The duke gazed out over the churned field of snow. The evening sun doused the slope in pale, pink light. Warriors with long poles were still searching for their missing comrades, although they had already recovered more than sixty bodies from the snow.

Orgrim shook his head. The humans must have known that none who stayed at the barricade to fight would survive. The barricade had blocked the narrowest point of the path up the mountain, the very place where the flood of snow, rocks, and smashed trees would be at its deadliest. They had sacrificed themselves to take as many trolls as possible with them.

His mind went back to the attack of the ice gliders in the Swelm Valley. With their fanatical willingness to perish, the humans had proven themselves almost as dangerous as the elves. Waging this war in the Fjordlands was foolishness. It was costing too much troll blood. They would do better to withdraw, to go back to the Snaiwamark or to the mountain fortresses far in the north, on the edge of the permanent ice. Orgrim thought of all the women waiting for him in the Nightcrags. He was tired of fighting. His people had won back a place for themselves in Albenmark. The humans had been punished. It was time to go.

He looked down to where the long rows of the dead lay at the edge of the snowfield. If he hadn't refused Dumgar's orders, he might very well be lying among them, he thought grimly. He knew he had to get away from the Duke of Mordrock—Dumgar's follies were becoming increasingly deadly.

Orgrim watched Birga pull a small dark-haired human out of the snow. The fellow was still struggling. The shaman turned him over and pushed a knee into the middle of his back. With one hand, she pressed his head down. In the other hand, she held a small bone knife. She cut the man's throat, and his struggles grew weaker.

Curious, Orgrim went to the shaman. The man's blood fanned out on the snow in small rivulets that crossed and recrossed before seeping away completely. Birga looked thoughtfully at the pattern the blood left behind.

"So what secrets is the future hiding from us?" Orgrim did his best to sound offhanded, but he was not particularly successful. He found the old hag's blood rituals unsettling.

Birga gestured sharply at him for silence. She turned the human onto his back. Where his neck had been, the warm blood had left a hole in the snow. "Disaster gathers from the north," the shaman suddenly said. She pointed to the dark clouds on the horizon; they had barely moved at all in the course of the day. "The wind will turn and bring arrows with it."

Orgrim hated it when the shaman spoke in oracles. In retrospect, you could read almost anything into her words. "What do you advise me to do?"

"Take your men and go into the mountains. Follow the humans. There is a woman you have to find. Their leader." Birga let out a short, barking laugh. "They call her Duchess. Her blood is of great power." The shaman glanced down at the bloody pattern in the snow at her feet. "Unlike this."

Orgrim observed the distant clouds. "How am I supposed to find her? When the storm comes, it will wipe out their tracks."

Birga looked up to him. Dark eyes gleamed behind her leather mask. "I knew that you would go if I told you, so I went to the woman's hut. Kneel before me!"

Orgrim obeyed. He did not like the shaman, but he hoped that she would speak for him when Dumgar made his allegations to the king.

Birga took a leather band from around her neck. The band had a single golden hair wrapped around it. She loosened the hair carefully and rubbed it into a small ball between her thumb and first finger. "Open your mouth, Orgrim."

She laid the small pellet on his tongue. With her rag-wrapped fingers, she stroked the duke's eyelids. The thin ragged fabric stank of decay. Birga murmured something unintelligible, then slapped Orgrim lightly on the forehead. "You will find the human's trail even if it is hidden beneath the snow or mixed with a hundred other tracks. She can't escape you anymore!"

"But if I take my men and abandon the rest of the army, I will look like a coward."

Birga slapped his forehead a second time. "Use your brain, Duke! Tell Dumgar that you've seen the wisdom of his words and that you're ready to toe the line. The puffed-up fool will be only too glad to accept your offer to take your men into the mountains and hunt for meat for the return journey."

"And what are you going to do, Birga?"

"I'll come with you. I want the woman myself. She has a courageous heart." The shaman clucked her tongue.

Orgrim thought of the promise he had made to the tyrant. He looked to the north. The wind had turned. Dark clouds were fast approaching.

HOPE

Alfadas had gathered the leaders of his small army around him: the veterans of the bloody days at Phylangan, and a pair of young jarls who had joined them two days earlier with their mounted troops, survivors of King Horsa's final battle. Brave men. Alfadas knew one of them, Jarl Oswin, from previous campaigns but now did not trust him. Oswin and his men had fled trolls once. Alfadas planned to lead them personally the following day.

The council of war took place in the open air. The men had pushed the sleds from Phylangan close together to give at least some protection from the wind. Torches were jammed into the snow, their flames dancing. At dusk, the storm reached them, its icy gusts sweeping across the fjord. Apart from the sleds, they had no protection from the tempest.

Alfadas took his sword and pointed at one of the small hills that Ollowain had formed from snow, a model of the pass that led up to Sunhill. Two small branches marked the positions of the palisades on the reindeer trail, and a few gray stones showed where the village lay.

With the tip of the sword, he indicated the higher of the two branches. "Our fathers and brothers are fighting here." He had to shout to make himself heard over the howling of the wind. "Our childhood friends. They're defending women and children and shedding their blood for us." The duke glanced at the young man that Lambi and the scouts had picked up on the fjord at midday. "Report on the battles, Olav."

The woodsman's voice was firm as he described how the defenders had held the first palisade for three days. Alarm and pride filled Alfadas when he heard how Asla had stood among the fighters on the wall-walk. His Asla! The way Olav told the story, it was mainly thanks to her that the fighters had held on as long as they did.

"The trolls' losses were so severe that they did not dare attack again for two days, although the second palisade is smaller and weaker. Last night, as I crept down the reindeer trail, things were still quiet."

The tip of Alfadas's sword moved down to the start of the pass trail. "Here, beside the ruins of the first palisade, the trolls have their camp. I have to believe that the defenders have held the pass for another day, but their situation is dire. They need us. From here, it's more than three miles to the trolls' camp. With a little luck, they will have pulled their sentries back because of the storm. Maybe we can take them by surprise. We break camp before dawn. We need to be in sight of the pass by first light."

"What if the storm hasn't passed?" asked Mag.

"We fought a battle in the Snaiwamark in a snowstorm. Have you forgotten how the trolls fled before us then?" Alfadas looked at the men around him, one by one. That battle on the ice had not been particularly successful, but they would not repeat the mistakes they'd made that day!

"Olav says that the defenders are at the end of their rope. Every hour counts. For their sake, we cannot let a storm slow us down. And it looks as if the trolls have no catapults this time. They did not fire on the palisade, at least."

Alfadas drew a thin line in front of the pass. "This is where you'll position the crossbowmen, Mag. You'll be behind them with the spearmen. You have command in the center of our battle line. If the trolls still haven't noticed us when our lines are in place, then we'll call them with our horns. Pull the crossbows back when the trolls get within forty paces. I'm relying on the line of spearmen not to break when the beasts hit you."

"We'll hold out, just as the men on the palisade held out," Mag replied grimly. "You might find the ice covered with our bodies when the battle's over, but none of my men will have a wound in his back. You can count on us, Duke!"

Alfadas drew a second line in the snow. "Here on the left flank is where our archers will be. Veleif, you'll have command there."

The skald looked at him in shock. "I'm no warrior, Duke! I can't do that."

Alfadas laid his left hand on his breast. "Battles are decided first in the hearts of the fighters. You know what it means to stir hearts, Veleif Silberhand. Make my archers too proud to run away."

He turned to Lambi. The jarl seemed aggrieved. "And where am I supposed to go? Aren't I good enough anymore to kick a troll in the ass? Aren't you ever going to forgive that thing with the doors? I . . ." He shrugged. "The elves won't miss 'em. I wish we'd pinched a few more."

Alfadas could not stifle a smile for long. He liked the jarl—*about whose nose one does not speak,* he thought—very much, and for him their quarrel in Phylangan was long forgotten. "You and your cutthroats will be right here." He carved a circle in the snow just behind the crossbows and spears. "You will wait there, at the ready. The moment the trolls charge Mag and his spearmen, you attack them from the flank."

Lambi grinned. "They'll piss on their own big feet when we grab 'em by the balls tomorrow."

"Don't just grab them. Tear them off!" Alfadas's hand sank to Ulric's dagger, which he carried in his belt. "Tear them off," he repeated quietly.

He could not think about his son now, he warned himself silently. His desire for revenge would muddle his thoughts. Alfadas looked across at Silwyna. She'd arrived no more than an hour before, astride a stallion nearly dead with exhaustion.

"The Maurawan will still join us?" he asked warily.

"Yes," she said firmly. "The trolls desecrated the forest. My people want vengeance. More of my brothers and sisters have followed your call than I dared hope, more than a hundred. Never before have so many Maurawan been moved to battle beyond our forests. They know about your battles in Snaiwamark. You have a good name among my race. They are coming for you, not for the queen."

Alfadas looked doubtfully toward the north, then he pointed to a small hill on the right flank of the battle lines he'd sketched in the snow. "This is where I need the Maurawan archers. I don't have enough fighters to reinforce our right flank."

"Where will you be in all this?" Lambi asked. Until now, Alfadas had always fought in the front line of his battles. And he knew that, among his troops, there was a running bet about which of them he went into battle with the most.

"I'll be with the riders." The duke drew a small circle behind the hill. "Here."

"But you're too few!" Mag said in dismay. "There's hardly twenty of you. The trolls will mow you down if they hit our right flank."

"I trust the Maurawan. They will hold this hill for us." Alfadas smiled, although he was filled with doubt. He knew better than anyone how unreliable the forest folk could be. They had only come through the Albenstar on the Hartungscliff at midday, and most of them had not come on horseback. He looked uncertainly at Silwyna.

"They are treetop runners," she said in the language of her race.

Was his doubt so plain to see?

"No one can move through the woods like we Maurawan. They will be on the hill tomorrow morning. I'll go now to take them the news. Trust me."

Her final words struck him like a dagger to his heart. Alfadas straightened himself. "With most of you, I've journeyed far. It may be that, tomorrow, some of us will not survive. I want you to be under no illusions. Our chances are not good." He pointed to the map in the snow. "When the trolls break through the second palisade, there will be another massacre. They've already spilled too much blood. Tell your men that I am ordering no one to be in this battle. I only want those beside me who want to be there, the way it was back then, on the shore at Honnigsvald. Tell all of them. Do not appeal to their conscience. Just say it, then go to bed. The night is short, and whoever fights with me tomorrow will need all their strength."

"My men are villains and cutthroats," Lambi said, visibly moved. "So you can count on us to be there in the morning, when there are throats to be cut. We're not the kind to let you down."

"I know it," said Alfadas wearily. He raised his hands to stop the others from interjecting. "I trust all of you. I know that all of you standing here in this circle of torches will be there tomorrow. But give me the time I need now, the few hours of night that remain. Leave me alone with my memories and prayers." With that, he left the circle of his officers and moved away, walking by himself, as had become his habit in recent nights.

Finally, his steps led him to Blood. They had found the dog that afternoon, more dead than alive, in a snowdrift on the shore. His fur was matted and stiff with ice. And yet, despite exhaustion and a broken leg, Blood had tried to drag himself on when Alfadas approached.

The duke had spent almost an hour with the dog. He had brushed the ice out of his fur and fed him with small pieces of dried meat. Now, Blood was tied to one of the sleds with a heavy rope. When the dog saw Alfadas, he barked and tried to jump to his feet.

"Easy, fellow. Easy. I know what you want." Alfadas kneeled beside him. "You want to take me to Kadlin, don't you? Be patient for one night. Tomorrow I'll go with you."

"Are you sure of that?"

Alfadas did not need to turn to know who was standing behind him. It had surprised him that Ollowain had not said a single word during the council of war.

"Are you sure you want to live? Your battle plan is sheer folly. I was there when the young woodsman talked about the trolls. He said there were four or five hundred of them. Your veterans may be brave, Duke, but you'd need four of them for every troll you need to defeat. If you fight tomorrow, they will all die. Think of Asla and Kadlin," Ollowain warned.

Alfadas stroked Blood's ragged fur. "I think of nothing else. They would not have sent the dog if they were not in grave danger."

"Don't start fooling yourself now, my friend! Asla does not even know that you've returned. Why would she send the dog?"

"She can sense that I'm on my way to her," Alfadas replied angrily.

"You're talking yourself into believing that, and you know it. There's only one logical reason why Blood is not with your wife and daughter anymore." Ollowain grabbed Alfadas by the shoulders. "Don't close your eyes to the obvious! Don't lead your men to their deaths to save those already lost!"

"They're alive!" Alfadas pushed his friend away. "They're behind the second palisade, and they're waiting for me. You don't have to fight tomorrow if you're afraid. The Maurawan will be there. They are the key to victory. Maybe Orimedes and his centaurs will make it, too. Lysilla must have found him long ago."

"You know I'm not afraid of death," said Ollowain sadly. "But a commander in the field who fills his battle lines with hope instead of troops . . . yes, that scares me. Still, I will be there with you tomorrow, my friend. If *you* will not look after yourself, then I have to."

Alfadas turned to the south. The gusting storm had eased, and it was starting to snow. "They are out there somewhere," he said softly. "And they need me."

SHE'S LYING IN FRONT OF YOU!

Ollowain looked out along their battle line. All had come, although Alfadas had allowed them to decide for themselves. Or perhaps because he had?

He gazed off to the right, toward the hill. The Maurawan had not appeared. Even Silwyna had not returned. But the trolls . . . the trolls were there. And though it did not look like five hundred, there were certainly enough of them to cut the humans to pieces.

Alfadas, stony-faced, sat astride the gray stallion that Count Fenryl had given him as a parting gift. It was too late to retreat now.

The trolls were advancing in a disorderly mob toward the right, in the direction of the unoccupied hill. If they reached it, they could outflank the humans' entire battle line.

Alfadas drew his sword. Forcing a smile, he turned to his tiny troop of cavalry. "It seems we'll have to make up for our elven allies from the forests."

The metallic clacking of crossbows sounded. Dozens of bolts slammed into the side of the trolls' formation. Warriors stumbled, screamed, and fell, but the advance on the hill did not slow. The giants put so little store in the humans' abilities that they did not even carry the massive shields that Ollowain knew from their battles in Phylangan.

The archers under Veleif's command fired salvo after salvo but were too distant to inflict much damage.

Alfadas raised his sword over his head. "Forward, men! You were beaten in Horsa's last battle. Show the world that you're the bravest of the brave today!" Without turning to see who would follow him into this hopeless battle, Alfadas let the gray feel his spurs.

Ollowain brought his stallion level with Alfadas's steed. None of the other riders stayed behind. They were twenty facing hundreds. The elf smiled thinly. He had no doubt which way this fight would go.

The horses made slow progress in the deep snow—the trolls would reach the hill first. Ollowain saw Mag react to the changed circumstances and try to swing a unit of spearmen toward the hill. In moments, the formation was hopelessly muddled. Lambi's men turned with them, but the spearmen were now blocking their path. With their advance toward the flank, the trolls had managed to bring the humans' entire battle line into disarray.

Ollowain drove his stallion onward. Another fifty paces and the trolls would reach the top of the hill. Another salvo of crossbow bolts brought down several of their warriors. The massive fighters roared battle cries at the humans, promising death and carnage.

Without warning, a wave swept over the crown of the hill. The snow curved upward, and slender white-clad figures emerged from their cover. Ollowain recognized Silwyna among them—the Maurawan! They let their arrows fly point-blank. Almost all the trolls in the first row fell, and those crowding from behind tumbled over the fallen. A second salvo destroyed any semblance of formation in the trolls' attack.

Ollowain could hardly trust what his eyes told him. The Maurawan must have taken up their positions on the hill during the night. They had dug hollows in the snow and covered them with their white cloaks and furs, then let the snow do the rest—it had filled their tracks until there was no sign left that anyone had set foot on the hill.

The trolls were slow to recover from their initial shock. But, determined not to give up on victory, they charged against the storm of arrows.

"Forward!" Alfadas cried wholeheartedly. "Attack the flank! Don't let our brothers-in-arms from Albenmark take all the glory!"

A high-pitched blast from a horn rang out, and a second wave surged through the snow. Horses and riders rose from their snowed-in hiding places. The elves swung into their saddles. In white armor of linen and leather and wearing silver helmets with light-colored horsehair crests, they looked like enchanted children born from winter itself. Mounted on white horses, snow-covered cloaks billowing, they charged down the hill. Their long lances shimmered in the morning light. Within moments, they formed an attacking wedge aimed straight at the heart of the enemy line.

Alfadas and his fighters had almost reached the trolls. Arrows buzzed overhead. Then the archers on the hills put down their bows, drew their long-swords, and stormed down the slope.

Ollowain now rode closer to the side of his foster son. Lances splintered as they galloped into the enemy's wavering battle line. Most of the trolls were still bent on victory. Horses whinnied. Ollowain leaned low in the saddle to duck a club. His spear struck a troll in the throat, but it was like stabbing a block of stone. The jolt knocked the spear from his grip. A troll snatched at his horse's reins and threw the animal to the ground. Ollowain's boots caught in the stirrups. Desperately, he tried to free himself. The snow broke his fall a little and saved his leg, which was trapped beneath the body of the stallion. Hooves flailing, the horse rolled clear, but the saddle horn jammed into Ollowain's thigh, and a burning pain flashed through his leg.

The stallion got back to its feet and reared up, its forelegs lashing at the face of the troll that had thrown it down. Half stunned with pain, the swordmaster managed to get up again.

The snow steamed with freshly spilled blood in the melee of horses, humans, and trolls. The air was filled with furious cries, the ring of weapons, and the curses and wails of the dying.

Ollowain's trousers were torn open. His thigh, crushed by the saddle horn, throbbed agonizingly.

A red-headed human fell beside him. An axe had split the man's back, and his lungs pulsed from the horrible wound like red wings. The man turned his head to one side. His mouth opened and closed, but no sound came out.

The swordmaster evaded a club, then swung his sword backhanded at the troll's wrist. Club and hand whirled together through the air, but Ollowain fell to his knees. His injured leg would not carry him. The troll howled and tried to stomp Ollowain into the snow, but a stab to the monster's crotch made the troll jump back, cursing. Ollowain followed it with a swing to the back of the troll's knee. As his enemy sprawled, Ollowain slashed his throat and rolled aside.

Alfadas was surrounded by a ring of trolls. He lashed out with his sword on all sides like a berserker. An axe crashed through both forelegs of his gray, and the big horse let out a shrill whinny and crashed to the snow. Alfadas was pitched forward over the horse's mane but was back on his feet in an instant, his sword flying in a glittering silver circle around him. The trolls kept their distance.

Now was the Maurawan's moment. Horns sounded wildly behind their battle cries. They raged through the trolls like a storm wind through dry autumn leaves.

Ollowain pushed himself up again. Behind Alfadas, a fallen troll swung his club back, aiming to smash the duke's legs. Ollowain's stab to the wounded giant's shoulder, however, ended the attempt. The troll turned with a snarl, his right arm hanging limp. Foul breath struck the swordmaster in the face, and the sword was jerked from his grip. Once again, his injured leg collapsed beneath him.

"I'll take you with me to the darkness, little elf," the troll hissed. He propped himself on his left hand—the fingers were reduced to stumps—and pushed himself around, trying to smother Ollowain beneath his massive body.

The swordmaster tried to crawl away backward, but a dead horse blocked his retreat. Laughing, the troll threw himself forward. Ollowain did his best to twist free, but his injured leg no longer obeyed him, and he was unable to escape his adversary. The troll pushed him down with his mutilated hand and bared his yellow teeth. "I'm not out of weapons yet," he snarled.

Ollowain's hand grasped at his belt. The gaping mouth came down. At the same moment, the dagger flew up. Teeth cracked and split as the silver steel sank into the troll's mouth, but even as the blade disappeared deep into the giant's gullet, he tried to bite Ollowain's hand.

"Luth, don't sword swallowers suffer some terrible accidents?" grumbled Lambi, spat out by the turbulence of the battle. He reached down to Ollowain with one hand and helped him to his feet.

"Thank you," murmured Ollowain, still dazed. Then he retrieved his sword from the dead troll's shoulder.

"You'd best save your own hide now, comrade. I can't watch over you all the time, and it looks to me like your leg's seen better days."

Ollowain gave him a sour smile. He was grateful to Lambi, but he knew he'd never be fond of the way the barbarian talked.

Lambi waved to a soldier who'd caught a riderless horse. "Bring that nag over here. The swordmaster needs some new shanks."

"My thanks, Jarl," Ollowain replied stiffly.

Lambi waved it off. "Forget it. If you really want to do me a good turn, tell me how you manage to keep those white robes of yours clean. See the nose I carry around? If I want to make an impression on the ladies, I need to be neat as an elf in every other respect."

Ollowain pulled himself into the saddle. "It isn't difficult," he said through gritted teeth. "You just have to avoid the muck."

The white stallion reared, almost throwing Ollowain, but he sank his fingers into the horse's mane. From the saddle, he had a good overview of the battle. The trolls were retreating. They were under attack from all sides now, and although they were still putting up a fight, their defeat was beyond question. The actual battle was over—the carnage would follow.

At the heart of the tumult stood Alfadas. He, too, now sat astride a new horse. *Is he looking for death?* Ollowain wondered. Alfadas had long ago crossed the line that separated suicidal daring from courage. The elf spurred his stallion forward, into the thick of the battle.

The dead and dying lay shoulder to shoulder on the ice, and the air stank of blood and excrement. The sky seemed to be holding its breath: not the slightest breeze stirred.

Some of the trolls broke free of their enemies and made for the palisade. If they managed to entrench themselves in the narrow pass, then the elves and humans would have lost the benefit of their superior numbers.

Ollowain drove his stallion onward. The dull, throbbing pain in his leg was agony. He left it to others to cut down the fleeing trolls. His target was the stocky warrior standing in the breach in the palisade and holding on to a small pale figure. Ollowain muttered a curse. They had Emerelle. Then the palisade had fallen, and the refugees were defeated. They were too late!

"I demand impunity!" the troll cried, his voice breaking. "I am Dumgar, Duke of Mordrock. If you harm me, King Branbeard's revenge for my death will be terrible." The troll lifted his right hand, in which he held a long bone knife. "And I'll cut the tyrant's throat from—"

An arrow tore the blade from Dumgar's hand, and the troll duke let out a cry. Emerelle let herself drop forward, attempting to escape.

Ollowain drew back on the reins and slid from the saddle. A hot wave of pain engulfed him as soon as he tried to put any weight on his injured leg. He hobbled toward the queen as quickly as he could. Dumgar tried to grab Emerelle again. He snatched at her long hair. In his left hand, he wielded a club.

Suddenly, a slim warrior was standing in front of him. Alfadas swept his sword across the troll's belly. Then he turned aside, ducked low, and rammed a dagger into the back of Dumgar's knee.

Ollowain reached Emerelle. The queen's hands were tied behind her back. She had a gag across her mouth and a leather blindfold covering her eyes. He closed his arms around her. "You are safe now, my queen."

Dumgar pressed his hands to his belly. Bloody entrails spilled from the gaping wound. Alfadas was standing very close to Dumgar. He held a long, slim dagger in his hand, its tip pointed toward the troll. "Do you know this blade, murderer? It belonged to a child. I'm going to cut out your liver with it and feed it to my dog. And if you're ever reborn, I swear I'll find you and kill you again."

"Ah, the elvenjarl, of course," Dumgar said. "You're too late!" A coughing fit racked his body. He dropped to his knees, still holding his belly with both hands. "You have a pretty, blond wife that you left with a fat belly, don't you? My hunters found her in the woods last night. There's not much of her pride left now."

Alfadas lowered the dagger. All the color had vanished from his face.

The troll pulled his hands back. Blue ropes of intestines swelled from his fat belly onto the snow. "It was delightful to meet her." Dumgar coughed again, causing more of his guts to spill out. "She's lying in front of you," he snarled, gasping. "She's lying in front of you!"

Coughing, he sank facedown onto the snow.

TO THE LIGHT

Ulric rubbed his bare arms. He was miserably cold. Gundar had been wrong. Their clothes had not gotten dry, and the fire had gone out. They had already been sitting in the dark forever. The cold woke him—he should not have fallen asleep! But he'd been so tired. He'd fallen asleep and hadn't put any new wood on the fire. He was so angry at himself that he wanted to scream. But it didn't help. He'd dug in the ashes, hoping to find even a tiny spark, but there was nothing. He should not have fallen asleep!

Halgard did not blame him. She had not spoken for quite a while. Her teeth chattered. Her hands felt icy.

If only Blood would return! Was he even still alive? Ulric listened into the darkness. He prayed that he would hear the soft splashing of water, but the cave was deathly still.

Deathly still! Ulric recalled Halgard's words, that they were sitting in a grave. Yilvina was not breathing. The troll. Sometimes Ulric thought he could hear the monster moving very quietly. Treacherous beast! Maybe he'd only played dead? Or he'd only been unconscious for a while and was just waiting for the moment to attack them.

Trolls were double-dealing, deceitful, unfathomable! He recalled how the troll with the burn scars on his belly had grabbed him in Honnigsvald and taken away his dagger. The bastard hadn't even condescended to actually fight him. He'd simply tossed the dagger away, then taken him to the place where everyone was screaming. Ulric knew what was being done there. He'd seen it for himself.

He, too, should have been killed there.

But then that other troll had come, the one with the stone hammer in his belt. The two trolls had talked. The troll with the stone hammer had looked at Ulric for a long time before saying something to him in their grunting tongue. Ulric, naturally, had not understood the words at all, but realized that he was free to go. He'd quickly found Halgard again—he was good at finding Halgard.

She had been extremely relieved to know that he'd come back, as relieved as she'd been in Honnigsvald when he'd jumped down from Grandfather's sled. He had told Erek that he was going back to Kalf and his mother. He'd lied. He hoped his grandfather would forgive him.

Halgard had gotten lost when the sleds were driven away, just as he had feared she would. But he had found her quickly enough, and they would have caught up with the last of the sleds if the guards had not been so quick to close the town gate. When the trolls had come to Honnigsvald, they had taken him and Halgard down to the shore with everyone else. Then they'd started picking out individual men and women. Ulric remembered the screaming. That had been bad. He'd better not think about that. Even now, it frightened him.

He stared into the darkness.

If he could only see just a little bit! Ulric raised his hands and moved them slowly toward his face. Even when the palms of his hands reached the tip of his nose, he could not make them out. It had never been so dark at home. Even when the heavy woolen blanket was pulled across the alcove where he slept, a faint shimmer of light found its way inside. It was as if he no longer had eyes in his head. He started at the thought. Was that possible? Maybe the troll had magicked his eyes away somehow?

Ulric touched his face. No. They were still there.

"Are you scared, too?" Halgard asked.

The boy could hardly understand her words, her voice was so weak.

"No!" he said resolutely. He was her hero, after all! He wasn't allowed to be scared. He protected her from the troll. And he went back to Honnigsvald for her. If only it wasn't so dark. It was easier not to be scared when you could see.

"Is it day outside, do you think?"

"I don't know." Ulric felt so useless. "I'm going to check on Yilvina," he said, and he stood and moved away from Halgard. In fact, he did not actually have to stand up to reach the elf. But men did things! They didn't just sit around.

When he touched Yilvina's body, he was shocked to find her as cold as ice. In all the hours of their escape, she had always had warm hands. The cold had never been able to touch her, and Ulric had accepted that it was always like that with elves. They simply didn't freeze. He wished that he could be an elf. But if she was cold now . . . Ulric swallowed. Then she was probably dead, too. Fear gripped him again. People died in this cave—it was no place for the living.

"How is she?" Halgard asked.

He could not tell her the truth. It would scare her more than it did him, he was sure. She was a girl, after all. "She's sound asleep. She's going to get well again."

"She felt really bad."

"Yilvina is an elf. Something like that can't kill her. She—" Suddenly, he could hold back the tears no longer. It was all so terrible. No one would find them there, in that cave.

Halgard crept across to him. Her hand stroked his hair softly. "Is it completely dark here?"

"Yes," he sobbed in a half-choked voice.

"Maybe we should go into the water? You said there were lots of broken-down trees knocked over by a storm outside, where I caught my hair. We're sure to find dry wood there, and a cave in the ground where we can crawl inside and light a fire. Yilvina has a flint somewhere. I heard her strike sparks from it. We'll take that with us, and her knife."

"I think they're in her hunting bag." Ulric felt around excitedly for the small satchel. That was a good idea! There in the dark, they would never be able to light another fire—you have to be able to see what you're doing for that. But outside he was sure he could do it.

He found the bag. Hastily, he rummaged through it and found a small dagger, some small leather pouches, and some sort of herbs that crackled between his fingers. Finally, he felt the flint. "I've got what we need," he announced proudly.

"Then let's go down to the water. But you have to hold my hand. I'm scared I'll get lost if you don't."

"I'll find the belt," Ulric said eagerly. "I'll buckle it around me. I'll need my hands for swimming and to pull us out of the hole in the ice. It'll work with the belt!" The idea of getting out to the light almost made him forget the cold. It was just dumb, though, that Halgard had come up with the idea. He could have thought of it, too. And he would have—he was certain of it!—if he'd just thought a little bit longer.

Ulric felt around on the cave floor until he found his belt. His fingers were so stiff with cold that he had difficulty getting the prong of the buckle through one of the holes.

Suddenly, Halgard was beside him. "You wouldn't go without me, would you?"

What did she think he was? He was her knight! He'd rescued her from a monster, just like in the games they'd always played. "No," he said firmly. "And if you say anything like that again, then I'm not going to talk to you anymore. It's mean to think of me like that."

"I didn't mean to upset you." She began to cry. "It's just . . . I suddenly couldn't hear you anymore. It was as if you'd already gone."

Ulric felt a pang of conscience. He couldn't stand it when she cried. He stroked her back. "I would never go anywhere without you. Never!" He took her hand and led it to the belt. "Hold on tight now. Don't let go of me, whatever happens."

He felt his way forward through the darkness, placing one foot in front of the other very slowly until he reached the water, then stood there with it just covering his toes. "We take a deep breath, then we run in together, all right?"

"Yes!" Halgard replied. "I'll count to three, then we'll do it. One. Two."

Everything in Ulric recoiled so much at the thought of re-entering the water that he felt as if he actually grew smaller.

"Three!"

He took a deep breath. Halgard pulled at him. She began to run sooner; he wasn't ready yet. He screamed! The water felt as if it were trying to cut through his skin. It gripped him. He slipped on the smooth rock and fell headlong, dragging Halgard down with him. He almost screamed again underwater. He pushed off with his feet. His hands probed at the smooth rock until, finally, he found the entrance. Gray light greeted him and renewed his strength. He swam toward the light and banged against the ice. Disoriented, he felt his way along under it. Where was the place they'd broken through? The hole was gone, frozen over!

Ulric took the small knife and stabbed at the ice. Halgard, beside him, beat her naked fists at their undoing. She began to bleed, and pale-pink streaks drifted beneath the crusts of ice.

Ulric's movements became slower and slower. The current caught them and pulled them along beneath the ice sheet. He could see the sun clearly in the sky. There was some solace, at least, to that: to not being in the dark.

The knife slipped from his numb fingers. He felt tired. He pressed his face to the ice once more. Something reached for him. Dark arms wrapped around his feet. *Branches,* he thought tiredly. He looked up. He did not feel the cold anymore. It was pleasant, there, being carried along by the water. The sun was so beautiful. So far away. So far . . .

THE PALE HAND OF A CHILD

T he big dog was almost dead on its feet. Mile after mile, it had led them down the fjord to a narrow side arm surrounded by steep mountain slopes. One of Blood's back legs was bandaged and braced with two wooden splints, but he still limped pitifully. He lost his footing often, and each time it took him a little bit longer to struggle back to his feet.

"He's leading us nowhere," said Lambi cautiously. He did not want to see the dog in agony anymore. "The survivors ran into the mountains. You won't find Asla and Kadlin here."

"You're mistaken," Alfadas replied. He seemed feverish, resembling little of the man that Lambi had once known. After the battle, Alfadas had cut out the troll leader's liver and fed it to the dog. Dealing with one's archenemies like that was an ancient custom in the Fjordlands, but if Lambi hadn't seen it with his own eyes, he would never have believed that Alfadas, the elven-jarl, was capable of doing it. Ever since they'd found the dagger in the pile of bones on the shore near Honnigsvald, something had been unleashed inside the duke, something that frightened even Lambi. It was a dark, destructive force. Some legacy of his father's, perhaps? Lambi knew many of the stories about Mandred. He preferred the axe as his weapon and fought with the fury of a berserker. If he once flew into a rage, then no one would be able to hold him back, it was said, and now Alfadas was acting the same way. Their calm, ever self-possessed leader was gone. He'd given way to a man hell-bent on following his path to the end, casualties along the way be damned. The duke had hardly slept for three days. By Lambi's reckoning, he ought to collapse at any moment.

Lambi looked back. The cold eyes of the elven queen met his. Did she know what was going on? Why had she joined the small party accompanying Alfadas on his desperate search? Maybe she was the one responsible for the dark side of the duke's nature. She was so cool and aloof, as if she were shut up inside a shell of ice. Lambi had seen her standing among the dead on the battlefield, in particular among the Maurawan, who had brought them vic-tory in the final battle. The death of the elves did not visibly move her, but her race dealt with death differently than humans did. They died without a cry or a whimper. It was rare for one of their wounded to so much as groan. A young woman, her body shattered by the swing of an axe, had dissolved into silver light before Lambi's eyes. He'd seen the same thing happen in the battles in Phylangan several times. But for it to happen there, by his fjord, among ancient, familiar mountains and forests, made it seem even more strange than before. The dying were absorbed into the light and ultimately smiled despite their terrible wounds. The memory of it rattled Lambi. The elves might be their brothers-in-arms, but they were still terrifying.

Beside the queen walked Ollowain. Both wore spotless white and, in their cold unapproachability, looked like the children of winter itself. Lambi did not understand the swordmaster at all. Ollowain knew Alfadas better than anyone else—he was the duke's foster father! So why did he not talk Alfadas out of this nonsense? If Alfadas did not rest soon, he'd kill himself. And it was up to him to determine the future of the Fjordlands. The surviving jarls had decided on that after the final battle, but Alfadas did not want to listen to them. And they would certainly not wait forever.

Apart from the two elves, only Veleif Silberhand and the young jarl, Oswin, had come along on their futile search. All of them, in fact, knew better, for they had found survivors who had personally seen Asla and the other refugees fleeing up the reindeer trail from Sunhill. Silwyna and anyone else still strong enough were searching there. Apparently, a large troop of trolls had also managed to escape along the reindeer path.

A weak bark made Lambi look up. Blood had reached a broad oak trunk frozen into the ice. From there, up the slope, stretched the signs of a past storm. The forest looked as if an immense and furious harvester had swung his scythe through it. Trees were smashed and fully uprooted, tossed, and tangled together. Some had crashed into the fjord. Blood pushed himself beneath a tree trunk that projected halfway out of the ice. Just a few steps beyond the barrier of dead wood, the side arm of the fjord ended at a sheer rock wall. Blood had led them nowhere—it was as clear as day. From where they stood, the only way out was through the fallen trees, and there was nothing on the ice.

Alfadas sighed and leaned against the fallen oak. The big dog dragged himself on a little farther.

"Our road ends here, I'd say," said Lambi softly. "Luth only knows what's gotten into the dog's head. Now let's talk, Duke. The jarls want to crown you king, and you'd be a dunderhead if you didn't accept. The Fjordlands need a man like you, a wise ruler, one who's strong enough for all of 'em to accept."

"How am I supposed to rule a land when I can't even protect my family?" Alfadas asked bitterly. "I don't want a crown! I will search for my wife and child. Nothing else matters more to me."

Enough! Alfadas had to get his head straightened out. In desperation, Lambi grasped him by the shoulders and shook him. "Wake up! What are you doing, chasing after this lame cur? I don't know what that troll said to you when he died at your feet, but the filthy bastards are liars. Forget him! His words were the last weapon he had, and all that shitpile wanted to do was hurt you. Get that into your skull! And it looks to me like he got what he wanted, hitting you right in the heart. You and me are brothers-in-arms. We've waded together through the blood of friends and enemies alike. You led me into a foreign world and back out again. Trust my words, not the words of that slobbering bastard of a troll prince. Now, I can see how you'd want to find your family. But why here?" Lambi pointed at the rock wall in front of them. "That goes nowhere. Why didn't you go up the reindeer trail and into the mountains? This makes no sense. I'm tempted to wallop you over the head just so you get a few hours of rest. Once you've slept, you'll see: you're chasing ghosts here, that's all."

Alfadas pulled himself free. "You don't understand. Blood is my daughter's dog. He doesn't obey anyone but her. He'll lead me to her. It has to be like that. You'll see." With that, the duke ducked beneath the tree trunk.

Blood had stopped just a few paces short of the rock wall. He scratched at the ice as if possessed, but his paws only slipped on the cold armor with which the fjord had outfitted itself for the winter. A chill wind swept the snow in thin veils across the fjord and howled among the rocks.

Tears of rage stood in Lambi's eyes. What else could he do to make his friend see reason? He wished he knew what that damned troll had said, but Ollowain, who'd been with Alfadas at the time, would not tell him. What kind of words could drive a man like Alfadas to the edge of madness?

Veleif stepped up beside Lambi. "Did you tell him?" the skald asked.

"He doesn't give a cold shit about the crown, and he'd be no man I'd follow if it were otherwise. Give him a few days, until he's found his wife and daughter."

Veleif shook his head. "People wait. Kingdoms do not. He has to understand that. I doubt that the jarls will ask him a second time. One does not turn down a crown."

"Who else are they supposed to ask? Each of 'em has too many petty jealousies. No, Alfadas is the only man they can all agree on. They'll ask him again," said Lambi emphatically.

"And if they asked you?"

The jarl snorted. "Me? Did you ever hear of a king with half a nose? Forget it, Veleif. I remember all the grinning faces when I was dragged off to Albenmark in chains—only too well. They don't even look at me as an equal. You'd as likely find a sheep that shits gold before those stuck-up whoresons would put me above them."

The skald crouched in the lee offered by the trunk. "Maybe I should compose a heroic song about you. In time, you'd be seen in a different light."

"What would you sing about? A hero who steals gold doors? No. If you want to write more than two couplets about my heroic deeds, you'll have to lie through your teeth." Lambi's gaze drifted to the elves. They were standing together a short distance away. The icy wind tore at their clothes. The queen wore no more than a thin dress and walked barefoot. Shivering, Lambi wished he'd been able to keep his golden amulet.

Oswin came over to them. Lambi felt uncomfortable in the jarl's presence. Oswin was too pretty for a man! With his green eyes, long red-blond mane, and hairless cheeks, he looked like a young woman. On top of that, whenever he was around the men who'd returned from Albenmark, he acted as awkward as a boy in love for the first time. For him, anyone who'd been to the elven kingdom was a hero.

"May I join you?" Oswin asked.

Lambi was tempted to say no just to see how the young jarl would react. Instead, he grumbled, "Course," and looked over at Alfadas. The duke was crouched on the ice, staring into the dark water beneath. The demented dog was still trying to scratch a hole in the ice.

"The things Blood could tell us if he could talk," said Veleif, rubbing some warmth into his arms.

"Dogs that talk? It takes a skald to come up with nonsense like that."

"Well, Blood will have had some reason for dragging Alfadas all this way."

Stupid talk. It made Lambi angry. "I don't have a reason for everything I do. Just imagine, sometimes I scratch my rear when it doesn't even itch."

Oswin looked at the ice underfoot, abashed. This was clearly not the kind of discussion he'd expected from heroes. Lambi's mood improved instantly when he saw how embarrassed the young jarl was.

"So you're comparing yourself to a dog?" Veleif said, his tone arch.

"Why would you think that? Is that meant to be a joke? Another quip like that, and I'll knot your fingers so hard you'll have to use your feet if you want any joy in your lonely nights!"

"But you—" Veleif began, then stopped as Oswin dropped to his knees.

"Did you see that?" He swept aside some snow. "By the gods! Those are children!"

All Lambi saw was indistinct, pallid figures. Something was caught among the dark branches, swaying gently with the current. A hand brushed suddenly across the ice—the pale hand of a child. A face appeared, just for an instant, but long enough for Lambi to recognize it. He had only seen the boy once before . . . but the elven dagger . . . how was it possible? The boy was back in Honnigsvald.

The current pushed the boy a little deeper until he was once again just a faint shadow. Lambi's stomach tightened. He glanced over at Alfadas. How could he tell him about this? Should he tell him at all?

"It's his son, isn't it?" Veleif whispered. "I thought . . ."

Alfadas looked up. The dog was still scratching at the ice. "The ice has been broken through over here," said the duke in a heavy voice.

Lambi, by the tree trunk, straightened up. Why had he come along? Alfadas had to be told. He had to be able to tell his son farewell.

PYRE FOR THE DEAD

Alfadas's hair clung to his forehead. He had been inside the cave and had read the traces he'd found there. He fought back tears and pressed his lips together tightly in his despair. His boy.

He had defended Yilvina and Halgard. Why had Ulric gone into the water? How long had he sat there in the dark? How long had he waited for Blood to bring help? Alfadas made a fist of his right hand and bit into the flesh, but the pain in his hand could not cancel out the deeper pain. He should not have waited! If he'd followed Blood immediately . . . he had come only a few hours too late. A few stupid hours.

Yilvina was still alive. Emerelle was confident that she would survive. She would be able to tell him what had happened. A single, bitter laugh escaped Alfadas's throat. He had believed his son to be dead, and now it was true. And yet it felt as if Ulric had died a second time.

Ollowain came to him across the ice.

Alfadas held up a hand to fend him off. He did not want to speak to anyone. Along the shore, a little way past the storm-ravaged patch of forest, was the pyre. The last gleam of sunset washed the mountainside in pink light. The night spread its wings from the east.

Lambi came up beside Ollowain. The elf held him back. Alfadas nodded a silent greeting to Ollowain, then turned and looked back at the pyre. This was how heroes were farewelled in the Fjordlands. In the end, they were not given to the worms. Their bodies became smoke and ash and were supposed to ascend like that to heaven. The fire was also a sign to the gods that a hero was coming to their halls. The gods observed the world and kept watch for that sign, said the priests. Alfadas wished he could believe that. It would be easier if he could, if he knew that Ulric would be more than just smoke, that there was something else beyond life.

If only Gundar were there. He had taunted the priest so many times. Gundar would have been certain to find the right words to send Ulric . . .

With heavy steps, Alfadas moved back to the shore. The darkness was rapidly displacing the sunset now. He owed it to Ulric to set fire to the funeral pyre at this hour, for this was the hour when the gods were especially watchful. Alfadas knew that Ulric believed those stories. He was still a child, after all, and he had loved stories about gods and heroes and trolls.

Again, the duke bit into his hand. Now Ulric himself was only a story.

Beside the pyre, a flaming torch protruded from the gravel on the shore. Ulric's final bed was built of layers of birch trunks. It smelled of fresh resin. Halgard rested at his son's side, and Ollowain had given his white cloak to cover the naked children. Their faces looked so peaceful, as if asleep, their arms folded over their chests. Emerelle stood by the children's heads. She was wearing her thin white dress. A plain-looking stone hung on a thin leather band, suspended at her breast. The wind toyed with the queen's untied hair. When she heard Alfadas's footfall on the pebbles, she looked up. Then she stepped back without a word.

Where they had erected the pyre, pale birch trees grew all the way to the water's edge. The wind whispered in their thin branches, a dying lament for his son.

Alfadas looked into Ulric's face. He had grown thinner since the last time he'd seen him. His face seemed harder, and the lips that had so often smiled at him conspiratorially were now pressed together.

The duke thought back to their playful duels with wooden swords and to summer afternoons when they lay on a mountain meadow and looked up to the clouds. He had told his son stories, faery tales, and sagas that spoke of a world filled with wonder.

"I was in the cave. I read the signs." Tears choked Alfadas's voice. "You loved them, my stories, and you lived them. For you, the Fjordlands were a place where brave warriors rescued enchanted princesses, a place where good always triumphed over evil. People like you are precious, my son, because they have not lost their belief in wonder and can give wonder to others." He took the elven dagger and pushed it beneath his son's folded hands. "Luth spun you only a short thread, Ulric, but you were what you always dreamed: a hero. Veleif, I know, will compose a saga for you. It will probably be as short as your life, but I believe that the people in this land will always remember you, just as they remember King Osaberg. You went to save your princess, and you killed a troll, all at an age when other children are still riding stick horses.

Halgard and you . . . you walked your last road together . . ." Alfadas faltered as his voice failed him. "You . . ."

Something that King Horsa had once told him came back to him then. *You know as well as I that the sagas of our heroes always end in blood and tragedy. That is how things are in the Fjordlands.*

"I wish you had not been born in the Fjordlands." Golden birch pollen danced in the last glow of sunset. Alfadas brought down the torch. The logs of the pyre were mingled with many young shoots and would not catch fire properly. Even as Alfadas looked at the pale trunks, a leaf unfurled on one of the green shoots.

He looked up. The air was awash with golden pollen. Fresh greenery embellished the birch trees by the shore, and they stood in full bloom . . . in the dead of winter.

"Put aside the torch," said Emerelle softly. "You won't need it. The life-light of the children was not completely extinguished. A spark still burned. I gave them some of my light. They will come back from the darkness. Give them a little time."

The queen looked exhausted. In the failing light, Alfadas saw small creases around her eyes that he had never noticed before. She stroked the plain stone at her breast. "You were right, Alfadas. Those who have not lost the belief in wonder are able to give wonder to others. Now lie down and rest. I will watch over your sleep."

THE KING

Filled with anxious hope, Alfadas gazed up the reindeer trail in the fading light of the evening. Ten days had passed since they had fought the trolls. He had now returned to Sunhill with the children.

Ulric and Halgard were both well. To Alfadas's surprise, Emerelle had remained in the human world. She took care not only of the children but also of others among the injured and infirm. She had changed. She was as distant as ever, but he had never thought that she would enter the stinking, overfilled quarters of the refugees to relieve old women of their gout, or save the frozen toes of children, or close his fighters' wounds.

From all around, the survivors of the troll war came to Sunhill, people who had lost everything but their bare lives. Gradually, it became clear just how savagely the troll leader had raged through the Fjordlands. Every town and village that lay north of Gonthabu had been razed. All along the shore, they discovered piles of skulls and bones like the one at Honnigsvald where Ulric's dagger had been found. Nobody was able to say how many survivors were still out there. Hundreds had frozen to death on the fjord and in the forests.

Alfadas had sent out riders and sleds to search for refugees. He looked out over the valley and saw the first lights were burning. Freezing figures huddled close to fires in the snow. Like a patchwork rug, the meager shelters of the lost were dotted along the reindeer trail below him. They had been built of whatever was at hand—sailcloth, old blankets, woven fir tree branches. Some had walls of snow, but many were nothing more than a roof. They were not suitable to withstand a winter that would last many weeks yet.

At Alfadas's order, all the sick and injured were housed in the few solid buildings Sunhill still had to offer. The very old and the very young had also found a warm place.

Although the twilight was rapidly fading, the valley still rang with the rhythmic clang of axes. Four days after the battle on the ice, Orimedes and his army of over a thousand centaurs had joined them from across the fjord. They came too late to drive out the trolls but just in time to take up the battle against winter and its miseries. They shared their provisions generously with the humans. Since their arrival, no one had had to suffer from hunger. At the start, many of the refugees had looked at the manhorses with awe, some even with naked fear. The huge creatures were too strange, half human-like, half horse. But with their rough, rude ways they were far more akin to the Fjordlanders than to the elves. They helped wherever they could. Orimedes had sent hunters into the woods to supplement their provisions with wild game. Most of the centaurs, however, helped build new huts from sprucewood. Seven plain windowless huts were completed every day. They continued to build more billets as new refugees arrived, and soon the patchwork village of tents and makeshift dwellings would disappear.

Emerelle had sent Yilvina to the heartland to request food and clothing from Master Alvias. Thanks to the queen's magical powers, the elven warrior had recovered quickly from her wounds. From her, Alfadas had learned about the terrors of the flight with his son. How would all that he had been through change him?

The stories that were told about Ulric among the refugees had already taken on a fabulous aspect. It was said that he had wielded the sword of dead King Osaberg and had killed a troll prince with it, saving the life of his maiden and an elf woman. In the stories, Ulric and Halgard had ridden through the woods on Blood's back, protected by the spirits of the trees. Others told of how the ghost of King Osaberg appeared to the children to lead them to his hidden grave and save them from a snowstorm.

Was it really Osaberg who lay in the cave? The winged helmet, the bronze armor, and the magnificent sword—it all fit with the legends of the dead king. But there would probably never be real proof.

Alfadas was worried about Ulric. It was not good to be celebrated as a legendary hero at the age of seven. What would his life bring? It was good that he had Halgard at his side. The girl would straighten out Ulric's head whenever his high spirits got the better of him. Alfadas had heard the story of the ghost-wolf that had stolen Halgard's youth. Emerelle had undone all that and had gone further: she had given Halgard sight. The girl had been blind from birth. Now she was slowly getting used to her new gift. She wore a snow mask to protect her from the bright light, but the sensitivity would soon pass, the queen had said.

Alfadas looked down over the makeshift village. Other wounds would take longer to heal, and for all Emerelle's efforts, many things in the Fjordlands would never again be as they once were. Half of its towns and villages had been devastated, and most of the men who could fight were dead or maimed. How were they supposed to defend themselves if the trolls came again?

When he thought of everything that lay ahead, he felt old and tired.

He turned away from the valley and peered up the trail above him. Where was Ollowain? The elf had been gone for five days. Was he so slow to return because he'd found them? Alfadas's heart began to beat faster, although he had forbidden himself any scrap of hope in recent days. The Maurawan had been unable to find Asla and Kadlin, and there were no better trackers. But his friend would search with his heart. If anyone was still able to find something that the Maurawan had missed, then it would be him!

Alfadas heard the thud of hooves long before he saw the rider. The big horse picked its way carefully down the snow-covered mountain path, and the rider held himself very erect in the saddle. He wore his cloak wrapped tightly around his shoulders. When he saw the duke, he clapped his mount on the neck and dismounted. He looked tired.

Alfadas glanced up along the dark path, but the rider had come alone. *I should not have hoped*, thought Alfadas bitterly. Hope was a fruit whose sweetness all too easily turned to bile.

"In the night after the avalanche, the snowstorm caught them unawares," said Ollowain, his voice toneless.

Alfadas looked at him in shock. "Did you . . ." His voice failed him. He tried again, but the question would not come.

Ollowain shook his head. "They were not among the frozen that I found. But I met a woman who had seen Asla and Kadlin walk off into the woods. Kalf was with them. It was not long before the storm came."

"And Silwyna? Did you meet her? I haven't seen her for days. Maybe she—"

"Yes. I met her. We camped together for a night. The Maurawan are still looking for refugees, but they hold no great hopes of finding any more. It is hard to survive in this kind of cold without food and a safe place to sleep."

Alfadas noticed that Ollowain was avoiding his eye. "What are you not telling me?"

The elf sighed. "The certainty you seek is something you may never find. The valley over there is vast. Asla, Kadlin, and Kalf may have lost their bearings in the snowstorm. No one can say where they went. As much as we search for them, it is more and more likely with every passing day that we will never know for certain. You should . . ." He shook his head. "No. Who am I to tell you what you should do?"

"What are you avoiding? Do you think the troll prince told the truth? Is that what you can't tell me?"

"It is true that some of the trolls went up the reindeer trail after the avalanche. The refugees saw them." He met Alfadas's eye for the first time. "You want to know what I believe? I believe that Dumgar was a liar. He could not beat you with a weapon, so he tried his best to hurt you with words. And he succeeded. I don't believe that anyone took Asla and Kadlin to him. But the problem with belief is that it has to exist without proof. Can you simply believe? Could you live with that?"

"In the camp below, by the palisade, they found children's bones and blond hair," said Alfadas dejectedly.

"And how many blond women are there?" the elf asked sharply. "It proves nothing. I camped with Silwyna in a cave in which we found the remains of a large fire. There were human bones there, too. Children's bones. And the cave stank of troll. But there were no traces of blood; most likely, they just cooked provisions over the fire."

"Or the bodies of the frozen."

"Yes, that's also possible. You will find no certainty, Alfadas. I rode into that valley as your friend to put your doubts to rest. I failed. But there is also freedom in uncertainty, if you are strong. You can choose for yourself what you want to believe. And I believe that Asla was not eaten by trolls. I have spoken with many refugees who survived that stormy night. They welcomed the storm. They preferred to freeze to death than be caught by the trolls."

Alfadas could well imagine that Asla had felt the same way. He knew how spirited and defiant she could be. In his mind, he saw her in front of him, her chin raised obstinately, her hands on her hips. None of fate's blows had ever been able to knock her down. She had always been stronger than him. When they had quarreled, he had almost always been the one to back down first. To never hear her voice again seemed to him unimaginable. But she would have done exactly what Ollowain said. With Kadlin in her arms, she would have marched away into the storm. She would have stayed on her feet for a long time; with Kalf's support, she would have gone on until she had no strength left. In the end, the fisherman would probably have carried both of them. Kalf was a strong man. And when he, too, was exhausted and unable to go on, he would have looked for a place out of the wind.

Tears stood in Alfadas's eyes. No doubt they would have taken Kadlin between them to warm her with both their bodies. Then Firn would have drawn his white mantle over all three. They fell asleep, never to wake. It was said that if the god of winter came to fetch you like that, you felt no pain.

Ollowain took him in his arms. The last time he had done that was when, as a young boy, Alfadas had been beaten again and again by the pupils in his elven sword-fighting class. As hard as he tried, he was never as agile or fast as the others. The swordmaster had told him then that he would still win if he could absorb more blows than the others. They had beaten him black and blue with their practice swords, and he had taken it all with gritted teeth. And, in fact, from that day on he had, at least occasionally, been victorious.

Alfadas gritted his teeth now, too, because it was that way again. He had to take the blows that life dealt him. At least he still had a wonderful son.

"I have to go now," he said, his voice calm. "You know what they want."

"Yes. And I believe it's right."

Alfadas was not so sure about that. He thought of how Lambi had left Phylangan. The accusations the jarl had leveled at him then had been justified: he hadn't given any thought to what would become of his men when they returned to the Fjordlands.

Alfadas walked beside Ollowain in silence as they descended the steep reindeer trail together. Then they turned to the left, onto the path that led to the large barn behind the village.

"And here I was thinking you'd snuck off!" Lambi stepped out of a patch of fir trees. "I've been searching for you for ages, Alfadas. Let me tell you, you're making a bigger fuss than a girl before her wedding. Come on!"

The jarl had something wrapped in a white cloth jammed under his arm. When he noticed Alfadas's gaze, he frowned. "Today's a special day. I don't want to fight with you."

"Why would we fight?"

Lambi threw back the cloth and showed him a gleaming golden winged helmet. "A king should have a crown. Try it on! I've got some parchment with me to pad it if it's too big."

Alfadas instantly recognized the helmet. "You stole it from the grave. You—"

"Its owner didn't bat an eye when I took it," Lambi interrupted him. "And a king needs a crown—or at least something that looks a bit like a crown."

Ollowain laughed. "Let him do it, Alfadas. You don't get to be king without a coronation, after all. And you can't do that without a crown. Even Emerelle puts up with it now and then."

The duke looked at the old helmet doubtfully. "You don't understand. The people believe that this is the helmet of a famous king. It's—"

"That's the whole damned plan!" Lambi almost shouted. "They said King Osaberg would return when the Fjordlands needed him the most. And that's exactly what's happened. He's been gone for centuries, a character in old stories. And all of a sudden, he's back—in our people's hour of greatest need. The old prophecy has come true. He came to give your son the sword with which he slew the troll, and now he's giving you his crown. Your rule begins—"

"With a lie!" Alfadas interrupted him, upset. "It isn't Osaberg crowning me, but my best friend, who I regret to say has no morals whatsoever."

"Trust him, Alfadas," said Ollowain. "What Lambi is trying to do is good and right. Kings are weighed with a different scale. The people will look up to you, and depending on what they see, they will find hope or lose faith. Use the stories that surround King Osaberg. Miracles don't just happen, Alfadas. They are made. Who are you hurting by making this helmet and its enchanted history your crown? Be generous! Give your future subjects a miracle that will lend them strength in these difficult times."

"Listen to a man who knows his way around kings and princes," Lambi said. "Now will you finally come along?"

Alfadas consented, although his misgivings had not left him. They led him to the barn, and he entered through a narrow door at the back.

Inside, it was stuffy and hot. The large room was overflowing. It stank of sweat, soot, and clothes that had been worn too long. Many of his veterans from Albenmark had come to be present at his coronation, but there were also the refugees—men, women, and children with careworn faces but hope in their eyes. Feeling ashamed of himself, Alfadas thought of Ollowain's words about miracles. It was up to him, now, to make them happen. He had to try.

At the end of the barn, a small stage had been constructed so that all could see the new king being crowned. As Alfadas climbed the steps, he felt like he was climbing a gallows. When he left that stage, he knew, his old life would be forfeit.

In the front row of those present, he saw his son beside Emerelle. Ulric was looking up at him, his face aglow with pride. He held Halgard by the hand. The girl's eyes were hidden behind a narrow snow mask.

Lambi told Alfadas to kneel. Then he unwrapped Osaberg's helmet from the white cloth and raised it high overhead. The jarl delivered a moving oration about the golden king and his return in their hour of direst need, the tale reaching its climax with a bony hand offering him the helmet, and Osaberg, in a deep, sepulchral voice, enjoining him to crown the elvenjarl as king.

The brazen lies took Alfadas's breath away. But he also saw how the warriors, farmers, and fishermen below, in front of the stage, accepted what Lambi was telling them. After all their suffering, they wanted to believe in the miracle.

Finally, Lambi crowned him with the heavy winged helmet. Alfadas rose to his feet and was greeted with rejoicing cheers. In the midst of all the noise, the notes of a lute sounded.

Alfadas felt the blood rising in his cheeks. He knew the melody. The cheers turned to singing.

> "There comes the jarl of Firnenstayn
> with his elven blade so fine.
> The lion heart of many a fray
> Sent by the gods to win the day."

He found Veleif's heroic song overblown and embarrassing. He had to remember to give the skald an important task in his court—anything to keep him from writing songs in the future. And he'd better keep Lambi close by, too. Maybe he'd make a good duke?

In the doorway of the barn, a slim white-clad figure appeared, her cloak billowing around her. Hardly anyone noticed her arrival, but Alfadas could not look away. She seemed to him like a child of winter, born of snow, just as she had on that distant day when he had first seen her at court in Albenmark—the day on which he had lost his heart to Silwyna.

SUMMER

Filled with love, the fisherman watched the blond woman on the shore. She sat on a rock in the sun and nursed her baby daughter. They had decided between them to call the girl Silwyna. If it had been a boy, they would have named him Luthson, for the weaver of fate had been generous with his gifts. Now Kadlin jumped out of the bushes. She had a long switch in her hand and held it over the water as if she were trying to fish. Quickly, though, she grew impatient and ran over to her mother.

The fisherman pulled in the line with the bird's foot. It had served him well so many times already. As he pulled it in, he thought back to the snowstorm and the trolls. He had never understood why the man-eaters had taken them to that cave. At first, he had believed that they would slaughter him. They had kindled a large fire and brought in a good supply of firewood. He could no longer remember everything that had happened, not exactly. A fever had overcome him, and when he awoke the trolls were gone. They had even left behind a few nuts and some beechmast.

Then Silwyna had come. The fisherman looked again to the woman on the shore: his woman. She waved to him. It had been her decision not to return.

Silwyna had helped them find this remote valley with the lake. It lay like a great blue eye among extensive forests, and there were fish and game enough to feed his small family. The fisherman said a silent prayer of thanks to the weaver of fate.

Again, his mind turned to the trolls and the elf woman. It was foolish, as a human, to try to understand what lay behind the actions of the Albenfolk.

The fisherman stood and poled his boat toward the shore. What did he care about the Albenfolk? He was happy. That was all that mattered.

APPENDICES
DRAMATIS PERSONAE

Aesa—Daughter of the farmer at Carnfort Farm

Aileen—Lover of Farodin; in Ollowain's parable, a legendary archer in the saga of Nazirluma and Aileen

Alathaia—Elven princess of Langollion; in a feud with Emerelle; it is said that she has walked the dark paths of magic

Alfadas Mandredson—Jarl of Firnstayn and prince of the Fjordlands in times of war; son of Mandred; grew up in Emerelle's royal household in Albenmark

Alfeid—Washerwoman in Firnstayn; mother of Halgard

Alvias—Elven chamberlain of Emerelle's court; commonly known as Master Alvias

Andorin—Elven healer in Emerelle's court

Antafes—Centaur warrior; member of Emerelle's ceremonial escort in Vahan Calyd

Asla—Wife of Alfadas

Atta Aikhjarto—Souled oak tree that saved the life of the hero Mandred

Audhild—Wife of the farmer at Carnfort Farm

Birga—Troll shaman; foster daughter of Skanga

Blood—Alfadas's dog; a gift from Asla's uncle Ole

Boltan—Troll artillery chief

Branbeard—King of the trolls

Brud—Scout in the service of Skanga

Dalla—Healer in the service of King Horsa

Dolmon—Kobold in Phylangan

Dumgar—Troll duke of Mordrock; adviser to King Branbeard

Egil—Son of King Horsa; heir to the throne of the Fjordlands

Eginhard von Daluf—Chronicler of King Horsa

Eleborn—Prince beneath the waves; ruler of the Albenkin that live in the oceans of Albenmark

Emelda—One of the names used by humans for Emerelle

Emerelle—Elven queen of Albenmark; one of the oldest beings in her world

Erek Erekson—Fisherman in Firnstayn; father of Asla

Fahlyn—Young elf woman from Phylangan; a member of the Farangel clan

Farodin—Legendary elven hero

Fenryl—Elven count of the Normirga

Finn—Oldest son of the farmer at Wehrberghof

Firn—God of winter in the pantheon of the Fjordlanders

Fredegund—Slave woman in Firnstayn

Freya—Wife of Mandred; mother of Alfadas

Galti—Fisherman in Firnstayn

Godlip—Jarl of Honnigsvald

Gondoran—Boatmaster of Queen Emerelle in Vahan Calyd; master of waters

Gran—Exceptionally gigantic troll warrior; rival of Orgrim

Gundar—Luth priest in Firnstayn

Halgard—Blind girl from Firnstayn; daughter of Alfeid

Hallandan—Elven prince of Reilimee

Horsa Starkshield—King of the Fjordlands

Isleif—Wilderness farmer; lives on a farmstead in the vicinity of Firnstayn

Iwein—The most important livestock breeder in Firnstayn

Kadlin—Daughter of Alfadas and Asla

Kalf—Fisherman and jarl of Firnstayn

Kodran—Ferryman at Honnigsvald; oldest of three brothers

Lambi—Jarl from the Fjordlands; banished by King Horsa

Landoran—Elven prince of the Snaiwamark and Carandamon; father of Ollowain

Loki—Orphan boy in the care of Svenja

Luth—Weaver of fate; in the Fjordlands, he is the god who weaves the strands of life into a wonderful tapestry

Lyndwyn—Granddaughter of Shahondin

Lysilla—Elf woman from the Normirga race

Mag—Ferryman at Honnigsvald; younger brother of Kodran

Mahawan—Elf; once lover of Emerelle

Mandrag—Brother-in-arms of the troll king; interim ruler of the trolls after their diaspora

Mandred—Legendary hero among humans and elves; father of Alfadas; jarl of Firnstayn

Maruk—Pack leader of the trolls in the service of Skanga

Matha Murganleuk—Souled magnolia tree in Emerelle's palace in Vahan Calyd

Melvyn—Son of Silwyna and Alfadas

Mjölnak—Warhorse of King Horsa

Murgim—Kobold from Phylangan

Nazirluma—Legendary king of the lamassu

Nessos—Centaur warrior; member of Emerelle's ceremonial escort in Vahan Calyd

Nomja—Elf woman; archer; once part of Emerelle's guard

Norgrimm—God of war in the pantheon of the Fjordlanders

Noroelle—Elven sorceress sent into exile by Emerelle

Nuramon—Legendary elven hero

Olav—Woodsman from Sunhill

Ole—Dog breeder in Firnstayn; uncle of Asla

Ollowain—Swordmaster to Queen Emerelle; a member of the Normirga

Orgrim—Pack leader, then prince of the Nightcrags; most competent commander of the trolls

Orimedes—Centaur prince of Windland

Osaberg—Legendary king of the Fjordlands

Oswin—Young jarl from the Fjordlands; standard-bearer of King Horsa

Ragnar—Warrior under Jarl Lambi

Ragni—A bodyguard of King Horsa; accompanied Alfadas on various military campaigns

Ralf—Name used by Egil Horsason to serve in Alfadas's army

Rolf Svertarm—Warrior under Jarl Lambi

Ronardin—Elven keeper of the Mahdan Falah

Sandowas—Elf from Phylangan; emissary in the service of Landoran

Sanhardin—Elven warrior; a bodyguard of Queen Emerelle

Sansella—Daughter of Hallandan, the elven prince of Reilimee

Senwyn—Elf; oldest of the Farangel clan

Shahondin—Elven prince of Arkadien

Shaleen—Wife of Count Fenryl

Sigvald—Wainwright from Honnigsvald

Silwyna—Elf woman; archer from the race of the Maurawan

Skanga—Important troll shaman

Slangaman—Legendary troll king

Slavak—Kobold servant; part of Shahondin's household, then in the service of King Branbeard

Snowwing—Falcon of Count Fenryl

Solveig—Woman from Firnstayn

Svanlaug—Goddess of victory; daughter of Norgrimm

Svenja—Aunt of Asla in Firnstayn

Taenor—Young elven sorcerer from Phylangan

Thorfinn—Farmer at Wehrberghof

Tofi—Youngest son of the farmer at Wehrberghof

Torad—Ferryman at Honnigsvald; younger brother of Kodran

Ulf—A bodyguard of King Horsa

Ulric—Son of Alfadas and Asla

Urk—Troll with a weakness for squirrels

Usa—Slave woman in Firnstayn

Vahelmin—Son of Shahondin; famous hunter

Veleif Silberhand—Skald in the service of King Horsa

Yilvina—Elf woman; a bodyguard of Queen Emerelle

Yngwar—Warrior under Jarl Lambi

LOCATIONS

Albenmark—Name for the entire physical world of the Albenkin

Albentop—Mysterious mountain in the north of Albenmark

Arkadien—An important principality in Albenmark

Carandamon—High plateau; permanently frozen; the original homeland of the Normirga

Drusna—Forested kingdom in the human world

Eaglescarp—A mountain fortress in Carandamon

Firnstayn—Small village in the Fjordlands

Gonthabu—Harbor in the south of the Fjordlands; residence of King Horsa Starkshield

The heartland—Province in Albenmark; location of Queen Emerelle's court

Honnigsvald—Small town about half a day's ride south of Firnstayn

Iolid Mountains—Mountain range on the edge of the heartland

Iskendria—Important trade center in the human world; famous for its library; notorious for its cruel town god

Kandastan—Legendary town/kingdom in the east of the human world

Kingdom beneath the waves—Principality on the bottom of the sea in Albenmark

Kingstor—The trolls' name for Phylangan

Langollion—Island to the southeast of Whale Bay

Mahdan Falah—The world bridge; inside the Skyhall of Phylangan

Phylangan—Also known as the stone garden; a fortress that watches over the entrance to the high plain of Carandamon

Reilimee—Important harbor town of the elves

Rosecarn—Elven settlement on the western end of the Swelm Valley; known to the trolls as the Wolfpit

Shalyn Falah—The white bridge; one of the entrances to the heartland

Slanga Mountains—Homeland of the secretive Maurawan race of elves

Snaiwamark—Original home of the trolls

Sunhill—Small mountain village on the reindeer path

Swelm Valley—Valley in the Snaiwamark that opens into Whale Bay; the troll fortress known as the Wolfpit lies at its western end

Vahan Calyd—Harbor town on the Woodmer; founded by the displaced race of the Normirga

Whale Bay—Large bay on the east of the Snaiwamark

Windland—Steppe landscape in the north of Albenmark; populated mainly by centaurs

The Wolfpit—Troll fortress on the western end of the Swelm Valley; known to the elves as Rosecarn

The Woodmer—Shallow sea in the south of Albenmark

GLOSSARY

Albenkin—Collective term for all the races created by the Alben (elves, trolls, centaurs, and so on); the humans refer to them as Albenfolk

Albenpaths—Magical paths

Albenstars—Intersection of two to seven Albenpaths; Albenstars are the entry points to the Albenpaths

Apsaras—Water nymphs

Bandag—Red-brown juice obtained from the roots of the dinko bush; used by the Albenkin to paint their bodies

Centaurs—A race in Albenmark; half horse, half human-like

Devanthar—Half man, half boar creature; archenemy of the elves

Dinko bush—Bush from which the Albenkin extract bandag

Elves—The last of the races created by the Alben

Farangel—Elven clan; part of the Normirga race in Phylangan

Fauns—A goat-legged race in Albenmark

Gry-na-Lah—A cursed or enchanted arrow that flies until it kills the victim whose name is written on its shaft

Holde—One of the kobold clans of Albenmark; they live in the mangrove swamps near Vahan Calyd; their prince is called the master of waters

Ironbeards—Carved wooden figures into which one drives items made of iron as offerings to the god Luth

Jarl—Title of the leader of a village in the Fjordlands; elected anew each year

Kobold—A race in Albenmark; not unlike humans, but small with large heads

Lamassu—A race in Albenmark; body of a bull, the wings of a giant eagle, and a bearded face

Liburna—A small galley, designed to be fast and light

Lutins—A race of fox-headed kobolds famed for their crude pranks and skill with magic

Maurawan—A race of elves that lives in the forests of the Slanga Mountains

Minotaurs—A race in Albenmark; steer-headed giants

Normirga—A race of elves that lives on the high plateau of Carandamon and the Snaiwamark

Oreaden—Shy mountain nymphs that live primarily in the Iolid Mountains

Riverbank sprites—Small, winged race of Albenkin

Shi-Handan—Soul eaters; creatures summoned by Skanga

Summoners—A subgroup of the trolls with the ability to form a spiritual connection with wild animals, to attract them and make them subservient to their will

Trolls—A warlike race in Albenmark; banished to the human world by Queen Emerelle

Warmaster—Elven title for the commander in chief of their military forces

Windsingers—A special group of elven sorcerers

Yingiz—Mysterious race driven by the Alben into the void between the worlds

ACKNOWLEDGMENTS

Despite the popular cliché of the author as a lone figure ensconced in a garret, hidden away from the world, the truth is that this book, at least, would probably never have been finished without the assistance of a great many unseen elves and kobolds. Those who helped me in my struggles with Albenmark were Menekse, who gave me my freedom when it was necessary; Elke, who knows draft horses better than I do, even though she can't stand them; Karl-Heinz, who dispensed advice freely, even at midnight; Eymard, who piloted me through the shallows of specialized nautical terminology; Gregor and Bettina, who were where I was not; and my editors Martina Vogl, who never lost faith, and Angela Kuepper, who ensured among other things that my readers were spared tapeworm sentences like this one.

Bernhard Hennen

December 2005

ABOUT THE AUTHOR

B ernhard Hennen studied archaeology, history, and German studies at
Cologne University, and he traveled extensively while working as a jour-
nalist. With Wolfgang Hohlbein, Hennen published his first novel, *Das Jahr
des Greifen*, in 1994. Since then, his name has appeared on dozens of historical
and fantasy novels, as well as numerous short stories. Hennen has also devel-
oped the story line for a computer game and has worked as a swordsman for
hire in medieval shows and as a Santa Claus mercenary. *Elven Queen* is the
third book in The Saga of the Elven, following *The Elven* and *Elven Winter*.
Hennen currently lives with his family in Krefeld, Germany.

ABOUT THE TRANSLATOR

Photo © 2016 Dagmar Jordan

Born in Australia, Edwin Miles has been working as a translator, primarily in film and television, for more than fifteen years. After undergraduate studies in his hometown of Perth, he received an MFA in fiction writing from the University of Oregon in 1995. While there, he spent a year working as fiction editor on the literary magazine *Northwest Review*. In 1996, he was short-listed for the prestigious Australian/Vogel's Literary Award for young writers for a collection of short stories. After many years living and working in Australia, Japan, and the United States, he currently resides in his "second home" in Cologne, Germany, with his wife, Dagmar, and two very clever children.